OR
HIS ADOPTED SON

BY
LYNNE MARSHALL

A KISS
TO CHANGE HER LIFE

BY
KARIN BAINE

WITHDRAWN

MILLS
BOON
&

Lynne Marshall used to worry that she had a serious problem with daydreaming—and then she discovered she was supposed to write those stories! Being a late bloomer, she came to fiction-writing after her children were grown. Now she battles the empty nest by writing stories which include romance, medicine, and always a happily-ever-after. She is a Southern California native, a woman of faith, a dog lover, and a curious traveller.

Karin Baine lives in Northern Ireland with her husband, two sons, and her out-of-control notebook collection. Her mother and grandmother's vast collection of books inspired her love of reading and her dream of becoming a Mills & Boon author. It wasn't until she joined her critical group UCW that she started to believe she could actually write—and only her husband's support enabled her to pursue it. At least now she can tell people she has a *proper* job! You can follow Karin on Twitter: @karinbaine1.

A MOTHER FOR
HIS ADOPTED SON

BY
LYNNE MARSHALL

Published in Great Britain 2016
By Mills & Boon, an imprint of HarperCollins*Publishers*
1 London Bridge Street, London, SE1 9GF

© 2016 Janet Maarschalk

ISBN: 978-0-263-25426-6

Dear Reader,

Writers are often asked where they get their ideas for stories. I can tell you I get mine all over the place! The spark that spurred *A Mother for His Adopted Son* came from an article about an ocularist in a regional magazine I subscribe to from Maine. I'd never heard of the profession, and was fascinated by this woman who'd been an art student but for the last thirty years had wound up making beautiful prosthetic eyes for clients. I clipped and held on to that article for a couple of years and it percolated in the back of my mind.

Another day, I was driving around doing errands and listening to the radio when an intriguing interview aired, about a sightless man who had become amazingly independent through using a technique called echolocation. The interviewer began by describing this man as having beautiful blue eyes and, yes, they were prosthetics. He'd lost both his eyes by the time he was eighteen months old to retinoblastoma, but his mother never let his blindness hold him back from exploring and being adventurous. That sparked my dormant ocularist idea and, as they say, a story kernel was created!

An ocularist isn't a 'usual' job for a Medical Romance character, so I ran it by my editor, who was open and encouraging about the idea. Soon the character Andrea came to be, and shortly after that a little boy named Dani, too. But who would be the hero of this story, and why? It didn't take long for the gorgeous pediatrician Dr Sammy to come into being—a dedicated doctor who believes in medical missions and adoption for very personal reasons.

I hope you enjoy the dramatic and often emotional love story between Andrea and Sam as they work their way to their happily-ever-after.

I always enjoy hearing from readers at lynnemarshall.com. And 'friend' me on Facebook! www.facebook.com/ LynneMarshall.Page

Love,

Lynne

To foster parents and adoptive parents worldwide,
who open their homes and hearts
and make a difference in young lives.

Books by Lynne Marshall

Mills & Boon Medical Romance

Cowboys, Doctors…Daddies!

Hot-Shot Doc, Secret Dad
Father For Her Newborn Baby

Temporary Doctor, Surprise Father
The Boss and Nurse Albright
The Heart Doctor and the Baby
The Christmas Baby Bump
Dr Tall, Dark…and Dangerous?
NYC Angels: Making the Surgeon Smile
200 Harley Street: American Surgeon in London

Visit the Author Profile page
at millsandboon.co.uk for more titles.

CHAPTER ONE

SAM MARCUS STOOD in the observation room above the OR suite in St. Francis of the Valley Hospital, waiting for his child to lose an eye. He'd seen his share of surgeries before, being a pediatrician, but never for someone he loved. This time he needed an anchor, so he leaned against the window to see his son better and to offer support against the threat of his buckling knees.

He watched as the anesthesiologist put his tiny boy under and while the surgeon measured the eye globe and cornea dimensions, the length of the optic nerve. His heart thumped in his chest, and a fine line of sweat gathered above his lip as the surgeon made the first incision. He swiped it away with a trembling hand, trying his best to get his mind wrapped around what was happening.

Enucleation.

His barely three-year-old newly adopted son had retinoblastoma and needed to have his left eye surgically removed. He swallowed hard and shook his head, still unable to believe it.

He'd fallen in love with Danilo, an orphan, on his last Doctors' Medical Missions trip to the Philippines. The mission had been in response to their latest typhoon, to tend to the countless new orphans. He hadn't been in the market for a son or daughter. No, it had been the last thing on his mind then. Yet there had been one particular one-year-old boy who'd lost his entire family in the typhoon and who'd miraculously managed to survive for forty-eight hours on his own. A little hero.

Over the days of the two-week mission, Sam and the other doctors had performed physicals and minor procedures, as well as arranged for other children who had required more extensive medical care to be transported to where they needed to be. Dani had used his new walking skills to follow Sam everywhere. It'd made Sam remember one of his favorite childhood books, *Are You My Mommy?* A story his own mother had read to him, where a little bird who'd fallen out of the nest went looking for his mother, asking everyone, even machines, if they were his mother, and it had broken his heart.

All the children on this mission were orphans dealing with their losses in their own ways, yet this child, Dani, seemed to have chosen Sam. He gave in and took the boy with him everywhere at the orphanage clinic, cautiously opened his heart, then fell in love in an amazingly short period of time. Then it was time to leave. Dani cried inconsolably, and one of the sisters at the orphanage told Sam that it was the first time the child had cried since arriving there six weeks before.

What was a man supposed to do? He knew how it felt to be homeless. He'd been taken away from his mother when he was ten. She hadn't abused him, but she'd had to leave him alone most nights so she could work a second job. Her plan had backfired and the authorities had taken Sam and put him into foster care. Yeah, he knew how it felt to be left all alone.

Fortunately for him he'd been placed into a big happy family and currently suffered from missing them, with everyone fanned out all across the United States. There'd been five natural siblings in all, and he'd become kid number six, yet his already overworked foster mother had insisted on bringing in more foster children—a long, long list of foster kids had come and gone over the years. *Why?* he used to ask whenever he'd been instructed to share his bunk bed with yet another new kid. *We don't have room for more, Mom.* She'd always insisted he call her Mom.

Even after all these years her response never left his subconscious. "We don't always know how we'll make ends meet or where they'll sleep, Sammy, but we just know we've got to bring them in because the child needs a home."

The child needs a home.

He'd been one of those children. And he'd been trying to prove himself worth keeping ever since.

When he'd returned home from the Philippines, he'd been unable to get Dani out of his mind. Missing his infectious smile and unconditional love, he'd decided to try for the adoption in honor of his deceased foster mother, because that child needed a home.

Though it had taken a year and a half to jump through all the hoops to arrange for Dani's adoption, six months ago he and Dani had teamed up and never looked back. And what an adjustment being a single father had been. It'd always been hectic, growing up with so many foster siblings, yet under the chaos there had been stability. Something he'd never had when he'd been a young boy. That was his goal for Dani, to give the boy stability, but he'd never been a parent before and they were both on a stiff learning curve, working things out, juggling the logistics of his busy career, child care and father-son time.

Then this cancer nightmare had happened, and any

stability they'd established had been replaced with utter mental and emotional turmoil.

They'd discovered the tumor on Dani's very first eye examination in the United States. The simple yet disturbing fact that his pupil had turned white instead of red when the ophthalmologist had shone a light into it had heralded the beginning of more and more bad news. The child had intraocular retinoblastoma.

The team of doctors, headed by the pediatric oncologist, had recommended the surgery after all other avenues of treatment—each with drawbacks and no guarantees—had been considered and rejected. Dr. Van Diesel, the pediatric eye surgeon, had come highly recommended, and since there wasn't a chance that Dani's vision could be saved, they'd opted for enucleation.

Sam watched from behind the viewing window as the surgeon, through a dissecting microscope, removed the outer covering of the eye. Next the four rectus muscles were detached from the eyeball, then the surgeon placed a hemostat on the stump of the last severed eye muscle. With special long, minimally curved scissors, he cut the optic nerve. Sam's battered heart sank, realizing the monumental change that single surgical incision had made to his son's vision. He stood motionless, unable to take in a breath, emotion flooding through his veins as next the surgeon removed the eyeball.

Unable to swallow the thickening lump in his throat, Sam watched as a nurse stood nearby with a small specimen container to collect a tiny piece of the optic nerve for histopathologic study. For their next huge hold-your-breath diagnosis—had all of the cancer been removed or had it spread? His stomach pinched at the potential outcome. The doctor worked painstakingly to also open the eye globe to harvest tissue from the retinoblastoma.

Before closing, he placed a plastic temporary conformer into Dani's eye socket to avoid a shrunken look and maintain a natural shape. They'd discussed in advance how this would be done in preparation to ensure the proper size and motility for the future eye prosthesis.

When he finally could, Sam took a deep breath. The worst was over, no, check that, the worst had been getting the damn diagnosis of cancer in the first place. Since he wanted to keep a positive outlook, he'd deemed today the first step in Dani's healing. He watched like a hawk as the anesthesiologist prepared his son for transfer to the recovery room and the surgical nurse bandaged Dani's left eye with a special patch to help decrease swelling.

He rushed out of the observation deck and hustled down the stairs to be the first to talk with Dr. Van Diesel when he exited the OR.

"All went well," the white-haired man said, as he tossed his gloves in the trash and removed the surgical cap then the mask from his face. "No surprises." He forced a smile that looked more like a squint. "Should be a couple of days before we get the pathology reports."

"Thank you." And Sam probably wouldn't sleep until he knew whether the tumor had spread or not. But he was determined to keep that positive attitude. As of right now the tumor was gone, his son was free of cancer. That was how it had to be.

The doctor continued on to the locker room. Sam stood outside the OR doors and waited for the team to transport Dani. Several minutes later the doors swung open and his son, looking so tiny on the huge gurney, got rolled toward the recovery room.

He followed the medical parade out of the surgical suite, down the hall and into Recovery. As he was a staff member as well as a parent, he was also allowed to accompany the boy rather than be instructed to wait outside until he was ready for discharge. The receiving RR nurses bustled around the gurney, transferring him to their bed, disconnecting Dani from the OR equipment and attaching him to theirs. Heart monitor, blood-pressure cuff, pulse oximeter, oxygen.

Sam remained by his son's side, taking his tiny yet pudgy fingers into his own, feeling their chill and asking for a second blanket to cover him. Every once in a while his son moved or took a deeper breath. His heartbeat was steady and strong, blipping across the monitor screen; his blood pressure read low for a three-year-old, but he was still sedated. One particular Filipino nurse looked after Dani as if he were her own. That gave Sam reassurance.

"Is your wife coming, Doctor?" Her Filipino accent made the sentence staccato.

"No." Sam shook his head. "No wife."

He'd lost the woman with whom he'd thought he'd spend the rest of his life. She'd walked away. But he'd committed to adopting little Dani and he couldn't bear the thought of disappointing the boy who would finally have a home and a family of his own. Even if it was just the two of them.

"I will watch him," the nurse said. "Don't worry. You should take a break."

He stretched and glanced at her name tag. "Thank you, Imelda. I could use a cup of coffee about now."

She nodded toward the nurses' lunchroom. "We just made some."

He thought about taking her up on the offer but realized how much he needed to stretch his legs, to get his blood moving again. To help him think. To plan. Maybe with more circulation to his brain he'd be able to process everything that'd happened today. "Thanks, but I'm going to take a walk."

He stood and started to leave, then blurted the first thought in his mind. "By any chance, do you know where the prosthetic eye department is?"

Imelda pulled in her double chin. "Do we have one, Doctor?"

He tipped his head. Good question. Hadn't Dr. Van Diesel mentioned it at one point? "I hope so."

As he left the recovery room, he made eye contact with the charge nurse. "I'll be back in twenty minutes but beep me the instant Dani wakes up, okay?"

She nodded, so he pushed the metal plate on the wall and the recovery room department doors automatically swung inward. With one more glance over his shoulder to his sleeping son, and another pang in his heart, he stepped outside.

The one-hour operation under general anesthesia was fairly routine, and because the eye was surrounded by bone, it made it much easier for Dani to tolerate. If all went well, his son could even be discharged later that afternoon.

He walked down the hall, entered the elevator. His mind drifted to Katie, wondering if this pain would have been easier to take sharing it with someone else, but that was never to be. Katie had stuck with him all through medical school and his pediatric residency at UCLA while she'd tried to launch her acting career. Sure, they'd talked about marriage and children, but mostly he'd avoided it. He'd been left by the most important woman in his life, his mother, at a tender age, and it had marked him for life. Toward the end of their relationship, she'd kept insisting on wedding plans and he'd kept sidestepping them. When he'd finally brought up marriage because of the adoption, after screaming at him for making such a huge decision by himself Katie had suddenly decided her acting career needed her full attention.

He'd screwed up by not consulting her, but he'd thought he'd known her, and she'd very nearly wrenched his heart right out of his chest when she'd walked away.

Not a great track record with the women he'd loved. At least his foster mother, Mom Murphy, had never sent him back.

The elevator stopped at the first-floor lobby and he headed to the information desk. "Don't we have a department that makes facial prosthetics here? You know, things like eyes?"

The silver-haired gentleman's gaze lit with knowledge. "Yes, as a matter of fact, I believe we do." He scrolled through his computer directory, then used his index finger to point. "It's called Ocularistry and Anaplastology." The man had trouble pronouncing it and made a second attempt. "And it's in the basement, with Pathology." He placed his hand beside his mouth as if to whisper. "I think it's next door to the morgue."

"What's the name of the head of the department?" Sam asked.

"Judith Rimmer. Or, as we volunteers like to call her, Helen Mirren without the star power. Hubba-hubba, if you know what I mean."

Sam's brows rose at the thought—so even old guys had crushes—but off to the dungeon he went. Once he exited the elevator, he wondered why the fluorescent lights even looked dimmer down in the hospital basement, but pressed on. He passed the Matériel Management department, then Central Service—the cleaning and sterilization area. He knew where Pathology was—

he'd visited there regularly to get early reports on his patients and to discuss prognoses with the pathologists. He'd also unfortunately been to the morgue far more often than he cared to in the line of duty. Nothing cut deeper than losing a child patient, and for the sake of science he'd sat in on his share of autopsies to help make sense of the tragedies.

Sam sidestepped the morgue double doors, refusing to even glance through the ocean-liner-style windows for activity, then squinted and saw the small department sign for Ocularistry and Anaplastology in bold black letters. How many people would even know what it meant?

The office was shoved into the farthest corner in the hallway, as if it had been an afterthought. The panel of fluorescent lights just outside the door blinked and buzzed, in need of a new tube, making things seem eerier than they already were. He wasn't sure whether to knock or just go inside. He glanced at his watch, he'd wasted enough time finding the department, so without a moment's further hesitation he pushed through the door of the "prosthetic eye people's" department.

A dainty, young platinum-blonde woman with short hair more in style with a 1920s flapper than current fashion arranged flesh-colored silicone ears under a glass display case, as if they were necklaces and earrings in an upscale jewelry store. She looked nothing like Helen Mirren but might pass as her granddaughter. What had that volunteer been talking about? On the next table sat a huge model of an eyeball. He narrowed his gaze at the odd juxtaposition.

The woman glanced up with warm brown eyes surrounded with dark liner and smoky underlid smudges. Not the usual look he noticed in the hospital, and the immediate draw caught him off guard. His son was in Recovery, having just lost an eye, for God's sake. He had no right to notice an attractive woman! The fact he did ticked him off.

"I'm looking for Judith Rimmer." Okay, so he sounded gruffer than necessary, maybe impatient, but it wasn't even noon and he'd already been through one hell of a no-good, very bad day, to paraphrase one of his son's favorite books.

"She's currently in Europe," Andrea Rimmer said. The intruder had barged in and brought a whole lot of stress with him, and her immediate response was to bristle.

The brown-haired man with intense blue eyes, of which neither was prosthetic, stared her down, not liking her answer one bit. He may be a head taller than she was, but she wasn't about to let him intimidate her. She'd had plenty of practice of standing up to men like that with her father.

"When will she be back?" He seemed to look right through her, which further ticked her off. Wasn't she a person, too? Was her grandmother the only one who mattered in this department?

"Next week." She could play vague with the best of them.

"I'll come back then."

It hadn't been her idea to take the apprenticeship for ocularist four years ago. Nope, that had been good old Dad's plan. She'd barely graduated from the Los Angeles Art Academy when he'd pressured her into getting a "real job" while she found her bearings in the art world. Now that she was in her last year of the apprenticeship, and since Grandma was threatening to retire and was expecting Andrea to take her place, she'd felt her back against the wall and resented the narrow choice being shoved down her throat. Work full-time. Run the department. The place didn't even have windows!

What about her painting? Her dreams?

Had the demanding doctor brushed her off by assuming she was an inexperienced technician because she was young? She didn't think twenty-eight was that young, but being short probably made her seem younger. If he thought he could be rude because she was young or a nobody, this guy with the tense attitude had just pushed her intolerant button.

"She may not *be* coming back." She sounded snotty, which wasn't her usual style, as she rearranged the ears again. But she didn't really care because this guy, who may be good-looking but seriously lacked the charm gene so who cared how good-looking he was, had just ruined her morning for no good reason.

She glanced up. He raised a brow and stared her down in response to her borderline impudent reply, and she saw the judgment there, the same look she'd seen in her father's eyes time and time again. *I'm a doctor. You dare to talk to me like that?*

The imaginary conversation quickly played out in her head. *What? Am I not good enough for you?* A feeling, unfortunately, she'd had some experience with on the home front most of her life. After all, wasn't she the daughter of a woman with only a high-school education? A stay-at-home mother keeping a spotless house for a husband who rarely visited? A woman so depressed she'd turned into a shadow of her former self? Half of her DNA might be genius, but the other half, often insinuated by her father, was suspect. Well, good ol' Dad should have thought about that before knocking up her mother if it meant so damn much to him.

The invading doctor continued to stare down his nose at her. Andrea wasn't about to back down now. The nerve. Did he think she was a shopgirl, a department receptionist minding the store while Granny frolicked in France? She'd just spent a week making this latest batch of silicone ears, measuring the patients to perfection, matching the skin color, creating the simplest and most secure way to adhere them to what was left of their own ears. And unless anyone looked really closely, no one would notice. Just ask the struggling musician Brendan, who'd had his earlobe chopped off by a mobster, what he thought about her skills!

"What do you mean, she may not be coming back?" His tone shifted to accusing as if he should have been privy to the memo and voted on the decision. Wasn't that how demanding doctors, just like her father, behaved? *I need this* now. *Don't annoy me with facts.* He stood, hands on hips, his suit jacket pushed aside, revealing his trim and flat stomach—wait, she didn't care about his physique because he was rude—refusing to look away from the visual contact they'd made. Something really had this guy bothered, and she was the unfortunate party getting the brunt of it.

"It's called retirement."

His wild blue stare didn't waver, and, as illogical as it seemed under the circumstances, something was going on with the electrical charge circulating around her skin because of him.

A beeper went off on his belt, breaking the standoff and the static tickling across her arms. He glanced at it. She was glad because she really didn't know how much longer she could take him standing in the small outer office, and most especially gazing into those intense eyes.

It was her job to notice things like that. Eyes. Yeah, she'd become quite an expert during her apprenticeship. If she kept telling herself that, maybe she wouldn't scold herself later for falling under the spell of a completely pompous stranger based solely on his baby blues.

"I've gotta go." Obviously in no mood to deal with her touchy technician act, he turned and huffed off, right out the door.

Wilting over her bad behavior, she tossed her pen onto the countertop and plopped into the nearest chair. Why had she behaved that way with him? She'd knee-jerked over the intruding and demanding doctor, but wasn't he acting exactly like her father? Arrogant and overbearing. Lording his station in life over her. *Where's the head of the department, because you're not good enough. Step out of my way.* He didn't need to say the words; she'd *felt* them.

Andrea caught herself making a lemon-sucking expression and let it go. Maybe she was the one with the attitude, and she hadn't even tried to control it. That man had just got the brunt of it, too. Truth was, she needed to be more accommodating to clients and doctors, especially if she actually ever agreed to take over as the department head. Which she sure as heck wasn't certain she wanted to do. Especially if catering to demanding doctors like that guy would be part of the routine.

She hadn't expected a young doctor with such interestingly pigmented irises—because that was what she'd learned to notice since beginning her apprenticeship—and penetrating eyes as that guy's to set her off on a rant. And she'd acted nothing short of an ass with him.

Shame on her.

Guilt and longing intertwined inside her. She'd fallen short of the mark just now, and it was a symptom of the battle she fought every day when she came to work. This was her job, creating prosthetic eyes for people who needed them, silicone ears, noses and cheeks for cancer victims and veterans, too, and it was a noble profession. She actually loved it. Loved the patients and making their lives better. But she liked things the way they were— working four days a week at the hospital and painting the other three. Her heart yearned to paint, not run a windowless department in the bowels of a hospital.

Andrea put her elbows on the counter and rested her forehead in the palms of her hands. If Grandma ever retired, some lousy department head *she* would make.

A week later...

It had taken Sam a good day and a half to calm down after his ridiculous encounter with the young woman in the O&A department. Where did they find the employees these days anyway? But to be fair, she didn't have a clue that he'd just come from watching his son have his eye removed in surgery. He may have been more demanding than usual, but he'd been in no shape to judge how he'd come off to her, or, at that moment, to care. All he'd wanted had been to ensure his boy could have the best person possible make a realistic-looking eye to replace the one Dani had lost.

That woman couldn't have been more than in her early twenties. How could she possibly have the skill...? Yet, he reminded himself, he'd eventually realized that Judith Rimmer had a reputation known all over the country for excellence in her specialty. He'd read up on her online while little Dani had napped one afternoon. She wouldn't leave her beloved department in the hands of a novice. Would she?

Now, having completely calmed down, and being back on the job with a miraculous break in his schedule that morning, thanks to a no-show patient, Sam prepared to return to the basement to discuss Dani's need for an eye.

He reached the ocularistry and anaplastology department door, took a deep breath and entered with a plan to apologize for inadvertently insulting the still-wet-behind-the-ears ocularist—if that was even what she was. How could he know for sure? They hadn't gotten that far. Because his foster mother hadn't raised an ungracious son—she'd knock him upside the head from the grave if she found out, too. Nor had she raised a son to judge a book by the young cover—not with the revolving door of foster kids with whom he'd grown up. He smiled inwardly, then swung open the door, and much to his surprise found Helen Mirren's double, not retired but standing right in front of him beside a row of unblinking eyeballs in all colors in a display case. She wore something that looked like a sun visor but with magnifying glasses attached and a headlight, examining one specific eye as if it were a huge diamond.

Sitting with an expectant gaze on her face was the girl, who, on second encounter, and with all that eye makeup, looked more like the iconic 1960s model from Great Britain. Twiggy, was it? But not nearly as skinny. This girl had curves. She obviously waited for Judith's approval on something, a project she'd made? Maybe, but, no matter what the scene was about, Sam was ticked off. Again.

The young woman finally noticed someone had entered and glanced at him, a quick look of surprise in her double take. Yeah, he'd caught her in a childish lie, so he glared back. He could act as juvenile as the next person, thanks to his four older foster brothers and two younger foster sisters, countless other foster siblings constantly coming through the family revolving door and foster parents who hadn't been afraid to make threats in order to tame the often out-of-control tribe.

"Reconsidering retirement, Ms. Rimmer?" His vision drifted to a perplexed Judith.

Judith's gaze flitted back and forth between the woman and Sam, obviously trying to figure out what their history had been.

"Technically I wasn't lying, because my grandmother plans to retire as soon as I'm ready and *willing* to take over." She stood, which hardly made a difference. What was she, five feet, tops? And jumped right in with an explanation. "And, for all I knew, she could've been swept away by the beauty of Europe and decided not to come home. To retire on the spot. It could've happened."

Her outlandish cover nearly made him smile. Nearly. But he held firm because he found himself enjoying her flushed cheeks and her mildly flaring nostrils as she explained, her raccoon-painted eyes taking on more of a fawn-ready-to-bolt appearance.

"Which makes it okay that you lied to me?" He wasn't ready to let her off the hook, though.

She stepped around the counter, taking two steps toward him, never breaking the visual connection, which was surprisingly stimulating. "You came in with a nasty attitude that day and proceeded to make me feel like a novice who couldn't possibly be of help to you. So I decided not to be any help at all."

So that's how she'd read him. For a second he felt like a chump, but she deserved the full story. An explanation for why he'd been that jerk. "I'd just come from watching my son's enucleation. I needed reassurance he could look normal again."

Her challenging expression instantly melted into an apologetic peacemaking plea. "Oh." Those huge eyes immediately watered. "I'm so sorry to hear that."

"Dr.—" Judith read his name badge "—Marcus, I'm sorry the two of you got off to a rocky start, I'm also very sorry about your son, but I assure you Andrea is as skilled as they come. And because I'm completely booked up with projects, having just returned from vacation, she'd be happy to help you with your son's eye prosthesis. I assure you, with her artistic background, she'll make a perfect match and fit."

Andrea sent a quick questioning glance toward her grandmother but immediately recovered, as if she'd gotten the clear message to play along. *Was* she a novice? Sam still wasn't convinced. She looked so young.

"So, what I'll need to do—" Andrea used an index finger to lightly scratch the corner of her mouth "—is make an appointment for you to bring in your son. Is he completely healed yet? We shouldn't take measurements until he is."

"It's only been a week, but he's doing really well."

"Let's make it next week, then, to be safe. I'll need to take photos of his other eye and make a silicone cast of his healed eye socket. After that I'll make a wax version, which I'll be able to mold as needed to fit. What's your son's name?"

"Danilo, but he goes by Dani."

She nodded, sincerity oozing out of those huge brown eyes. "What day is good for you?" She brought up a calendar on the computer—back to business—and he fished out his pocket phone, tapping through to his work calendar.

Back and forth they went, politely trying to work out an appointment day and time. His schedule was over-booked, since he'd taken off a week to be with his son after the surgery, which was why he was aggravated that one of his patients was a no-show today and would need to be rescheduled, further keeping him backed up. Yet that was the only reason he'd been able to sneak down here at this moment, which had turned out to be a good thing. Which would all be beside the point if he couldn't make an appointment.

At least for now, since his return to work, his for-mer foster sister Cat could be Dani's caregiver during the day. She lived within five miles of him and was a stay-at-home mom who needed the extra cash. Their ar-rangement worked out for everyone, since she also had two children under the age of five, and Dani loved to play with the other kids. He scratched his head, at a loss.

Why hadn't he considered his work issue when he'd known Dani would need the prosthetic eye right off? The bigger question was why hadn't he considered how difficult it would be to become a single father in the first place?

Of course, that hadn't been his original plan…

Yeah, he was in over his head, but it made no dif-ference, because he was proud and happy to be Dani's father, no matter how hard and complicated life had be-come because of it. Add another point to foster Mom's tally, *the kid needed a home*. "Do you do house calls, by any chance?"

Andrea dipped her head, thinking for a second. "No. But since I gave you a hard time last week, I'll make an exception for you, Dr. Marcus."

All was forgiven. Sweet brown-eyed angel from

heaven. "Call me Sam, please," he said, on a rush of relief. "I really appreciate that."

Their earlier glowering contest faded to a distant memory when she smiled at him. It was more of a Mona Lisa smile, but it drew his attention to her mouth and he noticed a pair of classic lips with the delicate twin peaks of a Cupid's bow.

"So how about this day next week, at your house, say, sevenish?"

"Sounds like a plan, Ms….?"

"Rimmer, but please call me Andrea."

"Are you related to Dr. Rimmer?" The tyrant of Cardiac Surgery?

"Yes. Andrea's my granddaughter," Judith spoke up, reminding Sam that Dr. Rimmer was her son. Why he hadn't made the connection earlier was beyond him.

"I hope you won't hold that against me," Andrea said drily, as though reading his thoughts and bearing the weight of her father's perilous reputation. She glanced sheepishly at her grandmother, a good sign that Andrea cared about her and didn't want to insult her son, though it seemed clear she knew what Sam's surprised reaction had been about.

Since they'd skimmed over last week's argument and had moved on to peace talks, he wouldn't bring up his multiple grievances about the curmudgeon cardiac surgery department head who wanted to throw his weight around the entire hospital. Instead he dug deep into his bag of tricks and pulled out a smile. Admittedly, since his breakup with Katie, and Dani's diagnosis, he'd nearly forgotten how, but seeing Andrea's immediate relieved reaction, her expression brightening and those lovely lips parting into a grin, he was glad he had. Plus he'd meant that smile and it felt pretty damn good.

Because she was the first lady to get him riled up in ages, and he liked how that jacked up his ticker. She'd made him feel nearly human again.

"Next Tuesday, then. Seven. It's a date, Andrea."

CHAPTER TWO

Andrea tapped on the white front door of the boxy mid-century modern home in the hills above Glendale. She was about to ring the bell when the door swung open. Admittedly nervous about facing the handsome Dr. Sam Marcus on his turf, she grinned tensely until she saw him with an adorable little boy balanced on his hip and wearing an eye patch, then she relaxed.

"Come in," he said, seeming more hospitable than she would have imagined considering their first two encounters.

"Hi," she said, stepping inside onto expensive-looking white tile in the narrow entryway. "This must be Dani." She moved closer to the little boy, raised her brows and gave a closed-mouth smile. He buried his face in his father's shoulder. *Ack, too much.*

"Bashful," Sam mouthed.

She nodded and pretended to ignore the adorable little person after that, as Sam bypassed the living room and walked her into the more inviting family room. It was large, square, open and with excellent sources of natural light from tall windows nearly covering one entire wall of the boxy '50s architecture. As it was late April, the sun stuck around longer and longer, and though his house abutted mixed-tree-covered hills and stood on metal stilts at the front, the angle at this time of day was perfect for maximum light. A thick brown carpet made her want to kick off her shoes and walk barefoot. Not sure what to do next, she set her backpack and art box aka fishing-tackle box on the classic stone fireplace hearth, then glanced up at Sam. The previously upturned corners of his mouth had stretched into a genuine smile.

She'd given herself a stern talking-to the afternoon they'd made the appointment for letting herself send and pick up on some kind of natural attraction vibes arcing between them. The man was a father! Probably married. How many do-oyers would she need with this guy?

Shifting her gaze from Sam, she secretly studied Dani so as not to send him into ostrich mode again. She was admittedly surprised that Dani wasn't a mini-me of Sam. He looked Asian, Filipino maybe? Was he adopted? And Sam didn't wear a wedding ring, which made her wonder if he might not be married, but she figured she'd find out soon enough once his wife or significant other made an appearance.

"That's as good a place as any to set up," he said, easing Dani down onto his own two feet. "I hope the lighting is good enough."

"This should be perfect."

Dani immediately ran toward his stack of toys.

"Um, should I wait for your wife?"

"I'm not married. I adopted Dani on my own." Sam sat on the large wraparound couch and put his feet up on the circular ottoman at the center.

"That's fantastic." *Don't sound so enthusiastic!* "The adoption part, I mean." The only men she knew in Los Angeles who adopted kids on their own were gay. Dr.

Marcus clearly didn't fall into that category if she read that subtle humming interest between them right.

"I knew what you meant." A kind gaze came winging her way, and she felt her anxiety over making a dumb remark take a step down.

"Does he speak English?"

"They spoke both English and Tagalog at the orphanage. He's superbright and picks up more and more words every day." Spoken like a proud papa.

She found the boy busy with a colorful toy TV controller, punching buttons and listening to sounds and jingles, and dropped to her knees. "So, Dani, may I look under your patch?"

The black-haired toddler, who was small for his age, kept his head down, staring at the gadget in his hand, as he let her gingerly remove the child-sized patch. She'd seen empty eye socket after empty eye socket in the four years since she'd started the apprenticeship, but this was her first toddler. Grandma had given her a pep talk that afternoon about how much she believed in Andrea's talent and technical skills, and truth was she knew she'd caught on quickly to the long and tedious process of re-creating matching eyes for the eyeless. But this was a beautiful little kid, and her heart squeezed every time she looked at him, thinking this was way too early for anyone to need a prosthetic. But was there ever a good age?

She'd worn stretch slacks, so she sat cross-legged beside him in order to be at his level. "I need to make a little cast to fit your face, Dani. Will you let me do that?"

The boy looked at his father, who reassured him it was okay with a slow, deep nod.

"It won't hurt, I promise, but it might feel strange

and cold for a little while." With adult patients it was so much easier to explain the process. She'd just have to wing it with Dani. "May I take some pictures of your eye, too?"

"Eye gone," he said, slapping his palm over the left socket, as if she didn't know.

"This eye." She pointed to the right one.

"Okay." She could hardly hear him.

"Thank you." She blinked when he glanced up. "Do you ever play with clay?"

He nodded shyly.

"This stuff is kind of like clay. Want to watch?"

"Okay."

"Here, you can touch it."

He did but immediately pulled back his hand at the feel of the foreign, gooey substance.

Andrea worked quickly to make enough casting gel to press into the empty socket area, and when it was time, Sam held Dani's head still while she gently pressed it into the completely healed cavity. "Cold?"

"Uh-huh."

"But it doesn't hurt, right?"

He shook his head and they smiled at each other. He understood she hadn't lied. A sudden urge to cuddle the boy had her skimming her clean palm across his short-cropped hair instead. "How'd you get to be so sweet?"

"Don't know."

A surge of emotion made her eyes prickle. This precious guy had already lost an eye to cancer. How was that for a huge dose of reality to a toddler? She swallowed against the moisture gathering in her throat. "I bet you were born sweet." Was this how it felt to flirt with a little kid?

The statement wasn't the least bit funny, but Dani thought it was and he giggled, his remaining almond-shaped eye almost closing when he did. She hadn't been around many children since way back when she used to babysit for movie money, but something about Dani made her want to kiss his chubby cheeks and touch the tip of his rounded nose with her pointer finger.

She wiped her hands clean and dug out her camera from the backpack. "May I take your picture?"

"Uh-huh." He watched her as if mesmerized, but also maybe a little afraid to move with the cast in place and taking form.

"I have to get really close to your eye. Is that okay?"

"Yes."

She leaned in toward his cute out-sticking ear and whispered, "I promise not to touch your eye, just take pictures."

He sat perfectly still and stared at her camera as she focused and zoomed in and shot photo after photograph of his dark brown orb. Later she'd study that eye until she had it memorized, then, and only then, would she attempt the intricate painting of his iris. Making eyes was a long and tedious process that took anywhere between sixteen and occasionally up to eighty hours, even though there was a big push to go digital these days. Mistakes weren't acceptable in Grandma's world. Neither was digital technology. Andrea had learned early on to take the extra time and effort at the beginning to save hours of do-overs. And she loved that part of her job.

By the age of three she knew the human eye was just a hair smaller by one or two millimeters than it would eventually become, and that by the age of thirteen it would reach the full adult size. Danilo would probably need a new prosthesis at that time, if not before, but she planned to make this one to last a full decade. The boy deserved no less.

After four minutes the timer went off, alerting her that the silicone was set. Tomorrow, back in the O&A department, she'd duplicate it in wax and later reform it until it fit Dani perfectly, which would give her another excuse to see the adorable little guy. There'd be multiple reasons to see Dani, since he'd have a trial period of wearing a clear acrylic beneath his patch for fitting purposes for the next month while she re-created his iris.

"I'm all done. What do you think about that?" She gently eased out the silicone cast from his eye socket, brow line and upper cheek.

"Okay."

"And it didn't hurt, did it?"

He shook his head. She showed him what the cast looked like and he made a funny face, which made her laugh, then she carefully put the partial facial and eye-socket cast into a protective carrying case. Dani watched every move she made, as if she might be taking part of his face with her. She handed him a mirror to see she'd left all of him behind. He stoically studied himself, missing eye and all, which made her want to brighten him up.

Andrea raised her brows and pressed her lips together before talking. "Did you know I brought you a present?"

His other eye widened. "No." So serious.

"I brought you my favorite stuffed frog." She reached into her backpack and pulled out the bean-stuffed toy that used to sit on her computer monitor at work. She'd grabbed it on a whim just before she'd left tonight. "His name is Ribbit."

Dani giggled again. "I like him."

"Here. He's yours. You earned him for being so good." She offered him the toy, and he reached for it without hesitation.

"What do you say?" For the first time in the entire process Sam spoke up.

"Thank you."

She couldn't help herself and kissed his forehead. "You are welcome."

Sam cleared his throat. "Can I make you some tea or coffee?"

"Tea sounds good. Thanks." There was a strange expression in Sam's eyes when theirs met, as if maybe he'd been touched by the interchange with her and Dani as much as she had.

Dani played happily with his frog as Andrea helped put the eye patch back on. "There. Now you look like a pirate."

"I don't like pirate."

"When I make your new eye, you won't need to wear the patch anymore."

He touched the patch and tugged on it. "Okay."

"Hey, is this your truck?" She crawled over to a pile of toys in the corner of the room. "May I play with it?" The boy quickly followed her and laughed when she made a vroom-vroom sound, pushing the red truck around the carpet, while waiting for Sam to make the tea.

Next they played building blocks, and Dani took great pleasure in letting her build her colorful tower, only to knock it down the instant she'd finished. She pretended to be upset, folding her arms and pouting, but the boy saw right through her. Mostly what they did was laugh, giggle, tease each other and horse around until Sam showed up with the tea.

"I hate to break up the play, Dani, but it's time to get you ready for bed."

Dani acted upset. He pushed out his lower lip and crossed his chubby arms just like Andrea had done a few moments before, but she knew it was all a show. He'd been rubbing his right eye when they'd played, like any little kid who was getting sleepy. When he thought she wasn't looking, he'd even yawned.

"Oh, jammies," Andrea said, to distract him from his pout. "I bet you've got really cool jammies."

"My jammies have trucks," he said, his sweet single-eyed gaze waiting for her reaction.

"Trucks! I think you already know how much I love trucks."

She was positive she saw him puff out his chest. Sam offered his hand and Dani took it, looking happily up at his father. The moment went still in her mind like a photograph, as she admired the sweet boy with the loving new parent he'd had the good fortune to find. But before he left the room she called after him. "Dani, don't forget your frog."

He trotted back to take it and gave her one last smile before running off to his father's waiting hand, then walking with him down the hall. Andrea sat on the plush carpet and sipped her fragrant chamomile tea, her heart aching for a precious little boy with one eye. The warm tea helped smooth out the lump in her throat, but there was no way she'd soon forget Dani.

A large framed black-and-white photograph on the opposite wall caught her attention. She carried her tea over to it and counted eight kids with a mother and father, all grinning, on someone's front lawn. She studied the enlarged grainy family photo and determined that the boy third from the end might possibly be Sam Marcus. Or maybe he was second in? Come to think of it, there wasn't a very strong family resemblance.

A tallish woman with a broad smile and clear-looking eyes stood next to a droopy-shouldered man with a soft, kind face. They both had dark hair. Two of the kids looked even less like the rest, a blonde girl and a gangly boy with a buzz cut, but somehow those two had earned the favored position of each standing under a draping arm of the mother. Maybe that was Sam under her right arm? Who knew? The date at the bottom of the blown-up picture read "1990." That would make Dr. Marcus somewhere around thirty.

Andrea's gaze wandered to another wall and a shiny silver frame with beautiful cursive penmanship on a weathered scroll inside. The title read "Legend of the Starfish" and the short allegory taught that though a person might not be able to save everyone, in this case starfish, they could at least help one at a time. She stood pondering the words, sipping her tea, wondering what this told her about Dr. Samuel Marcus, the single guy who'd adopted a little boy from the Philippines.

Ten minutes had passed. She'd put all of Dani's toys back where they belonged and had almost finished her herbal tea when Sam returned. He wore comfortable jeans that still managed to hug his hips and thighs, and a white with black stripes polo shirt he hadn't bothered to tuck in. It gave her a glimpse of his broader-than-she'd-expected chest and surprising biceps. He walked around in his socks, proving he was totally at home in his castle. His cell phone rang. He checked the caller and said, "Sorry, but I've got to take this. It's my sister." She nodded her approval.

"You're up late," he said, then walked around the room in brief yet very familiar conversation. She tried not to listen, though envying him having a sister to share things with.

His hair was less tidy tonight, and Andrea liked the effect, especially when a clump fell forward onto his forehead when he bent over to pick up an overlooked toy block. And the eyes that had practically drilled a hole into her the last time they'd met seemed smoky blue tonight without a trace of tension around them. She'd often heard the term "boyish good looks," but never understood what that meant until now. How could that uptight man who'd barged into her department be the same guy standing in front of her? A man who'd adopted a little boy on his own and appeared to genuinely enjoy a conversation with his sister. A man like that had to have a good heart.

She took in a tiny breath as he ended the call and approached, her enjoying every step. So this was what an everyday hero looked like. Feeling nothing short of smitten, she let out a beyond-friendly smile.

Sam didn't know why he'd choked up just before he'd put Dani to bed, but seeing Andrea with his son, and how effortlessly they'd gotten along, made him remember how much Katie had let him down. Evidently having her own kids would have been one thing, but it'd been too much for her to consider adopting someone else's child. "You never know what you'll get," she'd said. "You could be adopting a million problems." He'd argued that the same could be said for any child. Besides, he'd seen with his own eyes what wonders selfless understanding and generosity of love could work on most kids. His foster mother had been the queen of that, not only with her own children but with all the kids she'd brought into their home.

He wasn't about to go down Katie's road of disappointment and pain again, especially right now, not when the dramatic-looking, height-challenged blonde with big overly made-up brown eyes sat waiting for him. He smiled and she gave a flirtatious beam right back. He definitely liked that, even though he knew a smile like that could be dangerous.

"You've made quite an impression. Dani said to tell you good-night."

"Great. He's an awfully sweet kid."

"Yeah, he has a gentle nature." Now wasn't the time to go all soft over the misfortune of his beautiful adopted son, and how sometimes it reminded him of his own situation as a child, so he focused on his tea. "My tea's gone cold. Can I refill yours?" He scooped up his cup and took hers when she offered it to him, then headed for the kitchen. Surprisingly, she followed along in her bare feet. He liked it that she'd made herself at home.

He put their cups on the kitchen counter, and as he turned on the front burner to heat the teapot, he felt her expectant gaze. He glanced over his shoulder and found her still smiling at him, so he smiled back, letting her warmth pass through him. If they kept up this goofy grinning, things could get awkward.

"It's really obvious you're a good and loving father."

"I don't know how true that is, but he deserves no less." He kept busy, opening and closing drawers and cabinets, but talked freely.

Something about her easygoing and encouraging style helped him open up. "You know my greatest fear is that Dani might lose his other eye. They say the odds are low with a single retinoblastoma, but having gone through this with him I guess I'm still afraid it could happen again. And the kid so doesn't deserve any of this." He bit back his frustration.

Andrea kept quiet, cuing him to keep talking, so he did. "No matter what happens, my goal is to make as normal a life as possible for Dani."

"I can tell how much you care about him." She folded her hands on the quartz surface, and he thought the counter was high for her stature. She'd need a little stool to wash dishes at this sink. The thought tickled him and made the corner of his mouth quirk, imagining her standing on a stool in his kitchen, washing plates. So domestic, so different than the artistic impression she gave. Where had that thought come from?

She couldn't be more than five feet, but what a powerhouse. She'd probably never be caught dead washing dishes for a guy. He sensed she'd never let anyone take advantage of her. She sure as hell hadn't let him that day. Thinking back to her stern father, he was sure she'd probably had to grow a steel spine to survive. Yeah, no way she'd be a happy dishwasher.

He poured them both more tea and they sat at the kitchen table, and because she was so easy to be around, and seemed so sympathetic toward Dani, he decided to really open up. "I'm afraid people will look at Dani and pity him, which, by the way, you absolutely didn't do. Thanks for that."

She dipped her head and blinked slowly, then took a sip of her tea, so serious. "I've had a lot of practice with our clientele."

"I'm sure you have." He sipped, but the tea was too hot, so he put the cup on the table. "I also worry that other kids will be curious about his fake eye and make him self-conscious."

"I think all kids are self-conscious about something."

A quick flash of him being around seven or eight and having to wear faded thrift-store shirts that didn't fit to school, because that was all his mother could afford, reminded him firsthand about self-consciousness.

"The thing is, I don't want him to slip into the mind-set of feeling inferior. That could set the tone for the rest of his life. I'd hate for that to happen." He'd been fighting those feelings his entire life, and he'd obviously said something to move Andrea, because she leaned forward and her hand cupped his forearm and tightened.

"I'm going to make the most perfect eye ever for him. The other kids won't even notice."

"Then it'll be my job to teach him to be totally independent, not afraid to try things." His crazy, lovable foster family came to mind. "Hell, if he takes after any of his new uncles, he'll give me gray hair before my time."

"I think your plan is perfect. Dani's a lucky boy to have you as his father. By the way, is that your family in that big picture?"

He considered the Murphys his family, especially after he'd been taken away from his mother at ten and she'd officially given him up when he'd been twelve—which had hurt like nothing he'd ever experienced before and could never be matched until Katie had walked away—and they'd kept him until he'd been eighteen, then sent him off to college.

"Yep. The big clan, circa 1990. I was around ten in that one."

"Ah, you were the middle brother. I thought I recognized you." She laughed lightly, and he was glad she'd taken the time to look at his family picture, but didn't feel like going into the complicated explanation of who they really were. He hardly knew her. He'd let her think what he let the rest of the world think—he'd come from a big, happy family.

"Yeah, try being in the middle of four daredevil brothers. Those guys were tough acts to follow. Probably why I went into medicine." His professional choice had also been part of his determination to prove the positive impact fostering could have. It had been his way of giving something back. But she didn't need to know that, either.

She smiled and he grinned back. He found his smiles coming more often and easier, spending time with her. It felt good.

"I can only imagine." She went quiet.

They sat in silence for a while, him in deep thought about the responsibilities of being a single father, about how his parents had taught by example the importance of routine and stability in every kid's life, and having no clue what Andrea was ruminating about. Soon the tea was gone and she stood.

"Time to go?" How could he blame her? He'd gone quiet after the topic of his family had come up, then had gotten all maudlin about his lack of parental skills. Great company. Who'd want to stick around for more of that?

"Yes. I want to get an early start on my project tomorrow."

He stood now, too. "I'm really glad you're doing it."

"Really?"

"Yeah, you're not nearly as bad as I originally thought." They laughed together, and it lightened the shifting mood. He wanted that earlier ease back between them.

"Oh, yes, the impertinent ocularist strikes again," she teased. "But I could have sworn you started it."

"I was uptight. Give me a break."

He could tell from the benign look on her face that she *was* indeed giving him a break, that she totally understood, especially now having met Dani, and he truly appreciated that.

They headed for the family room, where her tackle box and backpack had been left, Dani's silicone cast safely tucked inside. "And I had no idea what you'd just been through." With the backpack over one shoulder she faced him, an earnest expression softening her serious face. "Please forgive me for being rude to you that day."

"I've already forgotten. Besides, after the way you and Dani became fast friends tonight, I kind of have to."

That got another smile and a breath of a laugh out of her.

He walked her to the door and allowed one quick thought about how great she looked in those black slacks and the pale blue sweater hugging her curves. It was so much better than those faded scrubs and that frumpy white lab coat.

They said good-night, and he asked when he'd need to bring Dani in for reshaping of the wax mold she planned to make.

"I'll be in touch," she said, "as soon as possible, I promise."

"Then I'll take you at your word."

They said their goodbyes. He closed the door and scratched his chin and let his mind wonder about the possibility of something more working out between him and the perky ocularist. That was a first since Katie, too, and a good thing. Wasn't it about time to start dating again? For an instant he realized how single mothers must feel, wondering if a man wanted to get involved with a lady with kids. Was that how it worked the other way around? Would it matter to Andrea, as it had mattered to Katie, that he was an adoptive father?

CHAPTER THREE

SAM STROLLED INTO the hospital employee cafeteria to grab a quick lunch before his afternoon clinic. He'd barely finished playing catch-up with his electronic charting and had about twenty minutes to spare. Going through the line, he grabbed the fish of the day, and his guess was as good as any as to what type of white fish it was. He went for the least overcooked vegetables, green beans, grabbed a whole wheat roll and a tossed green salad and was good to go.

After paying, he juggled his cafeteria tray and searched around the noisy and crowded room—which smelled entirely too much of garlic—for a place to sit. A pleasant surprise awaited him when he spotted the light blond hair of his new favorite ocularist, especially after the slam-dunk impression she'd made on Dani last night, and he made a straight line to where she sat. Fortunately, she was eating alone. And reading a book, so she didn't notice him coming.

"Is this seat taken?"

Andrea glanced up, totally distracted by whatever novel she'd been reading. "Oh, hi." An instant flash of recognition and a welcoming smile made him think he'd made the right decision. "No, join me."

"Thanks." The invitation, which he'd clearly forced,

still managed to make him happy. He sat, but not before removing the dishes from his tray and balancing that against the leg of the table. From this angle he could see the book was a biography on the artist Jackson Pollock. "Reading picture books, I see. No wonder you and Dani got along so well." He could always manage superficial conversations easily enough, had learned early on it was a survival technique in the foster care system, which had been pointed out to him by his "mom" when he'd tried the old you-can't-reach-me routine at first. The quiet and withdrawn kids got moved around more than the ones who knew how to socialize. All he wanted to do was prove he was worth keeping. That was the truth.

She rolled her eyes at his awful attempt at humor. "America's cowboy artist. Our very own van Gogh, torment and all." She closed the book and gave all of her attention to him. He liked that. Her naturally beautiful eyes were less distracted by makeup today, which he definitely also liked.

"How's our project going?" He pushed around the green beans rather than taking a bite, then decided to pile them on top of the piece of fish, thinking it might help the bland cafeteria food have a little more flavor that way.

"I'm off to a good start. I'll need to see Dani again, though, to exactly fit the wax mold."

"I can have my sister bring him by this afternoon, if you'd like." Yeah, piling the food together hadn't helped enhance the flavor at all, but watching Andrea, hearing her voice, made the taste far more palatable. Next he dug into his salad.

"I should be able to work that in. Can she bring him around two-thirty?"

"I'll see." He got out his mobile phone and texted Cat,

his foster sister, the one he felt closest to. Being a mother of two toddlers herself, plus the fact she lived five miles from him, it'd made sense to ask her to be his child-care provider when his parental leave came to an end and he had to go back to work. Not to mention the fact that her husband, Buddy, a welder, had agreed to her staying at home with their kids. They lived on a tight budget, and she could use the extra income that watching Dani brought. The way he saw it, it was a win-win situation.

Andrea took a dainty bite of her salad, and he smiled at her, then tore into his roll, slathering it with butter, then taking a bite. "So, do you eat here every day?"

"Not usually, but I came in early today to start Dani's mold and forgot to pack a lunch."

"Thanks for that." He got a return on his text. "She'll be here. Now I'll have to explain that you're located in the dungeon next to the ghoulish morgue." He finished his text and looked up to see her studying him. Had he been insensitive about her department and its location? Had he insinuated that hers was an inferior department? Hell, it didn't even have windows, even when right at this moment in time it was the most important department in the whole hospital for him and his son. "I'm sorry if that sounded mean. I have jerk tendencies. I blame it totally on the influence of four brothers."

"You do have a big family, I can't argue with that."

"Crazy big, but it made me who I am. Major flaws and all." He grinned at her and really liked what she returned. "Sorry." If he'd offended her about her department being in no man's land, she'd easily forgiven him, judging by the sweet smile that highlighted those gorgeous lips. He allowed himself a moment or two to check them out. And when was the last time he'd gotten carried away with wild ideas by a woman's mouth?

He took another bite of his food to distract him from thinking of what it would feel like to kiss her. "This has got to be the worst lunch I've had in a long time," he said, to cover his real thoughts. *But thanks for that luscious mouth of yours.*

"The salad's not bad."

He pushed his plate aside and pulled the salad bowl closer, deciding to take her up on her tip and stick with that and the roll. "Right about now I'm dreaming about Thai food."

"I love Thai food." She matched him bite for bite with the salad.

"Yeah? You like pineapple fried rice? Pad Thai?"

"Love it, and satay, peanut sauce, all of it."

"But have you ever had coconut curry with braised chicken and egg noodles?"

"No, and now my mouth is watering, thank you very much." She played with her salad, no longer taking bites.

"Sorry. Didn't mean to ruin your lunch, but sometime I'm going to have to take you to Hollywood Boulevard for my new favorite dish."

She tossed him a questioning glance over the vague remark. And, yes, he was testing the water. Playing it safe was a knack he'd developed, and always preferable to getting rejected.

"Uh, yes, I guess theoretically that was an invitation. You interested?"

"Well, you can't very well dangle coconut curry in front of me like that without inviting me. Theoretically speaking, that is. It wouldn't be polite."

"Agreed. And we both know I'm nothing if not polite." Considering their rocky beginnings, with his being pushy, demanding and rude and her giving him a taste of his own medicine right back, his absurd comment hit the mark and she laughed. He joined her. Good. She had a sense of humor. He'd try to keep her smiling, because she really was gorgeous to watch that way. "Truth is, since adopting Dani I don't get out much anymore. So are you really up for this?"

"Absolutely. But who'll watch Dani?"

Thoughtful of her to wonder. "I'll ask Cat again, since I haven't introduced him to Thai food yet." *And I'd like time alone with you.*

"Okay. Theoretically, that sounds good."

"Yeah, some Dutch beer, coconut curry—heaven."

"I know it's a gazillion calories, but I prefer Thai iced tea."

"Chicks." He tossed his paper napkin across the remaining half of his salad. "Only a lady would pass up good Dutch beer for sweet tea." He wasn't sure why he liked to tease her so much, but the instant she grinned he remembered. They were having something he'd almost forgotten. Fun.

"My prerogative." She feigned being insulted. "And guys. Always competitive. Please, don't tell me you'll force me into a hot curry tasting contest. I'm not one of your brothers."

He leaned forward and gazed into her truly enticing eyes. "How do you know us so well? You have a bunch of brothers, too?"

She shook her head. "Nope. I'm an only child."

"Really? I don't know many of those. What's it like to have a house all to yourself. To know what the sound of a pin dropping is? To never have to cross your legs and dance around in the hallway, waiting for the bathroom?"

After a brief and polite smile on the last comment she went serious, met his gaze and held it. "Lonely?"

That answer made him sad. He knew that kind of

loneliness, plus fear, having been left alone at night for a couple of years before he'd been taken away from his mother—he hated the memory and tried to suppress it as much as possible—plus, he wanted to put a positive spin on the conversation to keep things upbeat. "And quiet. I bet it was really quiet at your house, you lucky dog." Though the quiet used to scare him to death as that left-behind kid.

She'd finished her lunch and moved her salad bowl away to prove it. "So you grew up in a noisy house, big deal. Isn't that why they invented earbuds and playlists?"

Being around her kept him from going to that old and awful place in his mind.

"Headphones back then at my house with portable CD players. And anytime I used them one of my brothers would sneak up and pull them off my head. Made me all flinchy, waiting. Couldn't even enjoy the music."

He'd made her laugh lightly again and he really appreciated her putting up with his silliness, because he needed to get far away from bad memories. The fact that he'd fudged about his "family" really being a foster family didn't seem relevant now. "You know, if I didn't have to get back to work, I'd invite you to have lunch there right now."

"But I've already had lunch. Just finished."

She tipped her head, a suspicious gaze, clueing him in that he needed to do something. After all this big buildup about the great Thai food, the almost-but-not-quite invitation, he'd better make his move beyond the theoretical. And as his foster father used to say, there was no time like the present.

"Will you have dinner with me tomorrow night, then? I'm thinking Thai food. Hollywood. Beer or iced tea, but definitely fried bananas for dessert." He'd just asked out the first woman after his breakup with Katie and becoming a father, and it felt damn good. He was ready for this. Except maybe he should hold off on the triumph part until he got her answer.

A why-not expression brightened her rich mocha eyes, but only after a long moment's hesitation. This one wasn't looking for a date or a boyfriend—a good thing in general, but right this moment a little unnerving. "Sure," she said finally. "I'd like that."

Both surprised and happy, he grinned and rapped his knuckles twice on the cafeteria tabletop. "Great. It's a date, then."

"I'm sorry, Mom," Andrea said over the phone after lunch. "I've just made plans for tomorrow night." Why she'd agreed to have dinner with Sam Marcus was beyond her, but he'd lured her with a great-sounding meal, and to be honest the thought of spending a few hours with him hadn't seemed like such a bad idea at the time. Not even fifteen minutes later she doubted her decision.

Chalk another one up to dear old Dad, the first and worst man in her life.

"With a man?" Mom didn't even try to hide her surprise.

Andrea snickered. Yes, it was a rare occurrence for her to accept dates, so she couldn't blame her mother's honest outburst. Jerome Rimmer had done a number on both of them. "Yes, Mother, a man." A doctor, no less. Was she crazy?

"Well, that's wonderful."

"I don't know about wonderful, but there is Thai food involved, so it won't be all bad." No, she wasn't looking for a relationship, that was for sure, especially not with a doctor. Her overbearing, demanding, perfectionist father had pretty much messed her up forever in the male/female department. But a simple evening out, gazing at a way more than decent-looking guy, who also happened to smell really good—she couldn't help noticing during lunch—wouldn't be a total loss of an evening, would it?

"Oh, now, Andrea, maybe he'll be nice."

And maybe Dad was actually the greatest guy on earth, but somehow Andrea had never noticed it before? "He seems nice. But let's not read more into this than necessary. I'm making an eye for his adopted son, so I think he may just want to pay me back somehow."

"Oh, I see." Mom went quiet.

Her mother rarely invited Andrea to dinner, but now that she was on the new medicine regimen for her debilitating depression, she seemed to have more energy and to be more interested in interacting with people. Andrea hated to put her off. "Can we get together Friday night?"

"Oh, Friday is a bad night for your father. He's got a weekend conference to attend in Sacramento and he's leaving that afternoon."

"We could make it a girls' night out, just the two of us." Andrea had learned as a child how fragile her mother was emotionally, especially after marrying a guy like Andrea's dad, and her insecurity about being loved was still a weakness. The last thing Andrea wanted to do was blow her off without making replacement plans. Besides, she'd much rather have dinner with just her mother than both of her parents.

"That might be fun, but let me fix dinner," her mother said. "We can stay in and eat here."

Aware that her mother was still dealing with her reclusiveness and anxiety issues, Andrea wouldn't push it. "That's fine. I just want to spend time with you. Plus you know I love your cooking." Growing up, watching her mother always trying to impress her father with her cooking skills but always coming up short for her perfectionistic father, had taught Andrea not to even try to learn to cook.

"I'll keep it simple, but it will be great to see you. Seems like forever." Her mother's "simple" was fifty times better than anything Andrea could come up with.

"Barbara! Where's my gray tie? Did you iron those shirts for me?" Andrea's father's voice boomed in the background, demanding as always.

"Oh! Um, let me do that right now," Barbara said, her voice shifting toward trying-to-please mode from the relaxed state a second before. "I've got to go, honey. See you Friday. I'll tell Dad you said hi."

"I'll bring dessert!" She'd buy it from the local bakery.

And that was that. Dad bellowed, Mom jumped. Too bad antidepressants couldn't change that well-worn routine, too. And for the record, she hadn't said hi to her dad.

Sam picked up Andrea after work on Thursday, having removed his tie from a gray denim shirt and wearing a sporty black lightweight zip-up jacket and dark jeans. She'd dressed nicer than usual for work, had even worn wedge-heeled sandals, knowing tonight was their date, and had rushed to change when the department closed. She'd hoped her straight-legged beige pants and gentle yellow boat-necked sweater would be nice enough for dinner out, and, seeing his casual appearance, she decided she'd made the right decision.

"Hey." His genuine expression gave her the impression he was happy, and maybe a little excited about seeing her.

She was flat-out nervous, since he was the first guy she'd wanted to go out with in months, and worked hard to cover her nervousness and focus on the meal part, not the date. "Hi. I'm starving—how about you?"

"Definitely. Hmm, you smell great."

"Thanks. Sometimes I worry I smell like acrylics and wax after working here all day. I didn't overdo it, did I?" She'd used a sample she'd gotten at a cosmetic counter the last time she'd bought eyeliner. It had an almost stringent citrusy scent in the container, but softened on her skin. Or at least she hoped so.

He stepped closer and sniffed the air, but she got the distinct impression he'd wanted to test her neck, which kind of excited her. "Smells great to me."

Their eyes connected and something fizzed through her body. "Thanks." She pretended to hunt for her purse while she regained her composure. What was it about Dr. Sam Marcus that shook her up so much, especially since she'd seen him in another light at his house? This guy wasn't all boom and bluster, like her father. He was obviously a caring father who'd taken in a special-needs kid. One of the good guys, and good guys were even scarier than the bastards.

When they arrived at the Thai restaurant, it was only six, but the place was already crowded. Wall-to-wall tables lined up with little care for intimacy, just straight row after row from one end to the other of the modern Asian eatery. Though there were more secluded tables outside, enclosed by an intricate white wrought-iron fence to separate them from the boulevard, Sam thought the street noise would be too distracting and said so. So they took a table inside by a window with tall bamboo on the other side.

"It's not much for ambiance, but I endorse the food one hundred percent."

"I can't wait."

They grinned at each other all through dinner. Sam obviously enjoyed his Dutch beer, and Andrea savored her sweet Thai iced tea. She liked the end-of-day stubble on his cheeks and chin, and how his hair wasn't neatly combed. She thought the creases around his mouth made him look distinguished, but the one-sided dimple kept him cute, all-American-boy cute. She'd never call him classically handsome because he had so much more appeal as a good-looking, everyday kind of guy. The part of his face she hesitated to study was his eyes. Those baby blues seemed to reach right inside her whenever they talked, and she got occasional prickles down the back of her neck. It was a feeling she'd nearly forgotten, that "thing" that only certain men set off. Between eating all the great food, their conversation still managed to be nonstop.

Who'd have thought a stuffy, overbearing doctor could be so easy to talk to?

"No, no. I can't," she said, when he offered her one last bite of the fried bananas. "I'll burst." She was definitely thankful she'd worn her semi-loose envelope-hem sweater.

So he popped the last bite into his mouth and chomped down, shaking his head over how good it tasted. He sat back in his chair. "Do I look like a satisfied man? I'm just asking."

His frequent, silly outbursts always made her grin. "You definitely look like a man who's enjoyed his food so much he has a bright yellow curry stain above his pocket."

He pulled in his chin and glanced down, then frowned.

"I swear, I think Dani's eating habits are wearing off on me." He dipped his cloth napkin into the remaining glass of water and attempted to do a quick cleanup, which only drew more attention to the stain, which struck her as downright sweet.

"Dr. Sammy! Dr. Sammy!" A high-pitched child's voice cut into the moment. Sam lifted his brows and followed the sound.

So his patients call him Dr. Sammy, how adorable. Could this man be any more appealing?

"Hi!" He waved at a little redheaded boy who looked no more than eight, as he walked by with his parents on their way to being seated. The mother stopped.

"That new medicine you prescribed has done wonders."

Like a true gentleman, "Dr. Sammy" stood and spoke quietly to the boy's mom, though briefly. Andrea looked on with a strange feeling growing inside. Admiration. This was a good guy who took his job seriously, and who didn't just talk the talk but walked the walk. He cared about people. He was single and he'd adopted a son. With his profession, he could have indulged himself with everything from travel to grown-up toys like cars and boats to women, but he'd chosen to go on medical mission trips, settle down and raise a son…who'd lost his eye and needed special care. She'd never met a man like Dr. Sammy before.

The negative side of her allowed one little thought to slip past. What was the catch? Was he too good to be true? Maybe she'd seen the real Dr. Marcus the first day she'd met him, and for her taste that'd been way too much like dear old Dad. Maybe he was on his best behavior tonight and it was all a facade.

Andrea hated how her father still negatively influenced her life and her thinking toward men.

She took one last drink from her tea and stood when Sam offered her his hand. "We ready?"

"I'm going to have to waddle out of here," she said, "but, yes, thanks."

The odd thing was he didn't let go of her hand as they walked back to the car. The warmth of his solid palm flat against hers turned out to be far more distracting than the loud car noises, brakes and horns along Hollywood Boulevard, or the ugly earlier memories of being raised by a man like Dad. Sam's grip felt warm, and if hands could actually do this, it also felt sexy. She pursed her lips, wondering what to make of everything.

Sam walked Andrea to the apartment door. The sturdy Spanish-styled beige triplex dwelling had two units downstairs and a larger single unit upstairs. Andrea's was on the lower right, with rustic red Saltillo tile on the entry porch and an azalea shrub in a huge terra-cotta container right next to the door. He'd been surprised to learn she often took public transportation to work, and he wondered happily if maybe today she'd chosen to do it because they'd had plans for dinner and she wanted a ride home from him. He wouldn't let that fact go to his head, but it sure made his outlook optimistic about what might come next.

"Would you like to come in?"

Of course! "Sure. Thanks."

She unlocked the solid dark wooden door and flipped on lights. The funky yet hip apartment showed a different side of the Andrea he'd come to know at the hospital. The walls were covered in paintings that he knew for a fact he couldn't afford, and he wondered how she could. Rather than sit down in one of the boxy chairs or on the trendy urban home-styled sofa, he walked around the room and admired each one of the amazing conceptual modern paintings that featured mostly bright colors and abstract designs and patterns. "These are something else."

"Thanks."

Then his eyes caught sight of another one, very different from the others, in a corner by itself. It was a long rectangular canvas featuring a single eye peeking through a keyhole in an old door. From his own reading on the topic, he recognized this style as something called photorealism. "I'd buy something like this. It's really special." It spoke to him, seemed to nail how he'd felt as a foster kid at first, watching life through a keyhole, not really a part of it. Sometimes he still felt that way.

"Thank you."

"Who painted all of these?" He squinted to read the tiny signature but couldn't quite make it out.

"Oh, let's see. Um, me." She pointed to one of the bigger paintings, then another. "Me. Oh, and me and me." She ended by pointing to the door and keyhole, his favorite. "Me."

He did a double take and his brows had to have risen a good inch. "Wow. You're really talented." *She's an artist?* Hadn't he sworn off the artistic types after Katie, the actress, had chosen a recurring bit part on a TV sitcom to being his wife and an adoptive mother? "Now I get why you were reading that book on Jackson Pollock yesterday." Andrea possessed significant talent, he couldn't deny that.

"I don't paint anything like him, but I love his renegade approach to art." She threw her jacket over a chair. "He inspires me to take chances."

"So, let me get this straight. You're an artist who works at the hospital, making prosthetic eyes for people."

"Correct."

"But—" he glanced around at the spectacular paintings "—painting is your first love."

She stopped and sighed. "I have to be honest and say yes."

Uh-oh. Been there with Katie. "So if a millionaire bought all of your paintings, you'd walk out the door of St. Francis of the Valley and never look back?"

She stood perfectly still, clearly weighing the truth of her answer. Her eyes drifted over the walls of her apartment, studying her own work for just a moment. "In a perfect world, yes. But I have a grandmother I respect and a father who would hound me to death if I dared. And, honestly, I love my patients and the fact that I can improve their lives."

He didn't like the sound of the first part of her answer one bit. It meant she worked in the O&A department against her will. In fact, he hated the answer so much that a yellow flag waved in the recesses of his mind. Artists were flighty. People you couldn't depend on. Sign him on to the grandmother and dad's side. The thought didn't seem fair to Andrea, though. It felt kind of selfish, if he was honest, but after his experience with Katie his perspective was blurred. Then there was the second part of her answer—she loved helping people and obviously got a lot out of the job in that respect. Life was never black-and-white, and in her case he preferred the gray areas.

There was something about Andrea that called out to him. He genuinely liked her, she was attractive, talented, fun to be around, and she gave a damn about people. She also happened to turn him on. Very much. His instinct said to go for it, kiss her. Damn. Why couldn't he think straight? He'd blame it on the carb high from the Thai food, but the concern about her being an artist was still enough to trip him up.

"Would you like some coffee or wine?"

"The wine sounds great, but can I take a rain check? I need to pick up Dani." His son was a logical excuse, and an honest one. He really did need to go get him.

Sam glanced around the living room. He liked the feel of her home, especially liked her, and would've liked to stick around, yellow flag or not, because she was so damn hot. But he was a father and knew for a fact that Dani slept best in his own bed. Which was a great argument for finding a babysitter besides his foster sister—who couldn't do nights—one who would come to his house. Being a parent, especially a single father, had been a steep learning curve, and this moment had just taught him something else, besides caution about the new lady in his world—the value of a teenage, pay-by-the-hour babysitter. Did they still exist? He'd make a mental note to follow up on the idea ASAP so he wouldn't have to miss out on another invitation like this from Andrea, if she ever gave him one.

He noticed Andrea's disappointment over his rain check on the wine. It was in her nearly Keane-like eyes, which surprised and pleased him at the same time. Was she as interested in him as he was in her?

But she recovered quickly. "Sure. After that huge dinner I should put some time in on the treadmill anyway. A glass of wine would definitely interfere with that."

He'd enjoyed every second of watching her tonight over dinner. She'd eaten like a champ, and she'd parted her hair on the side and swept her bangs, the only long part of her hair, to one side, accenting her round face, big eyes and sharp chin. The short-haired style was definitely growing on him. She'd held up her end of the conversation throughout the evening, too, and he'd never felt the need to fill in lag time. She hadn't said a thing about her talent, either. Humble. Another good trait.

It made sense that a trained artist would be right for the job of re-creating eyes, and he assumed every eye was unique in some way, and an artist would be best to detect the difference. Now he was glad grandmother Judith had assigned her to his son's case. Glancing around her walls at the bright colors and splotches of paint that, though seeming random, still managed to grab an immediate reaction from him, he realized that Andrea was special, someone he wanted to know more. Even though he'd been kicked hard in the relationship solar plexus by Katie. Andrea was different. He had to keep that in mind.

Hell, Cat would be the first to chew him out for comparing the two women. And he didn't know Andrea well enough to pigeonhole her anyway, but she'd admitted art was her first love. She'd be willing to walk away from ocularistry if the artistic opportunity arose. Theoretically. But why should that matter? He wanted to get to know her better, and that part, the glutton-for-punishment part, the part that still insisted women didn't stick around for him, made him nervous. All because she was so damn appealing.

He was a father now, with a son who needed much of his attention and a job that needed the rest. Was there even room for a woman?

The silent pause had grown long and awkward. He'd been overthinking things, like always. That was another thing that being a foster kid had taught him—consider all possibilities, because life could change at a moment's notice. "I guess I better be going."

"Okay," she muttered, resigned. Disappointed? He hoped so because he sure was.

"Nice apartment, by the way," he said, thinking how lame he sounded, and turned to leave.

Andrea strode toward him with those crazy-sexy platform sandals tapping on the Spanish tile and something on her mind, and he stopped dead in his tracks. If he wasn't mistaken, she was giving a clear sign, so when she got close enough he held her upper arms and moved in for a kiss that evidently she had already been planning on. Great, the feeling *was* mutual. But was he sure it was a good idea?

Right now, who cared?

Her hands wrapped around his neck and that sexy fragrance he'd picked up on back at the hospital lingered in the air. He liked it. A lot. Her mouth felt fresh, tasted sweet, like her tea, and full of life. Every worry about her being an artist flew from his head. She kissed like a curious explorer, and he dived in with enthusiasm and soon did some serious investigating of his own. He liked the warmth of the inside rim of her lips, the feel of them on his, the fact that she opened her mouth and invited him in, then put him under her spell. She was a creative kisser, as she was a creative painter, and he soon got swept away.

With her body pressed against his, her heat and softness melding to his chest, a forgotten hunger came out of hiding. He wanted more of her. Confusion about pursuing his lust and whether it would be wise or not, and the more practical need to pick up his son at a reasonable hour, soon crept back into his thoughts and ruined the moment. He couldn't get carried away now. Was she trying to seduce him? Or had he made way too much out of her inviting kisses? She was a naturally passionate person, probably couldn't control it, so it made sense that she'd kiss like this. He was the one who'd blown everything way out of proportion because he was so out of practice, and still smarting, thanks to Katie. He cupped Andrea's soft cheeks and regretfully ended the kiss.

Neither said a word. He stared at her warm brown eyes and she stared back. The unspoken, mutual message being *Wow*. Yeah, there was definitely something there. Something between them. Sparks and fireworks and all. He couldn't very well jump into the sack with her, as he might have done back in medical school, not now that he was thirty-five, and a father, but he definitely knew, good idea or bad, he wanted to, and that was definitely a step forward.

"Will you have dinner with me tomorrow night?" he asked, his voice throaty with desire.

Her eyes went bigger, as if they could, and she smiled. Something told him to sell the deal, just in case there was any hesitation on her part about seeing a new guy two nights in a row. Three if they counted the night she'd measured Dani for his prosthetic eye. Oh, and lunch yesterday... But who was counting?

"I'm a great cook, and I plan to dazzle you with my culinary skills. And after Dani goes to bed, we can do more of this." He kissed her lightly but, practicing restraint, only once.

Her eyes went dreamy. Good, she liked his pitch.

"I'd love to but I've made plans with my mother for tomorrow night. I'm sorry."

What? At least she hadn't blown him off outright, but plans with her mother?

"Would Saturday work?" she said, before he had the chance to think any further.

"It does. As a matter of fact, it does." The blush on her cheeks may have been fading, but he was glad he'd put it there in the first place, and he was especially happy about her taking him up on his invitation, even if it was a day later.

Yeah, he was in trouble.

"Then I'll see you at seven on Saturday. How's that?"

"I'll be there."

He wasn't sure what he was getting himself into, seeing a woman—a yellow-flag-raising woman—several nights in a row, and maybe taking Friday night off would be a good thing, to cool down, but right at this exact moment he liked the possibilities.

"That was the greatest meal I've ever had," Andrea said on Saturday night, wiping her mouth with a paper napkin and pushing back from the table. "Even counting the Thai food Thursday night."

"You're awfully easy to please," Sam said, smiling. They were sitting at the small round table in the kitchen alcove, and he loved it that she liked his cooking. "Since it's the weekend I probably should have made something fancier."

"Are you kidding? I loved the shepherd's pie. The chicken was a nice switch, the spring vegetables were fresh, and I could tell your crust was homemade."

"You're okay with a guy who makes his own crust?" It was one of the first ways he'd bonded with his foster mom, by helping out in the kitchen. He'd wanted to be that good, likable boy whom they wouldn't send back, and helping in the kitchen had paid off. Not that they'd ever threatened or anything, but he'd been sent to a couple other foster homes before he'd wound up at the Murphys'.

Andrea gave a quick throaty laugh, one he'd already come to like. "I don't cook, so any homemade meal is a treat."

She didn't cook? Being artistic, he'd half expected her to be a gourmet chef, even worried she'd find his basic home cooking boring. Turned out that line of thinking had been a waste of time, since he was the one with the kitchen skills. "Then I'm especially glad you enjoyed it." He pushed another tiny yellow waving flag to the back of his brain. One: artist. Two: doesn't cook. And changed the subject.

"See, Dani? She cleaned her plate."

The little boy had eaten less than half of his dinner when he'd pushed away his bowl. Sam, being a pediatrician and often reassuring stressed-out mothers that their picky eaters were getting all the nutrition they needed, had been suffering from the same worries where Dani was concerned. The boy's all-time favorite meal was white rice. Period. Where was the nutrition in that?

"You sure you don't want another bite of baby carrot and new potato?" Sam remained hopeful Dani might want to show off for his new friend Andrea, but Dani shook his head vigorously, lips sealed tight.

Andrea scooted her chair closer to Dani in his booster seat. She picked up his fork and put a small mouthful of food on it, then made a buzzing sound and moved the fork around like an airplane. She lifted it upward, and Dani followed it with his one good eye, then to the right and the left. Dani might not be sure what was going on but she definitely kept his attention.

"Open wide for the landing," she said, buzzing and moving the fork in concentric circles toward his face.

Amazingly, Dani opened his mouth and let her place the food inside.

"You're good at that," she said, grinning. "Can you do it yourself?" Without waiting for his answer, she speared another small bite of dinner with his fork, but this time handed it over to Dani. "Bzzzzz," she began, and Dani moved his fork up then down, then around and round and right into his mouth. He laughed, mouth full of food and all, and Andrea clapped.

"You really are good at that. Want to do it again?" she said, sitting pertly on the edge of the chair in her layered tank tops of orange and blue, looking as colorful as one of her paintings.

Dani agreed to a third bite, but after that he was through, and she didn't push him. Good for her. She glanced at Sam and he nodded at her secret message. Yup, that was three more bites eaten that neither of them—them being him or Dani—had expected. Evidently, with the satisfied smile perched on that lovely mouth of hers, she'd never had a doubt it wouldn't work.

Sam had no sooner subtracted points from Andrea's scoreboard for not being a cook than he added some back for helping Dani eat, and several more for being so damn sweet about it. Not to mention the bonus points for being so easy on the eyes and the fact she was a damn good kisser. Sam stood to clear the table, and hopefully clear his head. Andrea had him all mixed up.

"Let me do that," she said, hopping up and taking the dishes from his hands. "It's the least I can do to thank you."

He stopped himself from making a wisecrack about not having a stool for her to stand on at the sink, choosing instead to enjoy having a woman like Andrea in his home, bringing such warmth and fun along with her. "Okay, if you insist."

She tossed him a sassy glance. "I do." Then she moseyed off to the kitchen sink, swaying her jeans-clad hips in an exaggerated manner. He and Dani weren't the only ones having a good time. The thought squeezed his heart the slightest bit. Was it a good idea to let Dani fall for her right along with him?

"Well, in that case, come on, Dani, are you ready for your bath?" He helped his son down from the booster seat and Dani ran straight for the hall.

"Yay, bath!"

"Be careful, remember the bookcase," Sam couldn't stop himself from warning Dani about the furniture, since they were still working on his loss of vision on the left.

Dani pretended to run into the wall, then made a big deal about faking falling down.

"You character," Sam said, grinning.

The boy got up again, squealed with delight and, having clearly gotten his dad's approval, ran into the opposite wall on purpose.

"You're a silly, silly guy, you know that?" Sam said, laughing and playing along with Dani all the way toward the bathroom. Realizing that his son most likely did it to impress Andrea, Sam shook his head. *Guys, even little guys, can't resist showing off for pretty ladies.* That moment of understanding, that Dani was a little guy who would one day become a man and who deserved all the fun stuff in life, just like anyone else, circled Sam's chest with warmth.

That clench of the heart from earlier squeezed about ten times harder. No matter how many times Sam had doubted himself about adopting Dani, the boy always proved what a perfect decision it had been. Adoption was just like a marriage vow, in sickness and in health. They were on this road together, and Sam never intended to let him down. The same way Mom Murphy had thought about him and the other foster kids she'd brought into her home. Damn, he missed her.

As he walked down the hall, just before he reached the bathroom he glanced back toward the kitchen. A whistling and singing-under-her-breath picture of beauty, Andrea stood at the sink as she organized the dishes and ran steamy, soapy water. Then he applauded himself for making another spot-on decision—asking her over for dinner tonight.

And God help him if he was setting himself up for another fall.

CHAPTER FOUR

ANDREA WORKED DILIGENTLY, polishing the clear acrylic replica of Dani's eye shape, taken from the mold in her office workshop. The sooner he was fitted, the sooner she'd know if the prosthetic was comfortable and therefore functional for a healthy and active growing child. The month-long adjustment period was probably the most important step in the process.

Then she'd begin delicately painting the subtle characteristics of his individual iris. The series of photographs she'd taken the other night were posted on her computer screen for her to zoom in on and examine. Everything from color patterns, striations and flecks would be replicated in Dani's final prosthesis. Even now red embroidery string had been draped in the configuration of minute red vessels on the white blob that would soon become Dani's sclera.

Sure, there was a new push for digitized replications for prosthetic eyes, but her grandmother was strictly old-school, and that'd made Andrea, even at the age of twenty-eight, an old-school diehard, too. Though she admitted to being interested in the new process popping up around the country. If it meant getting more high-quality eyes to more people in an efficient manner, it might be worth looking into.

When she hooked up the acrylic to a muslin-mopped buffing machine, her mind wandered.

A shiver snaked down her spine as she remembered the time-stopping kiss she'd shared with Sam on Saturday night. They'd been spending a lot of time kissing over the past few days. He was a good kisser. While they'd lingered in their lip-lock she'd explored the strength of his shoulders and chest, resisting the urge to continue on down his frame to his butt. That was definitely territory she hoped to check out in the near future. If she played her cards right...

A countertop pressure cooker dinged. An eye her grandmother had been working on had cured to rubbery toughness, so she took it out. With Andrea's thoughts securely back on the business of prosthetics and Dani, warmth opened and spread like a big floppy flower in her chest as she thought about her growing crush on the boy. He was so trusting and sweet and, well, she'd gone and let him steal her heart. A smile, urged on by tender thoughts, spread across her face until she thought about Sam and jitters replaced that warm fuzzy feeling. Would it be wise to fall for a highly driven doctor, like her father? She knew firsthand the consequences of stepping into that situation. What about Dani? Would he grow up feeling the way she had all her life, second best to his father's profession?

She thought about how caring Sam was with Dani, how attentive and alert to his needs he'd been that night. And after putting Dani to bed, how attentive he'd been to her. Another shiver shot down her spine. No. He was nothing like her father. That guy she'd met the first day here in the office had been an aberration. His son had just had surgery! He'd been stressed to his limit, and she hadn't helped the situation one iota. Of course they'd gotten off on the wrong foot.

Sam was *nothing* like Jerome Rimmer.

Her office desk phone rang.

"Hey," Sam said on the other end.

"Hi!" *I was just thinking about you.*

"I had a minute and wanted to call."

Because he was thinking about her, too? "I'm glad you did. I'm working on Dani's acrylic and need to fit him again."

"I'll ask Cat to bring him in, if that's okay."

"Of course. You've got a busy schedule."

"And it just got busier. Have you read the newspaper today?"

"Haven't had a chance yet." It wasn't a part of her routine because national news always depressed her.

"I'm part of a medical mission group, that's how I met Dani, and we try to set up clinics at least once a year wherever we're needed. I just got an email that our scheduled trip got postponed because of the drug cartel activity in Mexico, and they want to discuss it at a last-minute meeting tonight. I've been so busy with Dani I'd forgotten all about it. Anyway, I'm going to have to go to a meeting tonight." He went quiet.

She caught on to where he was going with the conversation. "And you need me to watch Dani?"

"As a matter of fact…"

After all the swooning thoughts she'd had about the boy, not to mention Sam, she didn't need to think. "I'd be happy to. That means I get to see Dani." *And maybe kiss you again.*

"Thank you so much." She heard pure relief in his voice.

On the verge of saying "Anytime," she stopped herself.

She'd already just jumped right in and offered to babysit without giving it a second thought. She didn't want to be taken for granted. "You're welcome."

"Is six-thirty okay? I'll try to have him bathed and ready for bed by then."

Again, she stopped herself from saying "No problem, I can do it" and instead went the efficient route. "That works for me."

"Can you stick around afterward?" His tone had gone quiet. Sexy. "Let's take that rain check on wine and…" Hadn't they already done that on Saturday night? But who was counting? She'd gladly keep rain checking over and over.

"Ah, sweetening the pot, I see. Now I'm all in." How was a living, breathing woman supposed to resist that kind of invitation and not play along?

His low, sexy-as-hell rumble of a laugh nearly had her hanging up the phone and marching upstairs to Pediatrics so she could plant one major, sloppy kiss on him right then and there to seal their deal.

"I'll see you later, then," he said. "I've got to run now."

"Okay, see you later." After hanging up, she quickly returned to her senses.

Sure, she liked Dani and Sam but things needed to proceed naturally and at their own pace. Plus she didn't want to come off like a welcome mat for Sam to take advantage of. She'd known the guy for a week and was already volunteering to be his babysitter. Sheesh. If she was going to get into a relationship with Sam, it should be for all the right reasons, not because of convenience.

She needed to stay focused and realistic.

Truth was, any night spent with Sam or babysitting Dani was a night away from painting. Since they'd bumped her up to five days a week instead of four in the O&A department, that left the weekends plus weeknights for painting, and she had minimal time for art as it was. Plus she worried about Sam always being taken away from his son. A medical mission meant travel. Who'd take care of Dani? Then it hit her.

Was Sam setting her up for that, too? If not her, how often did Sam expect to ship Dani off to his aunt Cat's? Little Dani had had no say in the adoption, but she was quite sure that wasn't what he'd bargained for. Kids needed their parents around as much as possible. That's how they felt loved. Again, she knew that from personal experience.

Hating how her relationship with her father shadowed her thoughts about Sam, but admitting she had some real concerns about him not being around enough for the boy, she refocused and went back to work on the prosthesis. But this time the job wasn't accompanied by dreamy thoughts or a wistful smile.

The next week...

Dani arrived at Andrea's office for the fine-tuning of the clear acrylic the boy had been wearing in preparation for his permanent prosthetic eye. They'd arranged for an end-of-shift appointment, so once Cat delivered the boy, Andrea could take Dani to Sam after his pediatric clinic ended. They'd also agreed to all have dinner out afterward, nothing fancy or exotic this time, just good old American food for Dani's sake.

Andrea replaced Dani's eye patch and patted his arm. "You're getting used to it?"

The boy shrugged his narrow shoulders.

"Does it bother you?"

"Don't know." He looked at his lap. She realized he didn't understand her questions.

"Does it hurt? Do you want to rub it?" She demonstrated rubbing her eye and made a face as if her eye hurt.

He stared at her with his one beautiful brown eye and slowly shook his head.

"That's good, then I did a good job." She smiled and he smiled back. "Want to go see your dad?"

His face brightened as he nodded exuberantly. After saying goodbye to her grandmother, off they went toward the elevator, Andrea feeling protective of Dani when people noticed his eye patch and reacted with sad pouts or sorry faces. She'd come to know the boy quickly in the past couple of weeks, and already she was attached to him, always eager to see him whenever she saw Sam. She also was beginning to understand Sam's deep concerns, not wanting Dani to see himself as inferior or pitied by others.

After they got out of the elevator on the pediatric clinic floor, they used the back entrance to reach Sam's office. Surprisingly, Sam was sitting at his desk.

He looked up and grinned. "My two favorite people!" he said diplomatically. Andrea knew, hands down, if it came to making a choice Dani would win, but it felt good to be included in Sam's world. With each kiss they seemed to be getting closer to crossing the line to making love. She wondered how that would change the dynamic, between not only her and Sam but her and Dani.

Dani rushed to his dad for a hug and the sight released bubble-like warmth in her chest, all floaty and happy feeling. Sam stood. "How'd the fitting go?"

"I only needed to make tiny adjustments and polish

the acrylic. Things are going great. I should be finished with his prosthetic by next week, and after another week we'll replace this one for the real thing." She grinned at Dani. "Then you won't have to wear the patch anymore. Yay."

Dani clapped. After smiling at her tiny patient, her gaze drifted toward Sam. He must have really liked what she'd said because he bore a look that mixed practical appreciation with nothing less than smoldering desire. What a combo! It set off a sparkling cascade across her shoulders and breasts, and she knew for a fact her peaked breasts pointed against the thin material of her blouse. It didn't go unnoticed. He stepped toward her, put his hand behind her neck and gently brought her within kissing range. His eyes flickered with pure desire just before their lips met.

It may have been a clinical office kiss but, wow, it thrummed right through her center straight down to her nearly curling toes. There they lingered on the outskirts of heaven until Dani tugged on both of their slacks and put a swift end to the moment, but not before Andrea saw a promise for much, much more…later. And she was definitely ready for that next step. Had been almost since the first night they'd kissed. Sam was a man she wanted to know completely, big scary doctor or not.

"I just finished my last appointment…" There was that post-kiss huskiness in his voice she'd come to love.

"Dr. Sammy!" A nurse appeared at his door. "There's a little girl having an acute asthma attack in the waiting room."

He instantly snapped out of their promising romantic moment. "Bring her to my exam room."

Andrea stepped aside and gathered Dani to her legs as "Dr. Sammy" strode out the door.

* * *

Down the hall, another nurse rushed in, with a panic-stricken mother following behind holding a limp child with her head on her mother's shoulder. "The urgent care triage nurse said she didn't hear any wheezing, so I left, but this happened before we got to the car."

Sam knew that wasn't always a good sign. The urgent care nurse may have heard a "quiet chest" but for all the wrong reasons. If the child had been suffering from a prolonged asthma attack, it may have turned into status asthmaticus, where the lungs had shut down, which could lead to imminent respiratory failure and, if not treated, cardiac arrest.

He strode to the exam room and saw a cyanotic toddler being propped up in a sitting position by her mother. The little girl used the accessory muscles of her upper chest, trying to breathe. When he had the mother remove the child's shirt, retraction was obvious between her ribs. The child was in acute respiratory distress. He instructed his nurse to measure the pulse oximetry, then put oxygen on the patient immediately.

"Mom, has she had a virus recently?" He pulled out his stethoscope, preparing to listen to the child's lungs. "Had to use inhalers more often? Been treated with steroids lately?"

"Yes," the stressed mother said, sounding as breathy as her child. "Last week. I knew I had to bring her to you, Dr. Marcus, but your appointments were full."

He shook his head, wishing for more time in the day and more appointment slots for kids like this, but also in disappointment over the UC triage missing the bigger picture than lungs without noticeable wheezing. They were supposed to be the safety net for situations like these, but today they'd let a patient and her mother down.

The pulse oximeter indicated a hypoxic patient with a loud alarm. Sam sighed at the reading. "Get a mask on her at eight liters. Start a line," he said to his nurse Leslie. "I'm going to give her a pop of adrenaline. Mom, how much does she weigh?"

The mother told him and he made quick mental calculations and drew up the drug, hoping to buy time before they set up a nebulizer treatment. He delivered the intramuscular injection, then stuck his head out of the examination room door. "Sharon? We need more hands in here." From the corner of his eye, he saw movement and turned toward Andrea and Dani. Concern covered her face.

"I'm going to take Dani home with me," she said, her brow furrowed.

He gave a grateful nod, trying to offer reassurance, but honestly he hadn't a clue how things would turn out for the little girl. "I'll come later as soon as I can. Thanks."

They left the department just before the tiny asthmatic took another step for the worse.

"Let's nebulize some adrenaline, try to open her up, then start the bronchodilator—oh, and add some ipratropium bromide, too." Why did he have the feeling he was running a precode? He studied the limp child. "Got that line in yet, Leslie?" His major hope was that her veins hadn't collapsed.

The nurse had just finished opening the tubing and the fluid flowed into the vein in the child's antecubital fossa. "Let's titrate terbutaline." He did quick mental math for kilograms of weight, then gave the amount for the piggyback to the IV. "Call the pharmacy, tell them we need methylprednisolone IV for a thirty-five-pound child, stat.

"Sharon, have someone call Respiratory, get someone up here pronto for blood gases." So far none of their efforts had increased the child's O2 sat, and if things continued on this trajectory they might soon be dealing with a code blue. "We'll keep the respiratory therapist around in case we need to intubate."

And so it went…

Andrea drove Dani slowly to her house, worried about not having a car seat for him and making him sit in the backseat of her car with the seat belt buckled tight. What would Sam have done if she hadn't been there? That wasn't all she worried about. Every time she'd seen him over the past three weeks, with each kiss she'd felt herself slip closer and closer to falling for him. Just now, seeing Sam spring into action like a hero for a child in need helped her understand how dedicated he was to his profession.

It also helped her put her own situation into perspective. Seeing his unwavering commitment forced her to take a good long look at herself, and how unsure she still was about her own professional path. She seemed to be standing with one foot in ancillary medicine and the other in the creative arts. And the truth was she loved both! Straddling the line hadn't paid off with her painting, she hadn't completed a picture in months, and it kept her anxious and unsatisfied when she worked her forty hours a week in the O&A department. She should never have agreed to add that extra day.

Add in starting to fall for a guy with a demanding job and an adorable kid who needed attention, and she nearly panicked, feeling completely out of control of her own situation. How had she let this happen? Sam had a way of taking over, just like her father, even when it wasn't obvious. Was that how it had all started with her mother? Little by little, because her mother hadn't figured out where she wanted to be in life, Jerome had taken over until there seemed nothing left of her mother. Until she'd practically disappeared!

Could the same happen to *her*?

"I'm hungry," Dani said from the backseat.

Thank goodness he'd broken her negative train of thought. "Want a hamburger?"

He clapped. "Yes!"

At least some decisions were still easy to make.

Fortunately, Cat had delivered Dani's day bag with him when she'd brought him by that afternoon. Andrea found pajamas and a pair of clean underpants plus some kids' books inside and so much more. Even Ribbit, the stuffed frog she'd given him. She'd been able to bathe him and read a book that apparently was his favorite, *Goodnight California*.

The author used the *Goodnight Moon* setup to say good-night in travelogue style to all the beautiful places in the state. Dani sat rapt, holding Ribbit, snuggled under her arm on the sofa, listening to every word as if he'd never heard them before, and pointing to his favorite pictures. The redwoods, Yosemite, the beach. Ah, the beach probably reminded him of home in the Philippines. She wondered if Sam had taken Dani to the beach yet.

Dani's day bag even had a toothbrush, so after one last glass of milk, where Andrea opened up Dani's world to the graham cracker experience of dipping them into the milk, she brushed his teeth and put him to bed, along with Ribbit, in her studio, which had a daybed and trundle bed combo left over from her childhood. Nowadays she used it to flounce onto when she needed to think about what she'd just painted and where to go next, or, as was often the case, to nap on when she'd painted so long she couldn't even bring herself to walk down the hall to her own room. When she'd been a girl, before her mother had gotten really depressed and hadn't allowed her to have friends over, her sleepover guests had got the trundle bed section, and she felt Dani, who had special toddler bed rails at home, would be safe there.

She kissed him good-night and started to tiptoe out of the room.

"Do I live here now?" he asked, just before she shut the door, having left a night-light on in the far corner.

Was that how orphans thought? "No, honey. You're just visiting, like when you go to Aunt Cat's house. Your daddy will come and get you later. But he needed to save a little girl at the hospital first."

"Okay."

It struck like a baseball bat how similar her explanation was to what her mother's used to be on countless nights when her father hadn't made it home in time for dinner or to kiss her good-night. The tender feelings she carried for Dani puffed up and made her eyes prickle.

It was scary to care so much for a little person.

Within a couple of hours of putting Dani to bed, a quiet knock on her door drew her from the art magazine she'd been reading in her living room. She opened the small peephole on the door. It was Sam, looking exactly the way a guy should after having a long, stressful day where lives had been at stake and family responsibilities had had to be put on the back burner. There was a combination of fatigue, guilt and gratefulness she read in his powerful blue gaze.

She invited him in with a quick kiss, pointed to the

nearest chair with an ottoman for his feet and offered him a drink of his choice.

"Seems like the perfect time for that rain check on the wine," he said. His shirt collar was unbuttoned and the sight of his throat looked sexy as hell. But, then, she found every little thing about Sam Marcus sexy, she may as well admit it. And she loved the way they'd made an ongoing gag about every glass of wine they shared being a rain check.

"Red or white?"

He closed his eyes on a slow inhalation, as if making one more decision was beyond his grasp, so she solved his problem.

"I've got a fabulous triple red wine open. How does that sound?"

Again, that grateful blue gaze, standing out all the more thanks to the after-five stubble on his cheeks and chin, nearly bowled her over. She turned to fetch the wine when a thought occurred to her. "Have you eaten?"

"No." He didn't need to think long about that.

"I told you I don't cook but I *can* make a pretty good omelet. Would that work?"

"Sounds perfect."

She understood he could probably eat cardboard if he had to by now, as it was almost ten.

"Dani in bed?"

"Yes," she said, as she got down two wineglasses and reached for the bottle on the counter. "Fell right to sleep in my old trundle bed. What a sweetheart he is."

"Okay if I take a peek?"

It was his kid, why did he need to ask? "You're not seriously asking me permission, are you?"

She imagined that Sam Marcus smile she'd come to know and adore spreading across his boyish but all-male face as she poured the wine and he padded down the hall. "Which door?" he asked with a loud whisper.

"First one on the left." She put his glass on the kitchen table and got busy gathering the things she'd need to make her one good dish. Sad but true, her cooking skills didn't go beyond sandwiches and eggs. But she was determined to make the best damn omelet of her life for Sam. She took a quick sip of liquid confidence from the wineglass and went to work.

After a couple of minutes Sam stepped into the kitchen, standing right behind her as she whipped the eggs. He put his hands on her hips, bent and kissed the back of her neck. She nearly dropped the whisk, it felt so heavenly. One touch from Sam. One kiss in the perfect spot, and she was covered in tingles. She stopped what she was doing, leaned back, giving him full access to the side of her neck, and enjoyed every second of this gift as he gently nuzzled and kissed her.

"Thank you," he whispered over the shell of her ear.

More sensations fanned across her scalp, down her neck and over her chest. "Anytime." Whoops, had she just given him permission to leave Dani with her anytime? "I should get this omelet going before you starve to death. Oh, and your wine's on the table."

He let go of her hips and stepped away, and she had dueling thoughts. She was either nuts to let him stop or smart not to let him take advantage of her right there in the kitchen. She took another sip of wine. Yeah, she was probably nuts.

"Good wine," he said.

"I thought you'd like it. How's the little girl?" Listen to them, a regular couple discussing the day and the kids. The thought almost made her smile, but the subject of the little girl fighting for her life kept Andrea serious.

A kitchen chair skidded along the tile as he pulled it out and sat, then took another drink and propped his feet on an adjacent chair. "She's alive, but not in great shape."

Something in Andrea's chest withered with the news as she heated the skillet and oil and when it reached the perfect temperature she poured in the eggs, listening to every word Sam said, giving him time to share as much or as little as he cared to.

"She coded shortly after you left. We intubated her, got her to the ICU in time for a second code." He sighed, and she glanced over her shoulder and saw him rub his temples with his thumb and middle finger. "She's on a ventilator right now, and hopefully the drugs will kick in tonight so we can get her off it as soon as possible."

"Oh, the poor baby." Andrea's insides twisted over the thought of a child fighting for her life. "If her mother hadn't brought her to you, she might be dead."

He nodded deeply and took another drink of wine.

"You look beat. Why don't you go make yourself comfortable on the couch, put your feet up, and I'll bring your dinner as soon as it's done."

He didn't argue, just took his wineglass and left the room. "Good idea."

She flipped the omelet, added grated cheese to the lightly browned side, waited a minute or two for the toast to pop and the eggs to set, then folded the omelet in half and put everything on a plate, then walked to the living room to find Sam asleep on her couch, her everyday hero breathing deep, peaceful breaths that did more for her libido than those butterfly kisses on her neck a few moments ago.

His long, sturdy legs stretched the length of her sofa. He'd kicked off his shoes, his sock-covered feet crossed at the ankles, arms folded over his trim middle, head tilted chin to chest. All he needed was a cowboy hat to complete the picture. He was a fine-looking man, and she could hardly believe he kept coming round. A quick fantasy of crawling like a cat over him and kissing the lips she'd come to long for started a deep yearning to be skin to skin with him. What would it be like?

Truth was she hadn't wanted a man this much since college. The complete opposite of the artsy fellow students she'd dated back then, Sam managed to turn her on wearing, as it happened today, a gray business suit. He hadn't bothered to take off the jacket, so she had to settle for looking at his naked throat and the top of his white undershirt as he slept. *Gimme, gimme.*

She glanced at the plate, steam rising from the best omelet she'd ever concocted especially for Sam, sighed, then took a bite to prove it really was as light and fluffy as it looked. She savored the egg and Cheddar cheese taste and the sight of the man she'd fallen head over heels for in record time passed out from exhaustion on her couch, then made a snap decision.

Tonight was the night.

She tiptoed to the kitchen, found a notepad and scribbled Sam an invitation. Then, making sure to leave one light on so he'd see it, she propped the note against his wineglass.

If you want to stay over, I'm keeping the bed warm for you. My room is at the end of the hall.

CHAPTER FIVE

SAM WOKE UP, a crick in his neck from the awkward position in which he'd fallen asleep on the not-so-soft modern couch. It took a moment to realize where he was. Andrea's cozy triplex apartment. He scrubbed his face to help him wake up. Dani was asleep in her guest bed. Right. No way would he disturb his son at this hour.

He took out his phone and scrolled with blurry vision for any messages from the hospital. He'd signed off with the on-call ICU doc and knew they'd only call with extremely bad news, so he gave a sigh of relief over the lack of "missed call" notices, texts or email.

In the dim light, his gaze drifted to the uneaten omelet on the glass coffee table. It touched him, knowing Andrea was a devout non-cook yet she'd offered to make the one thing she could, especially for him. He felt bad he'd fallen asleep before he could enjoy the fruit of her efforts.

From being so bristly at first, she'd turned out to be the sweetest lady he'd met since Mom Murphy. He thought about reheating the omelet in the microwave and eating it, so her work wouldn't go to waste, plus he really was hungry, but first his vision landed on the wineglass with a propped-up note. He didn't need to pick it up to read: *If you want to stay over, I'm keeping the bed warm for you. My room is at the end of the hall.*

She'd sketched a perfectly sexy eye in mid-wink at the end.

Suddenly wide-awake, Sam gulped down the rest of the red wine, the thought of making love with Andrea foremost on his mind. Hell, yeah, he wanted to. Had since the night he'd first kissed her, right here in her living room, and he remembered every second of that goodbye. Somehow, since then, their make-out sessions had never gotten beyond hot kisses and lots of groping and grabbing.

Why? Not because he hadn't wanted to. No. It was because he'd always sensed Andrea wasn't ready for that. Sure, she'd jump right into making out with him, he never doubted she wanted to. But something about their frantic kisses and fully clothed body sex had always ended with him backing off. Because of one message that always cut through the sexy haze. At some point she'd always tense up and there was no way, no matter how desperate he'd been to have her naked and to be inside her, he would force the next step—getting naked.

Maybe she'd sensed he was the kind of guy who kept his distance. Intimacy, trust, hell, how did a man make heads or tails of that when his own mother had ignored him and let him get taken away? Not to mention Katie leaving when he'd finally felt ready to commit to her.

But there was no doubt about the invitation from Andrea tonight. She was keeping the bed warm for him. It said so right there in her near perfect cursive. An ironic half smile lifted the corner of his mouth. She was an artist, of course she'd have beautiful handwriting, and the artistic winking eye was a great touch. He stuffed the note in his shirt pocket as a reminder. She wanted him.

The thought of her asleep yet waiting for him, her skin warm to his touch, relaxed and completely open, drove a spear of desire straight through him. Fatigued, who? It may have been a long and exhausting day, but he'd had a nap now, and he was fueled by pure desire for Andrea. More than ever he was ready to have his way with his artist.

He stood, took off his jacket, began unbuttoning his shirt and padded in his socked feet straight to her bedroom and the one woman he wanted right now. She'd even left the door open a crack. Once inside, he stripped, leaving a pile of clothes beside her bed before he crawled under the covers.

A blanket of heat and strength spooned behind Andrea as she stirred from her light sleep. Arms enveloped her, pulling her close, igniting excitement and, being honest, fear. She took a trembling breath when Sam kissed the side of her neck, his breathing steady, hot over her ear. She wanted him, God knew she did, so why was she so nervous about making love with him?

Because having sex was a big deal to her, it always had been. She'd tried her share of free and easy dates during college and had always limped away feeling somehow used, or like a user. Need had been a strong stimulant for the "right now" back then, but try as she might she'd always wanted much more. Could she ever actually say she'd loved someone? The truth? Not so far.

She turned toward Sam's chest, letting him capture her mouth with deep kisses as their bodies stretched along each other's. He felt great, every inch of him. Of course she'd gone to bed naked. She couldn't very well leave such a bold-faced invitation and not be ready when or if he took her up on it. She'd even left a condom on the bedside table.

Thankfully, he had followed through, because right now she felt the obvious length of him along her thigh, and the heat radiating from his body was lapping away at her every worry. His hands wandered everywhere, touching, testing, exciting her. Oh, how she wanted him.

She understood sex for sex's sake and wanted to be with Sam no matter what his desire was right this instant. There wasn't a single doubt in her mind that she wanted sex with Sam. Yet their coming together, wrapping, entangling, growing closer and closer still, seemed very different in comparison with others.

Sam rolled her, his weight pressing her down. She rocked against his strong thighs as he held her arms above her head with one hand and devoured her breasts with his mouth and tongue. Fireworks seemed to skip across her chest and burrow deep toward her core. She needed him. Soon, completely under his spell, she was lost to any thoughts beyond flesh and sensations, and the burning desire for him and him alone. With every cell in her body ignited from his touch, she bucked against him, opening, nearly begging for him to put an end to her frustration. She needed him inside. Needed to connect in the deepest way possible with him.

She held on to his hips, felt the muscular bulge of his ass as he followed her lead to the bedside table, sheathed himself, then slowly entered her. He'd already worked her into a frenzy and her moisture made their introduction smooth and, if possible, even more stimulating. The fresh sensations zinging throughout her pelvis made her gasp.

"Are you okay?" he quickly responded.

"Oh, God, yes. Don't stop."

He did stop, just long enough to deliver a broad, I'm-in-control smile. A shaft of moonlight caught that wicked twinkle in his eyes as he planted one big hand on her hip and began thrusting and withdrawing, never breaking their staring match. Wanting to close her eyes and crawl inside, to curl up with all the amazing feelings coursing through her body, she forced her gaze to stay locked with his, mainly because he willed it. And it both frightened and excited her to see the near wild look of passion on his face. He'd given in totally to their one point of connection—him being inside her—and his obvious desire to satisfy her.

Did it feel as astonishing to him as it did to her? His long, smooth thrusts seemed to pass over every single nerve ending. He treated her to minutes and minutes and more minutes at this heightened, sensitive place. Someday she would have to thank him profusely, but not now. Right now all she could do was experience everything he gave her. Her arms tensed, hands grasping the bedsheets, and she screwed her eyes tight as her mind drifted toward bliss. Then he pushed faster. Harder. The sensations tensing, tangling and balling up, building deeper, wider, threatening to overwhelm her. She held on to him with all of her might. Her gasps came quicker. She clamped her thighs tighter around his hips and lifted her pelvis just so, adding pressure and, oh, yes, yes, yes, pleasure, pleasure beyond her wildest hopes.

"Don't stop." Her voice sounded strangely disconnected from her body. Their body. Because they were a single unit now.

Sam didn't stop. He built and built and finally came at her with everything he had.

She sucked in air, held it, and as he drove at record

speed into the center of her universe she caught fire one spark at a time. A twitch, a rush of tingles breaking out from the hot gathering knot that grew and demanded release. Soon. Soon deep, breathtaking spasms exploded inside her, overtaking her, shooting down her legs and up to her breasts, holding her in suspension of time and mind. Out of control, her back and neck arched as he continued to push into her, prolonging her rush of blinding feelings.

Everything burst apart, flattening her, as a low, distant groan grew, building somewhere out there in the world she'd just left behind. Somehow, Sam moved even harder and his groan changed to a grunting as he thrust and pumped on and on until he joined her on the other side of their bliss.

Like rag dolls they landed in a clump of body parts on her mattress, sated and stunned by each other. Snuggling into the crook of his strong and inviting arm, feeling as she never had before, safe and completely claimed, she sighed and shut her eyes. No words needed to be said.

With only the occasional croak of a frog on the lawn, she drank in the contentment and silence, and the faint yet steady stroke of Sam's fingers along her arm. Then, knowing for this single moment all was perfect in her world, and as if she was having an out-of-body experience, she gently floated off to sleep.

Morning came entirely too quickly. Andrea cracked open one eye to find Sam blissfully asleep beside her. She began the slow process of stretching and slowly rejoining the living when crying woke her up. Dani!

She'd completely forgotten about the boy.

She shook Sam awake. "Dani's crying. Maybe you should get him."

Without a word, the once big puddle of flesh beside her came right to attention. Though he didn't look in the least bit sure of where he was just yet. He jumped out of the bed, searched for his clothes and hopped into first one leg then the other of his suit slacks, then strode out of the room, from the looks of him not anywhere near awake. "Coming, Dani. Hold on."

Being a single father, he'd probably gotten down the routine of waking up at a moment's notice to a science.

Andrea smiled. She lay there, drinking in the morning and the lovely body aches from last night's gymnastics with Sam, and the delicious lingering sensations between her thighs, thinking how lucky she was to have met him. Then one negative thought grabbed her by the throat.

Having him meant having Dani. How could she have forgotten about Dani so easily? Which made her wonder if she was ready to be a girlfriend to a guy who was still getting used to being a single father. Was that even what he wanted from her? If they got involved, would she be a girlfriend or a mother figure for Dani? What was Sam looking for?

The complications made her head spin, so she got out of bed to help ignore them, and made a quick bathroom stop before reporting for breakfast duty.

Sam helped Dani get dressed, then took the boy to the bathroom. Sitting him on the small tiled vanity counter, he washed his face.

"Why I sleep here, Dad?"

"I had to work late, so Andrea let you sleep over."

"I like *my* bed."

Point taken! "I know, Dani, and tonight you'll sleep there. Are you hungry?"

The boy nodded.

"Then let's see what we can rustle up for breakfast." He held Dani's hand and they walked down the short hall to the kitchen. Already he could smell coffee brewing and toast. The thought of seeing Andrea in the daylight, after ravishing her last night, excited him, yet he wondered how she'd receive him now. He hoped she wouldn't go shy or make things awkward, because from his standpoint things were going great. "Hey, good morning." He went the casual, oh-yeah-I-sleep-over-with-my-son-all-the-time routine.

"Hi!" Her eyes, without a trace of makeup, looked younger, oddly enough, bigger and browner, too. He'd noticed last night in the moonlight she hadn't had makeup on, but he'd been too distracted to comment. Very distracted, and gratefully so. "You two hungry?"

"Yeah!" said Dani.

"I've got plenty of eggs. Why not omelets?"

"I want cereal," Dani said.

"I think I have some of that," she said, opening a cupboard and pulling out a box. Sam could plainly see she was ready to cook more eggs.

"If you don't mind, I'll take you up on those eggs," he said.

"Done." She glanced over her shoulder and when their gazes connected a zing through his center served as a great wake-up call.

He could easily get used to looking at her in the morning. "Sorry I fell asleep too soon to enjoy your cheese omelet last night."

She found a small bowl and poured in a big helping of multigrain cereal for Dani. "I'll consider last night my practice session," she said, the double entendre making Andrea and Sam lock eyes again in a totally adult way. If what they'd shared had been practice, he couldn't wait for the dress rehearsal. "So you want more?"

Oh, yes, he wanted more of her. Hopefully soon. "Loaded question." She gave a quick, breathy laugh. "Yes. Definitely. I'll have—" he placed his hand around her upper arm and squeezed it the tiniest bit "—more."

She gave a coy smile as she looked up at him, and he bent and kissed her good morning. "Thank you," he whispered. "For a thousand things."

Her eyes widened the tiniest bit. "You're welcome, and thank you, too," she said, her gaze shifting downward and her cheeks turning pink before she got back to the business of pouring milk over Dani's cereal and whipping eggs for Sam's fresh omelet.

What did all this mean? He'd found a woman he liked. A lot. Had finally had sex with her. Which had been great. Beyond great. Of course he wanted to see her again. Often. But he was a busy doctor, a new and adjusting father. Were there hours enough in the day for all the time she deserved, too? Or was he already thinking up reasons to keep a distance between them? The safe route?

His phone rang. He quickly checked to see if it was the ICU. No. It was Bob Brinker, the lead on his missions team. "Do you mind if I get this?"

She puckered that sexy mouth of hers and shook her head, distracted and busy with making the omelet.

He'd missed the call but Bob had left a long message. They'd rescheduled the meeting Sam had missed last week for tonight. Did it work for him?

Hell, did it? He'd missed putting Dani to bed last

night. Then Sam read the last sentence. *It's the only night all of us are available.* How could he refuse?

He scrunched up his face and looked at Andrea. "I hate to ask you this, but could you possibly watch Dani for me at my place tonight? They've rescheduled the missions meeting. It's the only night that works for the rest of them."

She glanced cautiously toward Dani, then back at him. "If you don't have a choice but to go, then okay."

Did he have a choice? He really needed to rethink his priorities. He'd committed to this mission long before Dani's adoption had become final. Hell, if it hadn't been for his medical mission trips, he'd never have met Dani in the first place.

But things were different now. He was a father with a son who needed him as much as possible, and he'd just met Andrea, was already crazy about her and wanted to know her more. Juggling his job, fatherhood plus a new romance was complicated. Maybe Katie had been right—he wanted too much.

He looked at Dani. No way had Katie been right about not adopting. Dani was the best part of his life. Then he glanced at Andrea, putting a perfectly fluffy cheese omelet onto a plate especially for him. A lady who didn't cook had just given him the best she had, not to mention what she'd given him last night, and that meant something.

Who knew where the best of Andrea Rimmer might lead? One thing was sure, if they were going to pursue this "thing" going on between them, she deserved the best of him, too.

He pushed Dial on his phone. "Hey, Bob? Yeah, I got hung up in ICU last night. Never made it home. So, listen, I'm going to have to ask you to fill me in on whatever goes on tonight. I need to be home with my boy tonight."

A subtle smile crossed Andrea's lips as she handed him his breakfast, then their eyes met when she gave him a fork, and he knew he'd made the right decision.

A week later...

It was a big day. Sam had cut short his afternoon appointment schedule by two so he could personally take Dani to get his official prosthetic eye. Andrea had made a big deal about not showing it to him until it was inside the boy's eye socket, and who was he to argue?

They'd spent a couple more nights together over the past week, one planned and one, unfortunately, another last-minute "Can you watch Dani for me so I can attend the early morning staff meeting?" Turned out having someone to be there for Dani in the morning for breakfast and to get him ready for Aunt Cat's was a win-win situation. Andrea had opted to sleep over the night before, rather than get up at the crack of dawn and fight the traffic over to his house.

Any night making love with Andrea was a win-win, even though he felt tension mounting over the fact he'd yet to be completely honest with her.

He guided Dani toward the elevator. "After this appointment, you won't have to wear that darned patch anymore."

"Yay." Dani clapped his pudgy hands.

Sam's stomach felt a little queasy as he worried about how the prosthetic would fit and, almost more important, look. Would it be obvious that it was a fake eye? What if he didn't like Andrea's version of Dani's iris?

He took a deep breath and got into the elevator,

choosing to focus on more positive things, like how incredibly great it was to make love with Andrea, and to spend time with her. But where did they go from here? If he wanted an honest relationship, he'd have to come clean. He'd let her think he was from a big family—which theoretically he was in one sense—when he was actually the kid of a young single mother who hadn't had a clue how to be a mom or how to support both of them with the few skills she'd learned with only a high school education. She'd had to work two jobs, and Sam had had to spend nights alone in a shabby apartment, afraid and vulnerable, until he was ten and the courts had taken him away from his mother. And she'd let him go.

Soon enough they were in the basement, and knowing the routine Dani ran ahead. "Hey, hold on there, buddy, you don't want to wind up in the wrong place." He avoided saying "In the morgue."

"I want to see Andrea!" Dani eagerly kept going, knowing the way from all his prior appointments, so Sam picked up his pace to catch up.

"Okay, but let's go in together." He took his hand just in time to open the O&A department door, wondering why the dark, dingy hallway and office in the corner didn't creep out the kid.

Judith Rimmer met them in the display room, wearing the headgear getup and smiling. "It's your big day, Dani. Let me get Andrea," she said to Sam.

Almost immediately, Andrea emerged from the workshop, wearing a lab coat and a huge smile. "I wanted to give your eye one last polish," she said to Dani, as if preparing to give the boy a special gem. "Want to watch?"

Andrea had explained the entire process to Sam, and the final step was to cover the prosthetic in clear resin, and to polish the living daylights out of the new eye.

Being only three, Sam wasn't sure how much Dani understood about everything that was going on, but the kid couldn't look any more excited or expectant than if it was his birthday. "Yes!" Dani ran to follow Andrea into the back and the workshop. Sam chatted with Judith to pass the time. Soon enough Dani and Andrea reappeared.

Andrea helped Dani sit on a chair with a booster seat near the eye display counter. "Let's take off this patch." She gently removed it, and Dani watched and smiled the whole time. So trusting.

She checked the alignment of his new eye, had him open and close his eyes several times. She even checked for natural secretions and anatomical function before giving it her final seal of approval. Dani sat perfectly still like a little soldier the whole time.

Truth was, Andrea was a natural with his son. Her gentle touch, her care and concern for Dani, the way he trusted her. All systems seemed to say go, yet his lousy experience with Katie held him back from taking things further between them. Hadn't that proved he didn't know how to really love someone? He'd been completely convinced Katie had been the one for him, had been for all the years they'd dated, yet when he'd finally got around to asking her to marry him, her career had suddenly come first. How wrong could a guy be? What did it say for his judgment where women were concerned? Now he had a son who needed to come first. Sam knew firsthand that the less drama in life, the better stability for the kid. Wasn't that what the person who had really become his mother, not just a foster caregiver, had taught him? Since Mom Murphy had died, the person he'd trusted more than anyone, he'd struggled to let anyone get close. Hell, Katie could attest to that. Did Andrea deserve the same treatment?

Plus Andrea had been candid with Sam in one of their post-lovemaking talks. She longed to be the artist she'd set out to be at university, and felt for the past four years her dreams had been on hold while she'd apprenticed in ocularistry. Yet she obviously loved her clients at the hospital and enjoyed the work—Dani being a case in point—which proved she was as confused as he was. But had she been trying to warn him? Was she still holding out for her big break, the same way Katie had been?

He stepped out of his thoughts in time to see Dani turning around with his prosthetic eye in place. Sam had to do a double take to remember which eye was real and which was fake. Holy cow, she'd replicated his real eye perfectly. A mirror image. So much so, it brought a lump to his throat. "That looks fantastic, buddy." His grateful gaze met Andrea's. She looked relieved.

But Dani seemed puzzled, and usually when he did he asked Sam a question. This time, though, he turned to Andrea. "I can't see." He covered his good eye to make sure.

Sam's throat lump doubled. How the hell was he supposed to explain the truth?

Andrea went down on her knees to be at eye level with Dani. She cupped his shoulders and gave the sincerest look he'd ever seen. "Honey, the eyes we make here can't see. You'll always have to rely on this one." She touched him above his right eye. "This one will be good enough for both your eyes. This one—" she touched his brow above the new prosthetic "—is just to look pretty, so you don't have to wear that patch. Is that all right?"

Dani nodded solemnly. "I guess so."

Sam stepped closer, first giving Andrea an appreciative glance and nod, then studying his son's new eye up close. "It's amazing how perfectly matched this is to his own eye." He hugged Dani and looked at Andrea. "I can't thank you enough for making the most incredible prosthetic. Only a true artist could duplicate his iris so perfectly. My God. I'm shocked at how great it is." Maybe he was laying it on too thick, but he meant every word and gratitude got the better of him. "You really are a great artist."

"Now I think you're going overboard."

He touched her arm. "No. I'm not. This is fantastic. No one will know this isn't his real eye without looking really closely. You've just given him an amazing gift."

"It's my job."

"And you were made for it." From the other side of the room, Judith spoke up.

Sam could see a flash of rebellion in Andrea's reaction over the reminder from her grandmother of that continual war between practical day job and the artist itching to take flight. She chose not to say anything just then.

Dani jumped down from his chair and walked to a mirror, studying his image really closely. He made monkey faces and joked around, but Sam knew he liked what he saw. As for Sam, he couldn't be happier. His son wouldn't need to ever feel inferior, wearing a perfect eye like this one.

Andrea stepped up behind Dani, placed her fingertips on his narrow shoulders and spoke to him in the mirror. "You shouldn't fiddle with your new eye or treat it like a toy. If it bothers you or feels uncomfortable, you ask Daddy to bring you to me so we can polish it." She turned to Sam, her expression clouding with something unnamed, and she avoided making eye contact, instead seeming to look at his shoulder. "You'll need to clean it a couple times a day at first so it doesn't get gummy. Until his eye socket gets used to it."

"Will do. Are you all right?"

Her lower lip quivered the tiniest bit. "Yeah." She nodded, tried to brush off the emotions obviously building inside, doing anything rather than look him straight on.

Judith, as though sensing something was up, took Dani by the hand. "Would you like to see where I make eyes?" she said, leading the boy toward the workshop.

"Is that a hat?" Dani commented about her headgear, then took her hand, eager to follow her to the "eye" room.

"It makes things look really big. Want to look through it?"

"Yes!"

Once they were gone, Sam reached for Andrea and kissed her. "What's wrong?" He held her close, biting back his own mixed-up feelings, reliving all the reasons Dani had needed the prosthetic in the first place.

She shook her head against his shoulder. "Remember that first night I came to your house and you told me your biggest fear was the thought of Dani losing his other eye?"

He held her closer, kissed the top of her head. "Yes. It still is."

"I worry about that, too. I've fallen in love with your son and I can't stand the thought of him suffering or losing any more than he already has."

The lump in Sam's throat became too big to swallow so he couldn't speak. But he held on to Andrea with all his strength, hoping that maybe the two of them together could will away any future problems for Dani, even while knowing they were powerless. Life happened. It just did. There was no good-luck charm to ward off bad events or illnesses, or parents letting their kids go into foster care, no way to skip around the messy parts. What would be would be for Dani, and they'd have to deal with whatever played out. Andrea's support meant the world to him, helped him think he could get through whatever lay ahead.

As they stood holding each other it hit Sam how, without even realizing it, they'd become a kind of family where Dani was concerned. Yet he hadn't even gotten up the guts to tell Andrea the truth, and if he couldn't do that, how could he ever love her? Did he love her? Wasn't that how he'd started off with Katie, jumping right in up to his neck, deciding she was the perfect girl for him, only to find out several years later she had been anything but that girl. Even if he did think he might love Andrea, being a reasonable man he still couldn't believe that was possible yet, so was he ready to tell her something he wasn't even sure he was capable of?

Plus he had Dani now. There would be two broken hearts if things didn't work out. Yet Dani had fallen for Andrea right off, and kids were usually pretty good judges of character. Which brought his thoughts full circle back to Andrea, the woman in his arms who'd gone all weepy worrying about his son. Yeah, they'd become a modern-day melded family, whether they were ready for it or not.

Those astounding thoughts had him squeezing her even tighter, mostly for support. How had this happened so quickly, and was it even possible?

CHAPTER SIX

SAM HAD TALKED Andrea into joining him and Dani at the park closest to St. Francis of the Valley Hospital after the appointment. Still being spring, the sun was far from setting at 6:00 p.m. "Let's celebrate Dani's new eye," Sam had said.

Since she'd made it, how could she refuse?

Earlier Andrea had been hit with a world of worries about Dani. Sam had spoken of his fear the first night she'd gone to his house—that his son might lose his other eye. The thought made her feel queasy. It was also a sure sign she'd fallen for the kid. And his dad. How could her life get tipped on its ear in a month?

Maybe she should have put more thought into dating a man with a kid, a man with a huge family photo on his wall and a framed parable about saving starfish one at a time. None of which she could relate to and, honestly, was afraid she'd never be able to. But it was too late now to worry about "getting it" where Sam and his dreams and desires were concerned. She was already crazy about both of them.

Sam sat beside her on the bench in his work suit, a beige one with an Easter-egg-yellow shirt and, in typical Dr. Sammy style, a SpongeBob tie for the kids at the hospital. His legs were extended and crossed at the ankles, arms stretched wide along the back of the bench. Confident and relaxed. Instead of relaxing, like him, she perched on the edge of the bench, ready to run after Dani at a moment's notice in case he needed her on the kiddie slide or mini jungle gym. Sam was all about giving the kid independence. She was about keeping him safe.

A grin stretched across Dani's bright face. He tee-tered, then stood at the bottom of the slide before he galloped for the swings. Andrea hopped up and met him just in time to set him inside the toddler bucket-styled swing. That grin disappeared and he shook his head, pointing to the standard swings, the big-kid swings, down the line on the thick metal play set frame.

Andrea glanced at Sam, who was already up and heading their way. With a kind smile he lifted his son like a sack of potatoes over his hip, which Dani loved, then walked him down to an empty regular swing seat and put him in the center.

"You've got to hold on really tight," he said, making sure the boy's hands held the swing chain securely on both sides. Dani gave a solemn nod, as if realizing this was a big step in his playground life. A step worthy of his new eye.

She'd made plenty of eyes for patients during her nearly four-year apprenticeship, and she'd witnessed firsthand how life-changing that could be for them, which was incredibly satisfying. But with Dani—she patted one forearm, then the other—never before had the gratification been so intense that it raised the hair on her arms.

A few moments went by with only the sound of Dani's delighted squeals while Sam gently pushed him on the swing. Andrea stood enjoying the view and the light evening breeze, warmth pulsing in her heart. Beyond the huge sandbox area with all the playground apparatus, the grass was fragrant, freshly mown, spring green and dotted with young myrtles and ash trees. In a decade they'd offer shade in this newly opened park. For now, they were simply new and pretty to look at.

The vision inspired her, making her want to capture the essence of this moment with bright colors on a canvas. Thoughts swirled through her brain. Creative sparks made her come alive in a way she hadn't for months. On the verge of telling Sam she had to get right home, he looked up with an earnest expression, a man completely content pushing his kid on a swing, as if something had just occurred to him, too.

He started talking, but she was so lost in her thoughts she didn't hear him until she picked up at the point of new shoes. "What?"

"I said, when my mom used to take all of us for new shoes the week before school started, when we got home we'd all try them on and parade around for Dad. And Dad would say, 'It's a good day. All my kids have new shoes. Let's go have ice cream.'" He looked at her nostalgically over Dani on the swing, capturing her gaze. "Well, it's not just a good day today, it's a great day. Thanks to you, my boy has a beautiful new eye. What do you say we go get ice cream?"

Dani cheered, and there was no way right then Andrea could make an excuse to go home to paint.

That night, right after they'd put Dani to bed, they made love, then cuddled in Sam's huge bed. Sam surprised Andrea and opened up, telling her the entire story of how he'd come to be Dani's father. He shared every detail, including the heartbreak of Katie walking away over his decision, and it brought tears to Andrea's eyes.

Their relationship had grown so quickly, it seemed, and his willingness to share feelings normally left close to the heart was part of the reason. She thought how they'd both tiptoed into this new relationship, and she didn't want to upset the fragile foundation forming between them with one ongoing concern that he might want to be with her only because he needed a mother for his son. So she kept it to herself and they made love again.

Now stretched out side by side, they held hands and stared at the ceiling, letting the flush of fresh lovemaking spend its remaining moments covering them before dissolving into the dark.

Earlier Sam had asked her if she could watch Dani on Thursday night while he filled in for another doctor friend who needed to attend his son's sports banquet. After sidestepping the subject with sex, she couldn't, in the name of honesty, avoid any longer telling him what was on her mind.

Andrea first snuggled against his chest, which was lightly dusted with crinkly brown hair, thinking she'd never get tired of how sturdy he felt or his natural guy scent, and wondering over the difference in their skin tones. Then she broached the tough topic by sitting up and engaging Sam's full attention. Except his attention settled solely on her breasts, so she wrapped the sheet around her chest.

"You know how I love Dani," she said. He nodded. "And frankly you've given me lots of chances to get to know him. The thing is, I've been putting off painting a lot lately and I'm beginning to panic about it."

That got his full attention. He seemed uncomfortable,

realizing he was keeping her from her passion. "The last thing I want to do is stand in the way of your painting."

She leaned forward. "I believe you, and I have to admit it's always fun to watch Dani, but…"

He went up on his elbow. "Well, that's something, then, right? Because he loves you so much, and I trust you, I always know he's in good hands with you. And that means a lot to me."

"I'm glad you trust me, but it's clear you're the center of that boy's universe. He loves you so much and wants to be with *you*."

"Thanks. I know, but you two are really great together, too. You've got a very special friendship going on."

"So much so I'm beginning to wonder if this is what motherhood feels like, which scares the daylights out of me." She'd decided to tiptoe into the conversation.

He grabbed her and pulled her close. "Aw, you're just being a scaredy-cat about kids." Sounding like a typical pediatrician. "You're a natural."

A natural? Being raised by a deeply depressed mother and an oblivious father probably made her the furthest thing from that.

"Don't get me wrong," she said, glancing up at his chin, memorizing the fine stubble there. "I adore Dani, but he's your son and you need to be there for him as much as you possibly can."

"I am there for him, every day. I get him up every morning and put him to bed most nights. He knows I'm his dad, and I love being his dad." He squeezed her shoulder. "I even hope to have more children, too. I guess I should be up front with you about that, right?"

Now he tells her? She sat up again. "Yes, you definitely should."

Why did his hope for a big family make her immediately wonder where she'd fit in? He wanted more children? What exactly did he have in mind?

"Sam, you're a great dad, Dani is thriving living with you. But lately I feel like I'm doing as much, if not more, of the caregiving as you." She wouldn't dare mention that it also felt like being second best to his job, just as it'd always felt with her father. But it did!

"My job will always keep me busy, it's the nature of the beast. I *will*, however, get a babysitter before the end of this week. I promise." He looked sincere as all get-out, and she felt obligated to believe him.

"Thank you." It wasn't a perfect solution, but at least Dani could go to sleep in his own bed and she wouldn't be the one always putting him there. They kissed more, but she couldn't get into it. "You seriously want more kids?"

"Yes, but not, like, tomorrow. I come from a big family and I want the same. I've told you that."

Something about his answer didn't ring true, but she couldn't quite put her finger on it. Where did his need and desire to have a big family leave her? If they were together, would she have a say in the matter? This conversation was making her feel like a helpless child all over again. "But doesn't it take two?" Actually, he'd already gotten around that loophole by adopting. Would he do it again? Her head throbbed with questions.

"I'm not rushing things," he said. "I'm just being honest."

This obviously meant he was serious about her, and on so many levels she was crazy about him, too, but she couldn't discount her ambivalence about his desire for a big family. Not with her background.

Maybe he deserved to hear her side of the story. She

owed it to him. "I know how it feels, as a kid, to always want my dad home, because he never was. That's probably why I'm so sensitive to that for Dani. But unlike you with Dani, when my dad was home he'd be completely distracted with work. I'd be, like, 'Daddy, look what I drew,' and he'd glance up from his paperwork and say, 'Not now.' Sometimes I'd be quiet like a good little girl and wait for him, but I felt as though he didn't even know I was in the same room."

Sam pulled her closer, wrapping her in his arms. "You deserved better than that." He kissed the top of her head.

"I'm not asking for sympathy, I'm just saying that kind of experience doesn't make for 'natural' skills in parenting, like you've experienced."

He went still for a heartbeat, then sighed. "Trust me, if I can do it, you can do it."

Maybe she should be flattered that he felt open enough to tell her his plans, but she had plans, too. And she needed to think about those plans as well, but he pulled her back toward him. They snuggled down again and kissed a few more times. Her mind drifted to other points of anxiety in her life—ignoring her art, her love-hate relationship with her job, loving the patients but not the administrative part and feeling pushed to run a department. She stopped the kiss in the middle.

"My grandmother's retirement is getting closer and closer and soon, if I don't figure something out, they'll expect me to be the head of the department, which means administrative meetings and more responsibility. Where will that leave my painting? Honestly, I'm feeling trapped."

"Is this your father's or grandmother's idea?"

"Both, but mostly my father's."

"Then tell him you don't want that responsibility.

Tell him you want to go back to working part-time so you can still pursue your painting."

It sounded so logical, but Sam didn't know her father as she knew her father. "It's not that easy."

He didn't push her on the topic. Maybe he sensed what she knew firsthand, that there was no saying no to Jerome Rimmer.

He went quiet for a second. "Do I make you feel trapped?"

"No." She lifted her head to make eye contact. "No. But I can't be your babysitter, Sam, or a stand-in parent for Dani."

"That's the last thing I want."

"If we become a couple, I don't want to feel second in line to your job, because that's how I always felt with my dad. Nor do I ever want Dani to feel that way."

"I understand. That's the last thing in the world I'd want, either. And I really don't want to interfere with your art." He held her close, ran his fingers over her hair. "We'll work something out. I just need some time to think about this."

Right, men were task-oriented problem solvers. But this wasn't an easy-to-solve situation. She didn't have a clue what he'd come up with, but right now she was exhausted and couldn't summon a thought about what she should do, so she let him hold her, satisfied she'd said her piece. She'd let him know her fears, and why she was the way she was, totally ambivalent about his big family plans, and he'd accepted her concerns. But the most important thing of all was that they'd come closer as a couple tonight.

They'd taken their worries and fears and acted on them with caveman sex just now, the one thing they seemed to do best together. At least from Sam's view it was the least complicated part of their relationship. Plus it fit right in with his lifelong habit of trying to prove himself worth keeping. He knew how to make her lose it, and did it as often as he could.

He wasn't using her. He respected her completely, and he loved how she got along with his son. He could see a future for them, but they'd only started dating. Maybe it had been a boneheaded idea to announce how he wanted a big family. He was lucky she hadn't run for the hills.

It was his time-to-be-honest moment, and since Andrea had drifted off to sleep, he couldn't avoid thinking about it. He wanted to be around her as much as possible. They both led complicated lives, and he felt guilty keeping her from her painting. He understood her inner battle about always having to create time for her passion, as if it didn't mean as much as the more practical job of making a decent living while helping others. Maybe he could come up with a way that she could do both?

What if he asked her to move in with them?

If she did, she could paint every evening if she wanted to. He admired her talent, wanted nothing more than for her to feel fulfilled. He and Dani would learn to respect and honor her need to paint and stay out of her way when she did. He had a perfectly available spare bedroom he could turn into a studio for her, too.

Okay, his solution sounded more practical than romantic, and also scared the daylights out of him. Maybe he should think more about this first before he brought it up. But he had to be honest with himself.

I want her here. I see a future with her. I...I think I love her.

He shook his head, suddenly needing to take an extra breath. He did. He loved her. But she was all tangled up with job changes and a demanding father, not a great time for a woman to fall in love. And how could he tell her he loved her when he hadn't been completely honest with her about his family, and how he'd been the foster kid left alone until the Murphys had taken him in? When would he quit feeling unworthy of being loved because his mother had walked away from him? Wasn't he in charge of his life now? So why couldn't he come clean with Andrea and tell her he'd been an only child like her, and in two completely different ways they had both been abandoned.

Because it still hurt too much, and he didn't want her sympathy. He'd proved himself by becoming a successful doctor, yet why did he still feel unworthy of a woman's love?

It hurt too much to let the old pushed-down feelings out, so he focused back on Andrea and her issues. She needed to figure out how to deal with her father. It would be a shame if his overbearing attitude chased Andrea out of the profession. The way she'd painted Dani's iris was uncanny. No digital computer program could duplicate what she'd captured with her artistic eye. What she'd done for Dani was nothing short of a miracle. Just like that eye peeking through the keyhole painting. People were her canvases, and didn't the saying go that the eye was the mirror to the soul? What she did on the job was nothing short of art. Andrea had a gift that needed to be shared with the world, whether on canvas or with glass eyes and silicone ears.

There had to be some way he could help her. Should he confront her father for her? No, that was her business, but it ticked him off that Jerome made Andrea's life so difficult.

Now his head was spinning a mile a minute. He wanted to solve her problem because he truly cared about her. He knew he couldn't resolve her issues, that it was totally up to her to work it out with her father. But wasn't the hospital redoing the lobby? Wouldn't they be looking for new artwork once they remodeled?

Those big splashy paintings on the walls at her house would be the perfect style for a modern hospital. Who did he need to talk to about that?

Then the one painting in particular that stood out from all the others at her house came to mind, the single eye peeking through a door keyhole. In his opinion, it was a masterpiece, and no doubt featured the skill she'd developed in her apprenticeship as an ocularist. The iris. The mirror to the soul. And the world was filled with billions of people with their own individual versions.

She'd never run out of subjects to paint.

Sleep would probably never come tonight. He'd at least diverted his thoughts from old painful ones to Andrea's concerns. He smiled with satisfaction into the dark because he'd found a way for Andrea to share her talent with the world. At the hospital. Genius!

Now all he had to do was convince her to face her father and tell him to back off, to let her do her job the way she wanted, the way things were right now. Being a department head might hold prestige for Dr. Rimmer, but Andrea was a modern woman, why couldn't she have it all on her terms? Not everyone was meant to be a department administrator. She had an artist's soul.

CHAPTER SEVEN

TELEVISION NEWS WAS playing the minute Sam and Andrea hit the hospital lobby the next morning. The huge flat screen on the farthest wall ran pictures of death and destruction in Mexico, with captions. A drug cartel had bombed several places, one being the village where one of the drug traffickers who'd cooperated with the police lived. As usual, the innocents had paid the price.

The explosions and subsequent fires had taken hundreds of lives and caused countless injuries across the countryside, leaving only rubble and near total devastation in one quiet border village between Mexico and the United States. The hospitals were overflowing and emergency personnel stretched beyond their limits. The area needed help, and even the Red Cross didn't seem to be enough.

Andrea stood with her mouth open, reading the horrible story. Sam put his arm around her for comfort and it occurred to him that was the first time he'd made a public display of his affection for her at the hospital. Despite the horrible news, the comforting part felt good.

"Hey, Dr. Marcus," a passing young resident said. "Terrible stuff, right?"

"Unbelievable. So senseless," he replied, still trying to get his head around the incident.

"A few of us are making plans to head down to Mexicali this weekend to help out. Someone needs to triage those patients in Cuernavaca. Is your passport up to date?"

"Of course."

"Why don't you come, too?"

Sam glanced at Andrea, who wore an uncertain expression, and he held off accepting, saying he'd think about it.

The resident seemed gung ho on helping, and recognizing Andrea he continued, "Aren't you from the anaplastology department? You should go, too," he said to her. "The explosion and fire probably left a lot of people with facial injuries. There might be all kinds of ways you could help."

This young, long-haired resident's enthusiasm was almost palpable, and compelling, and it was quickly rubbing off on Sam.

"I, uh…" Andrea seemed stumped by his challenge.

Sam stepped in. "We'll definitely think about it and get back to you, Anthony. When are you planning to leave?"

"Tomorrow, 6:00 a.m. The sooner we get there, the better. The border town is only about four hours away—we've already arranged for four free vans from the local car dealership." He said that part to Andrea, as if it might help her make up her mind. "And we plan to come back late Sunday. We're trying to get the hospital to donate supplies, too. We're still working out the details, but I'll definitely get back to you later."

As it was Friday morning, the new doctor had a lot to work out in a very short time, but judging by his exuberance, and seeing a little bit of himself in the guy, Sam had no doubt all would be arranged in record time.

"Yeah, give me a call," Sam said, putting his hand at

the small of the back of the mildly stunned lady beside him to guide her toward the elevator. They didn't say a thing about the medical mission plans as they walked. Once at the elevators, where he needed to go up and she down, he pecked her on the cheek, liking the freedom of letting the world know—well, the hospital, anyway— that he and Andrea were a definite item.

"I'll see you later," he said, enjoying the subtle twinkle in her eyes after the kiss. She must've liked his public display of affection, too. "Oh, by the way, *is* your passport up to date?" he asked, just before stepping into a nearly full elevator.

Her eyes widened and she gave a closed-mouth huff in reply.

If Sam expected her to drop everything, pack up and head south at a moment's notice, he'd better think again. Though she had to admit that for one split second she'd found the offer intriguing. Frustrated about being put on the spot, she got in the next elevator going down.

What about Dani? Sam might not be married, but he wasn't a single guy anymore. He couldn't just drop everything and travel to parts unknown. He had a son to think of. If she did go, and there was a big "if" about that, who'd look after Dani? The mere fact that Dani was always her first concern made her stop and think. She was already in over her head with the Marcus men.

The elevator door closed. She was the only person heading to the basement.

More truth, who was she to judge how Sam and Cat bartered time and money? The lady cared deeply for Dani. Andrea had seen it with her own eyes whenever Cat had brought Dani in for his appointments, and she probably loved having him around her boys, as well. He was such a sweetie.

She got out of the elevator and headed down the dreary green and beige linoleum hallway toward her department.

Andrea had to admit, until she decided whether to go or stay, whatever Sam worked out in order to take this last-minute medical mission trip was between Cat and Sam.

What she needed to do was search her soul about whether to go or not. The thought made a band tighten around her head.

Andrea opened the door, checking her watch. Her first appointment was in ten minutes and she needed to get the custom prosthesis ready for attachment. She rushed around, gathering everything she'd need when the patient entered the department.

From his records she knew he was a veteran who'd survived two tours in Afghanistan, only to return home and get his ear bitten off by a neighbor's Rottweiler. From personal experience, he was an affable guy who just wanted to look normal again. Surgical reconstruction had been ruled out because the damage was too great, so he'd been coming to Andrea for custom prosthetic restoration. He'd decided against surgical magnet placement and instead had undergone a small but important bone anchor procedure, which allowed her to create a bar-clip attachment for the perfectly duplicated mirror-image ear, if she did say so herself.

Greg smiled widely, his ball cap tilting low over what was left of his right ear, hiding the fact he didn't have one. She greeted him, and after a little small talk about how his surgery had gone, she revealed the silicone ear she'd made to match his skin tone and the existing ear.

"Wow, this looks weird but great," he said. "I'll be two-eared again." He chuckled.

"You won't be lopsided anymore," she said, motioning for him to sit as she adjusted the lights for best visibility. She'd spent several hours replicating his other ear first with sketches, then in a mold, then touching it up to be a nearly perfect mirror-image match to the other side, but in silicone. "That's new." She always got a kick out of his tattoo sleeves, noticing he'd added a new colorful section just above his wrist on one forearm.

"Yeah, I saw the porpoise and thought it'd be cool there."

While they chitchatted she removed the large flat bandage covering the implanted bar and easily clipped the new ear in place, adjusting the tilt to match the other side. "See how easy this is? Now you try." She removed the ear and handed it to him.

Under her tutelage, he attached his new ear, then sat and stared at himself in the mirror for several seconds, turning first this way, then that. "Wow. It looks real."

"Of course it looks real." She couldn't deny the pride she always felt when clients were happy with what she'd made for them. "It should help your hearing by twenty percent, too. Those auricles are there for a reason, you know."

"Look at this!" He put his ball cap back on his short-cropped military-style hair, and it was now perfectly balanced between two ears.

"You look great." Her smile was genuine and heartfelt. "But, to be honest, I kind of like the tilted cap look, too."

"Thanks, Andrea." The sincerity pouring out of his gaze nearly melted her.

"You're welcome, Greg. Come back anytime you think you need an adjustment, okay?"

"You got it."

Next she had an appointment in the hospital to measure a young woman who'd lost most of her nose to cancer. Andrea had been studying the woman's photographs and wondered, since now was a perfect opportunity, if the patient might want a sexy new nose, or if she'd rather stick with a replica of what she'd been born with. It could be a touchy subject, and Andrea was working out in her head how she wanted to broach the topic when a text message came through.

Lunch?

She knew exactly who it was and texted back.

What time?

After she'd finished her bedside appointment, having discovered that the young lady would indeed love a new nose, specifically one like Reese Witherspoon's—which put a smile on Andrea's face—she met up with Sam in the hospital cafeteria, excited about her next project but even more excited about seeing him.

Then she ran into her father. "Andrea, you're just the person I wanted to see."

"Hi, Dad." Why did she always go on alert whenever he spoke to her? "You know Sam Marcus, right?"

Her father glanced distractedly at Sam, only acknowledging him with a quick nod. Sam had put out his hand for a shake, but when Jerome made no attempt to do the same, he withdrew it.

"Your grandmother tells me you still haven't filled out the job application."

"That's right. I've been pretty busy."

"Too busy to apply for the biggest job of your life? If they don't get applicants from inside—and let's be honest, you're the only person suited for the job at this hospital—they'll send the posting out to the public."

"Maybe that would be a good thing."

"You're talking nonsense and you know it," he scolded. The man never cared who was within hearing range when he berated her or when he was on a mission. "I'll expect to hear you've applied for the job before the end of the day."

With that, he walked away, leaving Andrea feeling humiliated and angry with him, like so many other times in her life. Did he still think she was ten? She stood and watched her father leave the cafeteria, then mumbled under her breath, "Jerk."

Sam bit his lip, watching her, probably realizing her old man treated everyone the same, including his only daughter. "You okay?"

She nodded. "Let's eat." Determined not to let on how upset she was, she led the way, taking some pleasure in the fact that Sam looked as if he wanted to deck her father.

They headed toward the line, filling their trays with the day's special soup-and-sandwich combo, tomato bisque and turkey deli. She'd been busy and hadn't realized how hungry she was, but now she'd lost her appetite, so with little thought she picked the sandwich combo. They found a table off in the corner of the cafeteria.

"You want to talk about what just happened?" Sam asked shortly after sitting.

"Absolutely not."

"Okay. Moving right along... I've been thinking about last night."

Even though she was still furious with her father, a naughty thought about their triple header last night crossed Andrea's mind and warmth trickled up her neck, spreading across her cheeks. Grateful for the respite from the tense encounter with her father, she couldn't hide her response.

"Not that, you bad girl," Sam said, lightly pinching her arm, playing along, embers igniting in those steel blue eyes.

She laughed, relieved she was back to her life as normal with the guy she was crazy about, especially those sexy eyes of his. "You don't know what I'm thinking." Yes, he did!

They shared a special smoldering gaze and smile that proved he knew exactly what she was thinking, and which set off a stream of liquid heat traveling through her navel and meandering southward. Wow, no guy had ever had such power over her that she could instantaneously forget yet another lousy meeting with her demanding father. Sam reached across the table and squeezed her hand, letting her know he felt exactly the same way. This, the sexual sparks between them, they both understood without a doubt or a single word.

She was in way over her head, with everything moving too fast, but there didn't seem to be anything she could do to stop it other than break things off. Which was the last thing she wanted to do.

He took in a slow breath and let go of her hand. They'd come to the cafeteria to eat after all. "So, anyway, what I was saying about last night refers to our conversation about your feeling like Dani's babysitter."

She'd just taken a bite of her deli turkey sandwich

so she just nodded deeply and lifted her brows. Yeah, she remembered that tense conversation very well. As she recalled, she'd started it.

"I don't want you to feel like I'm using you to watch my kid, or that you are somehow considered second best in my life. Anyway, I've devised a plan to make sure you won't feel that way about this weekend."

She hadn't yet swallowed, but she did so quickly in order to ask her question. "What are you talking about?"

He took a quick spoonful of soup and continued. "I've decided to go to Mexico this weekend and I want you to come with me."

She nearly choked on what was left of her next bite of sandwich. "You're going?"

He nodded, lips tight in a straight line, the quintessential look of determination.

Just like Dad. "Just like that?"

"Cat's agreed to watch Dani so we can go with the hospital team. Medical missions are life-changing. I can't wait to share it with you."

"But, Sam, I haven't made up my mind yet." She still hadn't painted one stroke from that inspirational moment at the swings in the playground. Was he planning on taking over her life and interfering just as her father did? She tensed.

"We could have a romantic weekend away in Mexico." There went his hand again, reaching for hers and grasping her fingers.

"With the drug cartels?"

"I get it. You don't have to go if you don't want to," he said. "But I was hoping you'd go with me. I want to share it with you, have you there so you can see why I feel so committed to these trips."

"But don't you worry about Dani losing more time

with you while you follow that passion for medicine and missions?"

"I know that's a touchy subject with you these days but, Andrea, as much as I love Dani, sometimes he'll have to understand that my job comes first. Not always. And certainly not because I put him second. Just that sometimes things come up that I feel called to do. This is one of them."

Why did the guy have to make such sense? "I need more time to think about this."

"You've got all afternoon and night. Those people could use your help just as much as they need mine. I can guarantee it." He shoved what was left of the half sandwich he'd been eating into his mouth and watched her.

She'd been in plenty of these positions with her father her entire life. Her back figuratively against the wall, but the words being used sounding like anything but an ultimatum. *Do this, it'll be good for you.* Part of her wanted to believe he was using one of her father's subversive techniques. But the other part, the part that knew this man was nothing like her father, nor could he ever be, understood he simply wanted to share his passion for medicine with her. This trip was special to him.

But having just come away from another tense encounter with her father, she wasn't in the proper frame of mind to give in so easily.

She sat spine straight, chin up, hands folded on her lap, not about to let him win this round, even while hating that a hospital mission to help the needy was at the center of the argument. What did that say about her? But she had to stand firm for now. "And I'd like to use all of that time to make my decision. On my terms. *If* I decide to go, it will be on *my* terms."

The man must be good at poker, because he didn't give away a single reaction to her holding out for more time. "That's perfectly understandable and reasonable." He spooned more soup into his mouth.

"Damn right it's reasonable," she mumbled. Okay, so she didn't sound quite as reasonable as he did, but maybe because she still felt as if she was talking more to her father than to Sam.

The way he lifted the corner of his mouth in a near smile proved she hadn't offended him. Did he think everything she did was cute?

When he'd finished his soup he wiped his mouth, stood, then bent to kiss her cheek. "If you make up your mind, we're leaving from the south parking lot at 6:00 a.m." He started to go but turned back. "Oh, and don't forget your passport." Then he left.

She shoved the rest of her sandwich into her mouth and chomped, irritated that Sam might be taking her for granted but also very curious about what a medical mission to Mexico would be like.

Sam was on the verge of feeling disappointed in the woman he was pretty sure he loved when he saw her beat-up champagne-colored sedan pull into the hospital parking lot at five forty-five the next morning. He'd purposely left her alone to make up her mind last night, though he'd thought about calling her any number of times. Relieved, he grinned all the way to opening the car door for her.

She tossed him a conciliatory glance as she got out. He hugged her, and she was receptive. "Glad to see you. Where's your bag?"

"In the trunk."

He found her duffel bag and several fishing-tackle

boxes, but having had her make a home visit to Dani he understood that was how she carried her O&A supplies. From the backseat of the car he saw her remove a large over-the-shoulder portfolio bag. "Planning on painting?"

"Maybe. Actually, as crazy as it may sound, if time allows, it might be a way to help the kids deal with stress. We'll see."

That was exactly why he loved this lady, she was thoughtful and caring and knew how to use art for therapy. What more could he ask?

He helped her carry everything to the van he'd been assigned, making room for her belongings despite the overflowing medical supplies. With very few words but a heartfelt kiss before they left, they set out on a nearly four-hour drive across the border to Mexicali.

It had been a long and, even though it was early morning, warm drive to Baja California, then on to Mexicali and the village on the outskirts of the city of Cuernavaca. The landscape looked much like the high desert in California and long flat vistas similar to the San Fernando Valley except without all the buildings, and it struck Andrea how similar the two states were. Though poverty was more apparent here. Slowly the roads got smaller and the towns grew poorer until they were on the farthest outskirts of Cuernavaca in a village decimated by a bomb and fire, thanks to a drug cartel.

The nearest hospital was small and overflowing, and though most of the severely injured patients had been taken there, many wounded and in need of care remained in the nearby area. Plus, as was always the case with these kinds of missions, word traveled fast and people who'd been dealing with medical issues for any number of reasons came pouring out of the countryside, looking for help.

The medical mission had been instructed to set up their makeshift clinic at the local school. They'd discussed it on the drive down and planned to divide classrooms into triage areas, patient education, easy procedures and exams, and more complex issues. A long line of people was already waiting to be seen when they arrived.

The vans were emptied of volunteers and supplies in record time and by noon the clinic was in full swing. Andrea glimpsed the dedication Sam had for helping those in need. He jumped right in and over the next several hours worked tirelessly to see and treat as many people as he could, along with the handful of other doctors, residents and nurses.

It was inspiring, and Andrea admitted she was glad she was there, even if she was nervous and felt a bit out of place. She saw her first patient with half an ear missing, made her mold of the other ear and took several pictures of what was left of the damaged side for fitting the prosthetic, then took all the information on where to mail the final product. Once again word got out and parents seemed to come crawling out of the woodwork with their kids. Some children were in need of prosthetics due to trauma and some due to a condition known as microtia. These injuries and conditions had nothing to do with the bombing, but Andrea was glad to help the community in any way she could. It turned out auricular prostheses were in high demand. Who knew?

By the end of the first day she'd seen no less than a dozen patients who needed everything from eyes to a portion of the nose and several who needed ears. She could do this, and what a joy to help little children look and feel normal again, not to mention the handful of adults who presented with missing facial parts. The only drawback was them having to wait until she went home to her workshop to make all the prosthetics and mail them back. And the prosthetic eyes wouldn't be custom-made or fitted as usual, but anything would be an improvement over an empty eye socket.

The gratitude was overwhelming, and because she didn't speak Spanish she'd smiled and nodded so much all day that by the afternoon her cheeks nearly cramped and her neck was sore.

During the evening she invited the young patients who were able to move around to come and draw pictures with her. She'd set up a little art clinic so they could dabble in just about any medium they wanted. Most stuck with pencil and drawing paper, but a few ventured into watercolors and one lone and talented teenager asked to try his hand at acrylics on canvas. She was thrilled to see them come out of their shells as they reached inside to their creative muses and worked out their fears and concerns through art. She knew first-hand the power of art and loved sharing it.

Sam caught up with her and grinned to see how engaged she'd become with the locals.

"Anyone ever tell you that you look like a canvas?"

She didn't get what he was saying until he took a rag and wiped away paint smudges from her cheeks. She laughed. "I do get messy when I'm in the zone with painting. I guess that's a good sign."

He hugged her, and after they'd shared a kiss she could see the passion for her and all things medical in his gaze, even though he looked exhausted from the long hours he'd put in. He belonged here. People in the world needed doctors like him, and a pang of guilt over her wanting him to stay home with his son made her stand straighter, and feel confused. As he'd said, sometimes Dani would have to understand that his job came first. So would she.

Life was complicated. Always would be.

"Have you got a minute?" he asked.

She looked at the group of kids deeply involved in their various projects. "Will you guys be okay without me?" She asked the one little girl who knew English to interpret for her. She repeated Andrea's question and everyone nodded and agreed they'd be fine without her for a little while. Andrea looked at the oldest boy working diligently on his small canvas. "Will you look after everyone for me?"

The little girl interpreted again, and the boy, named Rigoberto, nodded. *"Si, si."*

Sam took her hand and led her to a separate tent with a few cots inside. "Earlier I participated in surgically cleaning up a below-the-knee amputation. I want to check on Fernando."

"My God, you did major surgery here?" She glanced around at what was essentially a camping excursion setup, not a hospital.

"Actually, the bomb took care of that. The kid's leg was blown to smithereens. Good thing we brought a surgeon along. We debrided the flesh and cauterized the veins. Hopefully he didn't have too much nerve damage. For now he's stable and on pain meds and antibiotics." He went straight to a cot where a young black-haired boy slept deeply. He didn't look more than five or six.

Sam placed a gentle hand on his forehead and studied the kid, and Andrea's heart nearly broke over the compassion she saw in the man. He had so much to give, was heroic even, and didn't need to think twice about coming here once the opportunity had arisen. Unlike her. Plus he had to be an amazing doctor to do what he'd done for this young boy today.

What wasn't to like, or love, about Sam Marcus?

An IV flowed into one arm with a large fluid bag and several smaller ones, no doubt antibiotics to fight off infection in his mangled leg. In the other arm, blood was being given through the second IV. A nurse Andrea recognized from the hospital kept close vigil over the boy, who'd obviously been given something for pain.

"How's he doing, Gina?"

"Pretty good. No fever. Vitals are stable."

"Great."

A quarter of his tiny right leg was missing and heavily bandaged. "He's small for his age," Sam said to Andrea. "He's seven, and both of his parents were killed in the explosion. His uncle was the informant and they all lived together. Tomorrow we'll have to transfer him to the main hospital in Mexicali to wait for real surgery with excess bone removal and most likely skin grafts. Then after that he'll probably be put in an orphanage." He glanced up at Andrea, empathy coloring those blue eyes with concern. "Who knows what will happen to him after that."

Sam looked so sad. She understood the boy's future didn't look bright, and the ache in her chest made the backs of her eyes prick momentarily.

Sam noticed, and being the benevolent healer he was he put his arm around her. "The good news is with a below-the-knee amputation a modern prosthetic could let him walk and run almost like normal."

After one last check of the boy, Sam led her outside. "The bad news is he'll probably never get a prosthetic in an orphanage, or it will be some clunky outdated version, and he'll have to spend the rest of his life on crutches, feeling like a cripple."

"But you'll find a way to help with that, right?" If anyone could, Sam would.

He nodded, determination turning his blue eyes darker. She hugged him, thinking she loved how he couldn't walk away from children without helping in some way. He could make a difference for this one, just like the starfish parable. It was the mark of a good, good man. He had a near saint of a mother and a big family to thank for that. They stood for several moments comforting each other and Andrea considering the bad fortune in life.

Then it hit her. She didn't have the special gift Sam did, the compassion and love in his heart. She'd been left emotionally flawed because of her childhood, and it held her back in life. Her wounds weren't obvious, like Dani's or Fernando's, but they were nevertheless there. Her eyes burned and while holding Sam she let some tears flow, let him think it was because of the moving experience of the boy with the missing leg on this medical mission. Not because she felt broken inside.

Later, they slept near each other on the ground in sleeping bags, holding hands, and somehow it seemed as romantic as staying in a tropical B and B. Her world had opened up in ways she'd never dreamed of since meeting Sam. Maybe he could help heal her, too.

He'd been right about the medical mission. It had not only been life-changing, it had opened her eyes. The hard part was that she didn't like what she saw about herself.

Late Sunday afternoon they headed home. Andrea had seen how special Sam was with the sick children and finally understood without a doubt that he'd found his true calling. He was willing to make sacrifices for it, too. Though she'd been deeply moved by interacting with her share of patients, she, on the other hand, was heading home feeling a bit overwhelmed. She had a dozen or so prosthetics she'd promised to make for children and adults in the village, plus her regular work lined up at the hospital. How would she find time to do everything? Not to mention to paint that landscape she'd had on her mind since the evening at the playground.

How did Sam do it?

Why did she have to feel pulled in two directions, one practical and one artistic? Could she be a whole person if she gave up her art in order to help needy patients full-time? Wasn't there a place for art in life? Didn't it bring joy and beauty to people? She'd seen the sparkles in those kids' eyes as they'd drawn and painted, and shouldn't that be valued as much as the practical things? But she also knew she'd miss her patients. She loved helping people as much as painting.

Maybe she wasn't as emotionally deficient as she'd thought.

She forced herself to stop analyzing and worrying and once she weeded away those negative confusing feelings she realized she'd changed by coming on this mission trip. The experience had moved her deeply, she felt happy, and it had fed her creative muse in a way she hadn't experienced since college. It also made her determined to prove her father wrong. She could hold her head high and be both an ocularist and an artist, and she didn't need to run a department to prove her worth.

Now all she had to do was figure out how to make every single day longer. She'd have to get up earlier and put in time in her studio before work. She'd also have to stay late at the hospital to do the pro bono projects she'd agreed to for the people in the village. They deserved no less. She'd have to cut back on time spent with Sam and Dani, which pained her, but if she wanted to do it all, and she really did, there had to be sacrifices. A sick feeling dashed around her stomach and circled her heart. Sam would understand, but would Dani?

"How're you feeling?" Sam asked, taking her hand in his.

"Exhausted. Elated. Overwhelmed." She glanced at him through newly wise eyes and he still looked gorgeous. "Surprisingly, pretty good."

"Are you glad you came?"

"You know I am. Seeing you with the children, especially with Fernando, made me realize what a gift you have. It made me realize how lucky Dani is to have you as his father. But it also made me face myself. Your childhood turned you into the person you are and so did mine. But, unlike you, I don't think I'll ever have what it takes to be a parent."

"What are you talking about? You're great with Dani."

"Because I'm not his parent. I'm not responsible for him. You are."

Sam gave her a skeptical glance. "Something tells me there's more going on than meets the eye here. Are you okay?"

"To be honest, no. I'm not okay. This weekend I realized how messed up I am. You can open your heart and reach out to help people when I want to run scared. Loving others means something totally different to you than it does to me. My mother loves my father and it has nearly destroyed her."

"You talk as though your father is a monster."

"Not obviously so, but you saw how he was with me in the cafeteria. He still talks to me like I'm ten. He has zero respect for me or my mother. He was the kind of dad who'd demand I get straight As in school, then not bother to show up at the awards assembly. I'd be the only kid there without a parent in the room, because my mother was too timid to ever learn how to drive."

Andrea hated sounding so lost and needy, but she and Sam had been raised completely differently. He had the confidence to do whatever he felt he should, completely independent, interestingly enough, not needing anyone. Or anyone's approval. Sam needed to know why she was mistrusting and hesitant.

"My dad would holler and carry on if things weren't perfect at home, then rarely ever be there. I never felt love from him. All I ever felt was lonely and miserable, and I'm afraid I don't know how to feel or show love because of him."

Sam drew her near and snuggled her close. "You're not anything like your father. Don't try to fool yourself."

Bitter thoughts and intense sadness made her eyes prickle. Sam believed in her. He saw something worthwhile in her. He wanted to encourage her to branch out and experience a different kind of life. A different kind of love?

He put his arm around her on the van bench and pulled her near. "This probably isn't the ideal time to say it, but I thought you should know—" he kissed her cheek "—that I love you."

CHAPTER EIGHT

SAM HELD ANDREA close in the hospital parking lot. He cupped her face and kissed her as if they hadn't seen each other in weeks, even though they'd just spent two full days together. She let him kiss her, not caring what anyone thought. The man had already taken her breath away when he'd told her he loved her a few short moments ago, and she wanted to make sure he knew how happy that'd made her.

Especially after she'd just confessed how messed up her family was, and how it had affected her, and the man had still said it. She kissed him hard. Everyone was busy unloading the vans; they'd probably never even notice what she and Sam were up to.

Was she really worth loving? In Sam's world, yes. He had the capacity to love as she'd never experienced.

She wrapped her arms around his neck and leaned into his kiss with everything she had, and had never felt more beautiful in her life. Except for the fact they were both fairly grungy after a weekend of hard work without a shower, and her short hair, except for a few spikes, was nearly matted flat to her head. Yet she still felt beautiful...because Sam had said he loved her.

They'd made it back to St. Francis of the Valley Hospital parking lot by 8:00 p.m. There was much to be done, but his lips and the cascade of thrills they caused were the center of her world at the moment. She'd never been kissed by a man who loved her before. Wow, even her toes inside her practical cross-trainers curled from this most special of all kisses.

"Can we get a hand here, lovebirds?" said Anthony, the shaggy-haired, bearded resident who'd initiated the medical mission, standing over by one of the vans.

Nearly dizzy from the kiss, Andrea parted her lips from Sam's and looked into his eyes. She'd never seen such a dreamy gaze from him before and she savored the moment. Could she really do that to him? Well, it was a big deal when a guy told a woman he loved her. It had to be the honest-to-God truth or it meant nothing. Everything seemed surreal and it took a couple of seconds to check back in with the real world. She crawled out from the lingering love-hazed moment with him, not wanting it to end but knowing she needed to help with the unpacking.

"Welcome home," Sam said, sending a million possibilities through her brain for a meaning to that phrase.

"Thank you for inviting me," she said, heartfelt. The weekend had been inspiring on a dozen levels. Now that she realized how emotionally mixed up she was, she could work on fixing it. She could change if she tried. Sam would help her.

Sam tossed a look over his shoulder. "Theoretically, Anthony's the one who invited you."

"Yeah," Anthony broke in, "and I'm the one who needs your help unpacking now. Please, guys?"

Grinning, they got busy chipping in with the business of emptying and cleaning out the vans. Before long, when everything had been completed, Sam was at her side again.

"I've got to take off to pick up Dani. I promised him he'd sleep in his own bed tonight."

"I understand. Give him a hug for me."

"You're not coming over?" Surprise tented his eyebrows.

"We've just spent nearly forty-eight hours together. I love you, Sam Marcus, but right now I really need a shower and a good night's sleep."

She'd driven her own car over and had—despite the novelty of having a man tell her he loved her and her believing him—decided to go home tonight, leaving Dani and Sam time together. They needed father-son time, having been parted the whole weekend. Besides, she needed to get serious about a new routine, painting early in the morning before going to work. That special picture was fighting to get put on canvas.

He kissed her again, more a peck of understanding than a real kiss. "Okay. I'll see you in the morning, then."

"Lunch?"

"You're on."

She stood for a few moments, watching the man she loved walk away, wondering over the sudden change in her relationship status. She looked down at her feet to make sure they were still touching the ground. Maybe happiness was finally within her reach. The thought started a whole new tumble of chills.

Then she saw the text from her father.

We need to talk. ASAP. Come for dinner tomorrow night.

It wasn't an invitation so much as a summons.

The thought about falling in love and walking on air dissolved. Look what falling in love and marrying the man of her dreams had done for her mother. She'd often tried to make up for their being alone by telling Andrea about the wonderfully amazing man he'd been when they'd dated. Her mother's love for her father had turned out to be a deeply destructive emotion that had escorted her mother into a dark chamber, left her alone, moody and often withdrawn. Love had eaten her alive.

If she wasn't careful, could the same happen to her?

Andrea asked Sam and Dani to accompany her to her parents' house on Monday night as backup, but not before checking with her mother to see if it would be okay. Plus she needed to feel Mom out, see how her new meds were working. Was her depression under control? Was she really up for a dinner party, no matter how casual? They'd had a great time a couple of weeks ago, eating, talking, but that had been just the two of them. Adding Dad into the mix was always a gamble.

Barbara had promised she was in good spirits and would love to meet Sam and Dani, so Andrea had invited them along. It wasn't fair to use Sam as a buffer, but Andrea had something on her mind she wanted to be firm about, and having Sam there would give her more confidence.

Rather than knock on the door at the huge Rimmer family home in the heart of the Los Feliz hills above Los Angeles, she used her old house key and let them all in.

"Hello? We're here! Mom?"

"Come on in," Mom said, appearing at the kitchen door, wiping her hands on her half apron.

Andrea rushed to her mother and gave her a hug, grateful she had a spark of life in her brown eyes today. "Mom, this is Sam and Dani."

Perhaps overreacting a tad, Barbara put her hands

on her cheeks and beamed. "It's so wonderful to meet you," she said to Sam, taking his hand and shaking it enthusiastically. Then she bent forward to greet Dani. "Well, hello, young man. Aren't you a handsome boy."

Dani blushed and hid behind Sam's leg. "Sorry, he's a bit shy," Sam stepped in.

"We'll have plenty of time to get to know each other, won't we, young man?"

Still hiding, Dani peeked around Sam's leg to take another look at the new woman.

Barbara's voice actually sounded cheery, but Andrea didn't trust it. She'd had too much experience with her mother's mood swings over the years. She tensed, hoping for the best, but part of her was waiting cautiously.

Her mother twisted her wedding ring round and round her finger, a sign that underneath the cheery exterior she was nervous. "Why don't we go into the other room."

The Rimmer house was a grand old 1920s-style home with every room fairly small and neatly partitioned off, with a tendency toward being dark and dreary because of it. A perfect setting for her depressed mother. Andrea had forgotten how claustrophobic the house could feel at times. They walked through the living room section, with furniture that probably hadn't been sat on for months, and into the wood-paneled den that connected to the dining room.

"Can we help with anything, Mom?"

"You can get everyone drinks and set the table if you'd like."

Andrea and Sam pitched in and got everything ready at the table, letting Dani have a glass of lemonade while they did so.

In the dining room, Sam reached for Andrea's arm

and squeezed it. "Everything will be okay." She'd filled Sam in on her mother's condition on the ride over, and he already knew firsthand the blustery personality of her father. "I'm here for you."

"Thanks." She believed him and it reassured her.

The front door opened and a cool draft entered the house, traveling all the way to the den. Her father was home, and the loose knot that had been forming in her stomach over the family dinner tightened.

"Good evening," Jerome said, making his appearance wearing a dark blue work suit and still acting all business.

Dani went back into hiding behind Sam's leg. Barbara appeared from the kitchen, still twisting the ring on her finger but this time even faster, a new anxious expression on her face. Jerome went to her and kissed her cheek. "Barbara, something smells good."

Poof, tension disappeared from her eyes, and the ring-twisting stopped. "It's your favorite, Jerry, Santa Barbara–styled tri tip with onions and bell peppers."

Turning his attention to Andrea, Jerome ignored Barbara's reply. "I have a bone to pick with you, young lady." He said it as if she'd been truant from school.

Andrea squared her shoulders. "If it's about the job application for department administrator, I'm going to be honest. I don't want the job."

"You don't want the job? Do you know how many people would die for that job? The benefits, the stability, the future?"

"I like the job I have."

His jaw clamped down and his eyes went steely. Rather than wither, as she might have as a child, Andrea stood her ground.

"Do you honestly think I got you that apprenticeship so you could settle for working part-time?"

"Frankly, Father, I don't care why you forced me to take the apprenticeship. I've done what you wanted, will get my credential within the year, and after that I can do anything I want with it."

If steam could come out of a person's ears, it would have right then and there from Jerome.

"Why don't we all take a break from this conversation and have dinner," Barbara spoke up, sounding firmer than Andrea expected, which surprised and pleased her. Since when had Mom become a mediator? Out of respect for her mother, and little Dani, she'd bite back all the words she'd truly love to sling at her father right then.

As everyone prepared to sit at the dining table, Jerome cast a sideways glance at Andrea. "We're not through with this conversation."

Andrea pressed her lips together and passed her father an oh-yes-we-are stare, just long enough to get her point across.

The new medications for depression seemed to be doing wonders for Barbara. She sat at the dining table, head held high, making light conversation with Sam and teasing Dani to coax him to eat. Surprisingly, even Jerome settled in to a more welcoming mood as the family and guests enjoyed the grilled beef, fingerling potatoes and a vegetable medley casserole. Maybe he'd finally understood that his daughter could be as strong-willed as he was.

With Sam at her side, ready to back her up, Andrea had found confidence enough to make her point. It was her life. She'd make all the decisions from here on. Thank you very much, *Daddy*.

* * *

Things were going great for the next couple of weeks.
Andrea kept to her schedule of painting every morning
before work and only spending the weekends with Sam
and Dani. They might say they loved each other, but
she still longed for independence, and he needed special father-son time. Plus not going over to his house
during the week made Sam all the happier to see her
when she spent Friday nights through Sunday evenings
with him and Dani. Even then, Sam respected her need
to paint in the mornings. And after the boy went to bed
they definitely made up for those lost nights together.

With this schedule, the picture that had been impa-
tiently waiting inside her head seemed to pour out onto
the canvas, as if it had commandeered the brushes and
all she had to do was let her arms do the grunt work.
She hadn't been this inspired in ages, and whether it
was from being in a solid relationship with a good man
whom she loved or from going to Mexico and helping
out people in need, she figured her life had definitely
taken a turn for the better.

Soon that painting would be done, and she'd already
finished a couple of the prosthetics she'd promised to
the children in Mexico, too. And, as if her positive message was circulating in the universe, a long-ago friend
from art school had contacted her about a few of her earlier paintings. A new café wanted to display art on their
walls in the Gas Light District of San Diego. It would be
a huge help in getting her noticed, and Andrea was so
excited she wanted to personally deliver the paintings
and spend a weekend catching up with her old friend.
Sam understood and completely supported her going.

It seemed amazing what a woman could accomplish
when she was in love.

Even more amazing, Sam had found a second baby-sitter. The teenager of one of his colleagues from the hospital needed extra money for a big school trip in the fall. Ally was more than willing to babysit on week-nights if or whenever Sam needed her, and, most important, Dani liked her. Yes, all seemed right with the world.

On the eve of her trip to San Diego, a full two weeks from the night she'd lost sleep making her decision to take Sam and the young resident up on their offer to go along on the medical mission, she found herself in a very different situation. She was definitely losing sleep, but this time for a far more exciting reason.

Sam held her hips as she straddled him and rocked his world, doing a fantastic job of rocking her world, too. Quite sure there was no way her breasts could get any tighter or more tingly, he surprised her by rising up on an elbow and taking one into his mouth. She stopped briefly to savor the thrumming throughout her body, but soon craving more she lifted and curved over his length, with him solid and bucking up into her. The benefits of being on top and positioning him just so fanned the heat building between her thighs to a near inferno.

With early signs that there'd be no turning back, tension coiled behind her navel, knotting and threading down, spiraling deeper into her core. The small of her back buzzed with sensations. Every cell seemed awake and vibrating thanks to him. Sam's mouth soon found her other breast as she leaned over him, and he held her hips in place when he drove up into her again and again. Nearly helpless against his thrusts, all she could do was hold steady, willing her arms not to give out.

Rhythmical currents rushed along every nerve ending as he came at her over and over, licking at her mounting fuse, pushing and prodding harder, then faster, sustaining the thrill, and suspending time in that sublime state. He kept on until he set off a deep implosion in her. A guttural sound escaped her mouth, she trembled over him, the sweeping sensations annihilating every thought as her body tumbled and rolled through bliss.

Relentless, he carried on, pulling every last shudder and quiver out of her. Then, reading her perfectly, knowing she was basking in the afterglow, he rolled her onto her back. Determined and lost inside her, on his knees he came at her from the top, hitching her legs over his shoulders, grasping her pelvis tightly over him, holding her in place, bearing down on her. Deeper and faster still he came at her; hard and unyielding, he reawakened her center, then drove her passion so she soon needed him again like breath itself. His undivided attention lifted her, making her soar with inward spiraling sensations, then quickly dropping her into freefall in the nick of time to join him in his earth-shaking climax.

They crumpled together in a heap on the sheets, panting, their skin glowing with moisture as if they'd just run a two-hundred-meter dash. They clung to each other, Andrea never more grateful for knowing a man in her life. He laid a wet and wild final kiss on her and they moaned in mutual satisfaction. Damn, he was good.

She curled into him and they cuddled for several ecstatic minutes in the dark, their sweet love scenting the room. His fingers lightly dancing over her arm and backside, he drew her nearer and placed a kiss on her neck.

As she slowly emerged from her sexual stupor, something niggled at the back of her mind. Sam had seemed preoccupied throughout dinner. Was he worried about her going away? More than once she'd wanted to ask if something was bothering him, but in all honesty was afraid to find out it might be her. Or them. Or the new relationship they were forging.

The only example of love she'd had growing up had been her domineering father and her deeply depressed mother. It had definitely affected her ability to trust in love. But Sam had proved he was completely different from her father, and she was no longer afraid to hold back, to let herself trust and love him with everything she had. She was on the verge of feeling she'd found the right man, that she finally belonged somewhere, with him, and didn't want to upset her cart of dreams.

So she kept her concerns to herself about his earlier quiet demeanor. When he'd made it known that he wanted her after putting Dani to bed, she gave herself to him completely. It had quickly become second nature, almost like an addiction. Now, languishing in his embrace, she didn't want to be anywhere else.

He cleared his throat. Her ears perked up.

"I've been doing a lot of thinking," he said, his arm tightening around her as he spoke.

She hadn't been wrong about something being on his mind. She barely breathed for fear of missing what he was about to say. "Yes?"

"I've been thinking about Fernando in Mexico."

The weight of the universe seemed to come crashing down on her. Stunned, she couldn't take a complete breath. As thoroughly relaxed as she'd been a single moment before, she was now a ball of tension. "You're not saying you want to adopt him, too, are you?"

"I'm seriously thinking about it, and I want to know your opinion."

She sat up, because in her confusion she couldn't

bring herself to lie beside him right now, and she needed to see his face. "You want my opinion?"

His lower lip rolled tightly inward; he bit it. "I'm saying I can't get Fernando out of my mind. I swear the ghost of my mother is prodding me to get that boy, somehow, someway."

How could she be honest about her feelings and not come off as selfish when at the core was a noble desire? Sam's compassion seemed to be endless. Regardless, she owed it to him to tell him her thoughts. "You're setting this up to make me look and feel like a horrible person if I don't clap my hands and say 'Gee, that's great. Do it. Right now.' But if we're going to be a couple, you owe it to me to consult me on this kind of thing." Wasn't the decision to adopt a kid monumentally important?

He rubbed his hand along her shoulder and arm in an appeasing manner, and it irritated her. "Which is exactly what I'm doing."

She shook her head, refusing to make eye contact, reverting right back to not trusting him, to thinking he was just like her father. Old habits died hard.

"Life doesn't give us courtesy pauses, Andrea. You saw him. That kid needs a shot at a decent life."

Did this go beyond compassion to a savior complex? "Do you plan to save the whole world? Because the supply of kids who deserve chances is endless."

She may have hit hard and careless, but she stood by her comments. Stoic, he stared at the bedspread. Had he honestly thought she'd be overjoyed?

"You're a doctor, you help children stay healthy, isn't that enough?" He probably hated her right now, thinking she was callous and self-centered. Unworthy of his love.

She should have known the kind of person he was the instant she'd seen the Legend of the Starfish framed and hanging on his family room wall. In perfect calligraphy on parchment paper, the moral of the story came through loud and clear, that though one person can't save every single starfish stranded on the beach… *I can make a difference to that one, and that one, and…*

"I just can't get Fernando out of my head."

He was a true believer in the philosophy, thanks to his mother, a good, almost mythical woman she would never be able to measure up to. Who'd quite possibly died young from working herself to the bone with so many kids.

She hated letting her emotions take over, but feeling defeated before they'd ever even gotten started her eyes prickled and watered. No sooner had she fallen in love, finally giving herself permission for the new and amazing feeling, she'd had it ripped away by a guy who couldn't live with himself unless he adopted children in need.

"Aren't there ways to help him without adopting him? You could arrange for one of those high-tech prosthetic legs for him. Donate money to the orphanage where he'll live."

"You're right, but I'm just saying I can't get him out of my mind. It hurts."

There had to be more to the pain he mentioned than Sam's need to rescue kids. "Where does it come from?" His eyes darted away from hers but she couldn't let him drop the subject, especially with her going away in the morning. "This compulsion of yours, where does it come from?"

He looked back at her and his eyes, thanks to the dim moonlight, looked opaque and pleaded with her. "I haven't been completely honest with you."

A foreboding brick-like weight settled on her chest.

Oh, God, he hadn't already planned to adopt the kid and lied when he'd said he wanted her opinion, had he?

He reached for her hand and squeezed it. "There's something I haven't told you."

In fear, but needing to know the truth above all else, she held his hand with both of hers and engaged his eyes. "Tell me, Sam. What?" He didn't respond immediately, as if it was the hardest thing in the world to tell her, so her wild imagination took root. He really had already made plans to adopt this boy. The impact on their new relationship would be more than she could take. Hadn't he learned anything with Katie? "Look, I'm not your mother. I'm sorry for not being a saint. I'm just getting used to Dani, and to be honest so are you. It's too soon for me. I'm not even sure if I could be a decent parent to Dani. Don't you see?"

One eyebrow crimped upward. His look of disappointment may as well have been a dagger to her chest. The fairy tale of love with a wonderful guy evaporated into thin air. Hadn't she learned her lesson from her mother about how destructive love could be? Did he love her for herself, or did he just see her as someone he could mold into a version of his bighearted mother? Maybe he was like her father after all, wanting to change her and dictate her life. Would she only be a way for Sam to have that big family he planned to get by any means necessary? Her brain whirled with questions. None of them good. The thought of him giving her an ultimatum made her feel queasy. The words *the end* came to mind.

"That's not it. I promise I haven't gone behind your back and already made plans for Fernando." He squeezed her fingers, and she felt relieved. "I haven't been honest about my family."

Her mind went suddenly still, waiting, worrying, not having a clue what he was about to say. Sam had always come on like a steamroller, wanting that big family just like the one he'd grown up in, on his timeline and terms. Andrea had stood her ground, being honest no matter how unappealing that may have come across to Sam. One adopted son per single father was more than enough. But there was something about his family he needed to come clean about, and she suspected adoption had nothing to do with it.

"I've let you think I'd come from one big happy family, and in a way I did. But it wasn't my family."

She canted her head, holding her breath over what he might say next.

"That picture out there…" He gestured to his living room. "It's my foster family. *I* was the kid who got taken in by them. The Murphys." A blank stare overtook his face, as if a deeply sad memory fought to take control. "I was ten. I was taken away from my mother for being left alone at night. She was young and single and had to work two jobs to keep us from being homeless. It had been going on off and on since I was eight. She'd been warned on a couple of occasions, and finally one of the neighbors called the authorities. The Murphy family took me in and when my mother never tried to get me back, they kept me until I was eighteen. I've pretended to be something I'm not. I'm sorry. Truth is I'm an only child, just like you."

Love, sadness, anger, compassion and a dozen other emotions swirled around Andrea. How must a young child feel, being left alone night after night? Talk about feeling abandoned. No wonder he wanted to rescue kids. The hair on her arms stood on end over his revelation. She wrapped her arms around him, holding him tight, loving him more than she could bear to feel. "I'm so sorry, and so grateful to that family." She looked at him. He seemed to be in shock at reliving the toughest moments of his life.

"I wanted to be a part of a family more than anything, and they let me. When I was eighteen, my foster mom helped me look for my birth mother. She'd gotten married, started a new family, and when she could have tried to get me back, she hadn't." His face contorted on the last phrase, but only for an instant before he wrestled back control.

Andrea held him tighter, her heart aching for him.

"My own mother didn't want me, but Mom Murphy did. They accepted me as part of the family, and Cat, too. She was one of the other foster kids. Foster kids came and went, but the Murphys kept Cat and me. We bonded like sister and brother, right along with the other Murphy kids. I was lucky. I guess you could say blessed."

"Oh, Sam." She didn't know what to say. All she knew was that he was a special man. He'd received the grace of a strong woman after being left behind by his struggling mother. He'd had a second chance, like those starfish. No wonder that story meant so much to him. His foster mom had made a difference in his life, but Andrea suspected that even that wasn't enough to erase the pain of having his mother let him go and never try to get him back, even when she could have.

Andrea kissed the man she loved, in that moment knowing he could never be anything like her father. He knew what it was like to feel completely alone, to be frightened, to be saved. Because of that, she suspected she had a lot of making up to do for the women in his life who'd walked away from him, starting with his mother and ending with Katie. At some deep level would Sam always mistrust *her*? Would she have to prove herself over and over to him?

They held each other for several long moments, soothing, reassuring, loving, then found themselves back in bed, *showing* exactly how much they cared.

Late Sunday afternoon Sam jumped to answer the phone when he saw Andrea's number on the screen. He'd given her space by not calling her all weekend. Hell, after what he'd laid on her he was afraid to find out what she thought, because he loved her so much. He'd figured that out for sure over the past two days.

"Hi!" she said breathlessly. "I'm just walking into the house. You won't believe what happened in San Diego."

Wanting more than anything to see her, to hold her in his arms, he jumped in. "Why don't you come over for dinner and tell me all about it."

An hour later, she rushed through his door and into his arms, her excitement obvious.

He kissed her and she eagerly kissed him back. "I sold a painting yesterday! And another couple commissioned me to paint a modern art version of their cat!" She laughed. "It's absurd, I know, but I've already got an idea for it."

"That's fantastic," he said, meaning it. He was thrilled for her.

"For the first time since art school I see the possibility of making some decent money, painting and selling my art without selling out, you know?"

"Sounds like it's a good start." He measured his tone, not wanting to sound like the voice of caution, but part of him worried she'd take this bit of success and blow it out of proportion.

"I know! I'm ecstatic." Her eyes glimmered and her cheeks were flushed, and seeing her so animated and having missed her so deeply after she'd left early on Saturday morning, the only thing he wanted to do was kiss her again.

Of course he wanted to help her in any way possible to achieve success, had probably already overstepped his bounds by talking to hospital administration about her paintings. Coming from her background, with a manipulative and overbearing father, she needed to prove to herself she was in control.

Man, she's going to hit the roof if she finds out I put in a good word for her at St. Francis's.

They kissed more. He let his concerns go and focused back on showing how happy he was to see her. If Dani hadn't wandered out from his room and tugged on both of their jeans, they probably would have wound up having sex on the couch.

Oh, wait, right, since he'd become a father, those days were over...until later after he put Dani to bed, anyway.

Monday morning, after spending the night at Sam's, having incredible I-missed-you-for-one-whole-day-and-a-half sex, Andrea still managed to get up extra early with her alarm. She headed home, took a quick shower and put in an hour painting her favorite project. The enormous canvas as seen through a modern art lens, complete with a kid on a swing and a long-legged faceless dad pushing him, was really shaping up. The fact that the boy held a starfish in his hand was a new, surprising addition and tickled her.

She arrived at work to see a construction crew tearing down part of the hospital lobby. Was it an omen?

She remembered getting the memo about the remodeling project scheduled for this month, but had thought nothing about it until right now. Remodeling meant redecorating. Those tired old print excuses for art on the faded walls needed to come down and never be seen again. She had a damn good suggestion for their replacements, too.

As she headed toward the elevator she wondered who she needed to talk to about her own paintings. The display in the trendy café in San Diego had been a huge hit. Maybe the hospital might consider doing something similar here? Showcase local starving artists? Heck, she knew several artists in the area who'd give their eyeteeth to show their work in a busy place like the lobby of St. Francis of the Valley, including her!

She opened the O&A department with her mind spinning over the possibilities, then saw an envelope from Administration that had been slipped under the door. Once she read the contents, she rushed to call the one person she wanted to share every part of her life with—Sam.

"You won't believe this!" She didn't give Sam a chance to say hello, but he had a sneaky suspicion what she was referring to, since he'd started the ball rolling. "The hospital wants to discuss my art. They've gone to my website and seen my work, they're especially interested in my eye and keyhole painting, and they're interested in seeing more samples of my work in person! I've got an appointment with them on Wednesday. The note says, if they get approval, they'd put my pictures in the lobby entrance."

Since Andrea had finally stopped to take a breath, Sam jumped in while he could. "That's fantastic!" A twinge of guilt and a pang of anxiety gnawed at his conscience. Had he screwed up? What if she asked who had given them her name? Should he tell her first?

"I know! Nothing is definite but, wow, maybe with a few more sales and opportunities like this, I can actually support myself painting!"

What? Why should she immediately start talking about walking away from everything she'd worked toward over the past four years of her apprenticeship? That possibility had never occurred to him because of the great relationships she had with her patients. Shaken, he wasn't sure what to say. It seemed his great idea might have backfired on multiple levels.

"I mean, I may be getting ahead of myself but, really, Sam, do you see what I'm talking about?"

"I do. The hospital lobby display would be a huge opportunity."

"Oh, man, I never thought I'd see the day."

Still shaken, he wanted to ask, *Has it been that bad? Is it so terrible to use your gifts to help people replace missing ears and eyes?* Would he come off as a wet rag over her flame if he brought that up now? Or, worse yet, would he seem totally selfish and overbearing, just like her father, expecting her to stay in a job that she, apparently, could walk away from at the drop of a hat?

Perhaps his biggest offense—now that he understood how important it was for Andrea to step out from under her father's overreaching grasp—had been going behind the scenes and manipulating the outcome. Would she be furious with him for making that appointment for her in the first place if she found out?

Ah, so much for his big ideas.

CHAPTER NINE

SAM EXAMINED THE five-year-old Hispanic girl. His first observation made him think of Andrea. The child had been born with microtia, a condition where the pinna or auricle was underdeveloped. In this case, the right outer ear was extremely undersized compared to the normal left one. He hadn't seen this condition for a few years, even though the statistical incidence was one in six to twelve thousand births.

According to the chart, not only was the patient new to him, it was the first visit on record at St. Francis of the Valley. A small notation at the bottom referred to the family being new immigrants and first-time medically insured in the United States.

"The good news," he said, wanting to help the young mother's concerned expression, "is that the ear canal seems perfectly normal. I'll order a hearing test to make sure of that. Okay?"

The mother nodded eagerly.

"More good news," he continued. "There is surgery for this if you are interested."

Again, her eyes grew wide with interest.

"But Letitia needs to grow a little more first." He emphasized the fact by tickling the child, making her giggle. "You need to eat your vegetables, kiddo." The child laughed more. He turned to the mother. "You may want to think long and hard about the surgery. It involves using rib cartilage to make a graft and the surgery goes in stages, so there will be three different procedures over a period of time. We recommend the surgery the summer before Letitia begins school, and we have an excellent pediatric surgeon on staff who specializes in this."

"Three surgeries?" Worry lining her forehead like a pyramid, she shook her head.

"Another option is to have an ear prosthetic made. We have one of the best departments in the country right here. They can match your daughter's other ear with a silicone lookalike."

"She doesn't have to wait? No surgery?"

"There is need for one small procedure to create a way to attach the prosthetic ear, unless you want to use adhesive tape every day."

"One procedure?"

He nodded. "But Letitia would have to take the ear off every night. If she got sunburned, her ear wouldn't. That sort of thing. But I can guarantee that with our expert anaplastologists you'll have to look extra close to tell the difference from her natural ear."

"I have much to think about," Letitia's mother said.

"Yes. And I haven't even begun the actual physical. Let's get started, okay?"

Armed with options, the child's mother appeared more confident as Sam began the otherwise well-child routine physical examination of Letitia.

He understood that sometimes little kids made fun of anyone who didn't look like them. He'd thought long and hard about it regarding Dani. And as Letitia might start kindergarten soon, her mother would be worried about her, though the child's long thick hair did a good job of covering much of the tiny, underdeveloped ear.

He also suspected, from the mother's acne scars, that she may have been on a medication in early pregnancy that was known to cause the condition. The last thing he wanted to do was to make the mother feel responsible for a condition that really couldn't be pinpointed to any one thing she may or may not have done during pregnancy. So he kept his thoughts to himself. His job was to give a physical and maybe help the child look and feel more like the other kids in school, and that he could definitely do.

Andrea had been on his mind nonstop since her trip to San Diego, and especially since she'd hinted about trying to make a go of her artistic career. Did it mean she'd want to give up the one here at the hospital? Wasn't helping people, and especially children like little Letitia here, to feel good about themselves a noble job, too? Of course he'd support her in any decision she made because he loved her and wanted her to be happy, but he knew she had so much to offer St. Francis Hospital.

"Dr. Marcus." Sam's nurse tapped on the examination room door. "Dr. Begozian needs to talk to you."

Sam had just finished the PE. "Can you give Mrs. Juarez the instructions to the lab and Audiology?"

The nurse nodded, so he said goodbye and slipped out of the room to take the call. "Let me know what you decide," he said when he reached the door.

"I will, Doctor."

Sam headed to his office and the phone with the blinking light.

"I need a huge favor, Sam," said Greg Begozian, a young and bright resident whom Sam had taken under his wing.

"What's up?"

"I'm supposed to work the ER tonight, but I just got word my father's had a heart attack, and I need to catch a plane to Sacramento ASAP. But all the other residents are tied up."

"I'm sorry to hear about your father. Is he stable?"

"For now. Looks like he needs a bypass graft. I don't have the full story just yet."

"Hey, don't worry about tonight. I've got you covered."

"Thanks, Sam. You never let me down."

Sam hung up, thinking he'd be letting Dani down tonight, though, by having someone else read him his bedtime story and tucking him in. Ever since Andrea had brought up the touchy topic he'd thought a lot about it. But he was a doctor, and he felt responsible for his residents. At least he had an extra babysitter these days, one who would come to his house so Dani could go to sleep in his own bed. And Andrea didn't necessarily need to even know about tonight, did she?

Unfortunately, as it turned out an hour later, Andrea would need to know about tonight, because Ally wasn't available and Cat had other plans, so he needed to ask her to watch Dani. He hated making the call because he knew how seriously she was taking her painting now. Plus she had the appointment scheduled with hospital admin on Wednesday.

Fifteen minutes later…

"Uh, Andrea, I hate to interfere with any plans you have for tonight, but Ally has a volleyball playoff game and Cat has parent-teacher conferences, and one of my residents has a family emergency, so I'll need to cover for him."

"And?" Ever since seeing Sam in action in Mexico, she understood the demands of Sam's job and the pressure he was under, but before then she'd really given him a hard time about not being around enough for Dani. She understood the hesitation in his voice right now, but the guy had a serious problem with admitting he needed her.

"And I need someone to watch Dani."

"Was that so hard to ask?"

"I know you've got a lot of projects in the works now…"

"I'll bring my sketch pad and work after I put Dani to bed." Determination to make both her relationship with Sam and her personal achievements work was her new goal.

"You'll do it?"

Did he need to sound so surprised? "Yes. Since I'm your last resort, I'll do it."

"It's time to sleep, my love, my love…" Andrea whisper-read to Dani from an especially pretty book, as he settled comfortably into the crook of her arm. She'd personally chosen the children's book because of the beautiful pictures painted by the author. Each page seemed worth framing. But only after reading the truck book with all the bright pictures and hands-on activities. Reading this one, the time-to-sleep book, was her favorite way to calm the boy down.

Dani yawned wide and long after she'd read only a few pages of dreamy places with unusual animals and sleeping children. He rubbed his eyes.

"Are you ready for bed, sweetie?"

He nodded. She'd helped him brush his teeth already, and they'd had a fun game of hide-and-seek before that. To be honest, she loved being with Dani and when she was with him and Sam, her painting rarely entered her mind. That worried her. Wasn't art supposed to be first and foremost to a serious artist?

She walked him to his bed and helped him in, then tucked the sheets around him. "How's that?"

He nodded, smiling. "I like you to put me to bed." His speech had grown by leaps and bounds, too.

"I like putting you to bed." She kissed his forehead, savoring the preciousness of the little person and his fresh bath smell.

"I wish you lived with us."

She'd started to reach to turn out the lamp but stopped midway. How was she supposed to respond to that? Even wondered if Sam might have put his kid up to it. That made her smile, knowing how absurd the thought was. She decided to take the change-the-subject route. "You're a lucky boy to have your daddy."

"He works."

Too much. She didn't need to finish the sentence for Dani; she knew exactly what he'd meant. "Because he loves you and wants to take good care of you."

"I like you to put me to bed."

"That makes me happy, Dani. Thank you." *And sad for Sam. Oh, man, things are getting more complicated and downright awkward.*

"Will you hug me?" he asked in his usual shy manner.

How could she not hug this sweet, sweet boy? She wrapped her arms around Dani and held him until he gave a signal that he was ready to let go. "Sweet dreams, my little man."

Just as she got to the door he whispered, "I love you."

No doubt he'd heard it hundreds of times from his dad. What could she say? "I love you, too." It was true. She loved Dani with everything she had. She'd fallen hard for him the first night she'd met him. Now both of the Marcus men had declared their love for her. She gazed at Dani snuggled into his pillow, looking so small in his twin bed.

The poor kid had lost his parents before he could remember them, but he instinctively knew he wanted a family. Sam had been a blessing to the boy, just as the Murphys had been a blessing to him, and Andrea felt honored to be a part of his life. But Dani obviously wanted them together, like a real family. Which put both Sam and Andrea in a tough position.

After Dani had gone to sleep Andrea sketched some preliminary drawings, using the photograph of the cat from the couple who'd commissioned her to paint it. It was hard to concentrate, knowing that she had to tell Sam what she'd discovered tonight, but soon enough she got lost in drawing. It was almost eleven when he got home.

His eyes looked weary and his posture imperceptibly stooped, but enough for her to notice. Whenever she saw him her heart felt full, and that had never happened with anyone else. She walked toward him, and they hugged. He felt so good to hold.

"How'd things go?" he asked after she kissed him hello.

"Good. Dani's the sweetest kid I've ever met. But you already know that." She didn't mean to let emotion take over, but her voice had caught on *ever* and now there was stinging behind her eyelids.

It didn't get past Sam. "You okay?"

"Yeah. Can I make you a sandwich or anything?" She tried to recover fast, but moisture gathered at the sides of her eyes.

"To hell with the sandwich." His posture straightened, concern tinting his eyes. "Did something happen here tonight?" He came closer, looked into her face.

She swallowed against a sudden thickening in her throat. *Dani told me he loved me.* "Your son misses you so much, Sam."

A snap of emotion changed the concern in his eyes to irritation. She'd obviously hit a sensitive spot. "Look, a resident's father had a heart attack. He couldn't find anyone to replace him, so I agreed to work tonight."

"I get it. I know you have a demanding job. I'm just saying he misses you." *And now he's foolishly decided to love me, and I'm not ready for that responsibility.*

"And sometimes he'll have to understand that working late comes with the territory."

"But he's so young." She couldn't allow herself to get sidetracked. Dani's sad little-boy confession that his father worked a lot had set off bad memories. "Do you have any idea what it was like, never seeing my dad? Wondering if he cared?"

"You think you're the only one who ever wondered that? It's a fact of life. Being a foster kid with loads of brothers and sisters ensures you never get as much attention as a kid wants." He went quiet, turning inward.

How quickly she'd forgotten how frightening the first ten years of his life must have been. She needed to hear and understand his side of the story. "What's going on?"

"I was just thinking that, even though I didn't get the attention I may have wanted from Mom Murphy, I at least had my foster siblings to fill in the gap." He went still, and she filled in the blank… *Who did you have?*

No one.

Her lips tightened, fighting back the old hurt, confusion and anger, willing the first words to stay stuck in her throat. *I was so lonely. So was my depressed mother. Having each other wasn't enough.* Was that all she could promise sweet little Dani?

"Look," he said, obviously reading her expression of withdrawal, "I know you're still upset about my bringing up Fernando."

That was a fact also, but she had new concerns on her mind, which protected her from the ancient feelings threatening to make her break down right then. "Sam, I'm more upset with this Superman complex you seem to have. That you don't understand you can't do everything by yourself."

Sam and Dani's situation was too damn similar to the always-absent father setup when she'd been growing up. Because her father had been doing good things to help other people, she had never been allowed to express her true feelings of loneliness and longing for attention and his love. Nice little girls weren't selfish. Look where it had gotten her mother.

Though Sam was a completely different person than her father, she kept getting tripped up projecting those old awful feelings onto him. And now Dani wanted her to put him to bed every night. He'd told her he loved her. The kid needed a mother, and that was the last thing she thought she could be.

"Dani misses you, that's all I'll say."

He ground his molars and rubbed his temples. "Look, I've just had to tell a mom who brought her four-year-old into the ER last week, thinking he only had a bad flu, that he has leukemia. I had to admit him and get him started on chemotherapy. It's not a Superman complex, it's a job. Now, if you'll excuse me, I need to go give my son a hug."

That did it. *That poor mother.* The dammed-up feelings burst free and Andrea cried. Oh, could she ever have the emotional stamina to be a parent? Sam had seen it all as a pediatrician, he'd spent most of his life in a huge family with rotating foster kids, and though she tried to insist he was being selfish by even thinking about another adoption, the truth was he was anything but. The hard part would be trying to explain all of that to Dani.

She was the emotionally deficient one. She was the one who was selfish. Broken.

They hugged and kissed and comforted each other as no one else could. He wiped away her tears, even as she tried to smile through them. She told him she loved him and he did the same, then she left him for her house, so he could peek in on his boy and give that hug he so desperately needed just then.

Being a parent had to be a killer job. She'd never be able to do it.

The next night Sam was getting ready to put Dani to bed. The boy had been moody at dinner and throughout his bath. Maybe he was coming down with something. He felt his forehead, looked into his eye, and everything seemed fine, but Dani squirmed and resisted his intrusion.

"Ready for your bedtime story?"

Dani shook his head.

"What? No *Goodnight California* tonight? What about the truck book?"

Dani pouted and folded his arms. "I want Andrea."

To read to him? "She's at her house tonight."

"I want her to put me to bed." That was possibly the longest sentence Sam had ever heard come out of his son's mouth and, boy, had it packed a wallop.

Was his kid mad at him for not being around enough, as Andrea worried about? Or had the boy done the same thing he'd done, fallen in love with Andrea and wanted her there 24/7? Oh, man, this couldn't be good, two guys pining for the same girl. "She'll be back in a couple of days." Fingers crossed that wasn't a lie about the upcoming weekend. "Come on," he said, tickling Dani, hoping to tease him out of his sulking. "Want a bowl of your favorite cereal before I read to you?" No, he wasn't above bribing his kid out of a sour mood.

The offer got immediate consideration. Thank God for children and short attention spans. And endless appetites. "And don't forget you get to see the eye doctor for a recheck day after tomorrow. You need to be big and strong for that, and also get lots of sleep. You don't want the doctor to give you a sleepy eye report, do you?"

The child didn't have a clue what that meant, neither did he, but it definitely got Dani's attention. "No," he said, both his real and prosthetic eye wide.

After Dani had eaten his cereal and magnanimously allowed Sam to read him a bedtime story and kiss him good-night, he admitted that Dani thought of Andrea as a mother figure. How had he not thought that would happen? Probably unconsciously had wanted it. For a smart guy, sometimes he was a real bonehead. Had he inadvertently set her up to be his competition for his son's affections? That needed to change, unless she was interested in marrying him. The thought sent a little shock down his spine.

He finally got around to eating that sandwich, since the bowl of cereal before with his son had hardly helped quench his appetite. As he chowed down tuna salad on toast, he reran in his mind the entire conversation from earlier with Andrea. She understood loneliness and worried about Dani. She loved his kid as much as he did. Didn't have to say it, it was very apparent. And he himself loved her for a hundred different reasons.

He had proof that she'd wanted him once upon a time, too, since he still carried around the note she'd written him the first night she'd invited him to her bed, sketched winking eye and all. Yeah, he'd folded up that letter the next morning after they'd first made love and tucked it away in his sock drawer for times like these. When he got ready for bed later, he'd pull it out and take a well-needed look.

Seemed as if there was only one way to settle the issue.

Maybe it was time to make their relationship full-time?

The last bite nearly stuck in his throat. Was he ready to risk asking the big question of another woman finding her way back to her artistic passion? Proposing had totally backfired with Katie. But looking back, he realized all the obvious signs with her. Things were completely different with Andrea. He loved her. Trusted her. Wanted to make a life with her. He was pretty sure she'd want the same with him. But, still, maybe they should take things one step at a time.

Wednesday morning, Sam barreled into the ocularistry and anaplastology department to talk to Andrea about moving in together, not out of convenience but as a definite step forward in their relationship, with the intention of making it permanent not far down the line.

He found Judith, wearing her usual eye magnifier headgear, talking to a young man with scraggly blond hair. The guy moved confidently around the room, making clicking noises.

"I'm pretending to shop," he said, with a wry smile, immediately aware of Sam's entrance.

Pretending? Sam stopped and had to think for a second to realize that the twentysomething man must be blind. If so, his prosthetics were phenomenal. "Don't let me interfere."

"This is Ned," Judith said, smiling. "He's a longtime customer." She stood off to the side, like a proud parent.

Ned clicked more, then turned and nodded to Sam, uncannily nailing where he stood in the room.

"Ned rode his bike over to tell me he wants to change the color of his eyes," Judith said, pride brightening her face.

He rode a bicycle?

"I want to go blue. Tired of brown. Oh, hey, what if I get one blue and one green?" His wide, youthful smile was contagious, if not confusing.

Sam needed to clarify something. "You rode a bike over?"

"Yeah, been riding bikes my whole life."

"He's taught himself something called echolocation," Judith said. "Kind of like a sixth sense for the blind. Too bad not many use it or even know about it."

So the clicking sounds helped him find his way around? Kind of like bats using sonar navigation, bouncing sound waves off objects and pinpointing the location? His interest was definitely piqued. "If your technique works, why don't more use it?"

"Socially annoying," Ned spoke up. "Some folks don't want to hang out with a guy who's always making clicking noises. I call it BurstSonar, by the way. Sometimes it even drives my sighted girlfriend crazy." He laughed. "But she loves me anyway."

Sam couldn't get past the original statement. "You seriously rode your bike to the hospital?"

"Woodman Avenue is mostly a straight shot. I only live a mile away but, yeah, I even do off-road bicycling. Why hold myself back?"

"Ned is a great example of a totally independent sightless person. Lives by himself and does everything the rest of us do," Judith said.

"That's commendable," Sam said, stepping forward to shake his hand. "It's an honor to meet you."

He took his hand as if he'd seen it. "I'm a pretty damn good cook, too, if I do say so myself. Nice to meet you, too."

Amazed at what this guy had accomplished without sight, Sam shook his head.

"Ned is an outspoken advocate for independence of the blind, much to the chagrin of many who think of echolocation as annoying or disgraceful, even. Many of them are other blind people, too."

"Seriously?" Sam thought about Dani, and the horrible potential for him to lose his other eye. Wouldn't he want his son to know freedom and independence like this guy if he became blind?

"Yeah, some of my staunchest adversaries are blind people who think echolocation is offputting." Ned laughed, having said the last phrase as though it had tasted bad. "Like the whole point of life is not to bother other people. Unfortunately, that's what most blind people learn. That they're an inconvenience. That they are destined to spend their lives dependent on the kindness of strangers, the government and blind organizations looking out for them."

"It's a radical concept," Judith chimed in. "Ned has even started his own coalition to raise money and teach independence to the blind through his technique."

"This is fascinating, and, for the record, I think you should go with one green and one blue. Or get a pair of each and change eye color anytime you feel like it."

"That's a great idea." Ned smiled, as if really considering the suggestion. "Maybe I'll go violet."

They all laughed, but Sam suspected Ned might become Judith's first violet prosthetic-eyed customer.

"Well, it's been great talking to you," Sam said, suddenly eager to get back on track to why he'd come down here. "Judith, is Andrea around?"

"She took the rest of the day off after her appointment with Admin this morning," Judith said, unfazed, gazing happily at Ned. "She's painting. The hospital lobby needs new paintings, fast."

"I see." Sam winced over that expression with Ned in the room.

"And I don't," Ned said, not missing a beat. "But, you know, I've always wanted to try my hand at painting."

The quick levity may have gotten a chuckle out of Sam, but it didn't help the uneasy feeling crawling over his skin. Andrea had made connections and had found a way for her talent to be showcased. He certainly didn't begrudge her success, was happy about the hospital lobby deal, but she'd skipped work today because of it. Maybe it was her way of pushing back at her father?

She had paintings to paint, and a part-time job to hold down. Hell, he'd opened the door for her to showcase her work in the St. Francis Hospital lobby after the remodel. He should consider himself responsible for her taking the day off. If her art took off, lack of time might force her to make a decision about working at the hospital and helping guys like Ned look sighted, or going full speed ahead with her painting...and kissing this place, and him, goodbye?

His history with the women walking away who meant most to him still managed to step in and keep him insecure and off balance. He needed to get hold of himself. Stop the negative, insecure thoughts. But it was the first thing to pop into his head.

Of course he wanted the best for Andrea, wanted to support her every step of the way, whatever made her happiest.

Sam had big plans he wanted, no, needed to bring up with her today. But she wasn't here. She was home, painting. Having to postpone what he wanted to ask her made his stomach knot and kept the knot tight. Women didn't stick around for him. But what if he showed up at her house with the perfect secret weapon?

CHAPTER TEN

IT HAD BEEN an amazingly productive day. Andrea's arms ached from the nearly nonstop painting. The bright sun had helped make her small workroom ideal during the morning, but by afternoon she had to move outside to her postage-stamp-sized patio for the best light. That had never been a problem before because her painting schedule had been so irregular. Now, however, with a couple of commissioned paintings and, in one case, a cash advance, she needed to paint more and consistently.

Maybe it was time to consider renting space in a real studio. She knew artists who did that, shared studio space to make the rent more reasonable, and once she'd cleaned up she planned to make a call or two.

Someone knocked at her door. She glanced at the clock on the wall—it was six-thirty. Wow, she'd really lost track of time this afternoon. She looked a mess wearing a baggy T-shirt and the oldest, holiest jeans in her wardrobe, probably had as much paint on her face, arms, hands and her clothes as on the canvas, but there wasn't time to clean up before answering the door.

Not bothering to check the peephole on the old thick wooden door, she pulled it open a few inches and peeked around the corner.

"Surprise!" Dani blurted, tickled with himself and clapping.

"Hi!" She dropped to her knees, genuinely happy to see him, put her hands on his shoulders and kissed his chubby cheek.

"You look silly," he said.

"I know, I've been painting." Slowly she shifted her vision from the toddler to the long jeans-clad legs behind him, lifting her gaze until she saw Sam's handsome face looking a little more worn than usual. He'd combed his brown hair neatly, and his piercing blue eyes promised this was a no-nonsense visit. Her pulse fluttered at the sight of him, as it always did. "Hi."

"Hi. You get a lot of work done today?"

"Yes. Come in!"

"Don't know if you've eaten, but I brought you some of that take-out chicken you like with black beans and a side salad."

"How thoughtful of you. Thanks. I'd totally lost track of the time." She stood and hugged him hello.

They all went into the kitchen. "Share?" she said.

"We've already eaten. Thanks."

It felt so formal, and not at all the usual casual, comfortable routine between them. Something was up. She opened the bag and took out a chicken leg seasoned with the usual lime and pineapple juice, oregano, garlic and chili pepper—it smelled so good—and took a big bite. Loving the taste, the tenderness, she lifted her eyes to the ceiling, then, also loving the thoughtfulness from the man she loved, she smiled at him and took another bite.

But he wasn't smiling.

"I was surprised to find out you weren't at work today," he said.

Why did she feel the sudden need to explain, to

account for her actions, as if he were her father? She shuddered inwardly at the reference, feeling uncomfortably like her own mother. "I've been keeping up on everything, all the orders at work. I sent off the prosthetics I promised to the people in Cuernavaca last week. Even supplied a year's worth of special adhesive for the ears. I needed to get the cat in the bag, no pun intended, so I could get started on my next project. Hey, guess what, I've been commissioned for some paintings for the new hospital lobby."

"I heard that from your grandmother. Fantastic. I'm so happy for you."

"Thanks. I'm a little nervous."

"It'll be a big break for you, that's for sure."

"So you saw Grandma today?"

"Yeah, I stopped by the department, looking for you."

"Did I miss something?"

"A guy who clicks his way around the world."

"Ned! Isn't he an inspiration?"

"Sure is."

She could instantly tell Sam was done with small talk. He'd come here on a mission, and it was obvious he had something he wanted to get off his chest.

She wanted to love Sam and felt he wanted to love her, too, but regardless of their best intentions their pasts seemed to keep tripping them up, him always keeping a safe buffer zone, and her waiting for him to magically turn into her father. Would they ever get past that?

But the truth was she'd also missed him in twenty-four short hours, and that was a fact. Having finished the small chicken leg, she couldn't bring herself to eat another bite, as something besides hunger crowded out her stomach. Anxiety?

"Dani," she said, "would you like to play with the building blocks?" She'd gotten involved enough with Sam that she'd actually picked up a toy here and there for Dani to keep at her house. Remembering how much he liked his building blocks at his house, she'd bought a set for him to play with here.

He rushed at the chance, and soon sat contentedly in the corner of her living room, building a tower, knocking it down, then building another.

Andrea wiped her hands on a napkin, then glanced at Sam, who was still tense. "What's on your mind?"

"I've been doing a lot of thinking," he said, stepping closer, running his index finger along the curve of her jaw. "Anyone ever tell you that you look sexy with paint on your face?"

She gave a breathy short laugh, but tension took hold in her stomach as she waited for what he'd say next. Though the mere touch of his finger nearly made her lose track of her thoughts. How did he do that?

"I think we both know we love each other." He cupped her entire jaw, leaned in and delivered a delicate kiss to prove his point. Kissing always felt so right with him. "If your feelings haven't changed about me, I'm thinking we should join forces, you know, move in together."

Just move in. Like that.

Disappointed, she stared at him, eyes wide, not knowing how to respond. It certainly wasn't the most romantic proposal—in fact, the more she considered it the more she thought it was far too practical. But the man *was* a problem-solver after all. She had to be honest about what it made her think. "Shacking up out of convenience?" *How unromantic.*

He pulled in his chin, his eyebrows knitted. "No. Not at all."

If this was his idea of solving their problems, it made her angry. "Are you sure you're not just looking for a child-care provider with privileges?" she whispered, so Dani couldn't hear.

He grimaced, reacting to her low blow. "I thought you'd be in a good mood after painting all day."

Was he really that clueless? "I am in a good mood, but you seem to think about love as a business deal. You want what you want and I, well, the same. I love you, but a girl likes a little romance along the way."

He held her upper arms, looked deeply into her eyes. "Are you saying you're not interested in moving in?"

"Look, I do love you, and I love Dani so much I can hardly believe it. But I need to know you want me for me, not just to make your plans work out, but because you *need* me. Sort of like breathing."

"That's a bit dramatic, isn't it?" His comment fell flat, he knew it from the expression she tossed at him. So he tried again. "My plans involve making a life with you."

"Are you sure this isn't about putting all your ducks in a row for adopting more kids?" She narrowed her eyes for emphasis.

"Now who's being unromantic? I came here to ask you to move in, a huge step for us. You may not know it yet but we belong together."

Did they belong together? Him holding on to his secrets, giving the impression he was totally into the relationship but somehow always holding back some deep part of himself. She got it that his behavior was in no small part thanks to his childhood and feeling rejected by his mother, but nevertheless. Her with fears of becoming like her mother, giving up, giving in, lost and lonely on child duty while her husband pursued his profession and ignored the relationship.

Dani had stopped playing with the blocks, Andrea couldn't help but notice. "Dani, would you like a graham cracker and some milk?" Besides, she needed something to change the heavy atmosphere.

"Okay."

She led him into the kitchen and set him at the table with his snack. Then she went back to Sam, who was standing exactly where she'd left him, appearing dumbfounded, as if he already knew how things might work out. She pressed her hands together and placed them by her mouth, as if praying, as she approached.

"I do love you, Sam. I'm flattered beyond belief that you want us to live together, but maybe we're rushing things. The thing is, I need to know that it's me you want, and *need*, that I'm not merely a missing piece to fill that big puzzle you've created in your mind about the kind of life you want." She pleaded with her eyes for him to understand, to not be hurt by her honesty. "Don't get me wrong, it's a great idea. I'm just not sure about right now." Realizing she might have just hurt him deeply, she begged with a stare for his understanding. "We've got to be completely honest and open with each other, right?"

"I've been more honest with you than anyone else in my life."

"And I'm so grateful for that." *Was she so messed up that that wasn't enough?* "But you and your big compassionate heart scare me. I'm worried I'll never measure up to your standards. I don't know if I have the same capacity you seem to for reaching out to all those kids in need." Ironically, she worried he didn't need her anywhere near as much as he needed those kids.

Bewilderment filled Sam's eyes. "But you just said you love Dani."

"Yes, I do, and you, too. But I'm afraid I'll lose myself in your busy life, and I've only just started to find me." She pleaded for understanding with her gaze, her body tense and her feet bolted to the floor.

"How can you worry about losing yourself with me when I want success for you, too? I know how talented you are, hell, who do you think suggested you for the hospital remodel project?"

What? He'd set that up? It hadn't been her dazzling talent that'd gotten their attention? Roiling emotions made her face grow hot. Stupid her for thinking Sam was nothing like her father. He'd gone and done something behind her back, manipulating her life without her approval. *Jerome Rimmer strikes again.*

She nearly stomped her foot. Angry darts shot from her gaze, aiming to hurt. Because it ached to realize he'd misused her trust. "You just said how honest you've been with me, yet you listened on the phone when I crowed about how excited I was about the appointment. You never said a word that you'd set it up." He must have felt so proud of himself, not having a clue how much she'd *needed* to win that one for herself.

She wanted to run away to her studio and slam the door, rather than face the man she thought she loved. The man who'd just halfheartedly tried to fix their problems with an offer that they move in together, and to fix her professional problems by stepping in where he didn't belong. But she couldn't stand the thought of leaving Dani in the kitchen confused or worried. She forced herself to move and went to him. "Dani, honey, I think it's time for you to have your bath and get ready for bed."

"Will you read to me?"

"Not tonight, sweetie, but I promise I will soon. Maybe you can come here and spend the night with me sometime?" She tried to hide the slight tremble in her voice. Tried to keep it from breaking.

Sam cleared his throat at the kitchen entrance. She glanced up and saw total defeat on his face. Hell, he'd just asked her to move in with him and she'd essentially turned him down because she felt his big idea was for all the wrong reasons. He'd taken a risk and she'd shot him down.

"She's right, Dani, it's time to go." Sam said it kindly, but with a hint of dejection. The boy dutifully got down from the chair, having finished his milk and cracker, and took his father's hand. The pressure in her chest seemed to squeeze harder with each beat of her pulse.

Andrea rushed to Dani and kissed him good-night. "Have some fun dreams for me, okay?" He nodded. Then she stood, her heart feeling stretched to near tearing, took a deep breath and looked into Sam's tortured gaze. Words failed her.

He nodded his goodbye, skipped the kiss, turned and took his boy home, giving her the impression he totally didn't understand but knew when it was time to go.

She crumpled to the floor, never more tormented and mixed up in her life. How could she let a good man, a man who loved her and wanted to make a life with her, walk away? She'd sent him away!

Why did everything have to lead back to her childhood and her overbearing father planning every aspect of her life but never bothering to be around as she'd lived that life he'd prescribed? And her withdrawn mother letting her father run roughshod over her and never speaking up for her daughter or herself. Would it be the same with Sam? Why couldn't she believe him when he said he loved her and wanted to live with her, and not assume there was a big catch, that he only wanted her for his purposes, not simply because he loved her?

Because there *was* a catch, a huge one. He wanted her and he wanted that big family that he'd never felt he quite belonged in, and he wanted her to be like his saintly foster mother to make his world right again. Mother Murphy had died, the cruelest form of abandonment. Those were huge shoes to fit into.

Andrea felt she was barely ready for anything beyond loving Sam and Dani. But Sam expected so much more. She trembled with anger over his foolish and insensitive mistake, but more so with fear that deep down she just didn't have what it took to be Sam Marcus's woman.

Things couldn't have backfired any worse. Sam helped Dani into his car seat, even though his hands trembled. Pain, disbelief and a stew of other emotions kept him from thinking straight. He'd asked Andrea to move in, laid it all out there, and she'd brushed it off. Was that all he meant to her? He'd said he loved her. What did she want from him? Had her father messed her up so much that she couldn't trust his honest feelings? Maybe he should have asked her to marry him, but they obviously weren't ready for that!

Why did he feel so numb? Why had he run to her with a last-ditch plan to keep them together when they hadn't really even broken up, and now it felt as if maybe they were on the verge of ending everything they'd barely started.

Why did he never feel good enough?

Did he really expect her to give up everything she

held dear for the kind of life he wanted? He honestly didn't think so, but that was evidently how she saw it. If he could only figure out what she wanted from him, he'd do it. If she'd just given him a clue.

Did she really think she'd lose herself in his life? What about building a life *together*? He wanted what she wanted for herself. Hell, he'd spent twenty minutes talking to hospital administration about the new lobby remodel, encouraging them to brighten things up with pieces of art. Not cheap prints but real art from local artists.

As dumb as Andrea seemed to think it was, he'd given the executive secretary to the hospital CEO her website address to search for samples of her colorful artworks. He'd left the meeting with a grin on his face, and it had been for Andrea. All for Andrea. Now she had a commission for paintings.

But that had totally backfired. Man, had it ever. Did a guy who wanted to take over a lady's life do stuff like that?

Oh, man! That was exactly like something her father would do! Jerome Rimmer would go behind her back and set things up, as if she was a little puppet. No wonder she'd gone ballistic.

He'd screwed up royally just now on just about every level and didn't know how to begin to fix things.

Maybe he just needed to get his son home, to go through their nightly routine, then life would feel right again. But without Andrea he doubted life would ever be the same.

He hoped she wouldn't give up on them—he sure as hell wouldn't. He loved her too much. There had to be a way to work this out. But there wasn't enough time tonight.

As he drove into the garage at his home an image of her face appeared to him. "Maybe, instead of losing yourself with me, you'll come to *find* yourself in a life with me," he whispered. "And maybe I'll finally find myself, too."

CHAPTER ELEVEN

THE NEXT MORNING at the medical appointment, the doctor dilated Dani's eye, made a thorough examination, then had his nurse take him into a dark room to play while the eye medication wore off. Sam sat across from the desk in the office, waiting for the doctor.

The doctor looked grim, and Sam's instinct caused his entire body to tense.

The salt-and-pepper-haired ophthalmologist sat with a loud thump on his chair cushion, like a two-hundred-pound sack of potatoes, and sighed. A sound of defeat. "There are early signs of retinoblastoma in the right eye."

Stunned, Sam may as well have been hit with a two-by-four. He couldn't manage to breathe, his heart stuttered, and gut-wrenching pain for his son filled every part of him. He'd gone through this before, yet this time it felt twice as bad. Was that even possible? His head dropped into his hand, the burden of holding it up suddenly beyond his ability.

"We've caught it earlier this time, Dr. Marcus. We'll get a CT scan and an MRI, go through the staging process and see what our options are."

Sam couldn't think straight. Couldn't begin to string words together.

"Since you don't have any medical history on Danilo—I believe you said his parents are deceased?"

It took every last bit of strength Sam possessed to hold himself together. A simple nod seemed beyond his capability at the moment, but he managed to grunt a reply.

"I can tell you that *bilateral* retinoblastomas are always inherited, and therefore one of Danilo's deceased parents had to have been blind from the same cancer." The doctor continued as if Sam had agreed. "And with hereditary retinoblastoma, we must also be on the lookout for pineal tumors in his brain."

The mounting information tore at every nerve ending in Sam's body. Surely this was how it felt to have his heart ripped out of his chest.

"We have options this time around that we didn't with the last tumor because of the size. Even though before, without his family medical history, we didn't know he possessed a genetic mutation, and we hoped it might only affect one side, we might have handled things differently right off if we had known, but all is not lost. Once I gather the staging information, I'll know for sure if it's small enough to consider chemoreduction."

Sam glanced up at the doctor.

"The chemotherapy will be placed directly into the eye to reduce the size of the tumor. Then we can use laser light coagulation, also known as photocoagulation, to destroy any blood vessels leading to the tumor, starve it and destroy it."

"What about his vision?" Sam finally found his voice by focusing on the doctor's treatment plan.

"We might be able to save his sight."

He'd tossed Sam one tiny ray of hope.

"Our goal in shrinking the small tumor and essentially cutting off its blood supply is to save his remaining vision. All we can do is hope for the best and move forward from here."

"Thank you." They might be able to save Dani's sight. That was what he'd hold on to. That would help him through this horror show.

"We'll line up those tests ASAP and move forward as fast as we can," the stocky doctor said.

"I'm counting on it."

Sam left the doctor's office, seeing Dani playing contentedly in the dim room, and nearly lost it again. He inhaled, forcing himself to keep it together for his son. He walked down the hall, out of voice range, and fished out his cell phone with an unsteady hand.

His first thought was to call Andrea. But they'd had that nasty fight and she'd kicked him out of her apartment last night. And truth was he didn't know how he'd get the words out without breaking down. He needed to stay strong right now. For Dani's sake.

He dialed another number instead.

"This is Dr. Marcus. I need to clear my schedule for the next couple of weeks," he told the administrative nurse for his department. "I have a family emergency."

After a couple of days off, and without a word from Sam, Andrea returned to work, hoping she hadn't blown the best thing in her life. Selling her art only brought so much happiness. In fact, without someone to share the milestone with, it felt pretty damn empty. Paintings couldn't compare to a living, breathing man. Nothing could compare to Sam. She'd missed him and Dani terribly and had also missed being in the hospital, working on her projects for patients. By late last night she'd admitted she'd overindulged in painting for the past couple of days and the results on canvas were disappointing, to say the least. It was time for a change, a breather from creativity, and ocularistry was the answer. Plus she'd be closer to Sam in the hospital.

Feeling fortunate she had choices in life, she entered the department humming.

Her grandmother met her at the door to the workroom. "I thought you'd forgotten you had a job."

"Not for a second. But I did have some banked personal time off and decided to use it."

Before her grandmother could answer, her father strode through the department door. Andrea went on alert.

"Well, I thought you both should know they've hired an administrative assistant from inside to take over this department. Now, Mom, you'll only need to concentrate on O&A. Hell, you can work part-time, just like this one." He pointed to Andrea. "If that's what you want."

"Well, that's good news, but won't I have to train this administrative assistant?" Judith was all about business before pleasure, probably where Andrea's father had gotten it.

"Of course." Andrea's father looked at her, narrowing his eyes, though seeming far less imposing than usual. "I still can't for the life of me understand why you wouldn't take the job."

"You're the head of cardiac surgery, Dad, you don't have to understand what goes on in this department." *Or inside my head.* She knew her vague answer irked the heck out of him, and she thoroughly enjoyed it.

"You're right about that. I'll probably live a lot longer if I quit trying to figure you out." At last, a feeling they shared. His response wasn't to bristle, as it usually was. It actually seemed as if he just shook it off. Wow. That

was a first. "But that's not the reason I came down here."
He handed his mother a letter. "This came through Administration, and I thought your grandmother might like to read it to you."

Judith opened the letter and read it out loud.

Dear St. Francis of the Valley Hospital,
The community of Cuernavaca, Mexicali, wishes to thank you and your mission members for helping us in our time of need. You saved lives and helped us get back on our feet.

We are especially happy about the recent packages received by many families with new eyes, ears and even noses. These gifts seem like miracles for so many children. The parents of Jesus Garcia cannot thank you enough for giving him back a normal face.

We hope these pictures say what we cannot in words.

Forever grateful.

Moved by the heartfelt letter, Andrea stepped forward. "May I see the pictures?"

Smiling, Judith dug inside the envelope and found a photo, then handed it to Andrea. It was a grainy group shot of all the children she'd helped. Immediate fond memories, recognizing face after face, made her grin. A second picture remained inside the envelope. Judith took it out, studied it, then gave it to her. It was of a young boy that Andrea remembered well, beaming with pride as he now had both ears and a tip for his nose, and it seemed impossible to tell which ear was his and which had been made by Andrea. Though she knew it was the left one.

"This, my dear father, is why I need to be here in the lab, making eyes and noses, and not becoming one of the suits, running things."

Her father glanced at the pictures, then studied them more closely. "Nice work."

Had he just paid her a compliment? Had Mom started sharing her new medication with him? "Thank you. Now, if you don't mind, I need to show this letter to Sam."

"He's off on a family emergency," Jerome said.

Concern shivered through her. "How do you know that?"

"I just came from the monthly administration meeting, remember? He's been off since yesterday."

Anxiety sliced through Andrea over what the reason was for Sam taking family time off. Part of her plan for coming back to work today had been to invite him for lunch and admit she'd discovered that not only did she love him but she *needed* him in her life. And if his offer was still on the table…

Something must be wrong with Dani for him to take off so suddenly. She reached for her cell phone and dialed his number, walking into a secluded part of the department to talk to him, leaving her father and grandmother to chat.

"Sam? Is everything okay?"

"Oh, hi. Um, yeah. Dani's had a couple of tests and we're just keeping things low-key."

"What kind of tests?"

"A CT and an MRI."

He wasn't exactly forthcoming with information about why Dani had needed those tests. "Is he sick?"

Sam cleared his throat. "The cancer has come back in the other eye."

She gasped, couldn't help it, and spontaneous tears flowed. "I'm coming over right now."

"No. You don't have to. We're working through this. We just need some peace and quiet."

Shaken and taken aback that he'd dismissed her so matter-of-factly, she wasn't sure how to respond. "Uh, okay."

"Okay. Thanks for calling."

Still stunned over the horrible news for Dani, and feeling dismissed by a zombie version of Sam, she let him disconnect and stood staring for a few seconds, wiping the tears from her eyes, her fingers trembling. He didn't want her there.

Hurt wrapped her up and nearly squeezed the air from her lungs. She stood, stuck to the spot, thinking rather than panicking.

She'd spent a lot of time thinking while painting the past couple of days, too, and had figured a few things out. Sam kept her at a distance, even when he'd asked her to move in, by making it seem like a practical decision, having nothing to do with love or longing or—her new favorite word—*needing*. Because that was the missing ingredient she'd discovered while painting. Need.

That was how he'd learned to deal with his personal pain of having a mother who'd left him alone and vulnerable, who'd had to give him up and who had never tried to get him back into her life. He'd grown up feeling an outsider in a big family, always afraid he'd get sent away, pretending to be part of one big happy family but always keeping his distance, watching, waiting for the day to come. His relationship with Katie had proved he wasn't capable of committing until it was too late and the relationship was over.

From where she stood, Sam was repeating history

with her. He'd asked her to move in in a halfhearted way, not to get married, and had probably used her "no" as a reason to shut her out now.

Well, he wasn't going to get away with it this time because, unlike Katie, *she* loved him enough to fight for him. For Dani, too. *Oh, God, poor Dani!*

Rather than stand there and bawl helplessly, she grabbed her shoulder bag and marched toward the department door. Her father had left, and Andrea spoke to her grandmother on her way out. "I've got some personal business to take care of. I promise I'll be back tomorrow."

Judith raised her palms. "Like I could stop you? Do what you've got to do. Your job's safe with me—that is, until the new administrator takes over." She winked and smiled, as only a grandmother could.

"Thanks, Grandma."

Thirty minutes later Andrea knocked on the white front door of the boxy mid-century modern home in the hills above Glendale. It seemed she'd first stood at this door a lifetime ago. Sam's house. She'd been nervous then, but right now nothing could compare to the butterflies winging throughout her entire body—even her palms tingled. And her heart, it pounded hard enough to break a rib. She'd never taken a bigger risk in her life, but Sam and Dani were worth it.

Sam opened the door looking haggard and pale. He wore sweats and a ratty old T-shirt. His hair hadn't been combed in a while. "Andrea, I said you didn't have to come over."

"And you thought I'd listen? Sam Marcus, you'd better let me in or I'll roll right over you." Yes, it might seem absurd for a woman barely five feet tall to talk tough like that to a six-foot-tall guy, but right now she believed with all her might that she was capable of taking him down if he gave her any grief.

He didn't crack a smile but he stepped aside, letting her enter. "Dani's taking a nap." At first Sam avoided her eyes, but then those tired blues connected with hers and held on. There was so much pain there it made her ache inside. "Look, Dani and I will work through this together, just like we did the last time."

"How can you look me in the face and say that? Don't I mean anything to you?"

"Of course you do, but things have changed since the other night."

"You mean life got tougher, so you shut out the people you need most?" She'd play hardball if she had to. But, honestly, why hadn't his first phone call been to her?

"Didn't you kick me out of your house the other night?"

"I did, because you were being a bonehead. You asked me to move in—gee, how romantic. And you still don't think you need me. Or anyone, for that matter. You won't let yourself need anyone. But over the last couple of days I've done nothing but think about you and us and our situation.

"Now, are you going to let me sit down and get me some water or do I have to do that myself?"

She wasn't sure where this wild warrior woman had come from, but right now Sam needed someone to tell him what to do, and she was more than happy to do it. She trudged on into the living room and sat down. He brought her a glass of water, and one for himself, and she couldn't help but notice his hand trembled when he set the glass down. Her heart grieved for him in that moment, but she needed to say her spiel and get him to realize a few things before she could let out her true emotions over Dani's heartbreaking situation.

She took a sip for strength. "I say this as one only child to another. You've always felt like an outsider and kept your distance, even from me. Your foster mother loved you unconditionally, but you never believed it because it would hurt too much if she sent you back into the program, like some of the other kids that passed through her house."

"What's this got to do with anything?" He was definitely short on patience, and could she blame him?

"It has everything to do with us. Don't you see? You've always felt like you needed to prove yourself in order to be loved. Dani was abandoned. You knew how that felt. You could help him and return the favor your foster mother did for you. Loving a vulnerable kid is easy compared to a complicated grown-up like me."

She took a long drink to gather the confidence to bring up the next part. The part about her. "Then there's me, a girl who always felt rejected by her father. I didn't have a clue how to trust a guy, and you wanted to keep a safe distance, but the problem was that we had the hots for each other. We were crazy about each other's bodies. So we got in over our heads and tried to be grown-ups doing grown-up things, like falling in love." She'd been looking around the living room instead of at him because what she had to say was hard, but now she zeroed in on him. She had to, to make sure he was following her line of thinking.

"But we still weren't ready for that, even though we're both adults. Then there was the third ingredient of *us*, Dani. He needed both of us because he lost both of his parents. And like I said, you and I really got along great in bed, and we thought we loved each other. Which is fine. We should love each other. But, Sam, there was still something missing. *Need.* We had to need each other, and not just for practical purposes."

She stood, walked to him and knelt down in front of him, placing her palms on his knees. "After you left the other night, after you made the most unimpressive suggestion about moving in together, I had a lightbulb moment. You didn't need me in that deep-down, I-can't-live-without-you way every girl dreams about. It felt almost as if you could take me or leave me. Safe. You know?"

He didn't react in an obvious way, but she was quite sure there was a glint of something in his gaze, except she was too afraid to read it just then. What if he really didn't need her? "I had time to think and I realized I truly *needed* you in my life, whether you were ready for me or not. You made me come together. All my mixed-up parts finally came together. I needed you for that. Now I'm here because *you* need *me*. Because the little boy we both love is sick and *needs us* to come together and be there as a family unit for him. And you're right, that might not be any more sexy or romantic than your offer to shack up, but I'll settle for that right now. For Dani's sake."

She glanced up and saw a hint of gratitude in his gaze. "You need me because you don't have the strength on your own to go through this alone again." She squeezed his kneecaps. "You need me, Sam. And because of that I want to be here for you. For Dani." Her eyes prickled, her vision blurred. She'd gotten to the hard part, the part she'd promised herself on the ride over she'd beg for if she had to, and so far it looked as if she might have to. "I'll be your rock, I won't abandon you if things get too tough, I'll be your safe haven, I'll comfort you, I'll love you with everything I've got, because I love and *need* you, Sam." The tears came and she couldn't hold them back. "Can you admit you *need* me?" Her voice fluttered.

The invisible mask that held Sam's face together dissolved. His chin quivered and his eyes squinted tightly, forcing tears out the sides. He grabbed Andrea's hands, squeezing them like a man afraid to let go. "I thought I'd lost you forever when you asked me to leave. I might be the kind of screwed-up guy who asks a woman to move in because it's the practical thing to do, but underneath I meant it with all my heart, and I was too damn afraid to ask you to marry me."

She squeezed his hands. "Say it, Sam."

"Propose?"

She shook her head. "You know what I want to hear."

"I love you, Andrea."

"And I love you. But I *need* you even more. Now say it. Please?"

He grew very serious and stared down at her. "Honey, I need you. I can't face life without you."

She sighed as chills covered her shoulders and back. He reached for her and she climbed onto his lap, wrapping her arms around his neck and kissing his wet cheek. "Baby, I'm all yours."

Later, when Dani woke up, Sam made a simple dinner for the three of them, and afterward they played blocks and trucks and pretended that Dani's life hadn't been turned on its head again, until it was time to put him to bed. They'd take it one day at a time from here on.

"May I do the honors?" Andrea asked.

A week ago Sam had felt threatened by the fact that Dani had wanted Andrea to put him to bed instead of him. Tonight the request seemed like a godsend. How had he been so lucky to find a woman as strong and unyielding as Andrea?

"Give me a kiss," he said to Dani. The scrawny kid's arms circled his neck and tiny soft lips brushed his cheek, giving Sam a little taste of heaven, yet he ached inside. "I love you."

"I love you, too," Dani repeated, oblivious to what the near future would bring, as he trotted off to Andrea's waiting hand. She beamed at the boy who'd soon be facing the battle of his life, but for now he was suspended in sweet grace, surrounded by the two people who loved him most.

As Andrea and Dani walked down the hall Sam couldn't help but overhear his son's question. "Are you going to be my mommy now?"

Andrea laughed. "That's up to your daddy."

Sam grinned, the first time he'd done so since he'd gotten the dreadful diagnosis for Dani's remaining eye. Then he called out, "You can count on that, son."

EPILOGUE

One and a half years later...

DANI JUMPED ONTO the grass from the new wood swing set in the backyard. His independence always put Andrea on edge. He quickly utilized his newly learned skill of clicking to find his way back to the seat and climb on again. He'd been taking lessons from Ned, learning the art of echolocation and future independence, right along with Braille. They hadn't been able to save his vision but had successfully killed the cancer.

At first the blow from the news about Dani having retinoblastoma in his remaining eye had seemed insurmountable. But Andrea and Sam, together, had given each other strength and support so they could be the rock their boy had needed while he'd gone through the process of going blind.

They'd also, as the tight-knit family unit they'd become, agreed not to coddle Danilo unnecessarily. Their goal was to make a stable home for the boys, something they could depend on and trust, and that was now especially important for Dani. That's where the lessons with Ned came in, and the increase in Dani's confidence as a result brought joy to both Andrea and Sam.

With his prosthetic eye in place, and his sightless eye

looking exactly like the prosthetic, from this distance no one would ever notice he was blind. Dani jumped from the swing again, this time landing on his butt and laughing. Fernando may have a prosthetic leg, thanks to the drug cartel blowing up his village, but he ran like the wind, thanks to the latest high-tech prosthetics, and he swooped in to give his little brother a hand. Nando's determination never ceased to amaze Andrea, and he always touched her heart with his gentle spirit. She couldn't imagine a life without either of her sons.

Once Andrea had married Sam, she'd seen how much Sam had helped the orphanage in Mexicali and that he'd always stayed in touch with Fernando's caregivers. Opening her heart to loving and needing Sam had opened her mind, too. She'd been the one to suggest they go through with the adoption. It had taken over a year, but here he was, a great addition to their ever-growing family.

Nando tripped on a tree root as he rushed to aid Dani again, but she didn't run to him. These days it was too hard for her to get up. She and Sam had made a pact that the boys would be as independent as any other kids their age. She and Sam were determined not to let their sons' special challenges hold them back in life. That's why they'd let Nando try out for the junior soccer team in grade school, and he'd been accepted. He knew how to get back up, and he wasn't hurt from tripping just now, so she stayed put in the Adirondack chair.

In the meantime, Dani had found his way to the slide and, squealing with joy and hands held high in the air, he slid down a little too fast, and at the bottom he tumbled head over heels onto the grass. After a long motherly sigh, Andrea watched with interest to see how he'd handle things. He started to stand, but not before his big brother had offered him a hand and pulled him up.

"Thanks!" Dani said. "Did you see that?"

"Pretty cool," Fernando said, with a proud brotherly smile showing the gap from his newly missing front tooth.

Dani soon rushed back to his favorite outdoor pastime, the swing set and jungle gym complete with tree house, clicking all the way to the ladder for the slide. Back up he climbed.

Being eight and a half months pregnant made it almost impossible for Andrea to keep getting up and down. By the time she stood up, Fernando and Dani would have already worked out their problems, and wasn't that the way to raise two independent boys? So she just sat there and observed the fun, praying for the best.

"Dinner's ready!" Sam called from inside their new extra-large home. They'd found the perfect older house farther up the hills of Glendale, bordering La Crescenta, with four bedrooms, an add-on in the basement doubling as an art studio and prosthetics lab, including patient and/or client waiting area. So Andrea could work out of the house part-time for the hospital and part-time for herself. Judith had trained the replacement for herself and was now happily retired, but still working two to three days a week. The new house also had a rumpus room and a huge backyard! How could they raise two boys and their soon-to-be little sister without those essentials? And Grandma Barbara was a frequent guest, especially if Andrea had work or painting to do and Sam was at the hospital. Having grandchildren seemed to make her mother happier than Andrea had ever seen her.

Sam strolled toward Andrea, love openly twinkling in his eyes, and helped her up from the chair, then kissed her gently. She never grew tired of her husband's simple displays of affection. She'd made the smartest decision of her life in marrying him. Once she'd convinced him of how much they needed each other, old emotional walls had come tumbling down and they'd never looked back. Neither had they ever been happier.

"Eww," Nando teased.

"What happened?" Dani asked.

"They kissed. Again."

"Yucky."

The boys giggled, then rushed toward their parents.

"When are you guys going to get used to it?" Sam said, smiling, herding his sons along toward the house, Dani clicking all the way. "Wash your hands!" he called out when they overtook him, beating him to the back door, then he turned back to Andrea. "You coming?"

"In a second." She'd had a Braxton Hicks contraction when she'd been getting up and wanted to wait for it to subside. Using the time to gaze around, she grinned at nothing in particular and everything in general. The yard. The huge oak tree. The beautiful old house. The sky the exact color of her husband's eyes. The family that had just rushed inside for dinner. Her family. The people she loved with all her heart.

To some the life she'd chosen might seem super complicated, and it was, but the strangest thing had happened—she'd managed to find herself in the middle of that chaos. To Andrea the challenge of becoming Sam Marcus's wife had turned out to be the greatest adventure of her life.

* * * * *

A KISS
TO CHANGE HER LIFE

BY
KARIN BAINE

Published in Great Britain 2016
By Mills & Boon, an imprint of HarperCollins*Publishers*
1 London Bridge Street, London, SE1 9GF

© 2016 Karin Baine

ISBN: 978-0-263-25426-6

Our policy is to use papers that are natural, renewable and recyclable
products and made from wood grown in sustainable forests.
The logging and manufacturing processes conform to the legal
environmental regulations of the country of origin.

Printed and bound in Spain
by CPI, Barcelona

Dear Reader,

As a mother, I know that feeling of helplessness when my sons suffer any sort of illness or injury. For those whose young children have been struck by cancer it must be even more difficult to stay strong. It's a devastating disease which affects the whole family.

The research I did for this book taught me a lot about the patients and staff who inhabit the oncology wards. There are some amazing stories of courage and determination out there, along with some truly heartbreaking tales. However, one thing is clear—thanks to the ongoing research carried out in this field, survival rates are higher than ever.

My glamorous heroine, Jessica, is a survivor of childhood leukaemia herself. She's keen for her documentary to show the amazing work that goes on behind the scenes of cancer treatment, but finds opposition in Rob, a fiercely private oncologist. Behind their successful careers both are grieving losses of their own, but they can't hide for ever when they're working together in such an emotional environment.

I loved writing this book, even though the subject matter was so difficult it brought me to tears on more than one occasion. I have nothing but respect for the families and staff who deal with this illness every day. I will be making a donation to my local children's hospice from the proceeds of this book.

Love,

Karin x

For my bestie, Cathy. I still owe you a Mr G story!

A huge thanks to Charlotte Mursell
for working so hard with me on this book.
My afternoon with you and Laura McCallen
is one I'll remember for a long time. xx

I also need to give a shout-out to Brian and AJ,
who helped me with the technical stuff. Even though
I may have taken a few creative liberties with it…

Another book by Karin Baine

Mills & Boon Medical Romance

French Fling to Forever

Visit the Author Profile page
at millsandboon.co.uk for more titles.

CHAPTER ONE

THE BANK OF monitors filled with Dr Dreamboat's handsome profile as he strode past the remote camera in the hospital corridor. Jessica could see why the female members of the production team, and some of the men, had bestowed the nickname upon him. His strong stubbled jawline, wavy dark hair and piercing blue eyes made Rob Campbell perfect eye candy. With the rolled-up sleeves of his shirt bunched at his biceps and his sand-coloured trousers taut across muscled thighs, the guy looked as if he should be playing rugby and smashing into other huge beasts rather than holding hands with poorly children. As the consultant paediatric oncologist at the Belfast Community Children's Hospital, he was a vital link between the patients, staff and camera crew. It was a shame he'd been so reluctant for the documentary series to go ahead in the first place.

He'd voiced his considerable concern that they were violating his patients' privacy at the production meetings and it was in the project's best interest for Jessica to get him on board. Regardless of the hospital board's decision to allow filming and the crew's assurances that they would be sympathetic and respectful to all involved, the consultant had treated their presence here with quiet disdain. Jessica hadn't addressed him directly in the few days they'd been on-site to prepare for filming and instead had focused on building a rapport with the families on the ward. She had the signed consent forms of those willing to participate and didn't want anything to jeopardise everything she'd worked towards. This meant more to her than ratings and job security.

Cancer had been a huge part of her life; it still was in some ways. Not content to hijack her childhood, it had also tried to dictate her future. The after-effects of her treatment had followed her into adulthood and triggered early menopause. Just as she'd started to recover her femininity, that life-stealing illness had dealt the ultimate blow and made sure she could never be a whole woman.

Well, cancer had taken on the wrong redheaded warrior to tango with. It could take away her fiancé who couldn't deal with a barren future wife. It could take away the daughter she'd always dreamed of pampering like a little princess. But it couldn't take away her spirit. Nor anyone else's if she could possibly help it. If this series brought more funding to the hospital and helped even one child with their fight, it would be worth the pain it caused Jessica to relive her own.

The easiest way to allay Dr Campbell's fears that they'd trample over anyone in the pursuit of a good story would be to explain she was a survivor of childhood leukaemia herself. It would substantiate her plea that she simply wanted to raise public awareness of the incredible work that went on here. But that would mean exposing her weakness and the last time she'd done that it had cost her everything.

Adam, the man she'd thought she'd spend the rest of her life with, simply hadn't been able to cope with her health problems and who could blame him? When a man proposed to a vibrant young woman, he didn't expect to be marrying some prematurely aged, decrepit version of her. Their engagement had ended once Jessica's failings as a woman had become apparent. The hot flushes, mood swings and childless future had been difficult enough for her to deal with, never mind live alongside.

In tear-filled hindsight, he probably hadn't been the right man for her. Although he'd been right when he'd told her no man should be expected to take her on now that she was infertile. It would be selfish of her to ask that of anyone, not to mention detrimental to her well-being to imagine it a possibility. She'd only got through her body's changes and the break-up by accepting her fate as an eternal singleton and moving on. These days, her career was her significant other and these programmes filled that void where a family should be. They were her babies and she cherished every one. Each successful production she made was validation of her worth and all that she needed to fill her life. No man could ever make her feel as good as the awards and accolades bestowed on her for her work to date.

Now, not even an uncooperative oncologist could persuade her to divulge that deeply personal medical information lest it be used against her in some way. She'd worked too hard to put the pain of the past behind her to use it as a bargaining tool.

This was the first day of shooting and Jessica wanted to get it off to the best start possible. She'd done some reading up on Dr Campbell, enough to understand where his passion lay, and it wasn't a million miles from her own. He was leading the fundraising drive to pay for an MRI scanner for the Children's Hospital. There was no reason they couldn't use the airtime to promote the cause and perhaps cultivate a more harmonious relationship at the same time.

With that in mind, Jessica left the busy hub of the mobile production unit situated in the grounds of the hospital car park and went in search of her latest challenge. She'd learned at an early age to meet every obstacle in her path head-on and Rob Campbell was no exception. A liberal application of lip gloss, and a toss of her bouncy auburn curls later, she was ready to make contact with her target. She strode through the hospital entrance with a confidence that wasn't one hundred per cent genuine.

It was still early morning, the best time to do a recce around the corridors while it was relatively peaceful, quiet except for the sharp tap of her stilettos on the tiled floor. The impending sense of doom which descended as she navigated the maze of corridors had less to do with first-day nerves and everything to do with her residual hospital phobia.

The bright, airy atmosphere of the modern hospital was a far cry from the imposing Victorian building she'd attended for treatment. Instead of dark and imposing corridors, this wing was lined with colourful frescos designed to appeal to the children who attended.

Despite the visual differences and the time she'd had to get used to the surroundings, the glare of fluorescent lights and smell of bleach and antiseptic still took her back to a time when she wasn't so in control of her own destiny. Her steps faltered as a tide of nausea washed over her and forced a halt to her journey. She leaned against the wall, fighting to regulate her breathing and quell her rebelling stomach.

Inhale. Count to five. Exhale. Try not to puke on

your expensive red-soled shoes. Repeat until normal brain function returns.

Jessica pulled off her heels so her stockinged feet rested flat on the cool floor, back on solid ground. This wasn't about her. She was a visitor this time around, a grown-up replacing that pitiful figure who'd once resided here. When she'd first heard about this opportunity, she'd jumped at the chance to take part, regardless of her personal experience, perhaps even because of it.

Good or bad, hospital life had been a huge part of her childhood. Without the staff who'd looked after her, she would never have made it past adolescence, never mind the ripe old age of twenty-eight. Finally, she was in a position to pay something back. Replacing a husband and two point four kids with an impressive CV and impeccable professional reputation meant she could shine a light on a worthy cause. Nothing was going to stand in the way of that. Not her own personal issues and certainly not a difficult doctor who didn't know the first thing about her.

The double doors at the end of the corridor swung open and closed as staff walked in and out, giving a quick flash of the elusive consultant in his natural habitat. Every glimpse of Tall-Dark-and-Handsome reminded her how he'd earned his hospital heart-throb status. The nurses were flitting around him like groupies around a rock star and she was sure there were a few hoping to catch his eye for more than professional reasons. She could see why his good looks and high-ranking position seemed to attract every female within a five-mile radius but Jessica's focus had to remain on her project. There was no time for distractions. Certainly not a sexy, six-foot-plus real-life superhero one.

She gave herself a mental shake and coaxed her mind

away from the image of her new work colleague in body-hugging Lycra and tights. Fantasy rarely lived up to reality anyway.

With another deep breath, she drew herself up to her full five feet eight inches and made her way towards him, her shoes still in hand. Since any infection was potentially life-threatening to those on the other side of the doors, she paused only to squirt some hand sanitiser from the dispenser on the wall before she entered the ward.

Dr Campbell was standing at the nurses' station, his back to her, exuding a don't-come-any-closer authority without even trying. It took every ounce of her courage to edge closer to him.

'What do you want?' He didn't look up from the charts he was studying as he barked at her. It was the tone a busy and important professional used to fend off time-wasters so that only the bravest souls would persevere with their queries. She used it herself from time to time.

Having seen him in action on the ward from a distance, she knew how tender he could be under different circumstances. Clearly he didn't intend to make friends with her any time soon. Jessica reminded herself she'd taken on much worse than a doctor with a chip on his shoulder and lived to tell the tale.

'Hi. I'm Jessica Halliday, a producer for the documentary series currently being filmed. I was hoping we could have a quick chat before filming gets underway.'

'No can do. I have a full schedule this morning, even if I thought there was any point in speaking to you.' That gruff Scottish accent could've reduced a lesser mortal to a puddle of hormones, or tears. Not this girl. She didn't do swooning. Although when he did eventually turn around she might have shivered a tiny bit under his blue steel stare.

'It's important the viewers see the stories from the staff point of view as well as the patients'. I really think we could both benefit from working together and, as the man in charge, your input means a lot to the show.' As much as it galled her to sacrifice her pride, she wasn't averse to using flattery in order to get his approval.

'I'm sure there are a lot of men who would bend over backwards to keep you happy, Ms Halliday.' The doctor swept his gaze over her and, to her horror, a tingle of awareness danced across her skin. Male appreciation wasn't unfamiliar to her when a busy lifestyle ensured she kept her slim figure. However, she wasn't in the market for an inflexible male, and she didn't appreciate her body trying to convince her otherwise.

'I have no interest in reality television. If I did, I'd audition for one of those singers' got-no-talent shows instead of piggybacking on the misfortunes of the sick for celebrity status. I've consented to filming—that doesn't mean I'll pretend to be happy about it. These kids are going through enough without having cameras and microphones shoved in their faces. Now, if you'll excuse me, I have patients to see.' He broke off eye contact and returned to shuffling his paperwork.

The visual dismissal was the human equivalent of being hit with a fly swatter. Thanks to one life-altering break-up, Jessica didn't take rejection well. Her self-esteem demanded she leave more of an impression than an indistinguishable smudge in his day.

She shot out her hand to still his and demand attention. If she'd imagined him to feel like the cold fish he'd portrayed, the heat burning her fingertips where she touched him told her otherwise. Before she could linger on that thought, he snatched his hand away, frowned and took a step away from her as though she was contagious.

The snub stung like a sunburn in a hot shower. From her expensive clothes habit to her regular beauty treatments, she worked hard to make an impression on people. And to feel good in her own skin. She couldn't help but take any unwarranted slight against her personally and there was only one way to soothe the burn. With cool, hard facts.

'I'm sorry you feel that way about what we are trying to do here. For the record, this is *not* a reality show—it's a factual documentary series. As we explained before, our intention is to provide an accurate record of the process here and how serious illness affects the lives of everyone involved. I'll have to interview the staff and patients, so we'll need to draw up a schedule... I know there's a disused storeroom we can use for that once it's cleaned up... It would be great if we can organise a team meeting between my crew and yours every morning to coordinate filming. I hope we can find a way to work together, Dr Campbell, because I would really like to help—'

'I think you're under the misapprehension that we're somehow colleagues. I am not here to make your job easier, but to ensure my patients receive the best care available. For their sake I hope you don't get in the way of that.' He swept the files under his arm in one smooth motion and started to walk away before she had a chance to mention the MRI scanner.

As if sensing her mentally swearing at him, the consultant turned back. 'And please put your shoes on and at least try to be professional here.'

With her livelihood on a collision course with his ego, Jessica hopped across the floor after him, desperately trying to wedge her shoes back on her feet. As the go-to person on these productions, she didn't normally get flustered. She was the cool one in a crisis. Until now. She put it down to the surroundings rather than being nervous around this particular man.

'I am trying to be professional, if you would only cooperate.'

He stopped, arched a mocking eyebrow at her as she bobbed about like an inebriated socialite falling out of a nightclub, and walked on. She'd underestimated the strength of his objection and his unease was going to be even more noticeable on camera. She needed to fix this. Fast.

'I want to help with the fundraising for the MRI scanner.'

That soon stopped him in his tracks and he turned to face her.

'How?'

It seemed her determination had paid off as she located his Achilles heel. At least now she had an opening for a more civil conversation. She hoped.

'We can flash up the details of where people can donate on screen during the programme. Do you have a website set up?'

'Yes, but I suspect you already know that.' He watched her through narrowed eyes. So much for getting him onside. Now he was looking at her as if she was some kind of stalker.

She shrugged. 'I make no apologies for doing my research. This comes down to the fact that we can give the cause a boost.'

'If I play nice?'

'We appear to have got off on the wrong foot, Doctor. I'm not here to bully people into doing what I want. I'm simply trying to do right by all the families here. The scanner appeal will get a mention whether or not we can get along.' Jessica could produce a stunning programme in the worst of circumstances but she could do without this, frankly uncalled for, animosity when there were already so many emotional threads tying her to this.

'Don't take it personally. I'm very protective of my patients, as I'm sure you can imagine.'

'Of course. But we're on the same team here. Why don't we start again? I'm Jessica.' She held out her hand and attempted to erase their first frosty introduction.

The Highland Terror began to thaw as he gave her a smile capable of breaking the hearts of every hot-blooded woman in the vicinity. Thankfully, Jessica didn't let hers make decisions for her any more. These days she kept that vital organ out of her relationships with men and kept everything strictly casual. It was the only defence she had against the pain which would inevitably follow if she got too involved. Short and sweet was the way she ran her love life. That way there was no pressure on her to reveal her unsuitability as a prospective wife and mother further down the line.

'Rob.' He clapped his large hand into hers to shake on the proposed truce and startled her. It was probably just as well when her thoughts had turned to flings and relationships at the sight of one sexy smile. This wasn't the time or place, and he certainly wasn't her idea of fun.

'As a producer I'm well versed in getting financial backers on board, so I will definitely see what I can do with regard to your project. I've spoken to the director too and, if you and the other trustees are agreeable, we'd like to film some aspects of the fundraising initiatives going on. Perhaps we could get a sound bite from you on the subject at some point?' Jessica pushed the limits of their newly formed friendship a tad further but she hadn't got where she was today by playing it safe. Besides, they would probably need some lighter moments to balance out a lot of the difficult emotional subject matter. She'd flicked through enough pictures of the volunteers' antics on the website to know they had fun along the fundraising trail, regardless of whatever troubles they had at home or on the ward.

'We'll see.' He didn't commit to doing anything with, or for, her but at least he'd stopped scowling at her. She'd chalk that up as a win.

There was little more Rob could do. He'd made his objections known to the hospital board and the pretty redhead in charge of this madness. From here on in he'd just have to suck it up and put his personal feelings about the media aside.

He'd psyched himself up to do battle this morning over how this circus was going to play out in the department. On the few occasions he'd seen the producer before today she'd been placating the staff with facts and figures on why this would benefit the hospital. The lack of emotion she'd displayed on what was such a heart-rending subject for most people had led Rob to peg her as a cross between a stiff in a trouser suit and another overzealous reporter.

Well, Jessica had blasted the first part of his theory out of the water, bursting in here dressed as if she was going to a wedding. Her wedding. A short white lace dress wasn't the most practical outfit he'd ever seen on the ward. And those shoes—taupe…beige…nude…he wasn't sure of the technical term—he was sure they would send the health and safety lot into a tailspin.

One misstep on those spikes and she'd be heading back out to A&E.

The jury was still out on whether she lived up to his preconceived ideas of media types. It didn't bode well that she already had a list of demands with no thought to the daily running of the place. Unfortunately, cancer didn't work to a timetable and it would be down to her to fit in, not the other way around.

Perhaps he had been hasty in making assumptions about her character but he was extra-sensitive on the subject of privacy. And about intrusive investigators who unwittingly made their subjects' lives hell.

Five years after his wife and daughter had died, he was still trying to come to terms with the car accident and his loss, which had been splashed all over the newspapers. His grief had been compounded by the idea that he'd somehow caused the deaths of his family. If only he hadn't argued with Leah. If only she hadn't stormed out of the house in such a temper because of him. If he'd simply gone with her and Mollie in the first place. Then perhaps they would never have crossed paths with a so-called joyrider. Since the other driver had fled the scene, never to be caught, Rob would never know how events had played out, or ever find closure.

He'd been overwhelmed with so much support from friends and family he'd never been able to tell anyone the truth. That he was to blame and he didn't deserve an ounce of their sympathy. The claustrophobia of his guilt had escalated when the papers had run the story, making him out to be the victim, when he'd known differently. That primal scream had built inside him, ripping him apart in its effort to find release. But he hadn't been able to confess his role when everyone around him was already suffering so much. Instead, he'd taken the easy route and left everyone, everything, back in Scotland.

Of course it wasn't Jessica's fault that he was wary of the press but she'd already proved adept at her research. It wouldn't take much for her to uncover the tragic tale he'd kept secret since taking up his post here. He couldn't bear to have the details raked over again, or stand by and watch anyone else be put in a similar situation for the sake of one woman's career.

Still, she was right about giving the fund some much-needed publicity. As much as it might make him a hypocrite, they were a fair bit away from reaching their two-million-pound target and he would accept any offer of help. No doubt that had played a huge part in getting the families to take part when they were as desperate as he to get a scanner for the department. It would mean quicker diagnosis and treatment, as well as minimising the disruption to the children.

'By requisitioning the storeroom we'll have space for parents and staff to speak freely about certain aspects of the treatment without upsetting anyone around them. Can I pencil you in for a spot?'

Give these investigative types an inch and they took a mile every damn time.

'I have a very busy schedule. Speaking of which, I really need to start my rounds.' He put the first foot forward to escape Jessica's interference and check in with his patients so he could discuss their ongoing care later with the rest of the staff. Unfortunately, his new shadow refused to take the hint and teetered behind him in her high heels.

'I'll put you down as a yes anyway and you can give us a shout when you have a few minutes to spare. Now, the tech crew are set up on the ward, ready to roll. We thought it would be a good idea to film you talking to our little stars. I've already introduced myself but it might make things easier if they see a face they know and trust alongside the cameras.'

Tenacious. That was the word Rob would use to describe her. The most polite one he could think of, at least. It was also how he'd have described his late wife, along with *ambitious, stubborn, selfish, irresponsible* and *terribly missed*.

The argument that fateful day had been over what he'd perceived as neglect of their daughter while she chased her dream. Two adults should've been able to communicate better, discuss arrangements for childcare. Instead of one parent sneaking off to modelling assignments with a bored four-year-old in tow. If he'd handled the situation differently, been aware of his wife's struggle with motherhood earlier...

He dodged away from the dark cloud threatening to settle over him, as it always did when he thought of the accident. The years had done nothing to ease the pain of his loss but there was no room for it here. If these kids were able to wear a brave face through everything they were going through, he could too. After all, they'd done nothing to deserve the hand they'd been dealt and he was guilty of orchestrating his own heartache. He should've been there for his family when they'd needed him most.

'So...we'll make a start, then?' Jessica verbally prodded him.

'Yeah. Sure.' He could at least make preliminary introductions between the patients and the crew. That way he'd be around to make sure Jessica and co. didn't overstep the mark and upset people. He knew better than anyone who was strong enough to bare their soul to the world and who was too fragile to handle the spotlight.

Even with the best will in the world, the sort of attention a personal tragedy brought from the general public could break a person's spirit. There were only so many pitying looks and sympathy one could take before it became too much to bear. But he had the very family in mind who could keep them all on their toes.

'Hey, Max.' As soon as the cameras were ready to roll, Rob perched on the end of his favourite patient's bed, safe in the knowledge that nothing would faze this particular seven-year-old.

'You gonna play cars with me?' Max handed him a red pickup truck from the impressive collection of toy vehicles he had covering the surface of his bed.

'I'm not staying long this morning. I have to show this lady around the ward, but I'll come back later on to see you.' In private.

The demolition derby going on in the centre of the bed came to an abrupt end. 'She's gonna put me on TV.'

'Yes. If that's what you want.' Rob waited for the first indication that this was too much even for his resident funny man.

'Wait!' Max held his hand up to halt everything and Rob heard the collective gasp of the crew as they held their breath.

'Is everything all right?' All he had to do was give the word and this would end now.

'We can stop for a while if that's what you need, Max.' Jessica cut across Rob's concern with the practical solution of a timeout. Clearly she was used to being the one in charge. So was he.

The monitors were still holding steady as they charted the child's vitals, indicating that this wasn't a physiological problem. Max shuffled up the bed and sat straighter.

'I just want to make sure my hair is okay for the cam-

eras. Us TV stars have to look good for the laydees.'
He slid a hand over his little bald head, then slicked a
finger over his non-existent eyebrows.

'Maximus—' Rob tried to hide his own smile whilst
warning his tiny gladiator about making outsiders feel
uncomfortable. Max was too busy rolling on the bed
laughing at his own joke to take any notice. A sense of
humour was an important part of recovery but sometimes the dark nature of it could take others by surprise.

He half expected to see the efficient producer wide-
eyed with horror at one of the chemotherapy-based jokes
which flew about here on a daily basis between the kids.
Instead, those green-blue eyes were sparkling and her
pretty pink lips were curved up into a grin.

'Don't worry—you'll have all the girls falling over
themselves to get to you, Max. Perhaps you'd like to say
a few words to your future fans?' She wasn't the hard-
ass he'd taken her for as she played along, regardless of
the tight schedule she was probably on too.

With the air of a true pro, Rob's charge stopped
laughing and looked directly into the camera lens. 'Hi,
I'm Max. I'm seven and I like cars and strawberry milkshakes.'

'Excellent. Although I'm more partial to chocolate
ones myself.' Jessica wasn't appearing on camera herself but she certainly knew how to get the best from
her subjects. She even had good taste in milkshakes.

'Do you wanna see my central line?' Max pulled
down the front of his hospital gown to show off the long
thin tube inserted into his chest used to administer his
chemotherapy. He was so matter-of-fact about it there
was no room for sympathy or shock. As far as a lot of
the children here were concerned, they were sick and
this was how they got better. It was as simple as that.

The adults, on the other hand, had a much harder time of dealing with it. Max's parents were at his bedside now, happy to let him play up to the cameras, but it had been a long and tearful journey to get this far.

'Wow. That's cool. And can you tell me what it's for?' Jessica gently coaxed some more information from her subject. Since Max and his family seemed relaxed with the line of questioning, Rob would stay out of the conversation unless his counsel was needed.

'The nurses put the medicine in there and sometimes they take blood too.' The plastic tube apparently held no more fear for him than the toys scattered around him, even though he'd suffered some of the awful side effects from the chemo itself. Rob supposed this was simply part of life for the boy now, as it had become for so many of his patients. It was a scenario no parent wanted for their child but it was better than the alternative. He should know. If he'd had the chance, he would've done whatever it took to prolong his own daughter's life. That was part of the process he doubted these new visitors could ever really understand.

'You're a very brave boy, Max. Perhaps Dr Campbell could tell us some more about your condition?' Jessica directed the camera back to him.

Take a deep breath and think of the scanner.

He glanced over at Mr and Mrs Gardner in case they wanted to have their say first.

'I'm going to interview other family members later. For now, I'd appreciate your professional input.' There was no chance of dodging airtime with this eagle-eyed producer on the case. She had all the bases covered and all exits firmly blocked. Rob was back in the spotlight whether he liked it or not.

He cleared his throat. 'Max has Ewing's sarcoma of

the right tibia. This is a rare form of bone cancer usually found in older adolescent males. You're just one in a million, buddy, aren't you?'

Max high-fived him. 'You better believe it.'

'He's responded well to the chemotherapy and is scheduled for surgery to remove the remainder of the tumour.' Rob was savvy enough to understand that Max's surgery was probably another reason he would be top of the producer's wish list, along with his vivacious personality. The drama would be catnip to producers and viewers alike. Rob hoped it would have the happy ending they were all hoping for—complete removal of the tumour and preserving the limb without loss of function. Even then there were no guarantees the cancer wouldn't return or they'd face an eventual amputation down the line. Fortunately, this job was all about taking one step at a time and so far Max's treatment was on target.

'And that's under the guidance of a multidisciplinary team?' Jessica's stealthy research skills again made Rob wonder if they'd yet extended to his personal life.

That familiar churning started in the pit of his stomach, the way it always did when there was a chance he'd have to talk about what had happened with Leah and Mollie. There was no way he was going to be subjected to her questioning or, worse, her pity. 'Yes, Max's care plan has been tailor-made for him under the supervision of the surgeons, nurses, pharmacists and all the other health professionals involved in his treatment thus far.'

He shifted off the bed, not giving a damn if it upset camera angles or continuity; they could always edit. As far as this nonsense was concerned, he'd done what was required of him. More importantly, he'd checked Max wasn't anxious before heading for surgery. 'If you have any other questions, Maria, the senior nurse, can advise you. I really must get on with my rounds.'

Rob was counting on chatterbox Max to keep the crew busy until he'd seen the rest of his patients in peace.

'But…but…' Jessica was tempted to knock him back down on his butt and let her finish this segment. For some reason Dr Campbell seemed intent on sabotaging her at every turn. Just when she thought he was finally coming to terms with their presence here he'd closed up shop again. She was beginning to take it personally when he'd been such a sweetheart to Max.

Rob had switched the minute she'd opened her mouth about the MDT. Perhaps he was territorial and didn't appreciate anyone questioning his methods here. The truth was, she'd spent so long in and out of the oncology ward herself she was practically an expert in the procedures.

It had taken her a while to get used to seeing all the little kids attached to monitors and drips again and she'd actually welcomed having him to lead her through the ward. Sure, she had her hand-picked tech guys here but she was supposed to be the leader as far as they were concerned. There was such a strong association for her with pain and sickness she'd forgotten that there had been good times too. Max had reminded her that she'd had laughs with some real friends along the way. A few of whom hadn't made it out the other side of cancer. Rob had absolutely no cause to treat her as some sort of ghoul.

'Max, I'll come down later and walk with you to Theatre.'

Why couldn't he talk to her with the soft-talking Scottish lilt instead of that defensive bark?

'And maybe we could get that interview on tape while you're here too?' For now she could fire ahead with Max and his parents, but if she couldn't even nail him down for five minutes it was going to be a long couple of months.

'We'll see.' His eyes flashed with blue fire but this wasn't about him, or even her.

'Dr Campbell is one of my best friends. He brings me new cars every time I have to stay here.' Max said his piece on the subject, then resumed making explosion sounds as he caused a four-car pile-up on his bed.

It was a heart-warming statement that managed to smooth out the frown on the handsome doctor's forehead. 'You don't need to suck up, Max. We both know I have a silver Lamborghini with your name on it.'

These two together were cuteness personified. Jessica understood that the staff developed close bonds with the children—she'd become attached to the nurses she'd seen nearly every day—but it was rare for someone of Rob's status to take such a personal interest. He would probably relate more if he had boys of his own but Jessica knew nothing of his personal circumstances.

He turned his back on her to walk away but that terrier spirit in her wanted his name in her diary before he left. She reached out to stop him. 'So, we can go ahead and schedule that interview?'

The muscles in his arm bunched beneath her fingers and she had to fight to concentrate. This was a guy who worked out and someone she clearly had explosive chemistry with. Unfortunately, a quick check on his ring finger confirmed he was already taken.

'Why do I get the impression that not many people say no to you?' Rob cocked his head to one side as though he was studying some new incurable disease.

Goosebumps rippled over her skin. In her job she was used to being challenged; the thrill of it reminded her she was alive. Although, judging by her quickening pulse, it could be said she was enjoying it too much at present.

'They do. I simply choose to ignore it.' Something she was going to have to do about those hottie vibes radiating from her new *married* opponent.

CHAPTER TWO

Rob switched on the air conditioning in his car in an attempt to cool the after-effects of his early-morning workout and hot shower. He reckoned the gym was missing a trick with their opening times. A twenty-four-hour haven for members whose shift patterns and insomnia left them with too much time on their hands would make a fortune.

He'd stayed at the hospital until after Max's surgery, making sure there was a friendly face by his side when he came round from the anaesthetic. Even though he'd been exhausted by the time he'd returned home and fallen into bed, the tiredness hadn't overridden the all too familiar nightmares. Rob might not have been at the scene of the accident but it didn't stop him imagining their terror, hearing them call for him before the sickening crunch of the impact.

Sometimes he would even wake from his fitful sleep thinking he could hear Mollie crying from the room next door, a sound which always pulled on his heartstrings like a harp. He'd be out of bed and on his way to tuck her in before he realised his mind had played a cruel trick on him. Thanks to his own stubbornness and a dumb kid in a stolen car, he'd never have a chance to comfort his daughter again.

The first rays of the dawn light often came as a blessing, heralding the start of a new working day where he had plenty to keep his thoughts busy. It was the downtime, such as sitting in this logjam of cars, which let his mind wander towards those things beyond his control.

As he edged forward in the morning traffic, he spotted a familiar figure by the side of the road. Jessica, with her slinky grey silk dress hitched up to her thighs, was running after a bus, barefoot. Rob slowed the car to watch the spectacle. Sure enough, there she was with those ludicrous heels in her hand for a second time. Silver ones today. He wouldn't be surprised if she had matching shoes for every outfit in her, no doubt, vast wardrobe.

He wound down the window as he tailed her. 'You should really invest in a pair of flats.'

She slowed to a casual walk although her face was flushed from her exertions and he'd already heard her swear as the bus pulled away. Jessica leaned through the open window and the auburn waves of her hair tumbled over her shoulders. 'Are you going to sit there sneering all day, or be a gentleman and offer me a lift?'

He opened the door and turned off his MP3 player so he didn't lose the upper hand here by revealing his love of cheesy pop music. Even though she was the last person he wanted to spend time with, he could hardly leave her stranded when they were going to the same place. Next time he might be inclined to pretend he didn't see her and save himself from suffocating in her spicy perfume.

'I didn't have you down as the type to use public transport,' he remarked.

The expensive clothes and the matching pearly-pink mani-pedi she was sporting weren't in keeping with the thick exhaust fumes belching out from the bus in front. No, she'd be more at home in a sports car with the top down, cruising the streets of Monaco or somewhere equally fabulous.

'I never did get around to taking driving lessons. Besides, the buses run regularly into the city centre from here and I don't have to worry about finding a parking space. It's my fault I'm late. I slept in this morning.' Jessica leaned one hand on his leg to balance herself as she bent down to slip on her shoes. It was such an innocent, yet intimate, act but it burned his skin where she touched him. The rush of blood in his ears drowned out the majority of her chatter—something about missing breakfast—as she squeezed his thigh.

He hadn't expected to react so…primitively…to being in close quarters with a woman he'd barely spoken to until twenty-four hours ago. It wasn't as if he'd been a monk all of this time, where one touch from a woman could send him into raptures. He'd had a few flings but he lived by three rules—no one from work, no more than one night and keep things strictly physical. His partners knew the score from the start, so he could walk away without any emotional complications. No one would ever get close enough where he'd have to battle his conscience over replacing Leah in his life.

Jessica was attractive, successful and apparently incredibly tactile. What wasn't to like? Unless you only engaged in overnight shenanigans and the lady in question was at your place of work for the next four weeks. In other circumstances he might have acted differently, encouraged further exploration of his person, but this would only be asking for trouble. He shuffled in his seat as his body seemed to outgrow his trousers and he was glad when she removed her hand before things became uncomfortable for both of them.

'I…er…thought you might like to know Max's surgery was a success. The surgeon managed to remove all traces of the tumour.' He switched back to the topic guaranteed to draw out her ruthless side and remind him she was a no-go area.

'I already know, but thanks.'

'Oh, I wasn't aware you were still filming him?' He hadn't seen any cameras down near the operating theatre and it wasn't the sort of information the staff would've given her over the phone.

'We weren't. I got a text from his mum, Maggie, last night. I keep in touch with most of the parents to see how the kids are doing. Not everyone thinks I'm the devil incarnate.' She was trying to get a rise out of him but she'd managed that with one snippet of information.

He couldn't believe she was close enough to the families that they included her in their circle of trust. If what she was saying was true, that information on the children's health wasn't even gleaned for the benefit of the show. He would have to rethink what he thought he knew about her. His jaded perception of anyone in the media world had meant that he'd thought it impossible for her to be genuinely invested in these kids. To find out otherwise meant he might have to actually start being nice to her. At work.

'Well, I'm pleased you have such a personal interest in the families but I hope you understand we still can't have you breezing in and out as you please. We're not going to hold back treatment to fit in around your schedule.' The deliberately harsh words were an attempt to establish boundaries in a situation where he was scrabbling for an ounce of control. She was a member of staff by proxy and privileged to have been given access to the ward, after all.

'I assure you I'm deadly serious about this job. My timekeeping is usually impeccable. Unfortunately, I didn't sleep very well last night and didn't hear the alarm go off this morning. I'm sure even you've over-slept on occasion but you have my word it won't hap-pen again.' Jessica stiffened in the passenger seat, her hands resting very properly in her lap as she rose above his accusation of complacency.

'Good.' Rob jammed the car into fifth gear as they got a free run onto the motorway.

'Fine.'

An uneasy silence filled the interior of the car as they retreated back to their corners. Rob might have successfully asserted his authority over the crew's pres-ence in the department, but he'd also ploughed up any groundwork they'd laid for a semi-harmonious working relationship. All because he couldn't handle being this close to another woman without freaking out about it.

'Isn't there someone else who could give you a nudge in the mornings, or give you a lift into work?' He didn't know why he was pushing for more information about her home life. Whether she had a partner or still lived at home with her parents was of no consequence to him. Perhaps he was simply hoping there was someone else in her life to take responsibility for getting her to work on time so he didn't have to.

'I'm single and rediscovering the joys of indepen-dence. How about you?' There spoke the voice of a bitter break-upee. Someone who probably wasn't in a hurry to jump back into a relationship of any sort. Not that her love life was of any consequence to him.

He had no desire to get involved in the details of her

split, nor did he want to get caught up in an exchange of personal information with a virtual stranger. After a moment he decided to go with 'Unhappily single' to describe his current status. He wasn't alone by choice, and he wasn't too fond of the other label usually bestowed on him, since it portrayed him as some sort of tragic case.

'What, no Mrs Campbell to see you off to work in the morning with a kiss and some freshly cut sandwiches?' The sneer in Jessica's voice declared her judgement on the sort of woman she imagined married to him. How little she knew. Leah's free-spirited nature hadn't been dampened simply because she'd become a wife and mother. If anything, Rob had been the one in the relationship more suited to domesticity. Not that he would admit that to a woman who'd already challenged his authority and coerced him into making concessions for her benefit. A woman not unlike the one he'd lost.

'Not any more.' He tightened his grip on the steering wheel, trying to strangle the emotions bubbling up inside him, and put his foot down on the accelerator to get to the hospital as soon as possible. Post shift was the time for wallowing in his grief, certainly not before. It wouldn't do to cross his personal life with his professional one or he'd end up a complete blubbering mess every time a family reminded him of his. And what purpose would he have in life if he couldn't even do his job properly?

'Did she forget to cut your crusts off once too often?' The throwaway remark came with a snort but the subject was too raw for Rob to find any amusement.

'She died.' He didn't have to turn his head to know

he'd left Jessica open-mouthed; those words always had the same effect when he was forced to say them.

Usually he resisted telling people about his personal circumstances for as long as he could. This time, instead of reliving the horror by bringing it up, he found some relief in sharing his secret. It was somehow less painful than he'd imagined. In that brief moment he'd been able to actually be himself and stop pretending he was a man who had it all. As if he'd exhaled the toxins of the past in one deep, cleansing breath.

It was something he should've confided a long time ago. He knew Maria and plenty of others were curious about his wedding ring and lack of wife but he'd never been drawn to spill the details. It would only have led to more questions he wasn't prepared to answer.

There was something he recognised of himself in Jessica. Something about her which put him at ease in her company. Something dangerous.

'I'm sorry.' Jessica mentally facepalmed as she suffered a bout of foot-in-mouth disease. She would never have made such crass comments if she'd known he was a widower. In truth, she'd only said those things to remind herself that he was out of bounds. Her libido had pinged back to full strength when she'd felt those strong muscular thighs beneath her fingers. Now here she was having hot flashes which were more to do with lusting over a grieving man than her hormones. Mother Nature's timing was as atrocious as ever.

'Thanks.' Rob kept his eyes firmly on the road, leaving Jessica unable to read him. His locked-out arms and firmly set jaw told her she probably wasn't meant to, but it would be remiss of her not to probe further when he'd volunteered that first revealing nugget.

'Was your wife Scottish too, or local?' It was a question Jessica deemed not too intrusive but designed to give her an idea of the timeline involved here. He was still wearing his wedding ring after all. Rob had been at the hospital for a few years, so if he'd met his other half after he'd started his post here it could have been a recent passing. Even Jessica wouldn't put a newly bereaved doctor in front of the camera if he still had issues to work through. She made a note to quiz Maria Dean, the senior nurse on staff, who, unlike Rob, always seemed happy to talk.

'Leah was from Edinburgh, same as me.' The muscle in Rob's jaw twitched and Jessica could almost hear his teeth grinding together.

A name. An indication that he'd probably come to Northern Ireland after her death. Progress.

'Do you mind me asking—'

'Can we drop this, please?' This time he did look at her, shooting blue laser beams at her and leaving her under no illusion that the subject was a no-go zone for the foreseeable future. Apparently he did mind, cutting her off before she could enquire about what had happened to Leah.

'Sure. Sorry.' She was. Sorry she'd got him offside again, sorry he'd lost his wife and, most of all, sorry she'd brought it all back to him.

They spent the rest of the car journey to work in silence, Rob clearly lost in his memories and Jessica unwilling to say anything more in case she upset him further. If circumstances were reversed, she wouldn't appreciate anyone prying into her past to open old wounds either. Although her ex was still very much alive, it didn't make reminders of him any less painful.

Each time Adam came to mind, he brought thoughts of her own failings with him.

Perhaps Rob was going through something similar, taking the blame for events most probably beyond his control. She'd only recently begun working free of that guilt trap herself. That was why this job meant so much to her. Although she'd ultimately flunked the wife exam, she could still be a success in other areas of her life. It had taken a long time for her to come to terms with that.

It was possible she'd found a kindred spirit who'd also channelled all of his energy into his career rather than risk the heartache of another relationship. The thought comforted her even though the renewed awkwardness between them was palpable, since Rob didn't seem inclined to even switch the radio on. Jessica didn't dare defy him any further by doing it herself.

The heavy atmosphere in the car only began to lift when the familiar glass building came into sight. Most likely he was as eager to get to work as she was and check his personal baggage at the hospital door. There was nothing like deadlines and adrenaline to clear the head first thing in the morning.

Jessica unclipped her seat belt and reached for the door handle. 'Thanks for the lift. I'll jump out here.'

While Rob waited for the barrier to open at the entrance to the staff car park, Jessica made a swift exit from the vehicle to give him some time out. Maybe if he had some space from her for a few minutes he could forget she'd done the one thing she'd promised not to do. *Privacy* was his keyword and she'd tried to swerve his to satisfy her own agenda. Since he was the lead here it was going to take an extra effort to convince him she wasn't Satan's daughter recording peoples' suffering for kicks. He was the first man since Adam whom she wanted to know there was a soft heart beneath her crisp, ruthless producer shell.

'Did I see you arrive with Jessica this morning?' Maria interrupted Rob's thoughts as he flicked through his schedule for the day.

'My good deed for the day. Don't read anything into it.' He warned her off before she started her match-making mischief again. Ever since coming here he'd had to endure her futile attempts to see him settled down again.

He was sure Maria meant well but he needed a break from awkward dinner dates and disappointment. He didn't *want* to forget. Grief, Leah and Mollie were all part of him. He didn't want to move on and pretend that the best and worst things in his life had never happened. His wife and daughter deserved to be remembered and he deserved to live with the guilt of what had happened for the rest of his life.

Luckily for Maria, he could never get cross with her when she'd been his lifeline in a sea of despair. They'd immediately bonded over their shared devotion to their patients when he'd first started here. He hadn't told her, or any of his colleagues, about the accident even though it was clear he was on his own. He didn't want anyone to see him as anything other than a leader of his field. It was in everyone's best interests that he remained the strong stalwart during the hardships they faced here and not simply another grieving parent. Although it didn't stop her from setting him up with the nearest available spinster at every given opportunity.

'Why not? She's young, single, attractive…'

And definitely not the settling-down type. The ideal

woman for a no-emotions-required fling if they were both looking for one. There was just something about Jessica Halliday that set Rob's Spidey senses on high alert.

'I don't dispute the facts but you forgot to mention *nosy* and *incredibly frustrating*.' He'd known her only five minutes and she'd already unearthed more about his personal life than most of his colleagues were privy to. He wasn't in a hurry to share any more.

'Ah, she's got under your skin already.' Maria nodded with a knowing Rob-baiting smile.

'Not at all.' She was most definitely under his skin, to the point of irritation, but he didn't want Maria encouraging Jessica's interest, or vice versa. The last thing he needed was another concerned female hell-bent on getting him to dig deep into his emotion bank. That sucker was closed tight, hermetically sealed, weighted down and buried at the bottom of the River Lagan.

'I had several meetings with her in the lead-up to filming. She's no wallflower, that's for sure. Definitely not afraid to voice her opinion or ask difficult questions. Is that what you're afraid of?' Maria cocked an eyebrow at him. She knew him too well.

'I'm not averse to a strong-minded woman, as you very well know.' He gave her a flirty wink and hoped it was enough to end the conversation.

Instead, Maria rested her hand gently on top of Rob's in that sympathetic way that always made him want to push her away. He'd moved to Belfast to escape the pity party, not find himself as the guest of honour at another one. 'Don't give up on love. The right person is out there for you somewhere.'

Every time Rob heard those words he imagined a saxophone and some electric guitar playing him his very own power ballad. All he needed was a fog machine and a mullet and he'd be the epitome of eighties angst. He'd had the right person and she was gone. Nothing could change that.

Lucky for him he was in a busy hospital ward and not the dingy bedroom of his teenage self, so there was nowhere for him to sit and wail over the girl he'd lost.

Jessica's head was pounding and her stomach begging for something more substantial than the two headache tablets she'd consumed. She'd missed breakfast this morning and ended up skipping lunch in favour of a particularly fraught meeting with the director over content. He wanted more footage of Rob outside of his hospital role so that viewers were able to relate to him on a personal level as well as a professional one. That was akin to asking her to produce footage of the Loch Ness monster.

On top of that, she wasn't relishing the turn today's filming was about to take. It was going to be a tough one for all involved. She'd spoken to the family concerned to ensure they were ready to tell their daughter Lauren's story on camera and she was aware there would be no happy ending to this tale. Unfortunately, palliative care was part of cancer and it didn't discriminate against age. The treatment might help to make the patient more comfortable in the short-term but it wouldn't cure the illness.

Jessica didn't have to have children of her own to understand how incredibly distressing this would be. The professional producer in her agreed with the director that they had to include light and shade if they were going to chart the reality of the department. Her heart, however, wanted her to avoid any further reminder of cancer's destructive nature. This was a child, a baby, who'd been denied a second chance at life. In the end, it was the family who'd made the final decision to go ahead. They were keen to highlight Lauren's condition in the hope that a cure would be found some day. Jessica would simply have to try to remain emotionally detached from the subject. Easier said than done.

She massaged her temples as that heavy pressure seemed to bore down further inside her skull. The smell of coffee and cake hit her as she walked through the entrance hall on her way to meet the camera crew and she saw a few of the parents had set up a stall in the main foyer selling tray bakes and goodies to add to the scanner coffers. There were several tables and chairs dotted around for visitors and staff to take a timeout along with their treats.

Rob was there, talking and laughing with the mums with a box full of home-baked goodies in his hands. He really went above and beyond the call of duty for his patients and their families. The TV business wasn't exactly a breeding ground for that kind of altruism and Jessica found it refreshing. It was a pity she'd been such a cow to him this morning by prying into his private life. He was a nice guy and it had been a long time since she'd met one of those.

She started towards the stall to offer an apology and try to make amends but her legs wobbled beneath her. A heaviness settled over her entire body and she was helpless as she felt herself falling. Rob rushing towards her was the last thing she saw before darkness claimed her.

'Jessica?'

Lost in the swirling fog, Jessica could hear someone in the distance calling her name.

'Jessica?'

She wasn't ready to leave her peaceful slumber and cuddled further into the warmth surrounding her.

'Can you open your eyes for me, sweetheart?'

Jessica frowned. 'Go away.'

'I will as soon as we get you back on your feet.'

'What?' In her fugue state she swore she could hear Rob whispering in her ear to bring her body back to life.

'You fainted.'

Her eyes slowly fluttered open to find her dream date only a breath away. She didn't know what she was doing in his arms but she kind of liked it. His hard chest was pressed tight against her, his large hands splayed across her back so she was cocooned in his spicy musk and muscles.

'Can you stand on your own?'

Jessica blinked again and tried to focus. It soon became clear that their passionate embrace was more of a clumsy tango as Rob fought to keep her dropping to the floor like a sack of spuds.

'I'm so sorry. I don't know what happened.' She pushed against him to free herself from his hold and the embarrassing scene she'd created. The feel of his rounded biceps under her fingertips did nothing to help her equilibrium.

'Let's get you into a seat.' He lessened his grip but stayed with her until he'd deposited her into a chair at the makeshift café.

'I'm fine,' she insisted even though her head was still spinning. She hated showing any weakness, especially if it meant relying on a man to rescue her. Until now she'd been standing on her own two feet for some considerable time.

'I want you to put your head between your legs and take some deep breaths.'

She only complied since he was the doctor and she was apparently having difficulty staying conscious.

Rob rubbed her back as she inhaled. 'Do you feel dizzy?'

'A bit.' Another big breath in and his hand rose and fell with her.

'When was the last time you had something to eat? I know you missed breakfast and I doubt you've sat still long enough for a proper lunch break, have you?'

'Um…I had a cup of coffee this morning and some headache tablets. I've been busy with other things…'

'That explains it. You can't survive on a diet of coffee and adrenaline, you know. I understand your need to direct all of your energy into your work but it's important to stop and refuel every now and then.'

'Yes, Doctor.'

'You need something to raise your blood sugar and you definitely need to give yourself a break from these.' He crouched down in front of her and cradled her foot in his hands as the Cinderella scene played out in reverse.

Thanks to his open top button, Jessica had a nice view down the front of Rob's shirt. The smooth swarthy skin beneath contrasting against his crisp white shirt was not the usual skin tone of a fair-skinned native. Her feverish mind began to conjure up images of her handsome prince soaking up the rays in a lot less than a tailored shirt and formal black trousers.

She didn't do romance but she imagined it probably looked a lot like a burly doctor on his knees gently removing a girl's stilettos. He sat back on his haunches to face her again and reached up to brush the curls from her face. Her whole body tensed as if she was waiting for that one magical kiss that followed the princess's rescue at the end of every fairy tale.

One of the stallholders interrupted the tender moment to hand Prince Charming a glass of water, her eyes darting between Jessica and Rob as she clearly jumped to conclusions.

He thanked her and proceeded to tangle his free hand in Jessica's hair again.

'What are you doing?' She sprang back in her chair, now fully conscious and aware they weren't alone in the busy thoroughfare. Goodness knew what people were making of this whole episode but it probably wasn't anything which would improve her credibility here.

'You have cream in your hair.' Rob plucked at another strand to produce chocolatey proof that he wasn't randomly stroking her hair.

'*Oh*. Why?' This day was getting better and better.

'You squashed my buns,' he said with a grin and nodded towards the spot where she'd made her dramatic entrance.

Now cordoned off with safety cones, the area resembled something of a crime scene as efficient cleaners swept away the aftermath of an apparent cake massacre. The broken remains of cupcakes and caramel squares lay in a pool of cream and sprinkles on the floor.

'I can't believe you sacrificed cake for me. The actions of a true hero.' She clutched her hands to her chest in exaggerated appreciation, attempting to deflect attention away from the effect his touch had had on her. The hairs on her arms were still standing on end where he'd made physical contact. Obviously, in all the confusion her body had mistaken him for a potential mate. Her mind was having a harder time dealing with the idea when he represented everything that made her feel weak.

Sitting here, helpless and dependent on his instruction, took her back to a time when every decision about how she lived her life was taken out of her hands by doctors. Rationally, she knew it had all been in her best interests but she'd spent too long fighting for independence to relinquish it so easily now. Even to a doctor who could easily have made it as Mr June in the *Hunks* calendar currently hanging on her apartment wall.

'What else is a man to do when a beautiful woman swoons at his feet?' Rob moved to a standing position so Jessica was forced to strain her neck looking up at him. She ignored the tiny voice in her head squealing at the inadvertent compliment he'd paid her since the conversation between them had turned jovial.

Given their run-ins to date, Jessica doubted she was his type in any shape or form. Rob Campbell was destined to be part of a couple; her fate lay in a completely different direction. There was no point in even thinking there was any kind of entanglement on the cards. So she should really stop wondering if he had any hidden tan lines.

'I hate to burst your bubble but, as you said, it was probably from lack of food rather than a reaction to your good looks.' Jessica couldn't believe she'd actually fainted. She supposed she was burning off more calories than usual with all this toing and froing. In future, she'd keep a few snacks to hand to fend off further embarrassment.

'I can offer you some sweet tea and a cupcake for now but I'd advise you to eat a proper lunch as soon as you can.' He left her and took his place in the queue to purchase her temporary cure.

He wanted the best for everyone he treated, her included. At least this mishap had softened his attitude towards her. Even if it had come at the price of her dignity. Rob was sympathetic, passionate, dedicated…

everything a woman would want in a long-term partner. It was just as well Jessica didn't want one or she would be in real danger of falling for him.

CHAPTER THREE

JESSICA NIBBLED AT the slice of chocolate fudge cake and sipped the sweet tea Rob had provided until she started to feel like herself again. The fear of falling into a sugar coma prevented her from finishing it all. Rob had no such qualms and tossed his empty paper plate and cup into the bin.

'All better?'

'Yes. Thank you. I should head on over to the ward. I don't want to keep the O'Neills waiting.' This job didn't make allowances for illness or time off for busy producers who forgot to eat. She was responsible for everything that happened in front of, and behind, the screens. The success of the programme ultimately rested on her shoulders and she sure as hell wouldn't let a hunger-induced dizzy spell hold her back.

The next step on the career ladder was Executive Producer, where she could lead her own production from concept to completion. She wanted the responsibility for selecting and marketing a range of TV shows including dramas and documentaries.

'Ah, yes. They said you were doing a piece on them. I'll walk over with you.'

'There's no need. I promise we'll be respectful and sympathetic at all times.' Her hackles rose at the assumption she couldn't be sensitive, Jessica got up from her chair ready to march away. Only, the cold tiled floor beneath her bare feet reminded her she had to put her shoes back on before she could do that with any dignity.

'I'm glad to hear it. However, it's you I'm thinking about.'

Jessica's pulse beat a little faster and sent her head spinning again as Rob fixed her under that intense gaze of his. She knew he meant that he was concerned about her fainting spell but there was something inherently sexy in hearing those words. Especially when they were delivered in a spine-tingling Scottish rumble from a handsome doctor.

'Honestly, there's no need.' She was so used to fighting her own battles she'd forgotten what it was like to have someone watch her back. It probably wouldn't do her any good to get used to the idea when she was here only for a matter of weeks.

She wedged her shoes back on her feet so she was no longer at a disadvantage standing next to him. It wasn't as if she was some delicate creature who needed a man to make her feel safe. Not any more.

'I don't want to be held responsible for you swooning into the arms of another unsuspecting man.' He moved aside to let her pass.

'That was a one-off. Although I could be tempted to do it more often if it means I get force-fed chocolate cake every time.' She kept quiet about the bigger perk of having him hold her close, since it completely obliterated her ice queen image.

'That's not a bad plan. I might use it myself. Seriously, though, you should be taking it easy.'

Jessica opened her mouth to protest but Rob held his hands up and stopped her.

'I know, I know. That's never going to happen. Hence the personal escort. Shall we?'

He was being so courteous that Jessica wouldn't have been surprised if he'd offered her his arm like some nineteenth-century gent taking her courting. It left her no option but to let him accompany her.

If she was honest, as they stepped back onto the ward, she was glad to have his support for the next leg of her journey.

'Can you tell us something about Lauren's background? It would help the audience to understand the situation now.' Jessica's mouth was dry, her heart heavy as she addressed Mr and Mrs O'Neill at the bedside.

She admired their strength for wanting to share their story during what was probably the worst time of their lives. Their total devotion to their child made Jessica think of what her own parents had gone through. She'd always focused on how the cancer treatment had affected *her* but they must have gone through hell too. They weren't to know their only child would make it past the hair loss and sickness into adulthood. A comfort also denied to the O'Neill family.

'Lauren was first diagnosed with a brain tumour just after her second birthday. She had major surgery, followed by radiotherapy and chemotherapy.' Mrs O'Neill carried on stroking her daughter's hand whilst she was talking. Lauren was smiling up at her even though she was clearly very weak and the love they had for each other was tangible.

Despite the tragic circumstances, Jessica still had a pang to experience that mother/daughter bond from the other side of the equation. She knew how it felt to *be* loved by a parent but she could only imagine the strength of that love *for* a child. That was part of a relationship she would never get to experience and never fully understand.

A hush descended over the private room and Jessica sensed that they were all hesitant to go further into the details of Lauren's illness. There had been a purposeful attempt to make the hospital room as cheerful as possible with get-well-soon cards papering the walls and brightly coloured balloons and toys stuffed into every available space. It was difficult to be the one who had to make them face the reality of what the future held.

Jessica swallowed hard before she tried to coax some more information from the family. 'Can you tell me what happened after the initial treatment?'

The last thing she expected was to see Mr and Mrs O'Neill smiling as they were asked to cast their minds back to those days. Even Rob stopped looking so pained at the intrusion into his patient's business.

'They removed the tumour entirely and Lauren recovered well. We had sixteen fabulous cancer-free months catching up on all of the fun things we'd missed out on during the chemo. You loved the zoo, didn't you, sweetheart?' Lauren's mum was tenderly stroking her head as she recounted the happy memories.

'I liked the monkeys best.' Lauren's small croaky voice was so full of childish wonder it broke Jessica's heart. There was so much of life she would never get to experience.

Despite her residual health problems, Jessica was reminded how incredibly lucky she was.

'Yes, and Daddy bought you one, didn't he?' Mrs

O'Neill reached for the long-armed pink primate hanging from the corner of the bed and handed it to her daughter. Lauren cuddled into her treasured souvenir of the day with a smile.

'Does he have a name, Lauren?' Jessica was almost too choked up to ask.

'Pinky.' The unimaginative name from the four-year-old brought some nervous laughter from the assembled group.

'Lauren started to get sick again shortly after that day. The cancer had come back. To her spine this time. We'd already been told if it came back—' Mrs O'Neill's voice caught on a sob. She didn't have to finish the sentence for Jessica to understand there would be no cure.

Jessica had first-hand experience of the cruelty of false hope. Six months into her own remission she'd suffered a relapse. That period of respite where she'd been able to live like any other eleven-year-old girl had been brief. Birthday parties and girlie afternoons with her friends had been replaced once more with hospital appointments and sickness. Even now that fear of a decline in her health still shadowed her.

'Lauren's been having treatment to try to make her more comfortable so she can go home. We'll take another scan in a few weeks' time to see if the chemo has slowed the growth of the tumour.' Rob stepped in when it seemed Mrs O'Neill couldn't continue. Essentially, he was saying there was nothing more they could do for Lauren except make her last days more bearable and give her some quality time with her family.

Jessica didn't know how he managed to deal with this every day and still function as well as he did. Most of the time she was able to compartmentalise her life in a similar way. It was either file away this kind of trauma and get on with your own life or bawl your eyes out and eat your own body weight in chocolate. But it took a certain level of detachment not to be affected by the helpless babe, hooked up to bleeping machines and monitors, that even a hard-hearted producer didn't have.

She brought a halt to filming, not wishing to prolong the family's agony. Any further commentary could be added in the edits when she'd distanced herself from events. For now, watching these people whispering endearments to their innocent daughter as her life ebbed away was too much. It was intrusive and everything else Rob had said it would be. She wouldn't air anything they might later come to regret committing to tape.

'Thank you so much for letting us speak to you today. And, Lauren—' She wanted to offer some words of comfort but there would be no getting better, or second chances. All that came out of her mouth was a strangled cry and the tears she'd been desperately trying to hold back teetered on the edge of her eyelashes.

'Jessica will be back later to see you, Lauren. She has to go and finish making your TV programme so she can make you a big star.' Rob brought another smile to the little girl's lips so easily when all Jessica could do was see the sadness.

Two large hands rested on her shoulders and she didn't resist as they steered her away from the bedside and into the corridor. In other circumstances she would've shrugged Rob off and given him a dressing-down for undermining her. On this occasion she had to concede he was right. She wouldn't do anyone any good blubbing by the bedside when those worst affected by the situation were coping so much better than she was. That was the strength of a family, leaning on each other for support to get through the darkest days. Something she would never have for herself.

'I feel so, so sorry for them.' She exited the room in a daze, following Rob along the corridor simply because she didn't know where else to go. As much as she wanted to be able to do something for Lauren, she clearly wasn't in the right frame of mind to be of any use.

'We all do but they need *us* to be strong in order for them to remain strong. If you fall apart, they fall apart. Do you understand?'

Jessica bit her lip and nodded, doing her best to keep it together. She'd seen and heard some truly awful things while working as a journalist in the city centre before moving into TV and always managed to remain professional. It was the combination of such innocence tainted by the very thing which had wrecked her life which rendered her an emotional jellyfish.

'It wasn't my intention to upset them.'

Rob might be more understanding of her intense reaction if he knew her history. Indeed, had *she* been more mindful of how close she was to the subject matter she might have prevented upsetting a lot of people. Herself included.

'I accept that but we try to keep things as upbeat as we can here. We need to focus on the positives and take one day at a time or else we'd all go mad. Lauren's still here and she's not in pain. That's all we can hope for at the minute.'

Jessica hated not being able to do anything to help when she was so used to being in a position of power. Right now, the only thing still under her control was her personal life and she intended to keep a tight hold of the reins on that. Otherwise there was a chance she'd end up as one of life's victims. Again.

'Are you all right?' Rob turned back to check on Jessica, since she hadn't responded to his comment or bombarded him with a hundred questions about the next course of action. Despite her position, she wasn't very adept at hiding her feelings. This was clearly getting to her. He'd heard it in her voice and seen it in her eyes. It wasn't an uncommon reaction to being in the department; he simply hadn't expected it from *her*.

His first impression of her as a ruthless career woman was turning out to be false. From the moment they'd met, Jessica had made it very clear she was all about her work. He'd never expected her to have room for compassion along with her ambition, or let anyone see that side of her.

If anything, here was a woman who wore her heart on the sleeve of her designer dress. The very opposite of him. He went out of his way to disguise his emotions so no one ever came close to reading him. An air of mystery was preferable to people interfering or judging him.

In the space of twenty-four hours, however, he'd already seen Jessica irritated, vulnerable and sad. He found himself looking forward to seeing her happy and excited phases.

'I'm fine.' *I'm fine.* Those two words a woman could say and mean a thousand different things. In the end, though, it always boiled down to two facts. She wasn't fine, and she didn't want to talk about it.

The unusually high-pitched denial and trembling bottom lip told a different story. There was no way she could possibly go back to work in this state and not regret it.

'My office. Now.' Jaw clenched, nostrils flaring, Rob corralled her into a side room. There were some tricks to maintaining that aloof facade and he was willing to give her the benefit of his experience. Something he would do for anyone on staff. A timeout would give her the chance to compose herself before she went back on the floor firing out orders to her underlings. As he'd explained, they couldn't let their personal distress show in the middle of the children's ward.

The minute he'd closed the door behind them, everything Jessica had been holding inside came bubbling to the surface until a torrent of tears were streaming down her face.

'I'm…so…sorry,' she stuttered through her sobs.

'Don't be. You're only human.' Rob lost a piece of his heart to every child who came through those doors too, along with their families. If he was honest, he was glad to see that Jessica was developing an emotional attachment to the kids. It meant they were more to her than purely ratings fodder and that was all he could ask of her.

He took a handkerchief from his pocket to give to her and received a watery smile in return. The sniffing and spluttering started to subside. 'I'm usually not like this.'

'We all have our moments.' He'd shed a tear for every child they'd lost, albeit in private. The ones who reminded him of his own daughter took him a little longer to get over. A vision of his daughter's cute smile, so like her mother's, brought a lump to his throat. He swallowed it down and tried not to think how the nine-year-old version would've turned out. Would she still have been a daddy's girl? Or too embarrassed to be seen with him as she headed into those rebellious teenage years?

Jessica began weeping again and Rob automatically

moved towards her. As a doctor, it wasn't in his nature to ignore someone in distress. As a man, he couldn't stand by and watch a woman crying without doing something about it. Especially when that woman was only releasing the emotions he insisted on keeping locked inside. He envied her ability to express herself so openly.

'Let it all out,' he said as he stepped forward to fold her into his arms.

Moments such as this often made him wonder if the medical staff who'd been on the scene of Leah and Mollie's accident had cried for them. Had anyone offered them comfort?

There was only a slight hesitation before Jessica accepted him as a shoulder to literally cry on, her tears soaking through his shirt. Rob rubbed her back as he consoled her. Perhaps he should have prepared his new colleague more for life on the ward. He'd been too caught up in his own issues about what she did for a living to think about the woman behind the title.

She smelled so good. Like chocolate, tea and spicy perfume, mixed together to create all the comforts of home in one glorious package. For a split second, with Jessica in his arms, he let himself believe he could be part of a couple again, sharing fears and finding comfort in each other. But then what? He'd have to come clean about failing his family. Worse, repeat the same mistake over again and risk destroying more lives.

It was tempting to stay in this bubble and hide from the cruelty of the outside world but he was in serious danger of crossing a line here. Jessica wasn't one of his patients; she wasn't even technically a member of staff. Yet he cared about what she was going through. That didn't fit well with his no-emotional-attachments rule when it came to attractive single women.

'As soon as my shift is over, I'm taking you home.' He could still be sympathetic while creating some distance at the same time.

'Okay.' She sniffed as another wave of sorrow claimed her. It immediately called out to the protector in him which had once lived to serve the women in his life. He'd been there to patch up every cut knee Mollie had, to hold her when she'd cried, and suddenly that had all been ripped away from him.

Rob rested his chin on her head and stroked her hair until the storm subsided.

He missed being needed.

Jessica left the rest of the production team to view the dailies in the gallery while she went for a much-needed caffeine injection. As prescribed by Dr Campbell, she'd eaten a late lunch and intended to leave work at a sensible time. However, neither of those suggestions had managed to lift her spirits, or her energy, after the day from hell. It was unusual for her to be so drained by a shoot and she was going to have to get her head back in the game soon before anyone other than Rob noticed.

She still couldn't believe he'd been there to witness her epic meltdown. Not to mention the whole fainting episode. When the mood took him, Dr Campbell had the perfect bedside manner but her reputation as a no-nonsense ruthless TV exec was seriously in jeopardy. On a personal level, she had to admit it had been nice to have a shoulder to cry on. Despite having now earned her empowered women membership badge, Jessica had enjoyed having someone to stroke her hair and tell her everything would be all right. It was a shame it was nothing more than a fantasy. She would never rely on a man for any longer than those few minutes of madness today. It was the only way to keep her heart safe.

Jessica made her way to the vending machines by the hospital entrance, since the main catering was a bit of a hike away for someone balancing her entire body weight on the spikes of her stilettos. She was lost in thought watching the dark liquid fill the paper cup and wondering how bad it would taste when she felt a hand at her waist.

'Are you ready to go?' Rob's low voice in her ear sent a jolt right through her entire body, doing more to re-invigorate her than the iffy-looking coffee ever could.

She thought seriously about telling him to go without her. The snot crying and snuggling had been so out of character for her, she was tempted to walk home in the rain before letting him help her again. But a lift home meant she could be curled up on her sofa in twenty minutes instead of standing in the cold at the mercy of public transport.

'Sure. Let me grab my coffee first.' She carefully lifted the cup, looked at the contents and poured it back into the tray. 'On second thoughts, I'll make a fresh one when I get home.'

When she didn't automatically move to follow him, Rob rested his hand at the small of her back and nudged her forward. That slight contact buzzed her into action quicker than a tip-off on a dodgy politician. Either she'd developed some sort of allergic reaction to this man, or there was serious chemistry happening between them. Hopefully, she wasn't the only one who could feel it.

'Cheers for the lift. I hope I'm not taking you too far out of your way.' Jessica showered Rob with apologetic gratitude as they sped along the motorway towards home. She'd have to add driving lessons to the list of precautions to take before her next project, along with making sure to eat regular meals and steering clear of too-close-for-comfort subject matter. At least that way she stood a chance of avoiding a repeat of today's damsel-in-distress routine.

'Not at all. Which way now?' Rob was much more matter-of-fact about the whole business, as if he rode in to work every day on his white horse, gathering up swooning women in his path.

When Jessica sneaked a peek across at her chauffeur, she conceded it was entirely feasible. Everything about him—from those strong, thick forearms locked out on the steering wheel to the muscular thighs tensing as he shifted through the gears—said he was a man who could keep a woman safe.

It was important to her that a distinction should be made between a hungry and emotional professional and those needy members of the female sex. She didn't want him to think she was one more in what was probably a long line of women desperate to snag him as a life partner. Her interest in men remained on a more casual basis. No, her wobbly-legs episode had been a severe reaction to intense circumstances today. It was in no way a manifestation of her yearning for a significant other to lean on.

Jessica helped Rob navigate the maze of avenues and side streets until they finally reached her apartment block. 'Thanks again for everything.'

'Don't mention it.'

'For the record, I promise to never pull the wailing woman routine on you again. I'll also pay to have the shirt I cried on dry-cleaned and I owe you cake.' That should cover all of her debts. Apart from the counselling he'd provided in between all of her mishaps.

'That's really not necessary.' He wasn't making it easy for her to even up the playing field. In her eyes, unless she found a way to repay him she was resigned to playing the weak-female role in their working relationship for the rest of her time here. A title she'd fought long and hard to break free from.

'I imagine you have a standing order at the dry-cleaners for clothes stained with mascara and tears anyway.' Given the nature of his work and his white knight complex, it was probably a hazard of the job.

'Yeah. They know me as Dr Heartbreak in Soapy Suds. I've got a loyalty card and everything.' The doctor's self-deprecating sense of humour was unexpected. Unfortunately, so was Jessica's snort of laughter.

She buried her face in her hands but it was too late to corral the piggy noise, which had Rob creasing up with laughter. The price of his friendship apparently came at the cost of her abject humiliation. From chasing barefoot after a bus, to her banshee wailing, and now her farm-yard impression, he'd seen her at her absolute worst.

'Well, Dr Heartbreak, the least I can do is offer you a cuppa after everything you've done for me today.' Breaking her no-male-guests rule would be a small price to pay if small talk over a pot of tea helped her end the day with a modicum of dignity.

Rob had nothing but an empty house to rush home to but Jessica's invitation to come inside still waved up a red flag. He'd made that transition into friendship with her in the office today, albeit a different connection compared to the one he had with other acquaintances. He'd never felt the urge to hold Maria in his arms when she was having a bad day. There was a fragility about Jessica that called out to him and in that brief moment of comforting her Rob had relaxed his defences too.

It took a lot of energy to pretend that seeing Lauren and the others didn't get to him. He spent his days with other medical professionals who made it easy for him to keep that mask in place when they had to maintain a certain emotional distance from the patients too. Perhaps it was Jessica's empathetic way of interacting with her subjects which conned him into thinking he could drop his guard too.

He had hoped to abandon all thoughts of her on her doorstep once he'd fulfilled the promise to get her home. Now her offer to extend the evening made him think that she might need some company. Anyone would've been shaken up after everything she'd gone through today and there was a chance she didn't want to dwell on it alone. Wasn't he dreading doing the same thing himself? There couldn't be any harm in lending a sympathetic ear for a few minutes over a medicinal cup of tea. Especially if he could strike Jessica's welfare off the list of things which would keep him awake tonight.

'I would've done the same for anyone but if you've got any chocolate biscuits to go with the tea you can count me in.'

'I'm sure we can find something for that sweet tooth of yours.' Jessica went on ahead, leaving the front door open for Rob to follow.

The sound of a breaking dish and soft cursing led him towards the kitchen, where he found her picking up fragments of china from the tiled floor. The reasons he'd agreed to come into the apartment deserted him when he was confronted with the picture of her pert backside outlined in the tight grey fabric of her dress.

He said the first thing that came into his head that would excuse him for paying close attention to certain body parts he had no business staring at. 'It's highly recommended that you bend at the knees to prevent back pain.'

'You're off the clock now, Doctor, but I do appreciate your ongoing concern.' Jessica reached out and touched his arm as she straightened up again. Coupled with Rob's wayward thoughts, the unexpected contact practically singed his skin.

'No problem.' His eyes met hers and for a second he thought he saw his own desire reflected in those turquoise pools staring back at him. She blinked, breaking the spell and reminding Rob that all she'd offered him was a cuppa.

They managed to make the tea between them without any further inadvertent touching, which was a miracle, considering the cramped space they were working in. The living room they carried their tea and biscuits into wasn't any more spacious than the kitchen, made smaller by the collection of pictures and knick-knacks crammed in every available corner. Where one might have imagined modern furnishings and contemporary design, Rob saw comfy sofas and pretty floral patterns. It was homely and cosy, everything his house wasn't. He sipped his tea and perused the record of Jessica's life in candid photos lining the room.

The redhead with the boyish figure and short hair was a far cry from the curvaceous, glamorous woman standing before him now.

'Is this your mum and dad?' He lingered on the image of her sandwiched between a smiling middle-aged couple, taking pride of place on the mantelpiece. They looked so happy together it immediately made

Rob pine for the same close relationship he'd once had with his own parents. He'd severed all contact after the accident to start afresh in Belfast, with no ties to his past. Five years on and he was starting to see he'd made a mistake. He'd acted rashly, understandable when he'd suffered such a devastating loss, but it had only served to increase his punishment. That selfish decision to leave without explanation had come back to haunt him. Now he had no family at all to call his own.

'Yeah. Dad died not long after this was taken. Heart attack.' Jessica traced a finger over the figure of her father, whose Irish DNA she'd so clearly inherited, before wrapping both hands back around her cup.

'That must've been hard for you.' Rob knew that losing a parent was different to losing a wife and child but he clearly wasn't the only one having trouble moving on.

'It was. Is.' Jessica kicked off her shoes and folded herself into one of the two-seater settees, suddenly looking very small and weary.

She couldn't have been any more than eleven or twelve in the picture yet her pain was still there in her eyes. Rob saw the same haunted expression looking back at him every day in the mirror. It had taken him to battle his demons before he recognised it in her too.

He turned his back on the happy memories mocking them and took a seat opposite her. 'And your mum?'

'She's good, apart from her arthritis. Mum had me quite late in life, so we're dealing with a few health issues relating to her age now.'

'Does she live close by?' Rob hadn't even considered how his parents' health might've deteriorated since he'd seen them last. He was their only child and he'd failed them too because of his own selfish pride. As much as he was thinking about checking in with them again, he had concerns it could cause them more upset if he simply waltzed back into their lives after this length of time.

'Yeah. She's only a five-minute walk away. There are only the two of us left, so we've got each other's backs.' The strength of Jessica's bond with her mother was obvious in every word. Where death had brought her family closer, it had ripped his apart.

'You're an only child too? My parents always thought it would be unfair on me to have another child who needed their attention. I don't agree. I could have done with someone else to distract them.' Perhaps if he'd had a brother or sister to talk to, or act as mediator between him and his parents, matters might've been resolved sooner.

'I think Mum planned to have a big family but fate had other ideas.' Jessica shrugged but she couldn't fool him by feigning nonchalance when he'd already seen behind those shutters.

'It has a lot to answer for.' He gritted his teeth and silently cursed whatever powers had conspired to steal away his family's future too.

'What happened to your wife?' Jessica followed his train of thought and asked the question he'd been dreading. In the comfort of her living room, relaxing in a post-work chat, it had been easy to forget why he didn't put himself in this position of trading personal stories.

'Car accident.' That description could never adequately describe the ensuing carnage of that afternoon but he wasn't in a place where he was ready to discuss what had happened in any detail.

'Oh, my goodness. I'm so sorry.' There it was—the sympathetic head tilt and the wide eyes that said *Tell me more so I can weep for you*. The exact reason he refused to have this conversation any more. It was bad enough that people pitied him for losing his wife but he couldn't bear the sympathy and tears when he told them about Mollie too. He didn't deserve it.

He drained his cup and got to his feet before he said anything more. 'Thanks for the tea but I think it's time I was on my way.'

He could hear Jessica scrambling off her seat as he made his way to the door but he wasn't hanging around for her to dissect the story and make him the victim. Worse, she might just discover he wasn't the man she thought he was.

Damn it! Jessica had pushed him too far again. She'd only been trying to lend a listening ear, as he'd done for her. It upset her mother when she talked of her father and she wasn't exactly inundated with friends she could talk to. Some of the burden had lifted from her shoulders simply by having Rob to confide in and she'd wanted the same for him. His grief was evident in his refusal to talk about his late wife, not that Jessica would ever dream of forcing the information from him when she was still nursing her own heartache and secrets. It would be a shame for the evening to end on a bad note when she'd begun to get used to the idea of having a friend.

'Rob, wait.' She leaped up to say her goodbyes before he left.

He paused and gave her a chance to catch up. Standing toe to toe with him in the cramped hallway, with only the heavy tick of the wall clock to punctuate the silence, Jessica struggled to find the words she wanted to say. Especially when those liquid blue eyes blinking back at her were shimmering with hurt and loss.

'I didn't mean to make you uncomfortable. You've clearly been through a lot and I'm sorry I brought it up. I only wanted to be there for you, the way you were for me today.'

'It's okay.' He gave her a wobbly smile and battled to keep his alpha male stance even though his body language was crying out for a hug.

Tick-tock.

'Thanks again for everything.' She stood up on her tiptoes to give him a peck on the cheek.

'I'll see you tomor—' Rob turned to say goodbye at the same moment.

Their mouths met in an accidental kiss—a faux pas which could have been easily rectified if she'd apologised immediately and created some distance. Except his lips were as soft as they looked and she lingered there a little longer than was probably socially acceptable.

'Sorry.' She stepped back when common sense kicked in again. Kissing Rob when all he'd done was be nice to her was a stupid, impulsive move which screamed desperation.

Rob shot out his hand to catch her around the waist and pull her back. She was mid-gasp and flush against him when his mouth came crashing back down on hers.

He stole her breath away as he caught her bottom lip between his, and sent her head spinning from the lack of oxygen. She didn't know where the unexpected display of passion had come from but she wanted more. Who wouldn't want to be kissed by a hot doctor who tasted of sweet tea and salty unshed tears?

He thrust his tongue into her mouth and Jessica went limp against him, surrendering to the invasion. The sensation of butterfly wings on her skin tickled her from head to toe until every erogenous zone in her body was on high alert. She really shouldn't be enjoying this as much as she was. He was grieving. She was a mess. This felt so damn good.

Rob didn't often give in to acts of spontaneity but a chain reaction had begun within him once his lips had met hers, shutting off the rational side of his brain to let primitive instinct take over. Nothing else mattered except having another taste and her submission had given him the green light to take anything he wanted. The notion of progressing beyond a make-out session and carrying her off to bed got his blood pumping even more. She was so responsive, meeting every flick of his tongue with hers—he knew they'd be explosive together in the bedroom.

His erection was growing by the second, with Jessica pressed against him moaning her acceptance of the next step. She was trusting him with her body the way she'd trusted him with her emotions. Rob wanted her, needed her so badly it hurt—but not the complications which would come from sleeping with her. She'd shared so much with him already, she would never be simply a casual hook-up now. At some point she'd start to expect more than he could give her. The lusty haze began to clear as painful reality moved in. This was a mistake.

He must have said as much as Jessica quickly broke off the kiss.

'What?' Her desire-darkened eyes did nothing to help his current predicament.

He backed away from her. 'I don't want to make things weird between us at work. It's been a long day. We're clearly not thinking straight.'

'Right. It's been an emotional time for both of us.' She smoothed the front of her dress, creased where she'd been crushed against him, and could barely meet his eye. It was better this way. A kiss would be easier to forget than a passion-fuelled romp.

'So, we can pretend this never happened and carry on as normal tomorrow?' He always preferred to get these things straight to avoid any confusion later on. It wouldn't do either of them any good to be tiptoeing around each other for the rest of the month over a simple misunderstanding. They'd stupidly acted on their attraction instead of ignoring it but it wasn't too late to fix this.

'Sure. I mean we're not kids. One kiss is nothing to lose our heads over.'

'Right.'

They were both nodding their heads and shuffling their feet in an awkward dance around the truth. If it meant so little, they probably wouldn't feel the need to explain it away, but it suited Rob fine that they both kept up the pretence.

'I guess I'll see you tomorrow, then. Goodnight, Jessica.' He opened the front door and walked away before he did something he'd really regret.

CHAPTER FOUR

NOT EVEN THE NEWS that someone in the production crew had accidentally smashed a light fitting with a boom mike could dampen Jessica's spirits this morning. She'd spent all night replaying that Hollywood moment when Rob had pulled her back into his arms for a second kiss. It proved the attraction between them definitely wasn't one-sided even though they'd agreed to put it behind them.

That warm glow started inside her again at the mere memory. It had been a while since anyone had kissed her so passionately, made her feel so desirable, and she could easily get used to it. He'd treated her as a normal woman, not some pale, inadequate version of one. When the chemotherapy had robbed her of her beautiful hair, she'd thought no one would ever find her attractive again. At a time when friends were discovering make-up and boys, she'd been the pitiful creature tied to her sickbed, crying herself to sleep at night.

Adam had been her first serious adult relationship and since she'd been in remission when they'd met she'd been able to give everything of herself to him. Only for her useless body to let her down again and push him away when she'd needed him most. The menopause had zapped her energy, her libido and everything which had made her the woman she'd grown into.

They hadn't discussed children even after their engagement, each seemingly happy to focus on their careers. Or so she'd thought. The onset of early menopause had changed everything.

Her cycle had always been irregular but the irony of the situation was she'd thought she'd fallen pregnant when her periods stopped for good. For a short time she'd got used to the idea of being a mother and imagined having that little life growing inside her. It had been a double blow when she'd discovered the truth. After numerous negative pregnancy results and a battery of blood tests, her doctor confirmed his suspicion that she was still suffering the after-effects of her chemotherapy treatment. The high dosage of drugs she'd been exposed to for so long had finally stopped her ovaries from functioning as they should.

Neither of them had been able to handle the news that she would never be able to have a child of her own. The difference was, Adam still had the chance to walk away and start over. She didn't blame him for taking it.

The only consolation was that he hadn't been around to watch the humiliation of her going through HRT. Hormone replacement therapy might have reduced her symptoms but it didn't make a woman in her twenties feel any less of a failure. She'd had four years of dealing with this on her own and coming to terms with what it meant for her. There had been a few dalliances along the way but long-term relationships were no longer an option for her. She wouldn't let anyone get that close to her again and risk a rejection when things got serious after it had taken this long to learn to love herself again. Although she'd settle for a few more confidence-boosting smooches from Rob if he ever fancied a repeat performance of last night.

Neither of them were in the right frame of mind for anything serious when they were both carrying wounds from their past. That didn't mean they couldn't have a little fun for the duration of filming. All she had to do now was see if she could interest him in keeping things casual. More stolen kisses and passionate embraces with no ties or expectations sounded like the ideal set-up to her.

She had hoped to have caught him for another lift this morning so they could discuss what had happened but there'd been no sign of him. As she walked into the Teenage Cancer Unit to join the camera crew, she discovered why.

The unit was a separate ward for the older children, designed to have more of a relaxing vibe than the main hospital. The brightly coloured communal area, complete with comfy sofas and game consoles, resembled more of a youth club than a ward for sick children. There, in the middle of the room, Rob was already halfway through a game of pool with Cal, her lead story today. Apparently the doctor had had an earlier start than usual.

Jessica could have spent all morning watching Rob as he bent over the table, his black trousers taut around his backside, but the camera crew might've had something to say on the matter.

She walked over to view proceedings from a more respectable, if less intriguing, angle. 'Hey, you two.'

'Hi, Jessica.' Cal was first to greet her with his big beaming smile. Jessica was sure the handsome sixteen-year-old had broken the hearts of quite a few teenage girls before he'd become ill. Now he'd had the all-clear to go home again there would inevitably be a few more.

'Hey.' Rob barely lifted his head to acknowledge her before going on to pot another ball. It wasn't the scorching reunion she'd anticipated after a night reliving his hot goodbye. Even in the presence of a third party she'd expected him to be a tad friendlier towards her. Whilst she'd paid nothing more than lip service to their agreement to forget the kiss, he'd apparently followed it to the letter.

'How're you feeling today?' She focused her attention back on Cal instead of herself. His recovery was the reason she was here today and that was more important than a romance that apparently only existed in her head.

'Fine. As soon as I win a game against Dr Campbell, I'll be packing my bags for home.' There was no denying his excitement at the prospect as he high-fived his opponent. It was a far cry from the weak youngster she'd met a week ago when he'd been recovering from a virus. The chemotherapy weakened the immune system so much that even an innocuous cold was enough to floor a patient.

Jessica knew that desperation he had to get back to his own bed and belongings. The worst time for her had been when she'd had to spend Christmas on the ward, too sick to eat dinner or open presents. Cancer robbed people of more than their health; it stole childhood memories along with it. She was happy to see at least one of the children going home and getting back to his normal life.

'In that case you could be waiting awhile.' Rob showed no mercy as he cleared the table for another victory.

'You think he'd go easy and let me win one game.'

Cal shook his head and started to rack the balls up again. That stubborn determination would serve him well in the fight against his illness.

'Hey. You're the one who said you were fed up with people treating you like an invalid—' This time Rob gave Jessica a sly wink which said he was merely proving a point to Cal, not trying to hustle him.

She shuddered as her imagination went into overdrive, wishing that look was solely for her. A secret sign he was thinking about last night. It wasn't fair that this man was able to turn her inside out with one blink of an eye.

'You would have stood a better chance against me. I haven't as much as picked up a cue before.'

'It's dead easy. Here.' Cal thrust a cue into her hand and volunteered her as Rob's next challenger.

'I'm sure the doctor has better things to do than teach me how to play pool.' She tried to hand it back but Cal dodged away. Perhaps it was his way of getting out of another thrashing while still saving face. In which case she had no choice but to join in the game.

'I have a few minutes to spare before my next outpatient clinic.' Rob checked his watch but he was so hard to read; Jessica wondered if he was simply killing time or he genuinely wanted to hang out with her. Her ego wanted it to be the latter so her idea of a fling wouldn't come completely out of left field.

'So, you put your hand on the table and sort of seesaw the cue between your thumb and your forefinger.' Cal directed her first, standing with his arms folded across his chest until she did as she was told.

'Like this?'

'It's better if you make your fingers into an arch rather than have them flat on the table. Here, let me show you.' Rob came around the table to stand behind her. He leaned over and took her hands in his to demonstrate the correct posture. As his breath fanned the sensitive skin on her neck and his chest pressed against her back, Jessica was in danger of spontaneously combusting.

With his hands guiding hers she took her first shot and sank a red.

'See, it's easy. It's all about the angles.' His voice was husky in her ear, calling the hairs on the back of her neck to attention. Her imagination could've been working overtime but she thought he lingered with his arms around her for a fraction longer than he should have if she was a mistake never to be repeated.

She turned her head to thank him, only to find his mouth a few millimetres from hers. Given the hungry way he was gazing at her lips, there was every chance of another misdemeanour. A slight head tilt and they would fit together perfectly. Her breath hitched. It really was all about the angles.

'The very people I'm looking for. Cal, we need to take some more bloods before you go.' At the sound of Maria's voice in the room, Rob dropped Jessica so quickly she almost face-planted onto the table.

'Ugh. That's something I definitely won't miss.' Cal's shoulders slumped when he was faced with Maria's tools of the bloodsucking trade. Although giving blood samples became an everyday occurrence for inpatients and they were a vital part in the treatment, they certainly didn't get any easier to do. Jessica still winced when she had hers taken during her check-ups.

'Do you want to do it here, or—'

'We can do it in my room. I might have a lie-down after.'

Jessica's cheeks burned as she realised that her Rob

haze had blinded her to the fact that Cal was beginning to wilt. On closer inspection, he did seem more subdued than when she'd first arrived. It was easy to forget that even such a small thing as a game of pool could still wipe out a chemo-tired body, regardless of the strength of the spirit. Now that his cancer was in remission, hopefully he would recover quickly.

'You get your head down for forty winks and we'll get the crew to you when you're ready.' She could reorganise the running for today's shoot until he felt well enough to face the cameras with his parents. Despite whatever Rob or anyone else might think, the welfare of these kids took priority over her schedule. That was one of the perks of being top dog when they were dealing with such sensitive issues. A different producer might not have been as sympathetic to the children as one who'd gone through this herself.

Cal gave her the thumbs-up before he headed back to his room. Maria stopped halfway down the corridor and walked back towards them. For a moment, Jessica worried she was coming to give them a ticking off for tiring him out. Or to remind her that this wasn't the place to indulge her romantic fantasies.

'Rob, I wanted to make sure you're still on for tonight.'

Instead, the voluptuous Maria made her own overtures to the doc without any hesitation. The green-eyed monster tapped Jessica on the shoulder and rolled its sleeves up to prepare for a fight.

Except Rob was smiling and nodding to confirm Maria's plans.

'Of course. I wouldn't miss it for the world.'

'Good. I'll see you there at the usual time, then. Jessica, I'll give you a shout when Cal's parents come in so you can get set up.' Maria was so confident, so efficient, there was no room for argument.

'Thanks,' Jessica mumbled as Maria strode away again. Her thoughts about Rob were even more of a muddle now when clearly he and Maria had a relationship which extended outside of the hospital. There was no point in sharpening her claws over a man she had no claim on but he shouldn't have kissed her the way he had unless it meant something. She had to find out if there was something going on between Rob and the nurse before she let herself believe she had a chance with him.

Rob was glad of Maria's interruption. It dissipated the sexual tension radiating between him and Jessica. There'd been enough of that last night and he was still trying to figure out what to do about it. Every time he had her in his arms he seemed to lose his mind and that was the very reason he'd been trying to avoid her. Then she'd shown up in all her Audrey Hepburnesque glamour, ponytail swinging and eyelashes fluttering, to undo all his good work.

A gentleman would've chauffeured her to work again this morning and saved her from the horrors of public transport. Then again, a gentleman wouldn't have pounced on her the way he had last night. He'd acted on pure lust with no thought of the consequences of lunging at her like an overexcited prom date.

They'd shared a lot over the course of the evening, probably too much. For a moment he'd forgotten he would have to face her at work for the foreseeable future. She already knew too much about him to qualify as a one-night stand and starting something more than that was equally unthinkable. Even if she was agreeable.

At least he'd pulled on the brakes before doing something really stupid.

If he ever deigned to get involved again beyond a one-night fling, it would be with someone safe. Someone who wasn't always chasing the next thrill. He'd learned his lesson the hard way that family should always come before work. Perhaps he might still have his daughter with him if he and Leah had remembered that. Should he ever get a second chance at being a husband and father again, he'd strive to put that right. Only a partner with similar ideals could give him that feeling of completeness back. He was certain that someone wasn't Jessica.

'I should really get back to Outpatients.' He chose to ignore the herd of white elephants charging through the room.

'Are we really not gonna talk about what happened?'

He should've known Jessica wouldn't give him an easy out. Her style was much more confrontational.

'It was one kiss that shouldn't have happened. Let's face it—nothing was ever going to come of it. We have to work together and I don't want to complicate things. It's better if we just leave it in the past.' He glanced furtively around, as though they were discussing a matter of great national importance. In reality, he didn't want to give Maria any ammunition in her attempt to get him and Jessica together.

There was no doubt they had chemistry but Rob wouldn't be able to walk away with a clear conscience now he'd seen how delicate she was beneath the surface. His casual approach to relationships wouldn't work for her, or him, on this occasion.

'Of course. You're free to enjoy your night without worrying I'll say anything.' Jessica tilted her chin up with an air of superiority Rob didn't think was justified. They'd both acted rashly and he was simply trying to make working together less…awkward.

'I'm not sure a roomful of ten-year-old girls would be that interested in my love life but I appreciate the sentiment.'

Jessica plucked invisible dirt from her cute pink belly top and brushed her hands down her black swing skirt. 'I overheard you and Maria making arrangements for later.'

'Yeah. She railroaded me into giving a first-aid demonstration to her Girl Guide troop. You didn't think… We're nothing more than friends.' Although Rob's relationship with religion was strained these days, he was often roped in to help with church events, courtesy of his friend. He didn't mind. If he was pushed, he'd say he enjoyed the odd game of football at the youth club or chaperoning on Sunday school outings. Even though he was no longer a dad himself, supervising the kids somehow kept him connected to the role. He didn't know what that had to do with Jessica. Unless…

'Are you jealous?' Despite all his reservations about starting anything with her, he wasn't averse to the flattery of the situation.

'I didn't know… I thought that's why you didn't want me… It's none of my business anyway…' Jessica was gesticulating wildly as her cheeks glowed with a scarlet hue but he could read her as clearly as a front-page ad in the *Belfast Telegraph*.

'Maria and I have never been anything other than friends. She's more like a protective big sister than anything. Besides, I don't get involved with work colleagues. Which is exactly why that kiss between us should never have happened.' That didn't mean he hadn't wanted it but still, it was a mistake he couldn't afford to make again.

'Sure. Sure.' She was nodding now and avoiding eye contact. Telltale signs that he'd managed to screw this up even more.

'Tonight really is just a favour.' Rob didn't want them to revert to their former sparring ways on account of his actions. They could still be friends.

'You know, the director has been on my back about getting more footage of the staff outside the hospital to make them more relatable to the viewer. Do you think we could film a segment of you and Maria working with the Guides? It would really give us a contrast between your working life and what you do in your downtime.'

Jessica's proposal took him by surprise. Not least because it entailed them spending more time together outside office hours. Something which completely went against his decision to keep his distance from her.

'I wouldn't be comfortable with a film crew following me twenty-four hours a day. Besides, it would disrupt the girls too much and they're difficult to wrangle at the best of times.' This was outside the board's jurisdiction, so he had every right to say no to further intrusion. The trouble was, he'd already done Jessica a disservice by trying to pretend the kiss had never happened. Guilt often prompted him into agreeing to things which would normally be outside his comfort zone. It was the debt he felt he owed to Maria for taking him under her wing which had led him to volunteer in the first place.

'I promise we could do it with the minimum of fuss. All it would take would be a few shots at the start of the night. No muss, no fuss. Of course, I'll make sure we get consent from the children's parents before we start filming.'

'You'd have to check with Maria first.' Although Rob knew she wouldn't hesitate to agree in her endless quest to see him paired off.

'I'll do that now. Does that mean you're on board?' Jessica was the picture of innocence as she batted her eyelashes at him. And very difficult to say no to.

'I suppose I could do with another child wrangler at my side—' Rob had seen the rapport she'd built with the children here, so he trusted her to treat this as more than just another filming op.

'And I could do with brushing up on my first-aid skills.'

'In that case, I'll pick you up at seven.' Rob caved. With a roomful of giggly Girl Guides to keep him and Jessica busy, he didn't reckon they could get into too much trouble.

The 'visitor' sticker slapped on Jessica's chest wasn't merely a reminder of her status at the church hall; it was also a comment on her temporary role in Rob's life. No matter what feverish plans she might have had in mind for him, he'd made it clear he wasn't interested. If only his actions in her hallway hadn't said differently, she might have believed him.

For a split second when she'd seen him and Maria together, she feared she'd been spurned in favour of another woman. That dark cloud of self-doubt had begun to move in again, causing her to question her femininity. Despite Rob's ignorance about her fertility issues, she'd wondered if she'd still been found lacking next to the senior staff nurse. The knowledge that Rob simply didn't want her didn't make it any easier to stomach.

It was difficult not to take Rob's rejection personally but at least he'd asked her to come along with him to-night, so he wasn't averse to her company. Although this hadn't turned out to be the spontaneous, sizzling affair she'd imagined, a flicker of hope remained that spending time together might spark it to life.

She needed to know that, despite her inadequacies, she was capable of passion and evoking it in others. Her libido had taken a knock with her confidence but they both seemed to be getting back on track with Rob's help. She wasn't asking for romance and promises that couldn't be kept. All she wanted was a release for her pent-up desires and confirmation of his for her. If that didn't happen, the best she could hope for was that the friendly neighbourhood oncologist currently giving up his free time to babysit a group of Girl Guides might actually convince her there were some good guys out there.

'He's like a rock star when he comes here.' Maria stood at the back of the small room with Jessica, keeping an eye on proceedings. She was every bit as authoritative out of the hospital setting, even if she was in her casual wear rather than her uniform.

'Does he come here often?' It wasn't supposed to come out as a cheesy pick-up line from the seventies but Jessica was intrigued by the easy relationship he apparently had with everyone here.

She hadn't met many single professional men with the ability to talk to children on their level without being patronising and Rob's laughter said this was something he did for fun, not as a chore.

Until coming to the hospital, she'd never spent a lot of time with children. It was difficult being around other people's babies knowing she could never have one of her own. The nature of Rob's work meant he had a lot of experience dealing with them and it showed as he got them warmed up with a few parlour games. It was no wonder that a man who probably had family on his mind for the future wouldn't be interested in a fling.

Regardless of the inner strength Jessica had built up since her wedding dreams had ended, the longing for that perfect family life would probably never leave her either.

'Yes, he helps us out with the kids' clubs quite often, though he's never brought a friend with him before.' Maria's gaze flickered between Rob and Jessica. She'd become animated the minute they'd walked into the hall together. Unfortunately, there was absolutely no reason for anyone to get excited.

'As I said earlier, the director thought it would be good to get an idea of what our revered physician does outside of the department to show his fun side. Thanks for helping me get all the consent forms sorted out so quickly, by the way.' The director had actually said they needed to 'humanise' the man who dealt with life and death every day. Jessica had argued in the firm belief they'd captured his compassion perfectly but she'd consented that it would be nice to see more of him as a person in his own right.

She'd been reluctant to pitch the idea to Rob, given his initial reaction to filming the documentary, but Maria and the Guides had given her the perfect opportunity. It would be fair to say curiosity had also got the best of her about what he and Maria did together here.

'No problem. I'm stunned Rob agreed to this in the first place. He's a very private man.'

Jessica understood that fierce need to maintain control over personal information. Thankfully, the few relationships she'd had to date had been so one-dimensional she'd never had to reveal her personal shame.

Rob was different. He'd already found a way to get her to open up and that should've been the signal to cut her losses and walk away. For some reason, Rob made her want to stick around and figure out what made him tick too.

'I think he understands how important this is to the programme. I'm very grateful to you both for agreeing to do this.' Jessica didn't want to read too much into Rob's decision to take part when her hopes had already been dashed once on that front. She had to go with the positives that he was happy to work with her and that solved her professional dilemma if not her personal one.

As promised, after getting a few shots of Rob playing with the children, Jessica was able to send the crew on their way again. The footage, along with the long-awaited interview, should be enough personal insight into the man of the moment to keep the director happy. Even if she personally hankered for more.

Once all the recording equipment had been packed away and Jessica and Maria were the only spectators left, they fell into an uneasy silence while the rest of the room echoed with excited chatter around them. The girls were swarming around Rob as he produced a selection of bandages and splints from his medical bag.

He clapped his hands together to cut across the din. Playtime was over. 'Okay, can everyone please find a partner?'

The pack immediately followed his command and separated into pairs, all patiently waiting for further instruction.

'He is completely oblivious to the effect he has on young girls. I'm sure there's more than one who's developed a crush on him.' Maria watched him like a proud mother, putting all of those misconceptions about their relationship to rest.

Jessica forced a laugh, since she counted herself as one of those afflicted and was probably doing as bad a job at hiding it.

They listened to Rob give a short introduction about first aid and why it was necessary to think of personal safety as well as that of the casualty. He was adept at both fielding questions and making sure the girls understood the importance of the steps before attempting any treatment. 'I'm going to show you a few skills which might be helpful in the event of an accident. Of course, if there's a serious injury involved you should dial 999. Now, I'm going to need a volunteer to help me with the demonstration.'

A dozen eager hands shot into the air.

'Jessica?' He waved her to the front of the hall and Maria gave her a little shove forward into the spotlight.

She could feel the jealous eyes of every girl upon her as she made her way to Rob's side. 'I don't think I'm the right person for this. I thought I'd be handing out bandages and pouring orange squash.'

'You're perfect,' he whispered back, stealing her objection with a well-timed compliment. It was far from the truth; nevertheless, it had the desired effect on her. The idea of him accepting her, regardless of her flaws, set her heart aflutter and turned her brain to mush. Apparently those two little words were capable of reducing her from a strong, independent woman to just another love-struck girl.

'Now, lie on the floor for me.'

Her dreamy moment took a nightmarish turn.

'Pardon me?'

'I want to demonstrate the recovery position and I

can only do that if you kindly lie down. Please.' It was the plea at the end with a trace of panic which finally broke her down. This wasn't some sort of sick revenge for disrupting her workplace; he was asking her for help and she owed him big-style. She wouldn't let him down for the sake of her own pride.

'Fine.' Thank goodness she'd swapped her flouncy skirt for jeans or this could've been even more awkward. She thought she heard Rob's sigh of relief when she complied and fell at his feet for the second time that week.

Her pulse was racing as he knelt at her side.

'Try to relax,' he said as he unfurled her balled-up hands and moved her arms to her sides.

'That's easier said than done when I'm lying here at your mercy.' And wishing it was in altogether very different circumstances. Everything she'd seen of Rob at work said he was loving and giving and that was bound to extend to other areas of his life.

Jessica's mind wandered towards the bedroom and what a considerate lover he would make.

'I'll be gentle.'

The whispered words in her ear sent an all-points bulletin to body parts south of the border as arousal flooded through her. This was torture. Sweet, sweet torture.

'I'm feeling a bit hot.' The urge to flirt with him became too great to ignore. She wanted him to acknowledge that he wasn't as immune to her as he appeared.

'You do look flushed. Do you want me to loosen your top button?'

She bit her lip as she nodded. At this moment in time all she wanted was for him to touch her.

It might have been wishful thinking on her part that

his bright blue eyes had darkened to glittering sapphires as his fingers brushed the delicate skin at her throat but she really wanted him to rethink the boundaries on their relationship. She swallowed hard as he opened her blouse.

'Better?'

'Better,' she agreed even though she was burning from the inside out.

'I need you to close your eyes. You're supposed to be unconscious.'

Jessica was reluctant to block out the image of him smiling down at her as if they were the only people in the room, but she did as he asked of her.

All other senses heightened to compensate for the loss of her sight, the smell of his rich, woody aftershave enveloping her as he leaned over her. Rob explained to their audience that the recovery position was used for those who were unconscious but breathing, and only used if the person didn't have a neck or spiral injury.

'The first thing we want to do is check that the patient is responsive, by gently shaking and calling out to them. Jessica, are you awake?' Rob placed his hands on her shoulders and shook her.

How could she play the unresponsive patient when every part of her was tingling with sexual awareness? Had she known she'd spend her Friday night lying on a cold, dusty floor pretending she was unfazed by his every touch she might've found alternative entertainment for the evening. Although getting this close to him would be an incentive to do anything.

'If there is no response, call for help and move on to the next stage of checking the airways are open and clear. With an unconscious patient you can do this by tilting their head and lifting their chin.' Rob's hands were firm as he moved her into position. In her daydream she imagined this as her Sleeping Beauty moment with Rob playing the handsome Prince, come to kiss her into consciousness.

'Check the breathing now. Look for the chest rising and falling, feel the breath on your cheek or listen for the sounds.' Rob's breath was warm on her face, his mouth as close to hers as it could be without touching. She wondered if he could tell her breathing was *actually* becoming shallow. Perhaps if she acted her part well enough he'd give her mouth to mouth and put her out of her misery.

'If the person is breathing, then it is safe to move them into the recovery position until help arrives. Put the arm closest to you at a right angle to their body, with the palm facing upwards. Move the palm of their other hand against their chest. Lift the knee furthest from you so their leg is bent and their foot is flat on the floor. You can roll the person onto their side by pulling the bent knee towards you.' Rob manipulated Jessica's limbs so she moved at his will. Clearly she was long overdue some physical intimacy with the opposite sex for her to find this as erotic as she did. It wasn't often that she relinquished control but there was something about this man that made her trust him. That would make an interesting development in her love life, even if it was playing with fire.

'Rest the head on the free hand, with the mouth pointed towards the floor in case the patient should vomit. Make sure you push the chin away from the chest and keep the knee bent at a right angle to their body. Check breathing again while you wait for an ambulance.'

There was a whoosh of cold air around Jessica's

body and a sense of loss as Rob apparently got back to his feet.

'I want to see you take turns in your teams, repeating the process and talking me through the steps.'

Jessica opened one eye and squinted up at him. 'Can I get up now?'

'Sure. A round of applause, please, for my glamorous assistant.' Rob reached out to help her up. Jessica wobbled as she got back to her feet and steadied herself with a hand on his chest. In that instant back in his arms, they recreated that heat they'd had in her hallway. She recognised that lust in Rob's eyes as he stared down at her; it was the same thing coursing through her veins.

The clapping from the crowd grew so loud she knew there was no choice for them but to break apart. Jessica took a bow but secretly hoped this wasn't the final curtain. As far as this thing with Rob was concerned, she was waiting for an encore performance.

'Jessica, could you give me a hand going over the steps with the girls?' Rob called her back into action before she let her rampant imagination carry her too far away.

For the next twenty minutes she mingled with the pairs, helping them to remember the positions before Rob would give them one last test. In amongst the serious attempts to impress the instructor, there were also moments of fun as the group began to treat Jessica as one of their own. She fell into the role of agony aunt as they came to her seeking advice on boys and fashion, despite her warning she wasn't an expert on either subject. The innocence and honesty of the group was refreshing for someone who spent her time with cynical television types.

She'd forgotten what it was like to be part of something

fun without having to worry about the other parties' motives. Rob's participation in the activities here was beginning to make sense. Outside the pressure of work, this was the perfect place to unwind and still make a difference to the community. In some ways the split from Adam had turned her into the same self-serving monster she'd run from. Whilst she'd been cautious to protect herself from further hurt, she'd also been selfish, never taking into consideration how she could help others. Rob had suffered a tragedy which made her situation pale in comparison but he wasn't drowning in a sea of self-pity; he was still making a difference in other people's lives. Hers included.

CHAPTER FIVE

IN AMONGST THE throng of excited would-be doctors, Jessica noticed one young girl doubled over at the side of the room.

'Miss, I don't think Ciara's feeling very well.' The girl's partner confirmed Jessica's suspicions as she made her way over to the pair.

'Ciara? Do you need to sit down?' Jessica pulled a chair over and guided her into it. As soon as she saw the girl's grey pallor and heard her gasping for air, she knew it was time to call for help. 'Rob, I need you over here. Now!'

He was there in seconds, kneeling in front of the child and taking both of her hands in his. 'I need you to take long, deep breaths, Ciara. In and out.'

After a few controlled breaths the initial panic for all concerned began to subside. Maria distracted the rest of the girls with a promise of orange juice and biscuits once Rob assured her that he and Jessica could deal with the patient.

'Good girl, Ciara. Now, do you have your inhaler?' Rob's knowledge of the girl's condition said a lot about his relationship with those who attended the church. He was clearly more adept at making friends than Jessica had given him credit for.

Ciara nodded and produced the blue inhaler from her pocket. Rob shook it and uncapped it so she could take a couple of puffs to relieve her symptoms. They waited and listened as her breathing slowly regulated.

'We should really get you home, sweetheart.' Jessica rubbed her back and looked to Rob for further instruction. It was bound to be a frightening experience for Ciara every time her asthma flared up. Illness at that age was never easy and Jessica knew when she was sick the only place she wanted to be was tucked up in her own bed.

'I'll phone your mum and let her know what's happened. Jessica and I can give you a lift home if she agrees to it. Okay?' As soon as he got the go-ahead, Rob went off to make the call and Jessica did her bit to pacify Ciara until his return. She had to admit there were certain areas where she was willing to submit to his authority and she didn't let that happen with just anyone.

He was a take-charge kind of guy but he did it without arrogance or superiority. Nothing seemed to rattle him and she couldn't help wishing she'd had someone like him beside her when her world had been ripped out from beneath her. Things might have been different if she'd had a partner willing to be with her at any cost.

Rob called an end to the class. Now he had permission from Ciara's parents to take her home, he gave her another check-over and made sure she wrapped up before they headed out into the night. She was supposed to have been picked up by a friend of her mother's when the class was over but he felt more comfortable taking her himself in case of another attack.

It wasn't the first time he'd dealt with Ciara's asthma but the difference here was Jessica's support, for him and his patient. Instead of going into meltdown and causing Ciara to panic in return, she'd stayed calm and helped control the situation. There were no cameras rolling, no bosses to impress and no monetary gain to justify her actions. Her sole concern had been for Ciara's welfare and again that truly screwed with his idea that all media types were incapable of human emotion.

Bit by bit she was decimating his defences. Even now, with all three of them in his car, she was constantly reaching out to Ciara in the back seat to make sure she was warm enough and making small talk to keep her mind off her asthma. That sort of bedside manner would've made her a good doctor if she'd ever thought of following that path. Perhaps it was her choice of profession which had skewed his view of her from the start.

There was no escaping the incredible chemistry they had together. He was almost embarrassed about the display they'd put on during the demonstration, when he'd found every excuse he could for touching her. Perhaps it was because he'd tagged her as forbidden fruit, which made her all the more appealing. Denying himself something, someone who could give him so much pleasure only increased his appetite for it. He was craving Jessica the way a dieter craved carbs and chocolate. Given her sultry looks and breathy responses to his every touch when she was supposed to be unconscious, he didn't think she was against the idea either.

It was approaching the time when he might have to admit there was something going on and stop putting up imaginary barriers between them. Even the strictest dietary regimes left room for the odd lapse.

He parked as close as he could to Ciara's house so the cold night didn't trigger another attack. Jessica was first out of the car to help their patient and they both escorted her to the front door. Rob was acquainted with Ciara's mother but he was sure she appreciated having a female presence arrive with her daughter too. They refused the invitation for a cup of tea and he left his charge with instructions to watch her closely and phone the doctor in the morning.

'I'm sorry I ruined everything.' Ciara hung her head as they said their goodbyes but Rob couldn't let her go to bed burdened with so much unnecessary guilt.

'Not at all. We can pick it up again next week when you've all had time to practice.' That seemed to perk her up again, so he was free to leave with a clear conscience too.

'Will Jessica be there too?' Ciara's question left Rob and his new assistant staring at each other for the answer.

'If she wants to…' Rob didn't want to put her on the spot but he had no clue where things would stand in a week's time. She didn't need any more footage, so the answer would depend entirely on whether or not she wanted to spend her free time with him and a bunch of Girl Guides.

'I'd love to.'

Rob matched Jessica's grin as she committed to another evening with him. He was obviously a masochist when he was looking forward to another round of *Let's pretend we don't want to rip each other's clothes off.*

As they made their way back to the car, Jessica seemed to lose some of the spring in her step.

'Is there something wrong?'

She exhaled a slow breath, sending wisps of white whirling into the atmosphere. 'I just know how horrible it is to have to deal with that at her age.'

'You had asthma too?' A lot of things began to fall

into place for Rob. If Jessica had spent her childhood in and out of hospital, it would explain her empathy with the children. There was a possibility he'd mistaken her passion for the subject matter as naked ambition. Her admission changed his perception of her even more. Although she would probably see it as a weakness. It made him all the more privileged that she chose to share the information with him.

'Not asthma, but yeah, I was a sick kid.' It was a flat statement of fact with no plea for sympathy attached. Yet, as a doctor, Rob's interest was automatically piqued. Jessica was a fighter and he couldn't imagine her succumbing to anything, including illness.

'With any luck, Ciara's condition will improve as she gets older. I assume that's what has happened in your case?' He hadn't seen any residual physical evidence of whatever had ailed her. Except for the freckles left where the sun had kissed her nose, there were no scars or blemishes on her skin that he could see. And he'd been studying her form very closely these past few days. He knew her aquamarine eyes flashed with amber when she was annoyed and her cheeks flushed red when he was near.

'Yes, but recovery was long and not without challenges. I hope she does get better but sickness taints everything when you look back on those lost years. Hospital beds and blood tests aren't the stuff of nostalgic childhood memories. See, it's left me bitter and twisted.' Her humourless laugh was more disturbing than the sight of her unshed tears glistening in the darkness of the car. Whatever battle she'd fought had clearly left more than physical scars. Despite all his medical training, Rob had never found the magic cure for emotional trauma. If he had, he might have found it easier to open up the way Jessica could with him.

'And everything's okay now?' He didn't want to dig any deeper than she was comfortable with about her condition but if there was anything he could do for her in a professional capacity he wouldn't hesitate to do so.

'Yeah. I got the all-clear a long time ago.' There was a long pause, as if she was debating whether or not to go into further detail. Rob held off on starting the car ignition in case it broke the spell. He wanted to know what had happened in her past to haunt her still. He wanted to help her through it.

'Childhood leukaemia. Acute lymphoblastic leukae-mia, to be precise.'

Rob's breath caught in his throat. He'd seen many patients suffering that particular condition. ALL was such a devastating illness, with an average length of treatment of around two years. A long time snatched from a childhood, to be spent in and out of hospitals. 'You've been through the wars, all right.'

'I'm a survivor, if nothing else. My heart goes out to Ciara. The fight is never easy.' With everything else Jessica had been through, she was entitled to feel sorry for herself once in a while but she'd reserved her pity for another little girl. She was a remarkable woman who'd overcome so much and if she ever decided to give motivational talks Rob would be the first to sign up. Perhaps there was something to be said for this un-burdening of personal problems. After all, he'd slept a little better himself after finally telling someone about Leah. It was a type of therapy without paying a stranger to listen, or being tagged as a patient. Still, her empa-thy for others meant she was taking on other worries she could do nothing about.

'I know but you're here and you're healthy now. There's no reason why Ciara can't have that in the future too.'

'You're right. I'm just being silly.' Jessica reached for her seat belt and indicated she was ready to go.

'Not at all. You're caring and sympathetic. A beautiful person, inside and out.' In his mind, Rob was reaching out to her, cradling her face in his hands and kissing her. It was his heart telling him he shouldn't. The only thing he knew for certain was that he didn't want her to go home just yet. He couldn't dump her out of the car after she'd laid herself bare to him.

He hadn't been in this position before. Sure, he'd done his fair share of counselling families in the course of his job, but this was different. Jessica needed physical and emotional support and he wasn't sure he was capable of giving one without the other. If he kissed her, it would take them to a level beyond friendship and he didn't want that when she was so emotionally vulnerable.

He should really confess his sins and put her off from wanting anything from him at all, but he didn't want to do it here in the dark where they could barely see each other's faces.

'Thanks.'

Rob fumbled with his keys to get the engine started and break the tense atmosphere he'd created. 'I don't live far from here if you want to go grab a bite to eat? Your day has been every bit as busy as mine and we don't want you passing out again, do we?'

'I suppose…' Jessica's judgement where men were concerned was apparently still completely out of whack to have mistaken a compliment as a come-on. For a split second she'd imagined he was going to kiss her, only to find the hungry look in his eyes was for a snack, not her. She'd told him the very thing which had defined everything about her and she took his non-reaction as another snub.

If it wasn't for her growling stomach and an evening dwelling on her misfortunes alone to look forward to, she might well have declined the invitation.

She knew she'd made the right call when they drew up into the driveway. The large chalet-style bungalow was more of a family residence than the trendy bachelor pad she'd pictured him in. It was a new build and, with the acres of empty fields surrounding it, probably more expensive than a luxury apartment in the city.

It was immaculate inside; the order and precision he displayed at work clearly extended here too.

'Make yourself…er…comfortable and I'll see what we have in the way of food.' Rob led her through to the living room.

'No problem. Give me a shout if you need a hand with anything.' She took a seat on the shiny black leather settee. Everything in the room looked as if it had just been unwrapped. He'd been here five years and the place still didn't feel lived-in. Despite Rob's devotion to his wife's memory, there were no pictures of her around, no personal artefacts visible anywhere. As if he was in denial about what had happened. It wasn't healthy.

Rob returned carrying a few paltry grocery items which did not have the makings of a gourmet meal. 'We have tinned soup, eggs, some sort of vegetables, and I'm sure I saw a packet of sausages that are only days out of the best-before date in there somewhere too.

Sorry, I didn't think this through. I could whip up an omelette if you like?'

'There's no need. I love tomato soup and it means we can be eating in less than five minutes.' Soup had been one of the few things she'd been able to stomach during her illness and she related it to a comfort of sorts. She was ready for it after the day she'd had.

'As you wish.' Rob gave a sweeping bow and backed out of the room but Jessica was keen to spend more time in his company. Especially with this playful side of him.

'Wait, I'll come and help.'

The kitchen resembled something from a show home with its marble worktops, oak units and state-of-the-art gadgets. Her whole apartment would probably fit into one corner of it too. 'Are you telling me you have *this* to cook in and your diet is that of a penniless student?'

'Give me a break. I haven't had a chance to shop yet this week.' Rob poured the thick red gloop into two bowls and set the timer on the microwave.

Jessica wasn't buying it. The kitchen was so pristine, either he never used it or he had an army of woodland creatures under his command keeping it spotless. The size of this house would emphasise anyone's loneliness and she didn't understand why he would move here in the first place after losing his wife. She found it hard enough at times to fill the silence in her poky dwelling space, never mind this sprawling country estate—population one. At least she had her mother to visit when the loneliness became too much. From her restricted view of Rob's situation, it felt as though he was punishing himself by living in this vast empty space, as far from human company as he could get. Somehow she'd achieved VIP status which allowed her access inside his hallowed sanctuary.

'I'm sure you have a lovely view from here.' Although,

without the light pollution of traffic and civilisation, all she could see at the moment was eternal darkness.

'Aye. It's the perfect spot if you're fond of fields and sheep.'

Or brooding.

As beautiful as Rob's house was, this kind of isolation was never going to help his situation and Jessica had learned long ago it wasn't healthy to hold back on what she was thinking. Dinner could wait but if she didn't get this out now she'd burst. 'Do you really think Leah would want you to hide away out here for the rest of your life?'

Rob braced himself against the worktop, his back still towards Jessica and his hackles well and truly raised. 'You don't understand.'

'You're right. I don't. So explain to me why you're so damned hard on yourself.' After everything she'd shared with him, he should be able to trust her with his story. Unfortunately, trying to get information out of him was like banging her head off a solid, muscly brick wall.

The beep from the microwave barely registered for Rob as he was forced to turn around and confront the demons he'd grown tired of hiding from. 'I couldn't save her. I failed as a doctor, a husband... I wasn't there for her when she needed me the most.'

He'd been so caught up in his work, in saving other people's lives, he hadn't been there to protect the ones who mattered most to him. If only he'd shared the excitement of his daughter and joined the shopping expedition for her first day at school instead of dwelling on the argument he'd had with Leah at home, he might've prevented the tragedy.

Rob caught himself before he blurted out about Mollie, and how he'd failed as a father too. One shameful secret at a time. He didn't want Jessica to judge him or pity him any more than she did already. It wouldn't bring his family back. More than that, the memories he had of Mollie were his alone now and he wouldn't share her with just anyone.

'It wasn't your fault. It was an accident, something you could never have foreseen.' Jessica's naivety about the situation made her kitchen psychology all the more infuriating.

'We'd had a stupid row the night before and I was still stewing over it. Otherwise, I would've been with her when the so-called joyrider ran into her. I might've prevented it.'

They'd only been together a few months when she'd fallen unexpectedly pregnant and, if Rob was honest, Mollie was probably the reason they'd married so quickly. It had been Leah's decision to put her career on hold at the time but Rob would've supported her, whatever choice she'd made. That had made her deception all the harder to swallow. There'd been no need to lie to him about what she was doing or where she was going when he would've done whatever it took to make her happy.

They'd loved each other but he'd got the impression she'd started to resent him and Mollie for stifling her dreams. She clearly hadn't been content as a stay-at-home mum and he hadn't seen it until it was too late. The discrepancy between what Rob had thought was happening whilst he was at work and the reality of how Leah spent her time only came to light when their daughter had become cranky and out of sorts. In the end the truth had come from the mouth of his baby and turned his world upside down. The lack of communication between him and Leah, his ultimate failure as a husband to recognise that his wife was troubled, had cost him everything.

'The accident might have happened regardless if you were there or not.'

'Maybe, maybe not. I don't know what Leah's state of mind was when she took off in the car and they never caught the other driver. I'll never know how the accident happened and that's the killer. There's that small chance I could've prevented the accident, or saved her if I'd been at the scene.' And saved Mollie too.

'It's a terrible thing to have to come to terms with, but you can't blame yourself when you weren't driving either car.' Jessica's simplistic view didn't leave any room for survivor's guilt, or crippling thoughts that he could've somehow changed fate.

To this day the sight of policemen in the department still brought that lurching fear in his stomach that they were coming to deliver life-shattering news.

'Unfortunately, bad things happen to good people. Don't you think I've spent a lifetime trying to find someone to blame for my problems? Did I get sick because of something I or my parents did? No, it's just one of those awful things sent to test us and make us stronger human beings. You can't spend for ever letting the accident consume you. It's not your fault.' Jessica said those words his mother had played on repeat until he could hear them no more. It didn't mean anything when newspaper headlines were there to remind him that he was the doctor who couldn't save his own family.

Jessica cupped his face in her hands, insisting he look at her. 'It's not your fault and you deserve more than this half-life you're living. This tragedy happened *to* you, not

because of you. Trust me, I know the difference.' Jessica
was as passionate as ever, defending him from his inner
turmoil. He wanted to believe she was someone he had
an affinity with. For a little while he wanted to escape
from the inside of his head and let himself feel something
other than the guilt he carried with him on a daily basis.

'It's not your fault.' She repeated the mantra and
kissed him on both cheeks. Something he'd been too
afraid to do to comfort her in case she read something
into it. As usual, she acted without any of the intro-
spection he got bogged down into before every single
move he made.

'It's not your fault.' She kissed him on the mouth.
Perhaps she thought if she said it enough he'd start to
believe it. How different things would be if he could
share in her delusion and imagine he was nothing more
than a lonely man who needed comfort. That he had
permission to feel something more than the immense
sadness which engulfed his heart.

He closed his eyes and tried to block out the past to
focus on the present. On the soft pressure bearing down
on his lips, her exotic scent tickling his nose and that
taste of excitement on his tongue.

When he thought she was moving away, he went with
her, keeping their mouths fused together to prolong the
moment for a while longer. She relaxed into him and
Rob revelled in the warmth and comfort of her embrace.
He rounded his hand over her backside and brought her
flush against him to meet him at every contact point
guaranteed to fry his brain for good.

'Jessica…if we don't stop this now…' His voice was
ragged with desire but he didn't want to go any further
and live to regret it.

'What? We've both been denying ourselves this for too long.'

Jessica went to work on the buttons of his shirt, exposing his bare skin to the cold air and her warm mouth. His nipples hardened, along with other stimulated parts of his body, as she trailed kisses over his torso. With every touch, he was hurtling away from his pain. Jessica was a better cure than a kilo of chocolate and overtime any day.

He fought to think straight as she licked her tongue around his nipple. 'I don't want to get into anything serious.'

'Me neither.' She paid more attention to what she was doing rather than what he was saying.

'I mean it. I don't go in for anything more than one night with anyone.' He wanted to establish boundaries before they were past the point of no return.

She stopped what she was doing to look him square in the eye. 'I get it. Neither of us wants to get involved. That suits me fine. Right now I'd say one night of unbridled passion will get this thing out of our systems. In a few weeks' time I'll move on with nothing more than fond memories.' Trust her to verbalise her feelings so succinctly when he was struggling to find the words. He no longer had to worry about her agenda and there were no more barriers to stop him giving in to impulse just this once.

He drew her back up along his body so he could lose himself in the taste of her again and forget all the reasons they were so wrong for each other. Here and now, they were simply two lost souls clinging together, finding comfort in each other.

With his lips and tongue meshed with Jessica's, Rob finally released the passion he'd been holding back for so long. He slid his hand under her silky white shirt and cupped her breast, brushing a thumb over her nipple to bring it to attention. That small indication of her arousal launched his own into hyperdrive. He trailed kisses along her neck and unbuttoned her shirt with his free hand, exposing more of her body for him to tend.

Jessica's moans caused another rush of blood through his veins and called to his inner caveman. He yanked her bra aside and latched his mouth around the pink tip straining to greet him. She was soft and hard, spicy and sweet, so wrong and yet so right.

Fuelled by lust and adrenaline, Rob tugged Jessica's jeans and panties down out of his way. Clearly in as much of a hurry as he was, she kicked them off and returned the favour by unzipping his fly to let him spring free. He was on board a runaway train now. Even though he wanted to enjoy the sights, he was eager to get to the final destination. As he contemplated how to delay the journey, Jessica hopped on board and took control. With her arms around his neck, her legs hooked to his hips, she anchored herself to his erection.

Rob shuddered, fighting the instant gratification as they forged their bodies together. Jessica groaned into his ear and almost finished it then and there. He stilled inside her, adjusting to the tight heat taking hold of him, before he moved again. He backed her against the kitchen worktop, resting her butt on the edge so he had her where he wanted her.

With Jessica clinging to him like a second skin, he drove into her and found his sanctuary. Every thrust drew a gasp, pulling him closer to the edge of sanity. He'd denied himself so long, he gorged on this feeling of fulfilment without respite.

She raked her nails over his scalp, riding his demons

out with him. She seemed to gauge what it was he needed, what this meant, and kept pace until he was hurtling to the finish line. Rob's breath came in pants as the pressure built up inside him to bring this to an end. She clenched her inner muscles around him, squeezing him into immediate surrender. He poured inside her, releasing all of his frustration in a primal scream. Although he might repent his actions at a later date, for now Rob didn't have a care in the world.

CHAPTER SIX

JESSICA MADE IT back to solid ground on shaky legs and adjusted her shirt to at least cover her top half. Rob had literally taken her breath away. Although she'd always had an inkling of that fire behind the ice, she'd never expected him to be *so* impulsive, *so* hot-blooded. Everything about this was reckless and wild and everything she'd wanted to get out of her system. The trouble was, she couldn't wait to stoke the flames of passion again. Now she knew how great they could be together, once would never be enough for her. The spontaneity of what had just happened showed that he genuinely desired her above all else at this moment in time, but Jessica demanded proof that this was more than a temporary lapse of judgement on his part.

The doubt was already clouding his eyes as he rebuttoned his pants. She slapped his hand away.

'What the—'

'I'm not done with you yet.' She hooked a finger into his waistband and pulled him close for a lazy kiss.

'No?'

'We agreed on one night. One *full* night.'

She led him towards the door, in search of that elusive bedroom. Rob stopped in the doorway, a dead weight she couldn't hope to move without his cooperation. She knew he was debating whether or not to follow.

'If this is a one-time deal, we really ought to make the most of it. Don't you think?' She spoke softly so as not to spook him. One wrong move and this would be over before she even got him naked.

Rob unhooked her finger and took her hand in his. 'Then what are we waiting for?'

Brass bands heralded her triumph, white doves soared into the sky, and the sun broke through the gloom with the news. Jessica had definitely got her groove back on and she couldn't wait to dance the night away with her sexy new lover.

Now the initial frenzy had passed they faced each other across the vast expanse of Rob's king-sized bed in awkward silence. She was worried they'd lose momentum if they had too much time to think about what they were doing. Her hands trembled as she removed what little there was left of her clothes. Standing here naked before him was different from getting frisky still half dressed. She didn't have her pretty clothes to express her femininity for her. She was leaving herself open to scrutiny and Rob wasn't just a random hook-up she wouldn't see again. It mattered what he thought of her. She wanted him to want her.

When it came to getting value for money, she knew she was getting a good deal. Rob worked out, a lot. From his rounded biceps to his sinewy thighs, and everything in between, he was built for pleasure. She looked forward to uncovering every toned inch.

'Heels on or off?' She strode over to him with her hands on her hips, exuding a confidence she worked damn hard to convey. The business she was in had taught her to hide any weakness beneath a layer of bravado. Her body had let her down in the past and there was no better way to hide her insecurities than to strut around in nothing but a pair of shoes.

'Definitely on.' He made a guttural sound as he all but rugby tackled her onto the bed. Jessica shrieked, secretly delighted he found her visual stimulation irresistible. With Rob covering her body entirely with his, she was able to relax a little, but there was definitely an air of born-again virgin as she lay beneath him. It had been a while since she'd slept with anyone, never mind someone she'd swapped personal sob stories with. It brought the emotional element to intimacy she usually did her best to avoid. She arched up off the bed, keen to quieten that wounded part of her, and embraced this for what it was. A night to remember.

Each movement she made brought their bodies together. Not close enough. This time she wanted the full skin-on-skin experience. In seconds, she'd stripped him bare to see and feel the full evidence of his arousal pressed against her. There was no greater aphrodisiac for her than a hunky man who made her feel desirable. More than that, lying here beneath Rob, she could stop pretending to be anything more than she was. He knew almost all of her secrets—the ones that mattered for now.

He kissed her—a long, languid seduction of her mouth, promising a more thorough exploration of her body this time around. Something which made her shiver with anticipation and trepidation. Would he still find her this sexy if he knew her illness had taken away a vital part of her femininity?

'What about protection?' The irony of Rob's raspy request brought Jessica's tears closer to the surface.

She had to swallow them down before she could answer him. This was a chance to tell him the truth but she didn't want to start another discussion about her tragic history and break the mood. It was only supposed to be a casual hook-up designed to break the sexual tension between them once and for all. Not a proposal of marriage and an expectation she could give him babies.

'I've got it covered,' she said with a smile to hide her heartache. If it wasn't for her infertility, she might have fostered the notion she could have more than a one-night stand with someone like Rob.

He lifted his head to grin back at her before starting to kiss his way down her body again. Goosebumps popped along her skin with every feather-light touch of his lips. She didn't want to hold on to any of her baggage when he was intent on making her fantasies come true. He reached up to cup her breast in his large hand, rolling her nipple into a tight peak between his thumb and finger. Jessica had to bite her lip to stop from crying out as he dipped his head and drew the sensitive tip into his warm mouth. He trailed his tongue over her, flicking and teasing until she was bucking off the mattress like a wild thing.

For tonight, at least, her body was his to command. His mouth never left her as he made his way further down the bed, scorching a trail of wet kisses along her torso. As he manoeuvred himself between her legs and dared even lower, Jessica could no longer think of anything except her own desires.

He licked the seam of her womanhood and parted her with his tongue, her liquid arousal rushing to meet him. With every lick and swirl he demanded her climax until she complied, her cries echoing through the quiet house as that all-encompassing bliss claimed her. Only when he'd drawn the final aftershocks of her release did he replace his tongue with his equally breathtaking erection.

Rob braced himself on the bed with one arm either side of her and moved slowly inside her. He was already trembling with restraint, since the intensity of her orgasm had almost claimed him too. Now every one of his senses was heightened, every nerve ending zinging with energy as they forged together. He was lost to her heat, her sexiness and this amazing feeling of being alive. Despite their mutual agreement that this was nothing more than sex, somewhere in the back of his mind he knew this was wrong. Thankfully, carnal instinct kept it at bay.

She was hugging his waist with her thighs as she rode with him, punctuating every stroke with an erotic moan. Driving him to the point of madness. His thoughts, his whole being belonged entirely to her in that moment.

She clenched her inner muscles around him, hastening him towards that glorious peak of complete satisfaction. A roar was ripped from his soul with his final release, so powerful and strong it shook him to the very core. This was more than sex; he'd held nothing back as he'd made love to Jessica and he had no clue what that meant for the future. All he did know was that this euphoria wouldn't last. Not when they had to face real life tomorrow as a busy doctor and TV producer, only thrown together under temporary circumstances.

He lay down beside her and placed a kiss on her lips, thankful that she'd helped him to spend time in the here and now. For a while, at least.

'Are you okay? You're very quiet.' She was frowning at him and he knew he'd spent too long in his own head. It wasn't very gentlemanly of him to be thinking of anything other than the amazing time they'd just shared. The urge to flog himself with birch branches and repent his sins could wait until her side of the bed was cold again.

'You've worn me out, that's all.' He reached across and stroked his thumb against her cheek, keen to maintain some physical contact lest they broke the spell too soon.

'Do you want me to go so you can get some rest?' She sat up, trying to cover her nakedness with the sheet they were both tangled in. Her skin was flushed, her hair mussed from their exertions and her eyes wide with either fear or uncertainty. This had shaken her as much as him.

If they were to stick to their agreement, there should be no cause for panic. They could take things at their own pace. There'd be plenty of time for him to over-analyse tonight's events when she was gone. All he wanted now was for his mind to be at peace with his body.

'There's no need to rush off. I can drop you off later. Unless you'd rather go?' He didn't know if she preferred to cut and run but, given the choice, he'd rather lie with her awhile longer.

'No, I… As long as it's okay with you?'

'I'm enjoying the company.' Rob patted the pillow beside him, so she lay back down and cushioned her soft curves against him. He sighed. It was nice to have something other than ghosts to share his bed.

'I don't usually do this.' She almost whispered the secret into his chest. As if they were doing something illicit.

'What? Sleep with colleagues? Hang around after

sex? Snuggle?' He buried his smile in her cloud of red hair. There was no way he was going to judge her for falling into bed with him when they'd both acted on the same impulse.

'All of the above. You're covering a lot of firsts for me.' She placed her hand on his chest and he could feel her relax against him again.

Her admission flashed up warning signs that this was moving somewhere Rob wasn't ready to go. In a lot of ways it was already too late. 'This is new to me too.'

His love life didn't usually extend beyond hotel rooms and the rare time he did bring someone home, he certainly didn't encourage them to stay. It already changed the dynamics when he already knew he'd be seeing this bed partner every day until the end of the month. They might as well enjoy this for what it was.

'Don't worry. I meant it when I said I wasn't in the market for anything serious. I've been there. Still have the wedding dress hanging in the closet.'

'We have so much in common.' Rob deliberately made her laugh. The split from her boyfriend had obviously been more serious than he'd first thought. Another good reason they'd established boundaries before taking things further. He was never going to be the man who could repair her heart when he was still trying to piece his own back together. Although he and Jessica were both officially single, it would seem they were still married to their pasts.

'So I can lie here without worrying you've got the wrong impression?' Jessica traced her finger around his nipple and reminded him of the real reason they were here. Sheer heat.

'I promise I have no plans for *us* beyond right now.' Rob grabbed hold of the hand teasing him back to full strength and rolled over to pin Jessica to the bed with both wrists.

She was wide-eyed and panting beneath him. 'Then we really shouldn't waste what little time we have left.'

The alien buzz of an alarm clock ripped Rob from the arms of the deepest slumber. Any other morning he was awake before it had the chance to blare out its air-raid warning of daylight approaching. He attempted to roll over and switch it off but he still had a naked Jessica sleeping on his chest. Enthusiastic lovemaking had apparently cured his insomnia. He would include that in the pro column for sleeping with her when the doubts started to creep in.

His first instinct should've been to shake her awake and get her out of here as soon as possible. Neither of them had intended for her to spend the night. He'd underestimated how much it would mean to have her in his bed when he wasn't in a hurry to put an end to the dream. He closed his eyes again. An extra five minutes wouldn't hurt.

'What time is it?' Jessica mumbled against his skin, lost somewhere beneath her mass of wild curls.

His nether regions began to stir, reacting to the novelty of a naked woman in the bed.

'Playtime?' He ran his hand along her spine and down to cup her butt cheek.

Jessica leaned over his chest to peer at the clock. 'As much as I'd love to, we both need to get to work.'

Rob nuzzled her neck and did his best to persuade her otherwise. Once they got up, the fantasy was over and they had to return to the real world. Coming back to an empty bed tonight was going to be even harder than usual.

Jessica curled around him, rubbing herself provoca-
tively along his outer thighs, and plucking his nipple to
attention. 'I don't have a change of clothes.'

'You really don't need any.' He palmed her breast,
hungry for more than his porridge this morning.

'I think it might cause a bit of a stir if I turned up in
last night's clothes.'

Rob wrenched his gaze from her rosy peaks to the
rumpled clothes lying on a heap on his floor. 'You've
got a point.'

There was also the reminder of her standing in his
kitchen wearing *only* that shirt every time he saw her
in it. It definitely wasn't work safe, for either of them.

'I have to go.' At least she said it with great reluc-
tance as their one-night-only performance came to an
end.

'I'll take you home. As soon as I'm wide awake.' Rob
pulled the covers over their heads. He had no intention
of leaving this bed until they'd said goodbye properly.

Jessica imagined all eyes were on her as she did the
walk of shame through the doors, late for the first time
ever. True to his word, Rob had given her a lift home.
However, he'd also insisted on waiting for her. By the
time she'd showered, succumbed to Rob's suggestion of
one more 'last time' in the shower and changed, there
was no way of her making it in time to work.

'I had to make a few follow-up calls,' she mumbled
as she passed through the gallery. No one bothered to
question her and, since she was the one always pulling
overtime, she figured she was entitled to a bit of leeway.

The paperwork was piled up on her desk but her
brain was mush. The perks of her position here meant
she could position herself anywhere in the building

without having to give a detailed explanation. She wanted time out to think over what had happened last night, and this morning. Everything else could wait. It was on her head if this project failed and she would pick up the slack when she was in a better frame of mind. A coffee and a seat in the waiting room would give her some space. The people in there were too preoccupied with their own problems to take hers under their notice.

Sleeping with Rob had been all she'd expected, and more. Their verbal contract that it was a one-time deal could do with a few amendments. The evening had meant so much to her on a personal level she was reluctant to end it there. More than the self-confidence she'd gained from how much Rob had wanted her, she'd also had fun. So consumed was she by her distrust of men, and her own insecurities, she'd forgotten what it was to simply have someone to laugh and spend time with. Since Rob had technically made the first move, it seemed they'd both abandoned their hang-ups in the heat of the moment and taken a giant leap forward. Unfortunately, if he was now primed and ready to move back onto the market, someone other than her was probably going to reap the benefits.

While she wanted him to crawl out from his well of sorrow into her arms, there was no way she could compete with the memory of his wife. A man like Rob was always going to want the whole package. That house was waiting for the wife who'd have dinner waiting on the table every night, and a tribe of overexcited kids to greet him at the door. She already hated the woman he was going to fall in love with.

It was her own fault for being greedy. She'd got what she wanted, only to find it wasn't enough. That one night would haunt her for ever—knowing she was so close to happiness, only for her useless body to spoil everything again.

She stepped into the lift and punched the button for the restaurant floor. If she was going to cry into her coffee, she deserved something that didn't taste like tar.

A thick forearm shot through the metal doors before they could close. She couldn't even have two minutes of self-pity without interference. Resisting the urge to keep pushing the button, she plastered on a smile for whoever was about to join her.

'Hi,' accompanied Rob's sudden appearance.

'Hi, yourself.' So full of angry thoughts at herself and a woman she'd never know, she kept her gaze firmly ahead. She didn't trust herself to act like a grown-up around him and pretend last night had never happened.

The lift doors closed and sealed her inside the steel box with Rob. She could sense his eyes on her as the lift whirred into life.

'I'm sorry if I made you late this morning.' As soon as he acknowledged what they'd been up to only a short time ago, all bets were off.

'It was worth it.' Jessica turned to meet his gaze and, in that instant, the heat was back. They flew at each other in a tangle of limbs and mouths, as if they'd never made it out of bed.

She gave an inward sigh as he pulled her close. This lapse wouldn't help untangle her thoughts about him but it was exactly where she wanted to be. With temperatures reaching critical levels, they broke apart.

'We shouldn't be doing this at work.' Rob took a step back and scrubbed his hands over his scalp, mussing his dark locks to give him back that bed-hair look. It wasn't helping to put last night out of her mind.

'Did you have somewhere else in mind?' They'd

seriously underestimated the difficulty they'd have keeping their hands off each other now they'd shared naked time together. If he was intent on imposing a restraining order on close body contact, he should really stop seeking her out. And find a different topic of conversation.

Rob coughed, trying to clear the cotton wool suddenly lodged in his throat. From the minute he'd left her at the hospital entrance that morning, he'd been craving another fix. Far from getting closure on this thing he had for her, their liaison had increased his appetite. Life had to go on, and he would do it one step at a time. So far, Jessica had made no demands on him. He was the one obsessed with commitment and the havoc it could cause.

'Last night. Could we do it again?' This concept was so alien to him he'd apparently lost the power of coherent sentences.

Jessica arched an eyebrow. 'What happened to your one-night rule?'

Sticky sweat moulded his shirt to his back as his comfort zone disappeared into the distance. 'We had a good time, didn't we?'

'Yes. Does this mean you want us to keep on seeing each other?'

'The next few weeks are going to be hell if I can't touch you after what we shared last night.' Even now, watching those amber flecks blazing to life in her eyes, he was fighting a losing battle with his libido.

'I did think you were being quite stingy with your idea of a fling. It should at least last as long as a girl is in town. Say, another two weeks?' Jessica moved closer and toyed with his top button.

He swallowed hard as it popped open at her behest,

replaying the moment last night when the spark between them had exploded into a fireball of lust. 'We'll have all the benefits of being in a relationship without any of the drama of trying to make it as a couple.'

'You want us to carry on seeing each other?'

'I thought since we had fun last night and neither of us wants a commitment, we could keep this going until you finish filming here. If you want?' It was the perfect set-up, as far as he could see. All the benefits of being in a relationship without any of the drama of trying to make it as a couple.

'You mean by day we'll be working together, acting every inch the professionals we are, and by night... horizontal deviants.' Jessica's wink as she approved his plan sent the temperature, and his pulse, soaring once more. Rob really needed this lift to hurry up before they were both sacked for gross misconduct.

'Yes, we'll need to make sure we keep our professional and personal lives separate from now on. No more of these clandestine meetings.' He was saying the words but as he dipped his head to claim her mouth again he knew he was becoming seriously addicted to the danger.

CHAPTER SEVEN

ROB RESISTED THE urge to kiss Jessica when he met her in the car park. They were still technically on hospital grounds, which they'd deemed a no-go area since this afternoon.

They'd had a close call in the lift when the doors had opened mid-clinch to a group of elderly women who were thankfully too occupied with finding their car park ticket to notice. By conducting their affair at work, they were taking too great a risk of getting caught in a compromising position. Neither of them wanted to jeopardise their career for a fling which would be over before they changed the specials menu in the canteen. Instead, they'd reached the mature decision to wait until they'd clocked off before they dared touch each other again.

'I'm sorry if I've kept you hanging around all night. We had a new patient arrive with an aggressive stage three tumour, so we had to admit him straight away. In hindsight, I probably should've let you know so we could reschedule.' Timing was everything with these cases and cancer didn't take a night off simply because Rob had a beautiful woman waiting for him.

'Don't worry about it. I know you don't work a typical nine-to-five job. We were doing a follow-up with Cal and his family at home, so we've been off-site most of the day anyway.' Jessica's easy acceptance was probably because she worked similar fluid hours. That suited this no-strings arrangement but it also reiterated why it wouldn't work long-term between them. At some point he might want to settle down again and that would be next to impossible with two people who were slaves to their careers.

'How's he doing?' It wasn't often he got to find out about his patients in between hospital visits. Usually it was bad news if he saw them once they'd had the all-clear.

'Tired, but happy to be home. He had quite a fan club waiting to see him.' Jessica pulled out her mobile phone to show him a few photographs she'd taken of Cal with his mostly female friends.

'As long as he takes it easy.' He handed the phone back, his curiosity satisfied.

'Oh, he has an army of willing volunteers waiting on him hand and foot,' she said with a grin.

Now that Rob knew something of Jessica's background, he could understand the personal interest she was taking in the patient stories and how much their recovery meant to her as well as him.

He noticed Jessica shiver. Although the evening sun was shining, there was a definite nip in the air. Her floral strappy dress was pretty but scant protection from the Northern Irish weather.

'You're cold. We should get going.' There was no point freezing their bits off outside when they could be turning the heat up elsewhere. Preferably naked.

They made their way across the car park, the companionable silence punctuated by his growling stomach.

Jessica sniggered as they got into the car. 'I guess I'm not the only one who forgets to eat from time to time.'

'I hold my hands up to being foolish and missing lunch. Although, if memory serves, I was distracted on my way to the canteen this afternoon.' He leaned across to claim the prize he'd been waiting for all day. Unfortunately, as his mouth met Jessica's, his stomach protested again at being denied sustenance.

'You need food,' she murmured against his lips.

'I need you,' he insisted, deepening the kiss.

Another rumble.

'Right. That's it. We're making a pit stop for food on the way to your house.' Jessica resisted further overtures until he agreed.

'Okay. I'm sure we can manage that.' As long as it didn't interfere with their previously arranged plans, he was happy to grab some takeaway. He'd been reluctant to suggest dinner himself and take her to a more salubrious establishment in case it could be misconstrued as a date. They'd agreed to keep things purely physical to avoid any unpleasantness when it was time for Jessica to move on. Fast food was the perfect compromise.

'Good. You're going to need all the energy you can get.' There was a wicked glint in Jessica's eye, prompting Rob to get the engine started.

Tonight he had every reason to get home as soon as possible.

The steady rhythm of the car on the motorway played a lullaby for Jessica as she rested her head against the window and closed her eyes. Despite her best intentions, she was beginning to flag. They'd opted to sit in rather than take cold burgers and fries home and her full belly coupled with the long day was calling her towards sleep. Perhaps if she rested her eyes for five minutes she could recharge her batteries before the big night ahead.

'Jessica. We're here.'

'Mmm?' She heard Rob's voice calling her back to consciousness and struggled to open her eyes.

'You're home.'

When she was finally able to focus, it was to find they were parked outside her apartment block. 'What's going on?'

'You're clearly exhausted. We can do this another time.'

Jessica was wide awake at once. She'd promised him so much and let him down. 'Honestly, that was just a power nap. I'll jump in the shower, then I'm all yours.' She gave him her brightest, peppiest smile and prayed it was enough to convince him to stay.

Rob switched the engine off and she knew he was getting ready to see her off when he didn't take the keys out of the ignition.

'It's okay. I'm knackered too. Perhaps we overdid it last night. I think four times is a record for me and you can have too much of a good thing, you know.'

'Never. And, actually, it was five times, counting the shower. I think we were making up for lost time.' The thought that this wasn't a regular occurrence for him gave her some comfort. Not only did it mean she wasn't in competition with past lovers but that level of physical activity had clearly taken its toll. It would be impossible to repeat that on a nightly basis and function at work the morning after. Still, this wasn't the end to the evening she'd anticipated. She'd enjoyed having someone to talk to and lie next to as much as the sex.

'In that case, you've probably seen all my moves now anyway.'

'That doesn't necessarily mean I don't want to see them again soon. Won't you come inside with me?' She wouldn't beg him to stay, since that would make her look needy and fell outside the boundaries they'd drawn up. Although it would save her bruised ego if he did. Regardless of their pact, it was only human nature to be wanted for more than sex. Especially when even that had let her down in the past. What had there been to keep Adam when she'd lost interest in that too? Without children or passion, there'd been absolutely no reason for him to stay. They'd both known it. At least now she'd recovered part of what made her a woman, if not all of it.

'I'll see you to the door but I think we should call it a night before we burn ourselves out. We can pick up where we left off another time.' Rob had his seat belt off and was out of the car but there was no trace of anger or frustration at the change of plans. She wasn't used to a mature response in such circumstances.

'I guess I'll see you tomorrow, then.' She accepted her fate with a sigh as she rummaged in her bag for her keys on the doorstep.

''Night.' Rob leaned in and kissed her pouting lips.

It was amazing how revitalising one touch from this man could be, her body now fully alert. She dropped her bag so she could wrap her arms around his neck and pull him ever closer. Rob responded with two hands on her backside, turning this from a goodnight kiss to a lot more.

'We should take this inside before we really give the neighbours something to talk about.' She wasn't in the habit of snogging men on her doorstep and she could do without the inevitable 'Who's your boyfriend?' questions if they were spotted. There was no way of adequately explaining their arrangement to the well-meaning marrieds around here keen to see her partnered off too.

'I'm still not staying,' he mumbled stubbornly against the back of her neck as she opened the door. They practically fell into her ground floor apartment, giggling like a couple of teenagers. She was glad they seemed to have got their second wind, because she really didn't fancy a night on her own blaming herself for his absence.

'I'm going to grab that shower. You make yourself comfortable in the living room.' After a day trekking across the city for interviews, she wanted to freshen up. Stalling things for a little while might keep him here for longer than another fumble in her hallway too.

Rob groaned as she levered herself off him and headed towards the bathroom. 'Make it quick.'

She took longer than she normally would have under the lukewarm water for the simple reason she'd expected him to join her. Only when the temperature of the water dropped to gasping point did she admit defeat and turn off the shower. Teeth chattering and her skin turning a delicate shade of blue, she wrapped herself in a towel and went in search of her errant lover.

A quick check on her bedroom confirmed he wasn't lying naked on her bedclothes with a rose between his teeth either. He must've literally taken her at her word and stayed put in the living room. That would teach her to be coy about what she wanted in future.

Instead of the numerous romantic scenarios she'd envisaged of her man waiting for her, she found Rob had made himself a tad too comfortable.

'You've got to be kidding me.'

He'd left his jacket neatly folded over the arm of the chair, kicked off his shoes and was currently stretched out on her sofa, sleeping. She couldn't be cross with him when he looked so at home and so damn beautiful lying there. His lips parted on a soft snore, and the open top button of his charcoal-grey shirt was an invitation to get up close and personal.

She perched on the edge of the sofa and brushed a lock of hair from his face. His long dark eyelashes began to flutter as she touched him and she was almost sorry for disturbing him.

'Lie down with me,' he muttered without opening his eyes.

'My hair's still wet.'

'It'll dry.' He turned on his side to give her more room. Spooning was her weakness.

She snuggled in beside him. It was an age since she'd cuddled anything other than a cushion on this sofa. 'This is nice.'

'We don't have to do anything. I know you're tired.' Rob pulled the throw rug from the back of the sofa to cover them as he wrapped his arms around her.

'*I'm* the tired one?' She could already hear the change in his breathing as the past twenty-four hours caught up with him too.

'Shh. Go to sleep.' He buried his head against her neck and Jessica soon found herself following his command.

Rob wakened sometime in the early hours with a cramp in his leg and Jessica's hair in his face. It was far from an ideal place to sleep and yet there was a sense of peace lying here he was reluctant to abandon. With Jessica in his arms, there was no pain, or death or sorrow, only contentment. Unfortunately, her company was only a temporary solution to his problem and he suspected her departure would only serve to double his sense of loss.

The sound of birdsong outside burst the cosy bubble, signifying a new day and more firsts. It was unheard of for him to spend the night at a woman's home, never mind enjoy two consecutive evenings with the same one. By limiting liaisons to hotel rooms or a maximum of one night at his place, he maintained some control over proceedings. Those safety measures apparently went out of the window whenever he was with Jessica. This spontaneity was all well and good for a passionate affair but he hoped he wouldn't live to regret bending the rules for her. A sleepover at hers suggested a commitment he wasn't willing to give long-term.

Perhaps he could exercise some damage control by leaving before she woke. He shifted into an upright position and let Jessica fall back into his place. The blanket slipped onto the floor, leaving her in nothing but a skimpy towel. It would be so easy to simply tuck it back around her and walk away but he couldn't do that without coming off as a complete heel. At least if she wakened in her own bed it would show her he cared about her even if he couldn't stay.

He scooped her up into his arms and carried her to the bedroom, only her little moan against his chest indicating he'd disturbed her sleep. The towel came loose as he manoeuvred her under the covers and he made the decision to strip it away completely. It probably hadn't been the wisest move in the world to let her sleep in the wet fabric in the first place.

She was so serene lying there, scrubbed free of make-up with no glamorous clothes to hide behind. He understood why she dressed up even when she was so naturally beautiful. It was her way of protecting herself and covering her pain. She used cosmetics the way he used his position to maintain a certain distance from people but it must've been doubly difficult to keep the details of her illness hidden when she was usually so emotionally available.

He let out a yawn and checked his watch. There were still a few hours before he had to go to work. The bed looked a lot more appealing than the sofa. Jessica was naked. His shirt was damp from where she'd lain against him.

Suddenly he couldn't think of a single reason why he *shouldn't* strip off and climb in beside her.

'I thought you weren't staying.' Jessica curled into his side the second he joined her under the bed sheets.

'Temptation was just too great,' he said, running his hand over her shoulder and down to the curve of her waist.

Per their agreement, he didn't share the part about how she made him forget everything painful in his life when he was with her. He thought the first night he'd slept right through had been a fluke, simple exhaustion after their rigorous bedroom workout. Last night had challenged that perception. Fully clothed and in cramped conditions, he'd slept peacefully, free from nightmares and guilt. Jessica was the only common factor on both occasions. It would be telling if he noted any changes once he reverted to sleeping alone. Not that he was anxious to do that any time soon. Especially when there was a beautiful naked woman currently demanding his attention.

'How did we end up here, anyway?' The sheet slipped as she yawned and stretched, giving a tantalising glimpse of her full breasts. If she wasn't already snuggling back under the covers, he would've sworn she'd done it on purpose to make sure he didn't go anywhere.

Since they were both wide awake now with plenty of time to kill, it would be silly not to take advantage of the situation. He let his hand drift across her flat stomach and down towards her soft mound.

'I thought we might be more comfortable.' Although he was becoming anything but as his libido rose with the lark.

'And we're naked because…' She gasped as he slid a finger into her wet channel, and responded by raking her nails across his chest. It was an action he'd come to learn was a sign she was enjoying everything he was doing.

'I thought we might be more comfortable.'

'You're…so…thoughtful,' she said through panting breaths.

'I know.'

She was writhing against him, every stroke apparently bringing her closer to the brink. Rob threw the quilt over his head and burrowed down the bed, drawing a shriek of delight from Jessica.

He'd show her exactly how thoughtful he could be.

Two weeks into their fling and Rob still couldn't seem to get enough of Jessica. Even though they'd only parted a matter of hours ago at the hospital doors he was counting down the minutes until they could be alone again. She was a little ray of sunshine in the dark corridors every time she flitted past in her bright yellow outfit. A playsuit she'd called it and his thoughts were definitely playful when he caught sight of her long slim legs in the short all-in-one and strappy gold sandals.

He whistled the happy tune of a man secure in the

knowledge she was coming home with him at the end of the night.

'Someone's in a good mood.' Maria met him outside the door of the day unit.

'The sun is shining, I'm about to send one of my patients home...what's not to be happy about?'

'Hmm. It's just not...you. What's even weirder is I just passed Jessica humming that very same song.' She eyed him as if he'd been caught with his hand in the cookie jar.

'We must've been listening to the same radio station this morning.' It wasn't a lie. They'd both been rocking out to the same nineties music channel at the top of their voices in his car on the way to work. It turned out she was as bad a singer as he was, but equally enthusiastic.

'For goodness' sake, will you put me out of my misery and tell me you've finally made a move on her? Honestly, there's only so many meaningful glances a person can try to ignore.' Maria heaved a sigh as she waited for his confession.

His defences automatically shot up to protect his personal business from prying eyes, but Maria was his friend and invested far more than she should be in his love life. There seemed no point in denying it when he had nothing to be ashamed of.

'We're seeing each other but don't go buying a hat for the wedding. She's only here until the end of the month, remember?' Their relationship and this temporary high had an expiry date which would creep up on them before they knew it. He should mark out a chart or something to make sure he didn't forget.

'And what? You can drive from one side of this country to the other in a few hours. I'm sure you could still see her if you wanted.'

'I'm well aware of that but we've agreed this is for the best. You should be happy I'm having a bit of fun.'

Maria unfolded her arms and shrugged. It obviously wasn't what she wanted to hear but she was wise enough not to make another comment on the situation. They would never agree on what was best for him when she didn't know the circumstances which had brought him to Northern Ireland in the first place.

He followed her into the day unit and nodded hello to each of the patients receiving treatment. The oncology nurses were the ones who administered the chemotherapy drugs here once he'd devised the treatment plans. They were more than capable of removing the Hickman lines which were used for intravenous medicine and taking blood, when treatment ended. But he preferred to do this part himself when he could. That way he'd seen his patients through their illness from start to finish. It could be the most rewarding part of his job, performing this procedure when it meant the immediate threat to a child's life was over.

Maria was already in the cubicle with the ten-year-old girl and her mother waiting to be released from his care.

'I just need to check we have Katie Daniels, whose birthdate is the twenty-eighth of March here, in case I'm about to send the wrong person home?' He brought a nervous giggle from the child as she confirmed her details.

It wasn't until he went over her records again and saw those letters—ALL—he made the connection with Jessica. She would've been around the same age when acute lymphoblastic leukaemia had struck her too. He was eternally grateful for the fellow oncologist who'd saved her life. It proved to him how important his role here was for his patients and their families.

After he checked Katie's full blood count and clotting results were satisfactory he took off his wedding ring and gave his hands a thorough wash.

'Okay, Katie, I'm sure you'll be glad to know we're going to remove your Hickman line today.'

She bit her lip as she nodded but her mother's relief was more audible at having treatment come to an end.

'It's a relatively quick procedure. All you should feel are a few scratches when I numb the area around the line and some pressure as I remove it. You can stop me at any time if you're uncomfortable but it should all be over in a few minutes. Okay?' No matter how much he reassured her, it was only natural that she remained wary. He was glad when her mother reached over to take her hand to support her.

'I'm going to raise the head of the bed so you're more comfortable.' It also made it easier for him to access the site.

Maria stepped forward to lower Katie's hospital gown to expose her central line. Rob gently manipulated the tube so he could observe where the skin puckered and find the internal cuff holding it in place. He washed his hands again before donning sterile gloves and pulling a gown on over his blue scrubs.

He cleaned the area around the cuff carefully with copious amounts of disinfectant to create a sterile field and covered her chest with a sterile sheet, leaving just the site visible.

'I'm going to ask you to turn your head to the side and look at Mummy and so we keep the area clean we need to make sure you don't reach up and touch anything.

'Have you got anything planned to celebrate later?' he asked, trying to distract her from what he was doing.

'We're going to have a wee party at home,' Mrs Daniels replied as he drew up the local anaesthetic into the needle.

'My patients are always glad to see the back of me. I hope it's nothing personal.'

'You can come to my party if you want,' Katie said with her head still turned away as instructed.

'That's very sweet of you, Katie, but I'm happy just to know you're getting better. Now, you're going to feel those sharp scratches I told you about. If you want me to stop, you only have to call out.'

She nodded again and Rob could see her squeezing her mum's hand tighter.

He injected the anaesthetic in several areas around the cuff, careful not to hit the central line. Katie flinched when he broke the skin the first time but remained silent.

'I hope there'll be plenty of presents for you at this party too.' He stalled, waiting for the anaesthetic to take effect before he continued.

'I'm getting a puppy.' Katie's voice was positively shrill with excitement at the news. Although her mother was rolling her eyes at the idea, Rob knew from experience that the parents often promised their kids anything to help them through recovery.

'That's the best present ever. He'll be good company for you.' He lifted a scalpel from the tray Maria had provided beside him and made a small incision to release the cuff from her body. With stitch holders, he bluntly dissected the cuff until he could see the shiny white catheter.

'I need you to count to three and then I want you to hold your breath. One, two, three.' Rob applied pressure to the site and gently pulled the line free as Katie held her breath. It was important there was no air trapped in her chest, so he kept the pressure on her neck for a while after she started breathing normally again to make sure everything was sound.

'That wasn't so bad, was it?'

'Is it over?'

'As soon as we get you cleaned up.' When he was satisfied there were no complications, he cleaned the area again, closed the insertion site with Steri-Strips and covered it with a dressing.

'Can I go home now?'

'We need you to rest here for a little while, then you can go home and put all of this behind you.' There was no point hanging around reliving what had happened to her when she had the rest of her life to look forward to. The irony of that sentiment wasn't lost to him as he pulled off his gloves and retrieved his wedding ring from the sink.

'Maria will keep an eye on you until you're ready to leave. Watch out for any tenderness or discharge around the wound over the next few days, but that's us finished.'

'Thank you, Doctor, for everything.'

'You're very welcome.' He shook hands with the grateful mother, his wedding band mocking him every time it caught the light.

As soon as he was out of the ward, he wrenched it off his finger to study it. It hadn't occurred to him to take it off in five years and he knew Jessica would never expect him to do it for her either. The more he stared at it, the more he thought it was tying him to the past. Whilst he was wearing it, he was still half of a couple which no longer existed.

In the eyes of the world he was unattached; indeed nothing in his actions indicated he was still a married man. He certainly wouldn't be sleeping with Jessica if that was the case. The ring was nothing more than his security blanket now, his way to keep people at a distance. Except for the next couple of weeks at least, he wanted Jessica as close as possible.

Before he changed his mind, he pulled out his wallet and slipped the ring in beside the precious family photograph he kept there. As tough as it was to admit it, the only way his heart could heal was to let Leah and Mollie go. He would always carry them with him but that didn't mean they were still here. It was time to move forward without them.

Jessica turned the pasta down to a simmer and stirred crème fraiche, chilli flakes and tomato and basil sauce into the chopped peppers and tender-stem broccoli in the pan. The chicken breasts were in the oven and the table was set for two. She wasn't sure she could call this a celebratory two-week anniversary dinner considering it meant they were already halfway through their time together but at least someone was finally making use of Rob's fancy kitchen.

When it had become obvious he wouldn't be leaving with her, he'd insisted on ordering her a taxi and handed her the keys to his house. They both wanted to spend what was left of the evening together.

She'd made a detour to grab the makings of dinner and throw a few of her things into an overnight bag. It would save a lot of hassle in the morning when they'd invariably end up running late. The pressure was off now they'd established the nature of their relationship, so they could stop pretending she had any intention of going home.

She heard his car pull up outside as she assembled her ingredients into one spicy dish.

'Something smells nice.' Rob slid his arms around her waist and nuzzled into her neck.

It took great effort not to respond to his touch when she'd been waiting for it all day but she didn't want all of her effort to go to waste if they gave in to their hunger for each other. 'I thought it was about time someone christened this cooker.'

'How very domesticated of you.'

'Don't panic. I'm not marking my territory or anything. I thought we could both do with a proper sit-down meal.' She quite enjoyed cooking but it always seemed a terrible waste of time doing it for one.

'I'm not complaining. You're welcome here any time.'

If only that were true and there wasn't a deadline looming. She was getting used to this idea of domestic bliss and they were altogether too comfortable together, in and out of the bedroom, for this to remain a meaningless fling. She knew it but she didn't care. It was too late to retreat now when the damage was already done. The idea of no longer being with him was too hideous to contemplate and she was in this deeper than she'd ever imagined possible. All she could do now was enjoy the ride while it lasted. There was no other option but to walk away at the end of filming or she'd end up reliving that nightmare of rejection. Her appetite seemed to disappear with every mouthful.

After dinner they moved over to the sofa, where she'd grown accustomed to cuddling into Rob's chest at the end of a hard-working day.

'One of my patients finished treatment today,' he said with obvious relief.

'That's wonderful news.' Until he'd come into her life she'd forgotten the good parts of being part of a couple—sharing their stories and letting the stresses of the day ebb away in each other's embrace. It was a simple act which could be taken for granted when there was someone to come to every night but one which would be greatly missed in an empty house. There was only a fortnight left of playing the happy couple, then it was back to reality.

'How was your day?'

'Not as good as yours, I'm afraid. We had some technical issues with the remote cameras, so we've lost today's outside footage. We'll have some continuity difficulties to iron out in the edits.' It was a headache she didn't need but one she was sure they'd overcome. She wasn't one to give up without a fight.

'My poor Jess.' He dropped a kiss on her forehead and she felt better already.

She threaded her fingers through his, her heart almost stopping when she found the groove where his wedding ring once resided. There were any number of reasons why he might've removed it. Perhaps he'd forgotten to put it back on after washing his hands or caught it on a door handle and mangled it out of shape. Maybe he'd accidentally sewn it inside a patient. Anything seemed more plausible than removing it because of her but she couldn't bring herself to ask him about it.

The significance of that last scenario would scare her to death and force her to finish this earlier than expected.

A change of clothes and a toothbrush no longer seemed like the biggest step in their relationship.

CHAPTER EIGHT

JESSICA STOPPED BY the noticeboard in the corridor as one of the fundraisers took a red marker to the scanner appeal barometer.

'Every little counts,' she said, colouring in a few extra squares to take the total to almost three-quarters of the way to their target.

'Hopefully, exposure from the documentary series will boost it even more.' Jessica wanted the filming to benefit the patients and families as well as tell their stories.

'Fingers crossed.'

Once the wielder of the felt pen walked away, Jessica studied the pictures pinned to the board, charting the progress of the fundraising. They'd held bake sales, car washes and charity auctions—with Rob playing a part in every one. His dedication to the cause was admirable and completely justified now she'd met so many of the children herself. They were also the reason she was here and she never wanted to lose sight of that. After the events of the past weeks, there was a definite possibility of that happening.

She and Rob had made each other late again this morning but she couldn't complain. That reckless passion was more in keeping with a sizzling, no-strings fling than getting cozy on the sofa every night. The let's-talk-about-our-day level of intimacy was a different story, a one-way ticket to heartbreak. At the end of the day, someone like Rob needed someone more than her. She should never forget that.

'We still have a long way to go.'

For a second she thought she'd imagined Rob's voice until he cast a shadow over her.

'What? Oh, yeah, the scanner. I'm sure you'll get there.' *See, your focus is totally screwed. You thought he was talking about you.*

'Are you signing up?' He tapped on the latest money-raising idea pinned to the board.

'A fun run? Me?' It was a daytime event but in which context did he expect her to attend? Friend? Lover? Colleague? If she declined, she sucked as a human being in every category.

'It'll probably end up as more of a sponsored walk but it'll still be fun. We're taking the trail in Tollymore Forest Park in County Down, hoping to make a day of it. You're welcome to join us.'

'Next Saturday? I'll have to see if I can arrange a crew to cover it.'

'Actually, I think I'd prefer if they weren't there.' Rob ruled out the easiest option for her to justify being there by taking away her safety net.

He was close enough for her to see that he hadn't had time to shave this morning. The sight of his stubble and the memory of it grazing against her skin as they made each other late for work reminded her why it was dangerous for them to be alone together. She shivered in his shadow.

'We'll see' was all she would commit to for now.

'These might help make up your mind for you. I

forgot to give them to you last night.' He produced a gift bag from behind his back and a wave of panic washed over her.

'You didn't have to do that.' She had avoided the present-giving stage of relationships for a long time and took the bag between thumb and forefinger as though she'd somehow catch commitment from it. *That way madness lies.* At least that was what she told herself when she had only her mother to exchange gifts with over birthdays and major holidays.

'I know. Just open it.'

She held the package at arm's length while she opened it in case it exploded into a confetti of hearts and flowers. It was too heavy for jewellery or chocolates, and not tall enough for a wine bottle. A peek inside found a pair of trainers nestled in pink crêpe paper.

'What the hell…?' She pulled out a shoe in case the surprise was stuffed inside, but no, this was the actual gift he couldn't wait to give her.

'I can't stand seeing you in pain at the end of the night, after hobbling around in those heels all day. You should give your feet a rest every now and then.' He took the glittery pink footwear from her to display it in his hand with his best game show host flair.

'Thank you.' One pair of trainers bought with the welfare of her feet in mind suddenly became the most thoughtful gift in the world. And the scariest. Things were progressing too quickly to remain casual but she didn't want to quit him.

'And now you have an excuse to wear them.' He looked so pleased with himself, Jessica couldn't disappoint him by refusing them.

As she watched him walk away, she only wished

she had something more than long working hours and a dodgy medical history to offer him in return.

Despite her reservations, the glitzy footwear brought a smile to Jessica's face every time she donned them. At least the children approved of them, even if she'd received a few curious glances from her colleagues who were used to seeing her in more formal attire. A week's worth of shoe-focused attention was preferable to breaking in new trainers on a five-kilometre run and limping her way towards the finish line. That bit of forward planning ensured she was comfy in her own shoes as she started this race. At least, as comfortable as she could be standing in the middle of a forest dressed in a tutu.

She caught Rob sneaking another sideways glance at her.

'What?'

'I'm still surprised you dressed up and I definitely thought you'd be more of a glamorous princess than a sparkly fairy.' He shook his head as he assessed her choice of costume.

Jessica gave him a twirl so he got the full effect of her shimmering wings outside the confines of his car. She liked the fact that she could still surprise him even when they were virtually spending twenty-four hours together.

'Ball gowns and glass slippers aren't conducive to a hike in the country. Silver leggings, trainers and a pink tutu are much more suitable.' Today was about having fun and raising money; it wasn't a fashion contest.

'It's not like you to be practical.' He raised a dark eyebrow as he eyed her outfit again.

'I can do comfort when it's called for. I guess all of

that advice isn't completely wasted on me after all.' She tapped him on the head with her starry wand and danced ahead of him in the queue for their race numbers.

'Perhaps I should have worn the same?' He did a little shoe shuffle to show off the neon-pink leg warmers to go along with his eighties-themed outfit. Only the rucksack on his back, packed with medical supplies for emergencies, spoiled the look.

'I think you're rocking the Day-Glo singlet and Bermuda shorts perfectly well.' If he'd gone for the authentic tight white shorts, her heart might not have survived. She was having trouble enough not staring at his bulging biceps, never mind other protruding body parts.

'And I nearly forgot this—' He pulled a white headband from his bag to complete his ensemble and proved beyond doubt he had a sense of humour beneath the serious facade.

A lot of the staff had taken time over their costumes but there were a few whose ideas of fancy dress were based on novelty T-shirts. Jessica was glad Rob wasn't afraid to show off his fun side in public. It made him all the more endearing. As if healing sick children and catching fainting women wasn't enough.

They gave their names at the makeshift running station in the car park and received their numbers and route maps in return.

'You've got quite a turnout,' she remarked as they joined scores of people at the starting line.

'I recognise a lot of the faces too. There's a few of my old patients here with their families.' Rob grinned and waved over to everyone who caught his eye. It was obvious how delighted he was that they were far enough along in their recovery to take part. His big heart was one of the reasons she loved him.

She could try to fool herself that it wasn't true but all the signs were there. Why else would she spend every waking moment thinking about him and could no longer imagine sleeping anywhere but in his arms? Every layer she'd uncovered had made her fall harder and faster for Dr Robert Campbell.

The revelation was so great Jessica found herself sprinting away from it when they fired the starting pistol. She'd done the one thing she'd sworn not to and fallen in love. Now there was no way of getting out of this with her heart intact. Even if there was the slightest chance he could return the sentiment, there were too many hurdles for them to overcome. They would only be postponing the inevitable if they tried.

Twigs snapped beneath her feet as she tore up the ground in her bid to outrun the injustice of it all. She'd found someone who truly made her happy, someone she could be herself with, but there was still that skeleton lurking in her closet which would ultimately drive him away.

Before she could devise an escape plan, the object of her misplaced affection was speeding to her side.

'Hey, wait for me.'

'Sorry. My competitive instinct took over for a minute.' She slowed to a more realistic pace for a woman more chocolate bunny than gym bunny—one which didn't threaten to explode her lungs. Unfortunately, the deceleration didn't help regulate her thumping heart.

'Trust me, you're going to need to save that energy for the finish.' He gave her a wink and sped ahead, demonstrating his own competitive streak.

The track thinned out alongside a rocky stream, forcing them into single file and ending conversation between them. It gave her a chance to think about the consequences of her errant emotions, as well as ogle his backside.

She'd deliberately prevented him from staying at her house since that night to avoid this very situation. As if virtually moving into his would make any difference. In theory, setting time parameters was supposed to counteract such complications. In reality, feelings trumped everything.

Okay, so they travelled together to and from work when schedules allowed and they spent every night in bed together, but she hadn't planned this. What she did know was that he had permeated into every aspect of her life and it was going to be a Herculean task to remove all traces of him when she was expected to move on. Rob was part of her working day, as a doctor and confidante. At night, he was her companion and lover. And she didn't want to lose him in either capacity. This was exactly why she shouldn't have got attached from the start. They'd let emotion creep in where it had no business being, by nosing into each other's pasts.

Until this project began she hadn't entertained the idea of getting serious with another man. Adam had shattered her confidence and the belief that she could ever be enough for any man. Rob had showed her otherwise. At least on the surface. Now she was wondering if there was a way she could make this work with Rob. They were both single career people who so clearly enjoyed each other's company.

Although he was very good with the children, he hadn't made mention of a desire to have any of his own. It was entirely possible that Jessica had projected her insecurities onto him, making excuses for this relationship not to succeed beyond the length of the documentary shoot. For all she knew, he had issues of his own in that department. Perhaps he'd buried the idea of a family with his wife. Perhaps she should stop jumping ahead to the idea of marriage and children when he'd promised her nothing more than a few weeks in his bed. Even if they carried on, the spark between them could very well fizzle out before it reached the stage where it mattered.

There were only two ways she could see to deal with this serious breach of her heart and neither would necessarily end well for her. Either she could keep this new information to herself and pretend the end of the affair wouldn't crush her, or confess. Whilst she'd keep her fingers crossed that he could be prompted into declaring his undying love for her too, the likelier scenario was another rejection. He hadn't asked her to fall in love with him, never expressed an interest in extending their fling into an *actual* relationship. But if this was her last chance at having someone to grow old with, she would never forgive herself for walking away without a fight. Though he didn't know it, Rob held the key to her future happiness—a burden he might not be ready, or willing, to accept.

This new development in their courtship would change the dynamics between them for good. If she decided to share the news with him.

As the trail opened out again onto the forest floor, the throng of runners fanned out to create a colourful spectacle amongst the trees. The laughter and chatter of the group was a happy sound to behold, unless you were struggling to hear the decisions your subconscious was telling you to make. With a desire to be alone with her thoughts, she fell back from the crowd. She slowed to a walking pace and it wasn't long before Rob noticed.

'What's wrong, slowcoach? Are you admitting defeat already?' He was running back towards her, a vision in neon emerging from the dark woods. *Fit* in every sense of the word.

For fear of having to explain her sudden lack of commitment to the run, she doubled over and feigned injury. 'I think I've got a stitch.'

It wasn't a complete lie—there was definitely a sharp pain stabbing her insides that made her want to curl up into a ball. His face was a mask of concern as he jogged to her side, multiplying her level of guilt in the process.

'Take a few deep breaths and try to walk it off.' He fell too easily for the fib, enabling Jessica to keep the pretence going for a little while longer.

She straightened up with a grimace, making all the right groaning noises as she did so. Rob retrieved a water bottle from his backpack and instructed her to take a sip while they walked.

Whether it was a fake running injury or fainting from hunger, he was always there to catch her. Given his caring nature, he would probably show the same level of care for anyone in need, but he wasn't sharing his bed with them at night. Jessica had discovered for herself it wasn't so easy to keep love and lust separate at all times.

Her inner optimist held out hope that Rob's compassion would extend to all areas of her health problems. So he would understand her fertility issues, accept them and love her regardless. She was asking for the world.

Rob kept a close eye on Jessica as they made their way deeper into the forest towards the babbling stream. She was quieter than usual and he didn't think it was merely down to a stitch in her side. He'd seen her bounce back from worse than that. It wasn't like her to separate herself from the rest of the group either. Usually she would be right where he should be too—in the thick of things, keeping morale up. Not watching as the others disappeared into the trees. The imposed solitude hinted that she wanted to be alone with him for a reason and he wasn't about to complain. They'd grown so insular, cooped up at his place, it was nice to spend time together outdoors for a change.

With the documentary series beginning to wrap up Rob knew they were on borrowed time but he wasn't ready to say goodbye just yet. If there was a way they could keep on seeing each other when it ended, he would jump at the chance. He couldn't, didn't want to replace Leah and Mollie, but he couldn't stand the thought of losing Jessica either. Was five years of denying himself happiness punishment enough for his guilt, or should it remain a life sentence? Everyone else thought he'd been too harsh on himself but they weren't privy to all the facts. Jessica was the one person in whom he might be able to finally confide the truth. Her reaction would tell if he'd sufficiently served his time and they could see where this thing led them. He didn't want to throw away what he had with Jessica because he was afraid of being happy without Leah and Mollie.

He took the lead as they reached the crossing point of the river to scout out any hidden danger first. Although it wasn't necessary as Jessica skipped across the stepping stones after him like a woodland nymph. She was a shimmering light in the murky shadows of his world and he didn't want to be plunged back into darkness again once she was gone.

'Is everything okay?' he asked, holding out a hand to help her take the final leap.

'I'm feeling much better. Thank you, Doctor.' She fluttered her glittery eyelashes at him as she joined him on the riverbank and Rob couldn't resist moving in for a kiss.

Their lips met under the dappled shadows of the trees. The gentle swish of leaves in the breeze and the steady trickle of the stream serenaded them and created the perfect idyll for them to be together.

'I wish we could stay here for ever,' he whispered into her hair as he held her tight. He hadn't meant to say the words outside of his head but she didn't flinch at the sentiment. Everything seemed so easy here in each other's arms with nobody else to think about.

'Me too.' Her wistful sigh kept the dream alive as they rocked together for a little while longer.

Rob caught a flash of movement in the trees across the stream and the spell was broken. 'I think we have company.'

'It was too good to last,' Jessica tutted as a band of latecomers burst onto the scene in high spirits and full voice, disturbing the tranquillity. He hoped it was only the peace and quiet she was talking about.

'Come on. We can try to keep a few steps ahead of them.' He grabbed her hand and started back on the trail in the vale of the Mourne Mountains. If he was going to spill his deepest, darkest secrets, it would be somewhere without an audience.

Jessica giggled as they power-walked away from company like naughty schoolchildren caught playing truant. 'What happened to the affable doctor with time and a friendly word for everyone?'

'Even he needs a timeout now and then. Perhaps he's finally taking notice of those people telling him he should get a life of his own.' For the time being, that included Jessica and he intended to make every second count. That included days off and fun runs.

His partner in crime squeezed his hand in what he hoped was solidarity. Should he follow that advice to the letter, he very much wanted Jessica to be a part of that new start.

They circled round the duck pond and, once they were sure they were far enough ahead of the rest of the party, they came to rest on a bench. Jessica stretched out her legs and tossed her head back. Rob envied the sun as she gave herself to it without hesitation. He didn't know where he stood with her and he was sure she was still holding something back from him. Time with her had shown him he could still love his family and have feelings for her too. If he could get her to commit to something more than they had, he'd like to explore what that meant.

With his head in a whirl, he left her and walked down to the water's edge. He swung his backpack around and rummaged inside until he found what he was looking for. The ducks had always been a highlight of the trail for him and he never came empty-handed. Armed with a handful of oats, he knelt down to draw them closer.

'I'm sure Scottish wildlife love their porridge but I'm pretty sure the ducks around here prefer good old-fashioned bread.'

Rob shook his head. 'There's no nutritional value for them in it. In fact, it can cause bloating and generally damage their health. Not to mention the uneaten bread lying about which affects the water quality and attracts vermin. You're much better feeding them oats, corn or even grapes cut in half.'

'You've done your homework.' Jessica joined him, holding her hand out for duck bribes too.

'This was always Mollie's favourite part.' The words slipped out before he had time to think about it but even saying his daughter's name aloud parted the clouds of sorrow keeping her hidden from the world. It had been too long since he'd said it. To go from calling it out every day to avoiding any mention of her was as hard to accept as never seeing her sweet face again. He was thankful for one more chance to give her a voice. Regardless of his mistakes, she deserved to be remembered.

Her name hung in the air, waiting for Jessica to retrieve it.

'Mollie?' Jessica carried on chucking lunch out onto the water, oblivious to the significance of Rob's reminiscing. He was entrusting her with the memory of his daughter, the most precious thing in his life.

He closed his eyes and took a deep breath.

'It wasn't only Leah I lost in the accident that day. I had a little girl too.' It was as if he'd opened a valve, releasing all the pressure of his grief which had been building up inside him for so long.

He was starting to learn that remaining stagnant wasn't doing him any favours. Losing Mollie was the most traumatic event in his life and he'd tried so hard to bury it. As though it was something shameful. He wanted so desperately to believe he could trust Jessica with her memory.

Jessica gasped, inhaling the breath he'd just let go of. 'Oh, my God! No! I can't... I don't...'

It was a lot of information to dump on her and he understood how overwhelming the information was. What could you say to someone who'd lost a child? What could possibly make any difference?

He'd heard it all.

'At least she's with her mother.'

'She's in a better place.'

Every trite comment made him want to punch something. She was still his daughter and he'd lost her for ever. The enormity of that could never be expressed sufficiently. Perhaps it was better that Jessica said nothing, rather than trot out another meaningless cliché.

'How old was she?' Jessica's eyes filled with tears as they spoke and Rob was forced to turn away. It was a simple question; he hadn't expected it to cause him to well up more than he already had. There was no turning back now.

'Four. I have a picture here.' He fished in his back pocket for his wallet and the worn family photo he kept in it. There were no photographs in his house because he wanted to avoid awkward questions and his guilt. However, he'd kept this one close to his heart for the past five years. The small reminder of everything he'd lost when they started to fade in his thoughts.

'Is this Leah too? They're both beautiful. You all look very happy together.' Jessica's reaction held no trace of jealousy or exasperation as she was presented with his previous life. Rob was grasping at the idea that he'd found someone with room in her heart for all three of them.

'We were. Most of the time.' He tucked the photograph back where it came from, wishing he could hide his feelings just as easily.

'Why didn't you tell me?' Jessica's voice was a soft whisper invading his memories.

'This was supposed to be a no-frills deal, right?' He gave a humourless laugh. *'I killed my wife and daughter'* definitely didn't fall into line with that frivolous idea of fun she'd been looking for.

'I know, but we've shared so much these past three weeks. What made you think I couldn't handle knowing about your daughter?' The frown creasing her forehead and the defensive body language said she was hurt by his omission.

It was going to be difficult not to make this the 'It's not you, it's me' line.

He swallowed the ball of nerves lodged in his throat. He delivered life-altering news every day of his career but none which could potentially impact on his own as much as this. The real reason he'd kept Mollie a secret was to hide his shame at failing her. He didn't think he could bear it if Jessica turned her back on him once she learned the truth but he couldn't live a lie any longer. They wouldn't stand a chance at a future together unless she knew the *real* Rob Campbell.

'I didn't tell you everything about the accident. No one knows the full story. Which is why people are happy to paint me as the victim when I'm the one to blame. I told you about the row Leah and I had the night before the accident. We'd argued about Mollie's childcare. Leah was a model before she got pregnant and she'd started taking on assignments and dragging Mollie along with her without telling me. I thought our daughter deserved more attention. How much of a hypocrite does that make me for staying at home when I should have been with them, shopping for my little girl's first day at school? You can't imagine having to live with the knowledge that you sent your own wife and child to their deaths. I let them both down.' He sank down onto his knees. All that remained now was the shell of a man who'd once been a husband and father.

Jessica sat down cross-legged beside him, paying no attention to the mud clinging to her pink chiffon skirt, and took his hand in hers. He'd never fully appreciated the importance of hand-holding before now. She was showing him she was there for him, reminding him he wasn't alone.

'I still stand by the fact it wasn't your fault, regardless of any argument or that your daughter was there too. Surely your family can see that?'

'I never told them. I couldn't live with everyone knowing the truth and hating me as much as I hated myself. It was easier for me to just pack up and leave.' A decision he'd questioned at various points over the years but he'd left it too long to try to build bridges with his family now.

'Rob!'

Jessica nearly sent him sprawling into the dirt as she slapped his arm.

'What was that for?'

'You've spent so long beating yourself up I didn't think one more dig would hurt you. Seriously, though, five years cut off from friends and family is more than enough punishment for something that wasn't your fault. They didn't do anything to deserve that, did they?'

'No. I just couldn't cope with everyone telling me how I *should* be feeling, what I *should* be doing. I couldn't hear my own thoughts above theirs any more.' He'd been treading water on his own for years.

'Haven't you had enough space by now? What if you had been in that car? You might've been killed too. And what of the lives you've saved over these past years too? Do they mean nothing? You've accomplished so much in your career, made a difference to so many people. Isn't it time to reconnect with those who care about you?'

'I hurt them. Some of the things I said… I don't even know if they'd want me back.' He'd been hurt, angry, and he'd pushed away the few people he'd had left in his life. He'd packed up and walked away to start afresh. Except he hadn't. All he'd done was lock himself away with his grief in another country.

'Of course they will. They lost Leah and Mollie, and they lost you too. I'm sure a phone call would put their fears to rest.'

He'd never considered his parents', or Leah's parents' loss. The light had gone out in everyone's lives when they'd died. At the funeral and during the days following, all he'd been able to think about was the two white coffins and his own pain sealed inside. Leah's parents might have lost their daughter, but his parents had lost their son too. He'd been selfish and it took someone with Jessica's guts to point that out to him.

'We'll see. One thing at a time.' He was learning to deal with the here and now first.

'I think it would do you good to have someone here for you.' Jessica's understanding was the reason he'd finally shared Mollie with her. They'd come a long way since she'd come barging into his department and he'd wanted to show her and the film crew the exit. Now she was the one he wanted to be here for him.

'You asked me why I hadn't told you. The truth is, I've never trusted *anyone* enough with the full story. I don't want people thinking I can't do my job objectively because of what happened to me. It's private.

I've learned to be very selective about my friends over the years.'

'I would suggest "selective" to the point of friend, singular.'

'Look at it as your privilege, and not my madness.' He relaxed into a grin. After everything he'd told her, she was still here. Every time he'd imagined telling someone about losing his daughter through his thought-less actions, he'd pictured them running away as fast as their legs could carry them. Not sitting here telling him to pull himself together.

'I'm not sure what I've done to deserve such an hon-our but I'll accept it if it means you'll stop living in the past.'

That serving of tough love had stopped Rob from falling further into self-pity. He hadn't considered any-one other than himself in his actions and he could see it was time to let other people in to share his life. He was edging ever closer to making a commitment to some-thing other than his grief.

'Okay, okay, I get it. No more moping. You can be a hard-ass when you want to be, Jessica Halliday.' He'd already started to think more about his future over these past days and he was hoping she would be a part of it. With her help, he might just be able to free himself from some of the guilt weighing him down.

'I do have a certain reputation to maintain. As hon-oured as I am that you've shared all of this with me, I am curious why you've decided to tell me now.' She was almost daring him to say how he felt about her.

'I know we agreed to end things when filming fin-ished but now that it's approaching it seems foolish to set a time limit on what we have. We're good together, Jessica.' He stopped short of saying those three little words before he scared her off altogether. The next great reveal could wait until he knew there was a possibility she could love him back.

She didn't disagree but she was glad when the stragglers caught up and interrupted their conversation. This wasn't the time to reveal how she felt about him with people milling around feeding the ducks and taking refreshments. Especially when she was still trying to untangle the mess of emotions Rob had tied up even tighter in the past ten minutes.

The tension she'd sensed between them hadn't been leading up to Rob declaring his undying love for her, as she'd imagined. He'd given her something even more precious. Confiding in her about Mollie meant more than those three words, which didn't always turn out to be true. It was right up there with removing his wedding ring. Her pulse started to quicken as the implications set in. It was so much to take in.

He was telling her he wanted to be with her, something her heart ached for too. But her love could never be enough to replace everything he'd lost. Fate had cruelly struck her for a second time. Despite all her precautions, she'd fallen head over glittery running shoes for Rob and she was still going to have to end it. She couldn't take another rejection, which would inevitably follow once he heard about her infertility. This was a man who needed another family, deserved one, and she could never give it to him. It would be better for her in the long run if they stuck to the original agreement instead of dragging this out to the messy, painful finale. She wouldn't lead him on and let him think she was the special woman he'd been waiting for.

He'd held on to that loss for so long it was evident

how greatly it had affected him. The void in his life was as great as the one in hers for the child she would never have. Rob couldn't possibly find closure with her. How dare she expect him to move on from the past with her when she couldn't give him a future to look forward to. Her heart was aching, the pain of losing him tearing her apart inside, but she couldn't show him that. He shouldn't have to take on the responsibility of her pain when he'd made it clear from the start he wasn't ready for a relationship. It was her fault she'd let things get this far.

Adam had been right. She could never sustain anything meaningful without the resentment of her infertility coming between them.

'We should get moving before they send a search party out for us.' She got up and dusted herself down, ready to move on. She was good at that.

Rob scrabbled to his feet beside her. 'Thanks for hearing me out. I promise I'll think about contacting my folks.'

'Good.' Then the onus wouldn't be entirely on her to love and support him when she would inevitably let him down.

'We'll finish the rest of the discussion in private,' he said for her ears only. Apparently it didn't matter to her body that she'd already ended the relationship in her head as that growly Scottish promise brought goosebumps to her skin. This was going to have to be a clean break, with no lapses into his arms if she hoped to survive.

'Later,' she promised, although she planned something a lot less intimate than he probably had in mind. This break-up speech would serve her better when she was dressed in more sombre clothes, on neutral territory and preferably somewhere she could walk away from.

She steeled herself to tackle the rest of the run and was grateful that the last leg of their journey was mainly uphill. At least he wouldn't expect her to talk when she was gasping for breath.

CHAPTER NINE

ROB WAS FINALLY making peace with the past. After coming clean with Jessica he'd gone home and made that call to his parents. It had been a long, emotional reunion over the phone but one they'd all needed. The result of it was another weight lifted from him and an invitation to Belfast for them. They didn't believe he was to blame for what had happened any more than Jessica did. All they wanted was for him to be happy. And he would be as soon as he and Jessica found time for their heart-to-heart.

Now he was free to build a life after Leah and Mollie, he couldn't wait to take the next step with his feisty redhead. Unfortunately, the universe seemed to be conspiring against him getting anywhere close to her these days.

The fun run, coupled with the emotional baggage he'd unloaded onto her, had understandably left her drained on Saturday night. He'd agreed to the suggestion they spend the weekend apart for her to recover and take everything on board. But this was now Tuesday and paranoia was beginning to set in.

Logic said her busy schedule was to blame for the rushed phone calls and his quiet nights without her. These were the last days of filming and he knew she was trying to get everything wrapped up. It was the timing which made him antsy. He was trying not to link her sudden coolness to him spilling his guts about Mollie and the row he'd had with Leah before the crash. Jessica had been so understanding and supportive; he couldn't imagine she was now taking umbrage over it. The only other subject they'd touched on before she went AWOL was their relationship and he'd expect her to tell him straight if she wasn't interested in him any more. She'd never been behind the door in saying how she felt about anything since they'd met.

Time was running out and he'd wasted enough of it denying himself happiness. He intended to bring this to a head today so they both knew exactly where they stood before they let something good slip away. The best way to do that without interfering too much with her work was to combine the two. He'd scheduled that one-on-one interview she'd been so keen to get on tape from day one, so she had no more excuses not to see him.

Sitting here in a glorified storeroom with a camera pointing at him might have appeared an excessive way to get her attention but Jessica was worth it. He'd spent long enough with his life on hold and he would do whatever it took to ensure they had a future together.

Jessica bustled into the room a good five minutes later than they'd agreed, her arms full of papers and a coffee in her hand. 'I'm sorry I'm late. I won't keep you too long.'

He could've been any random off the street waiting to do a vox pop for all the interest she showed in him. There was no eye contact, no sly smile, no indication at all that they'd spent the majority of the past month in his bed. He frowned at the lack of familiarity even when they were the only two people in the cramped room. A matter of days ago they wouldn't have been able to keep their hands off one another and he didn't know what had happened to change that.

'No problem. It's just us, then?'

'Yes. Everything's set up, ready to go. I have enough technical experience to shoot these interviews myself with a static camera. It makes them more—'

'Intimate?'

'I was going to say relaxed, but I guess that works too. Basically, I'll ask you a few questions relating to your job and if you could answer directly to the camera it would be great.' She ignored the blush he'd brought to her cheeks and the reason for it as she maintained her professional stance in the face of his provocation.

'I get it. Then you'll edit out your questions so it looks as though I'm talking to myself?'

'I prefer to see it as a monologue to the camera, to the viewers who want to hear your personal experiences. Now, are you miked up?'

It crossed his mind to pretend otherwise and have her rummaging under his clothes with the microphone pack in the vain hope the contact would reignite the fire between them. In the end he decided against it, since she seemed keen to keep a camera between them at all times. 'Yes. I'm ready to roll when you are.'

He understood she had a job to do and this project was important to her. It was the only reason he was going along with this. For now.

Jessica willed her hands to stop shaking and prayed Rob couldn't see them. In hindsight, coffee probably hadn't been the best idea for her jittery nerves as she watched it spill over her notes. She wasn't looking forward to the conversation she had to have with him once the professional one was out of the way. She'd been deliberately avoiding it and the realisation she'd fallen hopelessly in love with him since the fun run. Hopeless when there was no possibility she could give him the type of fulfilment he deserved in life.

She'd justified the white lies she'd used to stay out of his bed as a way to create distance so the final blow wouldn't be completely unexpected. In reality she'd been too chicken to end things face-to-face. She was worried she would cave in at the last minute, afraid he'd see through her lies but most of all terrified he'd find out the truth and reject her anyway. Now they were here, alone, and she knew there'd be no more running away from him. As soon as she got what she needed from him.

She cleared her throat and took a sip of coffee, relying on the caffeine to see her through this without collapsing into a heap of jelly. 'Okay, we'll need an introduction. If you could just tell us your name, your role here and what your day-to-day routine is, it would be a good start.'

The irony of what she was asking wasn't lost on her. She knew everything about him, more than most people in his life. Rob had shared his most intimate secrets with her and she was pretending his life was a complete mystery to her for the sake of the camera. Worse, she was treating him like a stranger to protect her heart, with no thought for his. She salved her soul with the knowledge he'd survived a greater trauma than the premature end of a fling.

Once the camera was rolling Rob sat up straight to deliver his piece. He was making this easier for her than she'd anticipated. So far he'd followed her lead and swerved any mention of their relationship, or questioned her absence since Saturday. The insecure jilted woman inside her took it as a slight, ridiculous given the circumstances, but deep down she still wanted him to fight for her. Every closet romantic needed to believe they were worth loving even if it was a doomed venture.

'I'm Dr Rob Campbell and I'm the consultant paediatric oncologist at Belfast Community Children's Hospital. I treat young cancer patients and coordinate their care with a team of radiotherapy and surgical specialists. My job is to make sure each child receives the best possible care from the moment of diagnosis. This includes administering chemotherapy and deciding which combination of treatments will be most effective for the individual. I also liaise with the families to keep them informed at every stage of their child's treatment.'

His position here sounded straightforward when it was broken down into simple terms. The director had made the right call asking for more personal footage of Rob. Snippets of him in between patient stories could never adequately convey his emotional commitment to everyone who came through those hospital doors. At least the footage they had with the Girl Guides would show the rapport he had with children, whether they were patients or not. He'd probably been a fantastic father and she was sure he would be again some day.

She blinked away the tears burning her eyes to find he was staring at her, awaiting further instruction.

'That's great. Now, could you explain to the audience what chemotherapy actually is and what effect it has on cancer cells?'

He gave her a questioning glance as if to say *You know better than anyone what chemo is*, but this wasn't about her. Besides, they could use his definitive explanation to narrate any relevant segments involving chemo treatment.

'Sure. Chemotherapy is the name given to the drugs we use to kill cancer cells. These can be given as tablets, liquids or as injections into the bloodstream, muscle or spinal fluid. The drugs are then absorbed into the bloodstream and carried around the body to reach and destroy cancer cells.'

She appreciated that he didn't dwell on the inevitable side effects when normal, healthy cells were also damaged. They would be obvious on the faces of all those they featured over the course of the series. Unless you were extremely unlucky, those side effects subsided when treatment finished.

'Tell us why an MRI scanner is so important to the department.' Her promise to promote the appeal was the main reason he'd agreed to be interviewed, so she attempted to sweeten the blow coming by giving him what he wanted.

Rob leaned forward in the chair, his forearms resting on his knees and his steely stare directed down the camera as he prepared to do business. Shivers played along Jessica's spine. She knew how it felt to be the focus of his intense passion and her life was going to be colder without it. Without him.

'At present, we are the only specialist children's hospital in the UK without an MRI scanner. Unlike other procedures, an MRI scan is less invasive and exposes the patient to less radiation. Any child who requires a scan currently has to be transferred to the adult hospital, with some even forced to travel outside the country to receive one. An in-house scanner would cut waiting lists, diagnose patients quicker, and scans would take place in a familiar environment. The scanner will be completely funded by volunteers and we still have a long way to go to reach our target. We've undertaken bake sales, fun runs and all manner of sponsored events to raise money. These children deserve the very best healthcare we can provide, so all donations are welcome. Every penny counts.'

If Rob's impassioned plea didn't get the general public to open their wallets, nothing would. She'd be sure to play it to her contacts too. There were several she knew who made considerable donations to charity every year to ease their consciences about the extravagant lifestyles they led.

'I'll make sure we put all of the details up at the end of each programme, so people can donate straight to the fund.' Something more than bittersweet memories should come out of her time here.

'Thank you.' He was addressing her directly for the first time since they'd started the interview and she was grateful for the static camera when her hands began to tremble again. Every minute she spent here with him told her what a wonderful man he was and how much she would miss him. She had to get through this as quickly and efficiently as she could—wrap up the relationship along with the production and edit the highlights to air at a later date.

'We're on to the last couple of questions now. I know you have a lot of people to see.'

'I'll always make time for you, Jessica. Whatever you need, you only have to ask and I'll do everything in my power to give it you.'

She couldn't listen to those sorts of promises. They'd failed her once too often.

'All I need is five more minutes,' she said, deliberately misunderstanding his intentions.

Rob sighed and sat back in his chair. 'Then you have them.'

Jessica experienced another surge of disappointed relief when he conceded so easily. Perhaps the devastation of the break-up would be more one-sided than she'd imagined. She was the one who was going to have trouble getting over this for a long time. In some ways it could be harder to pick herself up after Rob than it had been with Adam. He'd gradually chipped away at all the defences she'd built since her doomed engagement. Until she was here, vulnerable, hurting and with no way out but to end the best thing she'd had in her life for as long as she could remember.

'Okay, back to the day job. What would you say is the best part of what you do here?' The faces of Max and Cal immediately popped into her head and the fantastic characters of the children she'd met in such a short space of time. There were definitely good memories to take away from here as well as the unhappy ones.

Rob's serious expression gave way to his beautiful smile. 'My favourite part of the job is definitely meeting all the characters on the ward. Despite what they're going through, the children always brighten my day. We do have a lot of fun in between the treatments. Undoubtedly, when I'm able to tell families their child's cancer is in remission it's a relief for me as much as them. I'm here to make them better and that's the outcome we all strive for. Oncology can also be an exciting field as we further our research and participate in new clinical trials. An estimated seventy-five to eighty per cent of children now survive cancer, thanks to the work that's being done.'

'And the most difficult part of the job?' They both knew what that was. She hated having to make him go to that dark place but she needed the viewers to hear it and feel it from him. Not all of the patients would be as lucky as her. Lauren's poor family had been able to take her home but in less happy circumstances.

'The worst part is having to deliver bad news to the family. Having to tell a parent their child's illness is incurable is something that stays with you for a long time. You're effectively handing down a life sentence when you say the treatment isn't working. I know what it's like to be on the receiving end of that sort of conversation. My four-year-old daughter died in a car accident, so I'm able to empathise a great deal with the families in those circumstances.'

Jessica paused filming until she was sure he was ready to share Mollie with the rest of the world. 'You don't have to—'

'I want to. No more secrets.' He waited until the camera was rolling before he spoke again. 'Losing a child is the hardest thing a parent can go through. It's only possible to get through it with the love and support of those around you. I wouldn't wish the pain I went through on anyone, which is why I'll do everything I can to prevent other families suffering. There isn't a day goes past when I don't think about Mollie.'

Jessica's vision blurred with tears when his voice cracked on his daughter's name. This was such a huge step Rob was taking by confronting his past so publicly. She was sorry she couldn't see it through to the end with him. He was moving forward but she'd remain frozen in time for ever. The only future she had now was her professional one.

She swiped the tears away with the back of her hand. 'Thanks. I think I've got everything I need now.'

Those blue eyes stared back at her from the other side of the camera. They seemed to reach deep into her soul and see her lies.

* * *

'Have you? What about us?' Rob couldn't understand the sudden drop in temperature between them. It seemed the more he opened up, the further Jessica withdrew. If he'd completely misread the bond they'd developed these past weeks together, he wanted to hear it from her.

'We had fun. That's all it was ever supposed to be.' She casually packed up her things as if what they'd shared meant nothing to her. Rob knew that wasn't true. Their relationship had stopped being casual when she'd stayed the night in his bed.

No longer content to sit and wait for her to validate their relationship, he got up from his chair and went to her. 'That's how it started but we both know it's a lot more than that now. These last days without waking up next to you have been hell. After losing Leah and Mollie, I never thought I would want anyone in my life again but you've made me realise that's exactly what I want. Maybe I'm wrong but I kinda got the impression you were happy being with me too.'

'I was but it's over, Rob. The job's done and so are we. I'm glad you're in a better place and I wish you all the best but I can't be part of this new life.' She turned and reached for the door handle but he couldn't let her leave until he knew why. He placed his hand on top of hers in a plea for her to stay.

'Talk to me, Jessica. One minute we're inseparable and the next you're waving me on my way as though we were nothing more than a holiday romance. Tell me what's changed between us since Saturday. I'm sorry if I overwhelmed you by pouring my heart out about Mollie but I needed to do it to give us a chance. All I'm asking is that you do the same. I know we're nowhere near the stage of discussing marriage and babies yet but at least I'm starting to see there's a future waiting for me out there. I really want you to be—'

'I can't do this.' Tears were streaming down Jessica's face as she shook him off and ran out of the door.

Rob didn't go after her when she clearly needed time out from him. He didn't know what he'd done to upset her except say how much he cared about her. If she truly didn't reciprocate those feelings, there would be no need for such an emotional reaction. There was pain in her eyes, sorrow in those tears, and he wanted to understand what was behind it. For the life of him, he couldn't fathom why she was causing them both unnecessary hurt. Perhaps he'd been too wrapped up in his own problems to see she had her own. Jessica had helped him exorcise his demons and he'd be there for her too if she'd let him.

They had something worth fighting for and he wasn't prepared to give up without finding out what was troubling her. If this was one of his cases at work, he would step back, assess the situation, find the source of the problem and treat it. He wouldn't accept the end until all possibilities had been exhausted.

CHAPTER TEN

THE THUMPING ON the front door threatened to drag Jessica back to consciousness. She stuck her head back under the pillows and waited for it to stop. After the agonies of the day, all she wanted was to fall back into oblivion and forget everything.

Her desolate womb had cost her another chance at happiness. Even for Rob, the man she thought could love her, flaws and all, her infertility would've been a deal-breaker. Right up until today she'd held on to that scrap of hope that he'd take her in his arms and tell her it didn't matter. In the end, she hadn't needed to mention it. He'd made it clear how important having children again would be to him and left her in no doubt about where she stood—on the outside, looking in at Rob while he played happy families with someone else.

She sandwiched her face between the mattress and the pillows and let her tears fall. With any luck, she'd simply drown in her own misery instead of having to go through this again.

There was more knocking. Louder. She lifted the pillow so she could call out.

'I'm not in!'

Whoever it was should really take the hint she wasn't welcoming visitors today.

They didn't.

'For goodness' sake!' She was forced to throw the covers back and get out of bed to confront the orchestrator of her unwanted alarm call if she was to stand any chance of sleep. Reluctant to be parted from the only source of comfort available to her, Jessica shuffled to the front door with her duvet still wrapped around her body. She yanked the door open, ready to let rip at whoever it was disturbing her already fitful sleep, only to find a persistent Scottish doctor on her step.

'I don't want to talk.' She instinctively tried to slam the door shut so she wouldn't be forced to have the conversation she'd done her best to avoid so far.

Rob wedged his foot inside. 'Well, I do. So stop being so bloody selfish and let me in.'

He wouldn't budge, leaving them in a ridiculous stand-off, made all the more absurd with Jessica cocooned in her bedcovers. She gave in with a loud huff and grudgingly granted him permission to cross her threshold.

Her mood wasn't further improved by how much better he looked coming off the late shift than she did. Bar some extra rugged stubble and his now wrinkled blue shirt, he was as handsome as ever. She, on the other hand, probably had mad bed hair, panda eyes, and was wearing her Super Sloth duvet cape.

'I'll keep this simple. There's no future for us. As a couple, I mean. We still have a future, separately, with work, and, you know, breathing and stuff.' She was rambling now but she hadn't expected to see him again. He'd turned up right in the middle of her grieving process and set her back even further.

Walking out on him had already left a crater in her heart the size of the Giant's Causeway. A void which no amount of casual affairs could ever fill. In some ways not having Rob in her life would be harder to come to terms with than no children. He wasn't making it any easier for her by being here when she'd made the decision to walk away from him.

'I don't believe you.' His you-know-you-want-me huskiness made her catch her breath.

No. No. No. It wouldn't do to give in to her weakness for him when she was already at an all-time low.

'Believe what you like. We're over.'

Anyone would think this guy had never been dumped before. Looking at that magnificent physique filling her eyeline, she could see why he probably hadn't. His refusal to let this matter go was simply prolonging her agony. All she was asking for was space to grieve this relationship so she could move on. Something he'd needed once too and an impossibility when he insisted on reminding her of what she was missing.

'I don't get to have a say?'

'This isn't about your ego. If it makes you feel any better, you can tell people you called it off.' Jessica was a cornered cat, hissing and scratching trying to protect herself. She needed him out of her life, not close enough for her to feel his warmth and smell his aftershave.

'I just want to know why.'

'I'm sorry but, trust me, I'm saving us both from a lot more heartbreak further down the line.' If he would only trust her judgement on this and let her go, he could find the woman who could give him everything he needed. And she could get back to something she had a chance of succeeding at.

'Do you have a crystal ball? Unless you've developed psychic powers, you have no idea how things might pan out. You can't tell me you don't want this.' He pulled her close with one arm around her waist and kissed her hard. His mouth crushed hers and he held her tight so she couldn't get away.

This was her chance to deny him, prove she was immune. She tightened her lips into a line of resistance, but Rob didn't stand down. He merely changed tactics. The hand restricting her movement now rested on the small of her back, the pressure on her lips eased as he skirted along her defence line.

She parted her lips for one more memory to cling to. As she lost herself in one last dizzying kiss, the rasp of his stubble on her skin vaguely registered. All she was doing now was opening up old wounds simply to satisfy her craving.

She turned her face away. 'If you're quite finished—'

Rob gripped her chin in his fingers and forced her to look at him. 'I love you, Jessica.'

She swore her heart screamed, *No!*

The words every girl wanted to hear made her want to run. There was no air in the room. She couldn't breathe.

First came love, second came possible marriage, third came a disappointed fiancé and a broken-hearted shell of a woman.

No, thanks. Been there, done that, got the tear-stained T-shirt.

'You might think you do, Rob, but really I'm nothing more than your rebound girl, your link back to the real world with whom you're mistaking lust for something more. You think you need to justify a sex life by concocting a fairy-tale romance to accompany it. Well, you don't need it. We're both consenting adults. You don't need anyone's permission to live your life the way you want.' *Ugh.* She hated herself for patronising him so much but she couldn't get sucked into this delusion for her own sake. A happy-ever-after was never going to be within her grasp.

'I know our relationship this far hasn't included talking about our feelings for each other but I'm leaving myself naked here. I'm being honest and I wish you would do the same. Look me in the eye and tell me you don't love me.'

'I'm sorry, but I don't feel the same.' The cruel lie burned her throat as it made its way to her lips.

Rob's face scrunched into a mask of hurt. 'Say it.'

'I don't love you.'

She confirmed her place in hell by denying the truth for a second time. Rob had gone through so much to get to this point and Jessica knew he would never have said those words to her on a whim. He *thought* he loved her but that was only because she hadn't been straight with him. To someone whose entire family had been wiped out, losing the chance to have another would matter some day. It was better to finish this now before she was in too deep.

'No? I would be more inclined to believe you if there weren't tears in your eyes.' Rob cradled her face in his hands so tenderly they fell all the more easily.

'I'm tired. Someone interrupted my sleep.'

'And I'll let you get back to bed as soon as you tell me the truth.'

'I don't love you,' she whispered, closing her eyes so she wouldn't have to look at him.

He brushed her tears and lies away with the pads of his thumbs. 'I'm pretty sure crying when you're dumping me invalidates that argument. For the record, you're a terrible actress. Forget saying those words if that's what's freaking you out but I don't see why we can't keep on seeing each other. I know you'll be moving on to the next job but it's not as if we live at opposite ends of the country. Why throw something good away?'

She snapped her eyes open, forced to defend her actions. 'We want different things. It would never work.'

'What? One of us wants to sit around brooding over her deadbeat ex, and the other wants to seize another chance at happiness?'

'You're not being fair.'

Neither was she and the truth was the only way guaranteed to get him to back off.

'I can't have children, okay? We both know that's a deal-breaker. Cancer and early menopause have pretty much ensured I will never be able to give you that replacement family you so desperately need.'

The great burden of her secret lifted from her shoulders to Rob's. She no longer had to fight her way free as his arms fell to his sides and he let her go without a word.

There was no jubilation to be had from her verbal victory. All she'd done was prove her point. When it came down to matters of the heart, she was no use to anyone.

It took a moment for Rob to come to terms with the reason she'd been holding back. Of course he knew infertility was a possible side effect of prolonged and intensive chemotherapy but Jessica was such a force of nature he never thought of her as a cancer victim. She'd been doubly unlucky. If she'd been older when treatment had started, they could've taken steps to freeze her eggs so she would've still had the chance to be a mother one day.

'I'm so sorry, Jessica.' He'd been here a hundred

times, offering sympathy to those whose lives had been destroyed by cancer and the words always seemed so inadequate.

Wrapped up in her comfort blanket, she looked very much the frightened child who'd probably gone through hell in those early years, but she'd come through it. Rob didn't want her to ever be sorry she had, simply because it had cost her the chance to have children. Perhaps he'd been *too* open about the effect losing Mollie had had on him. It would be easy to interpret that as a desperate need to have another child but that wasn't where his head was at right now.

'Yeah, well, there you go. The truth is out there. Don't let the door hit you on the way out.' She dropped her comforter and adopted her warrior pose—arms folded, lips pursed and defying him to love her.

'Why would that make a difference to how I feel about you? Do you really think I'm so shallow that I would stop loving you because of something you can't give me? What about everything you have given me—friendship, understanding…love?' He'd really messed up if she thought all he wanted was to replace Mollie. Jessica had given him so much by simply being there for him and he'd failed to do the same for her.

'I've been through this before, remember? I know how it ends. I've spent the last four years picking up the pieces after the last guy I broke that news to. You have permission to go back on the market with a clear conscience. I don't expect you to hang around and pretend we have a future when you have the pick of the fertile bunch out there. I'm sure there'll be no end of broody women lining up to make chubby-cheeked babies with you.'

Clearly he wasn't the only one having trouble letting

go of the past. It hadn't occurred to him that the walls around her heart were even taller than his.

'Do you remember the conversation we had about me hating people telling me how I should feel and how I should act? Yeah, that. I don't want anyone else but you.'

'You say that now but when it comes down to it—' She bit her lip and he could see the pain she was trying to keep at bay.

'I'll be there.' He needed her to believe in him, and herself.

'I'm such a catch. Remember, on top of my inability to conceive, there's the double whammy that the cancer could always come back again. I wouldn't inflict that on you when you've been through so much already.' She seemed determined to put him off by putting up more imaginary barriers but she'd forgotten she was the one who'd taught him to live in the here and now.

'I'd always had you down as a glass half full kind of girl, not glass half full of vinegar. Neither of us can base our futures on what-ifs. You're here, you're healthy, and that's all that matters.' And he loved her. If he was to take his own advice and stop focusing on the negatives in his life, he had to face up to the fact he was in love with a beautiful, smart woman who meant the world to him.

'But I can't have kids. That won't ever change.'

'Aren't you jumping the gun here? I only asked that we could keep seeing each other.' He managed to coax a wry smile from her. They both knew he wanted more than that.

'I know. I'm simply thinking ahead.'

'I'm not saying I wouldn't love to be a father again some day but if it doesn't happen, it doesn't happen. If the time comes when we would want a family, there are other options available. I would be more distraught at the thought of not having you in my life. When Leah and Mollie died, I went with them. For five years I've led a zombie-like existence. I was nothing more than an animated corpse cursed with life, forced to go through the motions of the daily grind. Then you came along and showed me what it was to love again. I can live without any more children but I can't live without you, Jessica.' He reached out and took her shaking hand in his. It wasn't only Jessica who was afraid of rejection. He wasn't sure if this—or he—was enough.

'Just so you know, if you turn me down again I'm going home to lock myself in a dark room with a family-size bar of chocolate. If I go into a sugar coma, it will be entirely your fault.'

'No pressure, then?'

'No pressure.' He was trying to keep the atmosphere light, since there was a danger of one, or both, of them dissolving into a snivelling mess. Given the burning in his throat and the moisture gathering in his eyes, there was every chance he would crack first. He couldn't lose her.

Maybe it was because she was in her comfort zone, maybe she was tired and emotional, or perhaps Rob Campbell was too damn understanding, but Jessica was starting to believe this could happen. If he really didn't think her infertility was an issue, it seemed only her insecurity was keeping them apart. She loved him, he loved her, but she was scared of leaving herself open again.

'Seriously, how can this ever work, Rob? We've got more baggage between us than the luggage department at Debenhams.'

Rob's hearty chuckle did more to warm Jessica than

her fifteen-tog duvet had. 'True, but who else would have us?'

'A family man without a family and a feeble, barren excuse for a woman. You're right. If we put that on a dating site, we'd be lucky to get a hit.'

'Ahem. *Feeble* is not a word I would ever use to describe you. *Stubborn*, *pig-headed*, *temperamental*, *compassionate* and *beautiful*, perhaps.' He stroked his thumb across her fingers. The tenderness coming from such a big man always surprised her. He'd never once portrayed the oaf which should have accompanied his height and build.

It was only one of the many things she loved about him. It was her own fear which stopped her from admitting it.

'Thank you.' Words could never fully express her astonishment that he still wanted to be with her despite everything she'd told him.

'You're wrong about one thing, though. I do have a family.'

'I know you do. I meant one of your own.' Tact wasn't one of her best qualities but he'd mentioned his parents so infrequently in the time she'd known him, she'd forgotten they existed.

'Thanks to you, I got back in touch with them last week. They want to meet up.'

'That's fantastic. I'm so pleased for you.' It would be good for him to spend time with his family. They had a lot to talk over and he might finally get some closure. She had a strange ache to be a part of that.

'I've told them about us and they want to meet you too.'

This was huge. Now there were no more excuses. She had to decide if she was going to take the leap of faith with Rob, or play it safe. As scary as it sounded to be someone's other half again, she owed it to herself to try.

She swallowed hard. 'I'd love to.'

'Say that again,' Rob demanded.

'I said, I'd love to meet your parents.'

'Oh. Sorry, I thought you'd finally admitted you loved me.' He wasn't that good an actor that she was convinced he'd misheard her.

She hadn't actually revealed that piece of vital information to him yet and she wasn't inclined to give it away so easily. 'Nope. I definitely said I would love to spend time with your parents.'

'Try again.' He pulled her into his arms and whispered into her ear, sending shivers tiptoeing across the back of her neck.

This time there was no denying how she felt about him. 'I love you.'

'Good, because I love you too.' Rob dipped his head and covered her lips with his. The kiss was a promise that everything was going to be all right.

Jessica had finally found her cure.

EPILOGUE

'IT'S TIME.' JESSICA gave Rob a gentle shake beside her. She was propped up against the headboard of the bed, trying to relieve the back pain, but it was getting to the point where she would soon need his help. There'd been something special in the quiet time between her contractions, knowing the child she'd thought she'd never have was on the way, but Rob wouldn't have wanted to miss a second of this.

'Uh-huh,' he mumbled into his pillow, still half asleep. With all the running around he'd been doing lately, he was bound to be exhausted. On top of his day job, he'd been attending prenatal classes with her and decorating the nursery. Not to mention all of the cooking and cleaning duties he'd undertaken since she'd started waddling into the final weeks of pregnancy.

She loved this man so much it hurt. Literally.

Another contraction started to take hold, tightening her belly and stealing her breath away. She squeezed her eyes shut and waited for it to pass.

'Jessica?'

She could hear her husband scrabbling to sit up beside her and the flick of a light switch as he finally came to. Once the pain began to subside she opened her eyes again to see his panic-stricken face staring back. 'The baby's coming.'

Rob leaped out of bed, clad only in a pair of black jersey shorts, and did a circuit of the room. 'Okay. Your bag's packed, we have your birth plan, I've got the hospital on speed dial…let's go.'

He was making her dizzy, pacing up and down the sidelines with the intensity of an athletics coach at a race meet. Any minute now he'd pull out a stopwatch and time her contractions, pushing her to beat her personal best.

'We've got plenty of time yet. I'm going to run a bath, have a cup of tea and relax as much as I can.' The contractions were far enough apart for her to indulge. There was no point heading to the delivery ward until labour had progressed further.

'Do you want me to phone the guys?' The way he said it left her in no doubt that having a camera crew here was the last thing he wanted. Her too. Since the success of the initial documentary series and the follow-up piece on getting the MRI scanner at the hospital, she'd started charting their road on IVF too. There were so many people going through the same process she thought it was important to record the trials and tribulations along the way. Rob had been supportive thus far but even she knew where to draw the line.

'They can wait. This is our time.' She didn't want to share it with anyone other than her husband.

'Good. I'll put this in the car and phone the hospital to let them know we'll be coming in.' Rob pulled on a pair of jeans and grabbed the overnight bag Jessica had ready to go.

He paused by the door and turned to look at her

with the biggest smile spread across his face. 'This is really happening?'

'Yes. It's happening. As soon as you help your pregnant wife out of bed.' Jessica swung her legs around to the edge of the bed and with Rob's assistance heaved herself up into a standing position.

'You need to take it easy.' He frowned as she took a few steps towards the bathroom.

'I think I can manage turning the bath taps on without coming to too much harm.' She shrugged off his concerns and shooed him out of the way. For someone who'd spent so long fighting her own battles she was still trying to come to terms with having a partner who looked after her so well. He'd been so attentive from the second they saw those two precious blue lines on the pregnancy test, Jessica knew their baby was going to feel as loved as she did.

These past two years with Rob had been the best of her life. He'd changed her from a relationship-wary, hardened singleton into a gushing romantic. Every day with him was filled with love and confirmation she'd made the right move in taking that leap of faith with him.

Things had progressed quickly between them once she'd finally admitted her feelings for him and let go of her fear. Meeting his parents had been emotional for all involved but they had welcomed her and Rob both into their lives. Talking everything through with them seemed to have finally brought him some closure and he'd proposed to Jessica within six months. By that stage she had no qualms whatsoever about the depth of his love for her and vice versa. After wasting so much time locked in the past they'd both been keen to marry quickly and make the most of what life had to offer.

Now they were about to have the happy ending they both deserved.

Rob insisted on making the tea whilst she walked the halls of what was about to become their family home, trying to ease the pain in her lower back. She managed only a few sips before she was forced to abandon it. Within seconds she was doubled over and squeezing Rob's fingers until they turned blue as another contraction took hold.

'Are you okay?' He waited until she'd stopped crushing his hand before asking. She could tell he was only moments away from bundling her into the car, regardless of her protests. This was definitely the anxious husband and soon-to-be father heading into the delivery room with her rather than the logical doctor. In some ways it was comforting to know he was still as overwhelmed by the situation as she was even though he wasn't a first-time dad.

'Just uncomfortable. I think I might climb into that bath now.' She hobbled back towards the bathroom with her Rob shadow trailing behind her to find her bubble bath lit by candlelight.

'I thought it would help keep you relaxed.' Rob unnecessarily justified his own thoughtfulness as she kissed him on the cheek.

'Thank you but I draw the line at whale song in case you were thinking about it. It's a bit too close to home under the circumstances.' As if to prove her point, she was forced to ask him to help her struggle out of her nightie and into the water. She'd loved every aspect of being pregnant but she would be glad when she could see her feet again.

'You're beautiful,' he said, kneeling at the side of the bath. Every time he said it she believed him a little more.

'Do you think the person who donated her eggs re-
alises how much she's given us?' Jessica stroked her
bump, rising out of the bubbles like an island in the
mist. After revealing her deepest, darkest secret to Rob
he'd recommended counselling for her to come to terms
with her fertility issues. It was during these sessions she
was reminded she still had options.

Things had deteriorated so badly between her and
Adam that she'd never explored other avenues. They
never would've survived the process they'd gone
through to get here today. Her bond with Rob had been
strong enough for them to face all the hurdles together.

Since marrying Rob the urge to have his baby had
become all-consuming. They'd considered adoption but
when it was explained to her there was still a chance of
her carrying Rob's biological child herself she'd been
determined to see it through. He'd been worried the
complicated process of IVF and donor eggs would prove
too stressful for her but this was one time the odds had
worked in her favour. The donor eggs, fertilised with
Rob's sperm in a lab, had been successfully implanted
in her womb first time around.

'Whoever it was deserves to be as happy as we are.
This is everything.' Rob rested his hand gently on her
belly and leaned over to kiss her.

Here with her husband, waiting for the arrival of their
baby, Jessica no longer saw herself as a victim. She was
one of life's winners.

Rob felt Jessica's abdomen tighten at the same time as
she flinched away from him. He hated seeing her in
pain and if he could've gone through this for her, he
would have. She'd been so strong and determined this

far, he knew it would be worth it in the end when they were holding their baby.

He held her hand as she panted through another contraction. 'Okay, water babies. They're getting closer. I think it's time to think about getting out.'

Jessica's grimace eventually softened into a grin at the same time the circulation came back in his fingers. 'I think Junior's of the same opinion.'

Rob grabbed a towel and helped her out of the tub. It didn't matter how relaxed she was about the birth, or the fact he was a qualified doctor, he would be relieved when they got to the hospital. There were so many possible complications in pregnancy, not to mention her chequered medical history, she would be safer in that environment than a remote house in the middle of the countryside.

'If he's as strong-minded as his mother, he'll be here in no time.'

'*He?* Do you know something I don't?'

'A figure of speech, I assure you, but Junior does lend itself to the possibility of a son…' He was teasing her. They'd decided against finding out the sex, having been blessed with this chance to complete their family. Rob didn't care if they were having a boy or girl as long as mother and baby were healthy.

'Hmm. We'll see. *She* could be as reluctant to join the outside world as her father had been.' As usual, Jessica parried back. Marriage certainly hadn't snuffed out that spark between them. There was never a dull moment with her in his life and he often wondered how he'd survived on his own for so long.

He'd never imagined he'd be given the chance to have this again and he would cherish every moment he had with Jessica and the baby.

'Er…Rob?'

It took only a second for him to register the shock in her eyes and the puddle of water between her feet and what it meant. 'Your waters have broken?'

'Yes.' For the first time since she'd woken him there was a hint of panic in her voice. Unsurprising when his own stomach was flip-flopping with anticipation of their imminent arrival.

'Okay. We got this.' It was affirmation to himself as well as Jessica that, come what may, they would get through these next hours together.

Jessica was lost in those blue eyes. Every struggle in her life had been worth it to get to this perfect moment.

'He's beautiful,' Rob whispered, his voice cracking as he stroked his son's head.

'He takes after his daddy.' With the mop of dark hair and brilliant blue eyes, he was definitely Rob's mini-me.

'Given the short time it took him to get here, I would say he has his mother's determination too.' Rob smiled and dropped a kiss on her forehead.

He'd held her hand the whole way through without flinching, even during the sweary, shouty stage of her labour. Thankfully, it had been a relatively straightforward delivery, so quick there hadn't been time for any pain relief other than the gas and air. At least it meant she was fully compos mentis to enjoy every second of this miracle.

'I can't believe he's really ours.' She might not be his genetic parent but after carrying him for nine months she was every inch his mother.

'We'll need to get used to it soon. The three of us are going to be together for a long time.'

Jessica watched as he cradled their baby in his arms,

smiling and cooing and totally besotted. She counted herself very lucky indeed. Rob had healed her heart and now, with a family of her own, she finally felt complete.

* * * * *

MILLS & BOON®

MEDICAL ROMANCE™

THE ULTIMATE IN ROMANTIC MEDICAL DRAMA

A sneak peek at next month's titles...

In stores from 28th January 2016:

- **His Shock Valentine's Proposal** *and*
  Craving Her Ex-Army Doc – Amy Ruttan

- **The Man She Could Never Forget** – Meredith Webber
  and **The Nurse Who Stole His Heart** – Alison Roberts

- **Her Holiday Miracle** – Joanna Neil
- **Discovering Dr Riley** – Annie Claydon

Available at WHSmith, Tesco, Asda, Eason, Amazon and Apple

Just can't wait?
Buy our books online a month before they hit the shops!
visit www.millsandboon.co.uk

These books are also available in eBook format!

215_MB16

MILLS & BOON®

Man of the Year

Our winning cover star will be revealed next month!

**Don't miss out on your copy
– order from millsandboon.co.uk**

Read more about Man of the Year 2016 at

www.millsandboon.co.uk/moty2016

**Have you been following our
Man of the Year 2016 campaign?**
🐦 **#MOTY2016**